THE

BLOODY

MARY

SAGA

A COLLECTION

Mary: The Summoning copyright © 2014 by Hillary Monahan
Mary: Unleashed copyright © 2015 by Hillary Monahan

First Paperback Edition, October 2018

10 9 8 7 6 5 4 3 2 1

FAC-025438-18229

Printed in the United States of America

This book is set in Century Schoolbook Std/Monotype; Bembo Book MT
Pro/Monotype
Designed by Maria Elias

Library of Congress Control Number for *Mary: The Summoning* Hardcover:
2014004254
Library of Congress Control Number for *Mary: Unleashed* Hardcover:
2014047136

ISBN 978-1-368-04123-2
Visit www.hyperionteens.com

SUSTAINABLE
FORESTRY
INITIATIVE

Certified Chain of Custody
Promoting Sustainable Forestry

www.sfiprogram.org
SFI-01054

The SFI label applies to the text stock

For the horror guy. Enjoy, David.

For Lauren, who's been there through every step of this journey.

BOOK ONE

YЯAM

THE SUMMONING

BOOK TWO

YЯAM

UNLEASHED

HILLARY MONAHAN

HYPERION
LOS ANGELES | NEW YORK

I grew up in an old New England town halfway between Boston and Cape Cod. Bridgewater was colonized in 1650, with West Bridgewater breaking off from the greater settlement in 1822. We were the smaller Bridgewater, at only about five thousand people, and part of the quasi-infamous Bridgewater Triangle. The Triangle is a cluster of paranormal activity in New England, people claiming to see everything from yetis to thunderbirds to ghosts walking along the backwater roads bisecting the Hockomock Swamp. This is mentioned in the second Mary book, *Unleashed*, where I send my girl protagonists into the swamp to defeat the murder ghoul.

Fun fact: "Hockomock" means "place where spirits dwell" in Wampanoag.

That said, the swamp is not the only source of oogedy-boogedy stories in West Bridgewater. Age breeds lore, and with lore comes lots of imagination fodder. My middle school was the Howard School on the main drag of West Bridgewater, but us kids grew up knowing the history of a previous Howard School, which looked like a cross between Harry Potter's Hogwarts and the Innsmouth Academy.

The original Howard School burned down in 1949. We're not talking a small-scale fire, either; it was toast, from top to bottom, save for a bell on top of the structure. That bell became a relic, positioned in front of the new Howard School as a reminder of the glorious and terrifying building that had come before. You couldn't walk through the front doors without passing it on the main green of the school property.

As middle schoolers, we were fascinated by the story of the fire, of how regular class was interrupted on a spring day, thanks to the blaze, and inevitably we assigned a ghost to it. In reality, there were no fatalities despite the intensity of the disaster, but that's not how legends are made, so we invented one. I'm not exactly sure who came up with it, but it was passed down from generation to generation, from class to class, that a girl had died in the Howard Fire. She'd been trapped in a bathroom and had perished when the building collapsed on her.

Her name was Mary Jane, and if you went into the bathroom alone, you might see her. But you could surely see her if you said the ritual words:

Mary Jane, Mary Jane
I believe in you, Mary Jane
And your golden blood.

I cannot tell you the number of middle-school girls who went into the bathroom, shut the lights off, and "played" Mary Jane in the Howard School mirror. Mostly I can't tell you how many because I refused *to do it*. I was quite content not partaking, and the taunting of being a chicken never really bothered me. I was safe and not ghost food. They were not.

Thus me > them.

I remember, distinctly, though, the tingle I got from the story being told over and over again, from kid mouth to kid mouth. I remember the weird details that got added onto the legend, too, like if you found four of anything identical together, it was a sign Mary Jane was near. (That one got awkward when you could look at four Tater Tots and associate them with a nearby ghost, by the way. We didn't discriminate in our terror.)

The love of that legend, of how unnerved I felt, compelled me to write the Bloody Mary books. I wanted to take a piece of where I came from and spin it for another generation. Obviously Bloody Mary and Mary Jane had two very different stories, but they were both bathroom bogeys (as I heard a Brit friend call them) and they were similar enough that I felt comfortable replacing one with the other. I set out to pen a scare with an all-female cast who spent their time focusing on the things that mattered—like escaping a ghost. Kissing in horror books can be great! But not *in* this story. I went for the visceral "jump scare" of a tried and true ghost story.

MARY: Unleashed and its sequel will always hold a special place in my heart, not only because it's my debut novel, but because it comes from something personal to me. This is my love of old lore, of scares and creeps shared not by a TV show or a movie, but orally, from generation to generation. The story changed over the years, and I'm sure it's gained some new quirks since my time in the Howard School, but I'm confident it's still there, somewhere, circling and sending kids into dark bathrooms with a name on their lips.

In fact, I know it is. The school sent me a picture of my book in the library, waiting for new readers.

—HJM, 2018

YЯAM

THE SUMMONING

HILLARY MONAHAN

HYPERION

LOS ANGELES | NEW YORK

September 2, 1863

Dearest Constance,

I regret to inform you that you are an abysmal sister. You snatched the only handsome Boston lawyer to ever grace Solomon's Folly, thus relegating me to a life of wedded torment with a sheep farmer or some other dullard. I will forgive this grievous insult, but please remember my graciousness come the holidays.

I wonder how long it will be before Mother suggests you take me to the city so I may seek my own gentleman. Am I terrible to confess that I would enjoy the sights more than romance? She may have married at seventeen, but I do not feel so compelled. It is likely my impatience speaking. An endless parade of soft words, flowers, and idiocy sounds quite grating.

Upon reconsideration, the flowers would be nice. I would be content so long as my ardent gentleman gifted me with flowers and had the good sense to leave immediately afterward.

You asked about my wellness, and though I do not like to complain, I must indulge this one time. Your departure was the first in a series of disappointments. Last month, our beloved Pastor Renault moved to a congregation in the Berkshires. I wish him the best, but miss him already. He had such a kind, loving manner.

The new pastor is as pleasant to me as Cain is to Abel. I'm convinced Philip Starkcrowe was sent to test my faith. He is tall and bird-boned with pitch-colored hair and eyes like night. He is young for his station, too—perhaps a few years beyond twenty. It is strange to see him donning the robes. He looks as though he wears the clothes of a man much larger than himself. He is a boy tromping about in his father's boots.

His voice is good, and his sermons are certainly impassioned, but there is darkness to his words. Where Pastor Renault spoke of God's love, Pastor Starkcrowe talks of God as an angry shepherd. We are sinful sheep bound for everlasting torment. I'm surprised he doesn't make us sing our psalms with mournful baa's in lieu of honorifics.

There's also the matter of his hypocrisy. You once jested that Mother is a princess torn from a storybook, but the pastor looks upon her like he has never seen a fair-haired woman. I may be innocent, but I am not ignorant, and there is an earthiness to his gaze that unsettles me. It unsettles Mother, too, though she'd never say as much. She is far too kind.

I, however, lack such grace. After Sunday's sermon, the pastor came to thank us for our devotion. While speaking to Mother, he stared too long at her—pardon my crassness, Constance—but he stared too long upon her necklace. It was so bold! I tried to hide my disapproval, but I must have failed because he turned a furious eye upon me. He drew me before the congregation then, and with that loud, fire-and-brimstone voice, proclaimed that "while Mrs. Worth has a pleasing disposition, I cannot say the same for her youngest daughter."

I may lack your sweetness and Mother's etiquette, but I never thought myself so monstrous. It was mortifying. Everyone in the church heard him. Elizabeth Hawthorne had the nerve to smile at my embarrassment! You would think being schoolmates for years would garner me some affection, but she will not forgive me for that

Thomas Adderly nonsense. It is not as if I welcomed his advances. He has onion breath and warts on his hands, yet Elizabeth still believes that I lured him away from her affections.

The rejection must devastate her Hawthorne pride. They do not breathe the same air as the rest of us commoners, don't you know.

I loathe the privilege money affords some people. I rest well knowing that you will never struggle, but if you become an inflated harpy like Elizabeth, I will strangle you in your sleep, Constance. On this I swear.

Since the pastor's histrionics, showing my face around town has become a nuisance. Just yesterday, Mrs. Chamberlain clutched her cross when I was in her presence like I could afflict her with a fiendish curse. I was tempted to hiss at her to see if she would hide beneath her bread counter. Mother would have murdered me, but I daresay it might have been worth it.

I apologize so much of this letter is ill news, my sister. Mother does say I spit vitriol when I am riled. Perhaps next time I will be a more uplifting correspondent. For that matter, perhaps I'll find a suitable sheep farmer in the meanwhile and will write of my impending nuptials!

I love you and miss you,
Mary

"Bloody Mary.

"Bloody Mary.

"BLOODY MARY."

Jess's voice echoed like we were in a cave. Darkness has a way of making everything seem bigger and more claustrophobic at the same time. Four bodies crammed inside Anna Sasaki's basement bathroom meant we were each nudged up against something cold and hard. Jess got the vanity, I got the toilet, Kitty was at the tub, and Anna had the linen closet door.

"Bloody Mary.

"Bloody Mary.

"BLOODY MARY."

The lights were off in the windowless room. According to Jess, Bloody Mary had to be summoned by the light of a single candle. Ours flickered on the edge of the sink below the mirror.

Though no one moved, and I barely breathed, the flame danced a jig on its wick as if held by invisible hands.

The whole thing felt eerie, despite my logical reasoning that the summoning was ridiculous. I'd played Bloody Mary at slumber parties with these same girls when we were twelve. Trying again in high school seemed a waste of time—but there was a strange exhilaration to it, too. The lure of the unknown. It was a good scare, the kind you got walking through a haunted house. The anticipation was far worse than the reality.

I bit my lip and stared at the mirror. Jess claimed there was a right way and a wrong way to summon Bloody Mary. This time we were doing it the right way. Positioning mattered. Salt mattered, too, because it purified against evil. Water mattered. Hand-holding mattered. Even the number of girls mattered. Before, the idea was to scream Mary's name in the dark and scare yourself pretending to see a ghost. This was more deliberate. More believable. This time, it felt like we knew what we were doing.

The mirror stayed vacant for at least thirty seconds. I didn't need to look at the shadowed faces beside me to know they were staring as intently as I was. It was so quiet. Seconds ticked by. The longer we waited for something to appear in the mirror, the less convinced I became it would. The thrill of calling Bloody Mary dwindled. There'd been goose bumps on the backs of my arms when Jess first said the name, but now they were gone. A sinking feeling of disappointment rippled around our summoning circle.

I was about to ask *Are we done yet?* when I saw a flash in

the mirror. I blinked, sure that it must have been one of our reflections. Then it happened again. A light streaked behind the mirror—a star across a night sky. Kitty's hand flexed inside of mine. She'd seen it, too.

The mirror filled with fog, like condensation after a hot, steamy shower. But the fog was on the other side. The *wrong* side. Droplets of water streamed down the glass, cutting black rivulets through the gray.

Kitty twitched again and I clamped my fingers down on hers so she couldn't jerk away. Jess had warned us about breaking the circle. We had to hold position or we'd be putting ourselves in danger. Bloody Mary hadn't gotten her name because she liked hanging out with teenage girls. To keep her at arm's length, we needed protective wards. The first and most important ward was the handhold.

Behind the mirror, the fog changed from a thick paste to a swirling mass of charcoal smoke. My goose bumps returned and my heart beat so hard, I thought it would pound through my lungs and splatter on the floor.

This couldn't be happening. I tried to think of ways Jess could have manipulated the glass, but I'd checked the mirror before we started. The frame was solid bronze, the mirror far too heavy for a single person to lift. There wasn't space for a movie projector in the room, and Jess didn't have the tech skills anyway.

No, this was legitimate ghost activity, and there I stood, witnessing it with my three best friends. Anna murmuring under her breath. Kitty wheezing louder and louder. Jess saying, "Come on—come on," over and over again.

"Look, Shauna. Look," Jess said. I looked. A black silhouette emerged through the fog, walking toward us down a tunnel that ought not exist. No, not walking—*shuddering*. There was no fluidity to the movements. It was one jolting, shambling step into the next, like a zombie movie monster.

Blood rushed to my face. My toes curled inside my sneakers. Bloody Mary was real and she was walking toward the glass! I didn't know what to do; I wanted to run away, but I desperately wanted to stay, too. It was horrifying and exhilarating, like that first big whoosh on an upside-down roller coaster.

Then she rushed us. An unnaturally fast blur of madness barreled our way from inside the glass. Her hand struck the mirror on the other side, though there was no sound to punctuate the strike. I yelped, the desire to crouch and hide warring with my mind's insistence to absorb every last detail.

Most of Mary was masked by the fog, but her hand was as clear as my own. Her fingers were long and twiglike, with twisted, swollen joints. A sheaf of gray, shriveled skin hugged each appendage, peeling away from the tips. A deep gouge bisected her palm from pinkie to thumb, revealing her rotten, ragged flesh. Tarry blood seeped from Mary's wound, smearing the glass in streaks of blackish maroon.

Gross.

And it got grosser when Mary curled her fingers over to rake them down the glass, her nails in a state of decay. Some were broken off at the nail bed, others had snapped into sharp, serrated razor tips. I expected to hear a shrill squeal from the mirror, but there was nothing. My mind filled in the audio track with nails on a chalkboard, the imagined sound sending another ripple of fear through my body.

I was so consumed by terror and fascination that I had forgotten about Jess, Kitty, and Anna. I should have been more careful. When Mary lifted her second hand to the mirror, this one just as desiccated as the first, Kitty jolted next to me like she'd been struck by lightning. She tried to wrench away, forcing me from my stupor. My fingers dug into Kitty's sweaty palm to keep her steady, but I felt her pulling. She'd become a hundred-and-seventy-pound eel at my side, and there was only so long I could keep control of someone so slippery.

"Kitty, stop," I whispered.

"No. Nooooo," she groaned, another violent twist nearly pulling my arm from the socket. I doubt her resistance was conscious on her part. Kitty knew the dangers of breaking the handhold as well as the rest of us, but she was panicking. I clutched her wrist to anchor her to the group.

"Jess," I hissed. "Do something."

"What? Oh..." Jess said, seeing Kitty struggling beside me in the dark, Anna manhandling her on one side, me on the other. Before Kitty could escape the circle, Jess's voice rang out strong and clear through the bathroom.

"I believe in you, Mary Worth!"

The hands and blood vanished immediately. The fog dissipated, as though a gust of wind had swept it away. We were left in a dark bathroom with an empty mirror and a flickering candle.

We never saw Mary's face.

2

It started with the letter.

Jess had gone to Solomon's Folly during April school vacation to stay at her grandparents' lake house. Solomon's Folly—or the Folly—is a sleepy old town without much going for it beyond its strategic access to other, more interesting places. Go south on the highway and you're on Cape Cod. Go north and you're in Boston. Farms, trees, and a lot of creepy graveyards constitute most of the town. Our hometown of Bridgewater isn't much more exciting, but at least fast food and a movie theater exist here.

I'd spent half the summer at the lake house last year, canoeing and grilling and getting bitten by mosquitoes with Jess, my best friend since before I could remember. We met in kindergarten and have been friends ever since. Even when she'd graduated from "the girl I was in Girl Scouts with" to "blond, blue-eyed beauty queen," we'd stuck together. I'm good-looking enough with my red hair and dark brown eyes, but Jess is a stunner. The all-American-girl-next-door flavor of stunner. The rest of us pale in comparison.

I declined the invitation to the Folly that April so I could perfect the art of laziness at home. I was working my butt off to make honor roll, and with four advanced placement classes, it wasn't easy. Junior year is college transcript year, and if I wanted to go somewhere that wasn't the University of Loser, I needed good grades for scholarship money. April vacation was the last chance I had to relax before finals came crashing down.

Jess had been positively industrious by comparison. Sometime during her vacation, she'd rediscovered the Bloody Mary legend. The letter from Mary Worth to her sister, Constance, was her sales pitch. The photocopy of the original was her way to get us on board with the summoning.

"There's a rumor that Mary Worth is Bloody Mary," Jess said, dropping a pile of papers into my lap as I devoured pizza in Kitty Almeida's downstairs media room. We were gathered around a glass-top coffee table, me on the center cushion of the couch, Kitty seated to my left, and Anna perched on the floor by Kitty's knees. Jess hovered behind us, looming over my shoulder like an oversize parrot.

"You mean that stupid game we played a million years ago?" Anna asked between bites of pizza. She had tomato sauce on her face. I threw a napkin at her so she could clean up. "Thanks," she murmured, wiping her chin, then tying back her hair. Anna's dad is Japanese, her mom is Irish. From Mom, she'd inherited a stocky build and freckles. From Dad, she'd gotten pretty brown eyes that she hid behind a pair of gold-framed glasses and perfect black hair that felt like water and hung to her waist.

"Yeah, the one where you nearly puked because I slapped the bathroom door when you were inside? Remember?" Jess asked with a snicker. It took me a minute to pluck that memory from the banks. It had been a slumber party at the McAllister house to celebrate Jess's twelfth birthday. Someone got the brilliant idea to play Bloody Mary. Every one of the ten girls there went into the bathroom individually, shut out the lights, and called for Mary. And every one of us insisted we saw something creepy in the mirror—except we hadn't.

Poor Anna was the last to go. By then, Jess had grown bored of the game and decided to up the ante by grabbing the doorknob and shaking it to make Anna think the ghost was there. Anna hadn't puked, but she had cried, and we'd all had to tell Jess what a jerk she was at her own birthday party. She'd always had a talent for being the biggest ass in the room. I loved her, but that love came with a great responsibility, like whacking Jess whenever she got out of line.

"Yes, that one. And thank you for reminding me!" Anna said. "This conversation is now a total waste of your time."

"Wait. No, hold on. Read the letter." Jess reached down to grab the papers from my lap, waving them under my chin. My choice was either to accept them or suffer the torment of a thousand paper cuts. The script on the pages was small but legible despite the cursive flourishes. Someone had taken great care to make it as neat as possible, and glancing at the signature on the last page, it was evident that someone was Mary Worth. Little black ink spots dappled the corners of the paper, and there were shadowy rings in places that indicated the original letter had some water damage.

When Kitty swooped in to read over my shoulder, the motion a little too "starving seagull on popcorn" for my taste, I shooed her away and read it aloud. The language was stiff, but the September 1863 date explained the tone. This was Civil War–era stuff, all "Four score and seven years ago," and somewhere, my U.S. history teacher totally appreciated that I'd immediately linked the year to the Gettysburg Address.

"Whoa, this is over a hundred and fifty years old? Where'd you get it?" Kitty asked.

"Solomon's Folly," Jess said. "The town claims to be the source of a lot of urban legends. At least, that's what my grandfather says. He's a little weird, but sometimes he says cool stuff."

Jess was failing to mention that they suspected Grandpa Gus was in the early stages of dementia, but I wouldn't bring that up in front of the other girls. Jess loved her grandfather, even if he sometimes forgot his pants and wore a kitchen colander as a helmet for fun.

"That's neat," Kitty said, taking the letter to skim it. When she was done, she slid it onto the coffee table between two pizza boxes, narrowly avoiding a run-in with a puddle of grease. "It'd be cool if it's really Blood Mary's letter."

Anna shrugged. "There's nothing in that letter that screams

'scary ghost chick.' Husbands and pastors and mean girls? So what?"

Anna was being harsh, but that edge was part of her personality. She was blunt to a fault.

"Well, it could be Bloody Mary," I said. "I mean, yeah, there's the possibility it's not, but if everyone in town says it is, why is it so ridiculous to consider it?"

"Seriously," Jess said. "Have a little imagination, Anna. Grandpa had me talk to my great-aunt Dell. She's as weird as he is, by the way, Shauna. Like, seriously creepy old lady. Anyway, she filled me in on the summoning details. She says there's a real way to do it. I think she was trying to scare me, but I want to try it anyway."

"So do it. Why do you need us?" Anna pressed.

"The summoning has to be four girls, that's why. Otherwise I'd ask Marc and Bron—" Jess cut herself off with a muttered curse. She wasn't supposed to mention Bronx. He'd dumped Kitty three weeks ago, and Kitty had spent every day since weeping and listening to their song while one of the three of us stroked her hair and told her it was okay.

The problem was that Bronx was best friends with Jess's boyfriend, Marc. Jess couldn't exactly ditch Bronx in a show of solidarity, and so there was static. It wasn't like Jess talked about Bronx a lot, but saying his name was enough to make Kitty go slouchy and cast her eyes to the floor.

I had to swallow a groan. After three weeks, Kitty's kicked-dog routine was getting old, but my irritation was tempered by the knowledge that her melancholy wasn't a manipulation tactic. She had zero self-esteem. Kitty was a solid forty pounds heavier than the rest of us and she seemed to think it made her disgusting. Bronx had certainly liked her curves, but Kitty saw herself as the ugly duckling no matter how many times I pointed out her stunning green eyes and gorgeous caramel-colored hair.

Jess didn't have the same kind of patience. She'd done her best to overlook Kitty's moroseness, but lately, Jess rolled her eyes to the ceiling and gritted her teeth. "It makes me feel like a bad friend," she'd told me in confidence, "like she thinks I'm trying to hurt her, and I'm not." I understood Jess's perspective. Intentionally or not, Kitty was laying a major guilt trip on Jess's shoulders. If she could stop being passive-aggressive, they'd probably be fine, but that wasn't Kitty's way.

Looking between the two of them, I knew we'd skated onto thin ice. Kitty was shriveled in the chair next to the television while Jess's mouth pinched into a grimace, her eyes narrowed to feline slits. Kitty was about to get a massive blast of Jess fury to the face. I *really* didn't want to have to pick up those pieces, so I grabbed the pages of the Mary Worth letter and waved them over my head, a red flag before the bull. I knew it'd at least distract Jess from the imminent danger of a meltdown.

"This. We should do this," I said. "The Bloody Mary thing. It'd be cool."

Anna caught on to my great distraction plan and hauled herself up from the floor to reach for the letter. "Sure, why not?

It's not like anything will happen. But if it'll shut Jess up, I am totally down for it."

Jess ignored the jab. She was too busy erupting into excited, ear-piercing squeals, like we'd crowned her prom queen for the second time this year. She vaulted the couch to throw herself into the seat beside me, her arms snaking out to jerk me into a spine-crushing hug. She may have been a skinny chick, but she could give hugs that'd make a grizzly bear squirm.

"Awesome! Kitty, you in?" she asked. Kitty was nodding her head before Jess even got the question out. Depression or not, Kitty fell into line with the rest of us because that's just what Kitty did.

If I had known that days later we'd be watching Bloody Mary scratch at Anna's bathroom mirror, I might have thought twice.

3

"That shouldn't have worked," Anna said, slumping on the floor between the toilet and the wall. Her hands kept raking through the hair at her temples like it needed to be patted into place. "There is no way that should have worked. How? How did it work?"

Kitty nodded her agreement from inside the tub. After we'd broken the handhold and turned on the light, Kitty jumped inside the bath to lie down, her head tilted back like she wanted the shower to rain a better reality over her. She was stiff with fear. Her eyes bulged, a flush stained her cheeks. Her right hand was white-knuckled on the side of the tub, like she needed something solid to hold on to while she reconciled the impossible thing that had just happened.

"But it *did* happen," Jess said gleefully. She pulled a red notebook from her backpack and perched on the bathroom vanity, her butt in the sink, her back to the salted mirror like it hadn't just had clawed ghost hands menacing it. She recorded every detail of the summoning, including the time and which cardinal points people stood on when Mary appeared. There were papers glued to the first few pages of the notebook, presumably the letter she'd shown us. Jess was keeping everything in one tidy place for all her Bloody Mary needs.

"How are you not even a little bit bothered by this?" I asked. I didn't look as rattled as Anna, and I wasn't catatonic like Kitty, but I had my own issues. My head pounded like a one-man band was doing laps across my forehead.

"I am freaked out a little, too, but it was so cool. Wasn't it? It was awesome!" Jess insisted. She grinned at me and rubbed her shoulders like she was cold. Maybe she was a little more bugged out than I gave her credit for, though it still took massive stones to sit on the sink with her back to the mirror like that. "Bloody Mary. We did it. Like, really for real. How awesome is that?"

"Awesome in the broadest sense of the word, maybe," Anna returned. "I'm not so sure what we just did was smart. Some stuff is better left to books and movies. The reality is too... I don't know. It's too something. And that something isn't necessarily good."

"No way," Jess said, hopping down and turning around to scoop the salt off the vanity. I wished she wouldn't do that. It made me feel safer to have it around, but she'd brushed it aside before I could make my mouth form the request to keep it there. The headache was wreaking havoc on me. "We've done something only a handful of other people have ever done. We've done something historic. Yes, it was scary, but she's a ghost! Ghosts are *supposed* to be scary."

I started to see Jess's point. It had been exciting until it turned terrifying, and even then the terror was pure adrenaline. I'd only felt uncomfortable when Kitty began her freak-out dance beside me. "I guess," I said. "I just got...I feel a little sick. I got scared it'd go bad at the end. We never really talked about what would happen if we screwed up."

"There's no point discussing it if we're not going to screw it up. Which reminds me. You," Jess said, whirling on Kitty. Jess leaned over the tub so far, her profile was hidden behind a veil of blond hair. The only thing I could see from my position on the floor was Kitty's bewildered, slightly gassy expression.

I swallowed a groan. Why had I brought it up? I knew Jess would go after Kitty sooner or later. I didn't have to make it sooner. I braced, ready to intervene if Jess got bitchy. For all that she was my best friend, she had a mean streak, and Kitty was the poorest equipped of our group to handle Jess when she was riled.

"What'd I say about the handhold?" Jess demanded.

"I'm sorry. I got scared," Kitty replied. I watched her sink farther into the tub, shrinking away like Jess was going to unhinge her jaw and swallow her whole.

"I said there were three things we had to do. One, line the mirror. Two, light the candle. Three, and most importantly..." Jess let the thought linger.

"Hold hands, I know," Kitty said. "I'm sorry."

"Sorry won't cut it if you screw it up next time. Hold it together, or if you can't, I'll have to get someone else." Jess's hand reached down to pat Kitty's shoulder. It was supposed to be a reassuring gesture, but Kitty flinched like Jess was going to beat her to death.

"Wait, there's a next time now? You want to do this again?" Anna asked. I was guessing she was less interested in a repeat performance than Jess was. Or I was, to be fair. I was curious about the rest of the Bloody Mary package. I wanted to see what was attached to those hands, but there was no way Anna would listen to me.

Jess, however, stood a chance of convincing her. Jess was one of the most charismatic people on the planet when she put her mind to something, and even the iceberg that was Anna Sasaki would melt in the wake of an impassioned Jess speech. Jess wasn't stupid. She didn't get great grades like me or Anna, and she spent most of her time texting instead of paying attention in class, but she was clever. She understood people. If she wanted us to do something, she'd appeal to us in whatever way would get her results.

Jess slithered past me to sit down in front of Anna. The bathroom was so small their knees touched, but that didn't stop Jess from worming her way in so Anna was forced to look right at her. "How are you not seeing how amazing this is?" Jess asked. "I know it was scary, and scary is usually bad, but this is different. It's a miracle that it worked. Doesn't that excite you? That you're doing something other people can't? I bet fewer people have seen Bloody Mary than have . . . I don't know. Climbed Mount Everest. Or gone into space."

"Well, yes." Anna groaned, leaning her head against the tiled wall beside her. "It's scary. I'm also not sure it's safe. She clawed the glass. What if she's violent?"

"She's violent on the other side of the mirror. She can't hurt us while our hands are held. We control the summoning, we control her. You know?" Jess grabbed Anna's hand, giving it a long, reassuring squeeze. "One more time. What can it hurt?"

Anna jerked away with a sigh. The moment I heard that sound, I knew Jess had won. "Fine. Fine! But if something happens to me, I'm going to come back and haunt you. I will haunt you when you pee. I will haunt you when you're making out with Marc. I will make you miserable for the rest of your life."

"How's that different from any other day of the week?" Jess flashed Anna a grin before whirling around to look at me. "Tomorrow for another summoning, yeah?" She glanced between me and Kitty. Both of us nodded, though mine was more enthusiastic. Kitty was afraid, but Jess had already given her the out if she didn't want to come along. There were more than enough second-string friends to replace her. Laurie Carmichael and Becca Miller came immediately to mind, two girls from Jess's softball team who followed Jess around like puppies.

"Cool. One thing, though." Jess whirled in a circle so she could look at all of us, her finger pointed at each of our faces. "No parents. My mom would flip if she knew what I was up to. They won't believe you, anyway, so unless you want to look stupid, keep it quiet."

I hadn't considered telling my mom, but Jess had a point. If I told my mother that I'd conjured an evil ghost in a mirror, she'd probably look at me funny before asking if I needed to see a doctor.

"Right," I said, Anna and Kitty nodding along with me.

"Good. Okay, I've got to get home for dinner. You coming, Shauna?" Jess asked.

"Sure," I said. My mom had worked doubles since Monday, so Jess had dragged me home with her every day this week. Mrs. McAllister always seemed happy to have me, and I always thanked her profusely for the meal, feeling like a charity case.

"Let's go," Jess said, slipping out of the bathroom. She handed me my backpack as I followed her into the hallway.

I could hear Kitty and Anna talking quietly behind me. I poked my head back inside the bathroom to say bye to them. They waved, both looking tired and scared, and in Anna's case, a little irritable. She had her glasses off and was rubbing her eyes. Her hair had escaped its clip and had slithered over her shoulders like a black waterfall. Kitty had cried so much, her eyeliner had smudged down her cheeks in black tracks.

"See you two tomorrow," I said.

"Later," Jess echoed, and we climbed the front stairs to get to the driveway. Jess drove a hybrid car so green, it practically glowed in the dark, but she liked it and that was all that mattered. I climbed inside and buckled my seat belt, my hand already looping around the handle in the ceiling. One too many car rides with Jess had taught me to hold tight or risk massive head trauma when she took corners.

"Can you call your mom and make sure it's okay that I come over?" I asked when she climbed in beside me. "I don't want to crash again without asking."

Jess nodded and pulled out her cell. Two minutes later we were headed back to her house, four neighborhoods away.

The whole "honorary McAllister kid" status was fine until Todd, Jess's seven-year-old brother, decided to annoy me like I was his real older sister.

"Shauna, guess what?"

"What?"

"No, you've got to guess."

"Uhhh..." I said, concentrating on putting my napkin across my lap so I wouldn't have to answer.

"Shaaaauna. You have to guess!"

"Todd," Jess warned, slapping a wad of green bean casserole onto his plate so hard, bits of it splattered over the front of his blue T-shirt.

"Eat your dinner before it gets cold," Mrs. McAllister said. She leaned over the table to stuff a buttered biscuit in his mouth to muffle him. "I'm sorry, Shauna. 'Guess what' is one of the lovelier things he picked up in school. Oh, Jess, Marc called while you were out. He said he couldn't get your cell. Give him a call after dinner."

Jess had shut off her phone when we were summoning Mary

so we wouldn't have any interruptions. Marc must have called while we were incommunicado.

"Thanks," Jess said.

The thing I liked best about coming to Jess's house, besides the food, was the noise. Being an only child with a mother who worked all the time meant my apartment was tomb-silent. Sometimes it was okay. I could hear myself think to get my homework done, I could read or go online without any interruptions. But it was isolating, too. Here, with Mr. McAllister's loud deejay voice, Mrs. McAllister's propensity to drone on about anything that came to mind, Jess's phone ringing off the hook, and Todd's unbridled energy, I was distracted. I let the family's whirlwind swallow me.

"How was studying today, girls?" Mr. McAllister said with a mouthful of green beans I really wished he'd kept to himself. Apparently, instead of telling her parents she'd convinced her best friends to summon a deranged ghost, Jess had told them we were studying. Her parents should have known better. Jess didn't know the meaning of the word *study*.

"We didn't get as much done as we'd like. We'll probably finish up after dinner," Jess said, the lie sliding smoothly off her tongue.

"Then I don't want to hear the TV on." Mrs. McAllister gave us a pointed look. "And this isn't going to be an all-night thing, either. Bed by midnight, Jess."

"Can you talk to me like an adult? Seventeen, not seven." Jess hunched in her seat, stabbing her chicken like it was the dead bird's fault her mother nagged her.

"Maybe if you hadn't spent all last term on the phone with Marc, you wouldn't have gotten C's and D's on your report card. You're far too smart for bad grades, and softball's only going to get you so far."

The amazing thing about Todd, besides his ability to get anything in the universe stuck up his nose, was his complete lack of survival instinct. For some ungodly reason, he picked that exact moment to launch into a string of whining that was so high-pitched and irritating, I couldn't understand a word he said. Eventually, I figured out something about giant robots and dinosaurs and going to the movies, but it had practically required a translator and a Todd-to-English dictionary to reason it out.

"Saturday, Todd. Your father already told you that. Whining's not going to get you there any quicker. Now finish your dinner," Mrs. McAllister said.

"But Moooooom. I want to gooooo."

"Oh, my *God*, will you shut up about that stupid movie? It's all you talk about. You're so annoying sometimes," Jess snapped. The combination of Kitty's flip-out, her mom's scolding, and Todd's Toddness had frayed Jess's last nerve. I knew it was coming, but I'd hoped to be clear of the shrapnel before the bomb went off.

Mrs. McAllister's hand jerked out to grab Jess's wrist, her expression dark. "Knock it off. Seventeen, not seven, remember?"

"Whatever."

"Not 'whatever.' It wasn't so long ago that you were throwing tantrums, and you'd better believe we didn't treat you like you just treated your brother. Check the attitude."

"Apologize," Mr. McAllister said.

Jess rolled her eyes. "Fine. Sorry, Toad."

"Jessica!"

"...Sorry, Todd."

Dinner conversation petered out after that exchange. I helped clear the table, meticulously scraping each plate before putting it into the dishwasher. Jess was already halfway up the stairs to her room when I asked if I could be excused. Mrs. McAllister smiled and nodded, her voice getting louder when she said, "Your friend *still* has better table manners than you, Jessica."

Another one of Jess's *whatever*s floated down the staircase.

I grabbed my book bag from the floor of the kitchen and followed Jess to her bedroom. In the McAllister stairwell, there was a decorative mirror hanging among the family portraits. I caught a glimpse of my reflection mid-step and a shiver racked my spine. For all that I'd come down from Bloody Mary during dinner, seeing that glass made the unrest slither back. I ran the rest of the way to Jess's room, my eyes pinned to the floor.

The second the bedroom door clicked behind me, Jess pulled out the red spiral notebook from her backpack and looked over her Bloody Mary notes. I sat on her bed and grabbed a stuffed pony Marc had won for her at the summer carnival last year. It rested on my stomach, and I bent its ears back and played with its hooves while Jess plunked down in front of her computer, her hand shaking the mouse to clear her screen saver.

I could see the reflection of my sneakers in the sliding mirror doors of Jess's closet. I averted my gaze.

"You okay?" I asked, knowing she was upset with her mother.

"I will be. My family's irritating."

"I think all families are."

"Yeah, well, mine wins a prize," she said. She thumbed through her Mary notebook, past the photocopied letter she'd pasted to the first few pages and the notes she'd taken after Mary appeared. She read a few lines, typed something into her Web browser, and began reading from her monitor. I squinted to see, but it was too far away and I was too lazy to get up to snoop.

"I'm trying to find out about Mary Worth. Like, who she was. All the books I've found had mixed reports on Bloody Mary. Some say she was crazy and killed her children, some say she was a vampire. Others say she was a girl who died in front of a mirror and she got trapped inside it."

I'd heard these stories before and I nodded, making the stuffed pony dance at the back of Jess's head to amuse myself. "That's an old folklore thing. They used to cover mirrors in a house when someone was dying or dead. They thought the glass would swallow their souls," I said.

"Yeah, that," Jess said, her head jerking around toward me. I dropped the pony back onto my chest. "We'd have to find out if there was a mirror nearby when she died."

Jess clicked a few more Internet links, and I stifled a yawn against the back of my hand, my eyes straying to her alarm clock. I may have been a little tired, but I was still wiggly and nervous over Mary. Sleep wasn't coming anytime soon.

"I do have to study tonight," I said. "I have a McDuff essay on the Battle of Antietam due, so I can't stay late."

"That's fine. I'll bring you home soonish. So what did you think of Mary?"

I rolled onto my hip to look at her, my head perched on her mountain of pillows, my arm wrapped around the carnival pony. "What do you mean?"

"I mean, did you have fun? Did you like summoning her?"

"I don't know if 'like' is the right word, but it was fun. Terrifying, but fun." I fussed with the pony's ears again. "I wish Kitty hadn't scared me more than I already was."

Jess whirled around in her desk chair, her head falling back against the headrest of her seat. "Right? If she does it again, she's out. I've got way too much invested. Like, I got the letter, I went and talked to Aunt Dell at the library. I even called this woman Cordelia Jackson, who supposedly summoned Bloody Mary a billion years ago. She didn't want to talk to me, but that's beside the point. I worked for this. I don't want Kitty screwing it up for me."

I realized then I'd never asked Jess what would have happened if Kitty *had* broken the handhold. Stranger, it hadn't occurred to Anna to ask, either. "What happens if she does?"

Jess lifted her head to peer at me before letting out a long sigh. "Nothing confirmed, but she can scratch at people, grab them. That's just a rumor, though! Like I said, Aunt Dell was trying to scare me when I talked to her, but obviously there was some truth to what she said if the ritual worked. Cordelia survived Bloody Mary, so—"

"Survived?" I interrupted. That wasn't the verb I was expecting. *Summoned* maybe, or *encountered*, but *survived* made it sound like our lives were in peril if we kept messing around with the ghost, and frankly, I wanted to see her, but I wasn't willing to do it at the expense of my life.

"Well, yeah. Cordelia's here to talk about it, so that makes her a survivor. We're survivors in the same way. It's just too bad she hung up on me when I called her." Jess leaned forward in the chair to look at me, her hands balanced on her knees. "It was just a word, Shauna. If Kitty screws up, I'll send Mary away. I summoned her; I can dismiss her. She *has* to listen to my voice. That's how it works."

At one in the morning, I was too tired to work on my Antietam paper and too nervous to sleep. Jess dropped me off at eight, and while I'd done all right with the Bloody Mary thing when the McAllisters were around, the moment Jess drove away I was left with the thought of those ghoulish hands, the creaks and groans of an old building, and my imagination. I jumped every time a pipe rattled or my ancient upstairs neighbors went to the bathroom.

The post-summoning jitters afflicted everyone but Jess. Anna had glued herself to her dad's side all night and refused to go downstairs. Kitty had brought Kong, their Doberman, inside to sleep with her.

Jess, however, insisted she was fine. She texted me little tidbits of information she'd found online about Bloody Mary.

Jess: *Mary 1st appeared in the US in the 1960s.*

Me: *Why did she wait a hundred years?*

Jess: *Dunno. Still lookin.*

I didn't know how to respond, so I left it at a *cool*, all the while trying to keep my head on straight whenever Mrs. Zajac upstairs paced her way from her bedroom to the bathroom and back again.

It still struck me as weird that Jess wasn't the slightest bit freaked out. I finally asked her how she was so calm.

This is science, she texted. *Like an experiment.*

Not only was this *not* science, but real science was terrifying. Hadn't she ever cut a cat open in Mr. Sanno's anatomy and physiology class? That was Frankenstein-level horror, but when I said as much, Jess texted back *lol.*

I forced myself into bed at half past one in the morning. Fifteen minutes later, my mother came home from her closing shift at McReady's. The squealing door and the movement in the halls should have bothered me, but her presence quelled my nerves. She was my own fleshy night-light. I heard her pad toward my room and open my door to check on me; I closed my eyes and feigned sleep. Fleshy night-light or not, if she saw me up this late, she'd lecture me. Lucky for me, fake sleep translated to real sleep and I managed to drift off.

When I woke to the bellowing of the alarm clock, I heard my mother rummaging around in the kitchen. I oozed out feeling like I'd been hit by a garbage truck. I must have looked that way, too. Mom gave me the hairy eyeball over the top of her newspaper.

"You look exhausted. Are you okay?"

"Hey." I shuffled to the coffeemaker to get myself a cup, loading it with milk and sugar.

She pushed a chair out with her foot. "Want some waffles? They're frozen, but I'm a little short on time."

"You worked a double yesterday. I can get them myself," I said.

"You're still my kid. Let me pretend I'm good at this parenting thing." She put the newspaper aside and walked to the toaster, popping a pair of cardboard-looking waffles into the metal slots. She pressed a kiss to the top of my unshowered head as she passed me. "Why are you so tired?"

For a moment, I thought about telling her about Bloody Mary, but I had given my word to keep silent. I didn't *have* to do as Jess said, but the truth was, I wasn't sure how Mom would take it. I'm not one of those kids who's into darker stuff. I don't love horror movies, I don't talk about ghosts or aliens. I don't even read my horoscope. If I started babbling on about ghosts in mirrors, Mom would think something was seriously off with me.

"History paper took me longer than it should have," I said.

"No fun. I hope you weren't up too late." Her fingers drummed on the counter as she waited for the waffles to pop. The dark circles under her eyes made her look tired. Eighty-hour work weeks would do that to a woman. She was pretty in spite of it, though; prettier than me, anyway. Where I'm short, she's tall. Where my hair goes to frizz in the rain, hers stays curly and glossy and bounces around her shoulders. She has flawless, model-like skin. I'm riddled with freckles from forehead to toes. I'm not ugly, but my mom's in a different league.

"A watched pot never boils," she said under her breath,

turning away from the toaster to rummage around for maple syrup, a plate, and a fork. "Oh. I've got tomorrow night off from McReady's. You up for tacos and chick flicks?"

"Sure."

"Awesome. There's a Sandra Bullock thing I've been meaning to see, and I can hit a drive-through on the way home." The toaster popped. She pulled the waffles out, tossing them back and forth between her hands so she wouldn't burn the tips of her fingers. I watched her smear them with butter and maple syrup, my stomach grumbling. She served me the plate and dropped a paper towel over my head like a hat. I grinned, not bothering to move the paper towel even when it slid down to cover half my face.

Mom winked at me and drained her coffee cup. Her eyes flicked to the clock on the wall, a deep furrow appearing in her brow. "Shit, got to go. I should have been out of here five minutes ago. See you later tonight?" She lunged for her purse on the counter, jogging through the kitchen and living room to get to the door faster. Her hands slapped at her jacket pockets in search of her keys.

"Bye, Mom," I yelled after her with a mouth full of waffles. It came out more like "bah mot," but she understood, wagging her fingers in a wave.

"Bye!"

Her feet pounded down the steps of our apartment building a minute later. A door slammed and a car engine roared to life. When I looked back down at my waffles, I realized my appetite had left with my mother. I pulled the paper towel from my head and went back to my room to get ready for school.

The morning was one boring class bleeding into the next. I turned in my homework, bombed a math quiz because simple addition was beyond my tired brain, and shuffled to the cafeteria like a zombie. By the time I found my usual lunch seat, Jess was already waiting for me, Marc at her side and Bronx at Marc's other side.

Marc Costner was everything Jess ought to be dating—popular, arrogant, athletic. She was also smarter than him, which worked out well. I couldn't see her with someone smart enough to tell her to shut up when she ran her mouth. Jess was a pretty girl, and pretty girls were supposed to date cute guys like Marc. Sandy brown hair, green eyes, and a broad, square jaw.

Bronx wasn't quite that good-looking, but he wasn't unattractive by any stretch. He had black hair that curled around his ears and golden tan skin. His eyes were the color of good fudge. He was stockier than Marc, but not fat. He was the star football player on our team. When he hit other guys, they fell over, and when other guys hit him . . . well, they fell over. Bronx was a big dude.

Anna and Kitty weren't there yet, which was probably good. Kitty was going to lose her mind when she saw Bronx, and I hadn't had enough caffeine to deal with her drama yet. I grunted my hellos at Jess and the boys before dropping my bag onto the floor and lurching to the lunch line.

Once I had my food, I could see Kitty and Anna in the doorway of the caf, looking at our table as if sitting there would give them Ebola. They spotted me and I lifted my fingers in a feeble wave. Anna darted toward me, Kitty dragging behind her.

"Are we not supposed to sit with you?" Anna said in greeting. Despite her own sleepless Bloody Mary night, she'd been perfectly pleasant to me in the two classes we'd shared this morning. But seeing Bronx and Marc at our table now, all that pleasantness was gone. She looked like she could breathe fire.

"You can sit wherever you want," I said, dropping my gaze forlornly to my pizza. Hopefully she'd let me eat it before it got cold. The way she ground her jaw, I wasn't sure that was going to happen. The sad part was, I hadn't gotten that caffeine yet, either, so I was operating on two and a half exhausted brain cells screaming for a can of Coke.

"Well, it upsets Kitty. Jess is making problems," Anna said.

"Is she? Jess is allowed to sit with her boyfriend at lunch. We're fully capable of finding another table." I glanced over at Kitty. She looked like a deer about to be flattened by a bus. "I'll move my stuff and the three of us can sit together somewhere else. I'm sure Jess will understand."

Kitty took a moment to think the option over. While I waited, I finagled the cafeteria tray into the crook of my elbow so I could shove my pizza slice into my mouth. I loved the girl, but some things had to come first. Not dying of starvation was one of those things.

"We can sit there," Kitty said after a minute, her chin notching up. She wanted to look tough, like she could handle the situation, but the effect was ruined by the slight twitch in her cheek.

"Are you sure?" Anna pressed.

"Yes. I can't avoid him f-forever." Kitty tugged her arm away from Anna and went to make her usual salad. Anna followed her, and I took the opportunity to flee back to my seat. I positioned myself opposite of Jess so Anna and Kitty could sit on my right. This way, Jess and I acted as a Mason-Dixon Line where the northern boys and the southern girls never had to meet. They could stare at one another if they wanted to—I wasn't the eyeball police.

"Hey, Shauna. How you doing?" Bronx asked, smiling at me over his carton of milk. He had four empty ones on the table in front of him, and I glanced at my crappy sugar cola with guilt. He got vitamin D. I got stuff that would take the rust off of a car fender.

"Good. Tired."

"Oh? You out late last night?"

"Not really, just studying."

"I did that once. It hurt my brain," Marc said. He slung his arm over Jess's shoulder and made kissy faces at her until she gave him one of her fries. He bit her finger, and they shared a nauseating giggle.

Bronx smirked and shook his head. From the corner of my eye, I saw him glance behind, his eyes locking on Kitty. His face hardened and then fell before he leaned across the table to half whisper, half yell to me. He didn't want everyone to hear him, but the din of the cafeteria was so loud, it was hard to be inconspicuous.

"She doing okay?" Bronx asked. "Jess said she's had a bad couple weeks. I wasn't trying to . . . you know. I feel bad."

Jess eyed him and then me. I peeked past Jess's shoulder and saw Kitty coming our way, Anna at her elbow. This wasn't the time to talk about this, though I did want to know why a seemingly decent guy would dump his girlfriend with no warning. Maybe if he explained himself, Kitty could wrap her mind around it more. It'd give her closure or something.

"Not now. Text or call me later," I said.

"What?" he asked, the cafeteria suddenly noisy.

"Text or call me later," I repeated. Only I said it too loud and Kitty was close enough to hear. She looked between me and Bronx, and I knew something terrible had just happened.

"It's not like that," I said to Kitty, and she nodded, but she wouldn't look at me. All evidence that she was going to be brave about Bronx was gone as she scampered to the seat farthest away from him. Anna cast me a look, but it wasn't unfriendly. It was pity. Kitty knew me better than to think bad stuff about me, but when it came to Bronx, Kitty wasn't thinking straight. All Kitty knew was I'd been friendly with Bronx because he was her boyfriend, but there was no Bronx-and-Shauna dynamic. Now there suddenly was, and it scared her.

It was Jess who broke the uncomfortable silence—and managed to make the situation more awkward. I hadn't thought that it was possible, but Jess shouldn't be underestimated. "Oh, come on," she snapped, rolling her eyes at Kitty and then over at Bronx. "Like Shauna would do that to you. I can get your being upset, but do you think she's going to hop on Bronx's junk the moment you're off it?"

While I appreciated that Jess was defending my honor, I wanted to hide under the table for the rest of my life. The urge to crawl into a hole wasn't made any better when Marc whispered to Bronx, Bronx nodded, and they vacated the table.

"Jess, don't," Anna snapped.

"Don't what? Point out that Shauna would *never* do that to Kitty? Ever? Come on. You know she wouldn't," Jess said.

I felt that I should speak up, maybe assure Kitty that it was okay, but Anna picked up a piece of broccoli and flung it across the table at Jess. It hit her forehead and tumbled down into a puddle of ketchup. "Yes, I know she wouldn't. And Kitty knows she wouldn't, but it's still too raw. Don't be a bitch."

"It's been three weeks. Three weeks!" Jess got up from her seat to sit down across from Kitty. "We love you—I love you—but this has got to give. If you're so crazy upset that you can't deal with Bronx talking to your friends, or him being around or whatever . . . I don't even know. I'll start sitting with Marc at lunch and the four of us can hang out after school. But I'm not going to watch you psycho yourself into thinking Shauna's out to get you. Okay?"

Kitty nodded, but still she said nothing. Anna glared daggers at Jess, and Jess arched an eyebrow. There was no other way to interpret that gesture. It was an invitation to escalate this into an argument. Jess and Anna normally poked each other like sisters, but with all the weirdness at the table, it couldn't go anywhere good.

"Enough," I said. I'd been toying with my cookie, but I put it on the corner of my tray so I could address them with my serious face. "I would never hurt you, Kitty. If I talk to Bronx, it's to find out what's up—that's it." I glanced at the other side of the table. "And Anna, Jess—it's over. Let it be over. We've got plans later. I think we're all tired and a little on edge, yeah? So let it go."

Anna gave a curt nod. Jess shrugged and retrieved her book bag from the floor. Her expression was flat and irritated. For all that she'd bull-in-a-china-shopped that conversation with Kitty, she was making an effort to rein in her temper. Jess grabbed her tray and walked off to go sit with Marc and Bronx, abandoning the three of us to a quiet, joyless lunch.

I was staring out the window at the empty football field for most of my last class and missed the assignment my English teacher had given. At the last bell, I darted for the door. Yes, I'm a good student, but there are days I need to get away from school and give my brain a break.

I quickly shoved my books into my locker, though I still managed to be the last one to the parking lot. I stiffened seeing my friends together by Jess's car, expecting more static, but the hours apart must have mended the rift. Kitty was talking, Anna was nodding, and Jess was smiling. I wouldn't question how it happened. I was too relieved.

"Let's do this," Jess said when I approached. She opened the trunk of the car so I could throw my bag in with everyone else's. Kitty and Anna slid into the backseat while I buckled myself into the front. Jess peeled out of the parking lot with a spin of wheels and flying grit.

Anna had the house to herself until her parents came home from work, so we crashed at her place for the second day in a row. Anna opened the front door while Jess rummaged around in her trunk for supplies. There was a big box of kosher salt, a beeswax candle, a compass, and the red notebook.

Kitty and Anna went upstairs to take a small break before we got started, but not Jess. She went right at it. She dropped her stuff in the sink and removed the pictures from the wall—a Sasaki family portrait from some camping trip and a *Starry Night* lithograph. She hadn't done this the last time we'd summoned Bloody Mary. I watched her stack the pictures on the bottom step, curious.

"It's a precaution. The frames are shiny. Like, you can see yourself in them," she said. "I don't want Mary to come through in a weird place."

I grabbed the portrait to look into the brass frame, my distorted reflection peering back at me. "Does it work like that? Like, she can be summoned somewhere other than a mirror?" I asked, horrified at the idea of Mary's appearing in places she didn't belong.

"I won't take any risks. I told you I was being safe."

I watched Jess arrange the candle and grab the salt before flipping open her notebook. Everything she did was so organized, and I tried to find solace in her system, but my stomach clenched. The ritual worked *because* Jess was so careful. These precautions weren't for safety so much as for success.

I wanted to bail right then, but leaving would infuriate Jess. I'd be mad at myself, too, I supposed. "I had the chance to see

Bloody Mary but I settled for her hands" felt pathetic. I didn't want to be that person. I took a deep breath and replaced the family picture on the step. One good look at Mary and I'd be done. I just had to swallow my nerves and go for it.

I could handle it. I'd be fine.

"Hey, can you go get me a water? I'm thirsty," Jess said, interrupting my thoughts.

"Sure," I said.

I could hear Anna and Kitty in the kitchen murmuring, and I wondered if they were feeling the same way I was, that maybe this wasn't such a good idea. I crested the top step and peered at them. They were standing side by side near the kitchen sink, their heads tilted together. Kitty looked pale; Anna looked angry.

"Everything cool?" I asked.

Kitty nodded; Anna scowled.

"I'm not so sure I want to do this again. I don't want to be afraid of my bathroom forever," Anna said.

"Do *you* want to be the one to tell Jess that?" Kitty asked. I pointed at Kitty as if to say *That* before opening the fridge for Jess's water.

Anna shrugged. "I really don't care. She'd get over it. I just . . . I don't know. This seems like a bad idea."

"It's a terrible idea," I said. "But I do kind of want to see Mary's face. I mean, just to finish it. We never have to do it again."

Anna lifted her glasses to rub her eyes, her mouth puckered like she'd smelled something bad. A moment later her shoulders dropped and the glasses slid back onto her nose. She shook her head and shouldered past me to get out of the kitchen. "Fine. Let's get it over with, but I hate you all a little right now."

The three of us went downstairs looking like we were marching to our executions. By the time we crowded the hallway outside of the bathroom, Jess had finished with the salt and was skimming her notebook one last time, the compass in her left hand. I offered her the water and she pointed at the side of the tub, indicating I should leave it there.

"I'm making a small modification to the positioning this time," she said. "Kitty, you come stand here." She motioned at the spot Jess had taken the first time, next to the vanity. Kitty squeezed past her, frowning that she was now closest to the mirror. She opened her mouth to protest, but Jess cast her a sharp look and Kitty kept quiet.

"I can stand there," I offered, but Jess shook her head.

"No, you're going to be where you were. Kitty's going north to the vanity, Anna south to the tub, and I'll take the linen closet so I can see better." I'd still be holding Kitty's hand this time, just on the opposite side. I eyed her, hoping she wouldn't spaz out again. She looked nervous, but not nauseated like yesterday. Maybe that was a sign we were in the clear. Jess would be on her other side this time, too, and I knew she'd be a little better at reining Kitty in than Anna had been.

We wedged into our positions looking nervous and grim. I had a terrible case of the jitters, adrenaline pounding through my body. Jess leaned past Kitty to light the candle before flicking off the lights. Anna let out a shuddering gasp, Kitty groaned, and I held my breath as Jess fell into place opposite me. We were ready.

"Bloody Mary. Bloody Mary. BLOODY MARY," Jess shouted.

The candle on the vanity cast eerie shadows, our forms tall and distorted against the walls. Our hands were clenched together so tightly, our fingers trembled. This time, it took only seconds for condensation to cover the glass. A thick fog swirled, gray tendrils of smoke spinning in a maelstrom, before a black figure appeared, the vague outline of a woman. I braced myself, expecting more of the slow, shambling gait we'd seen last time.

SLAM.

Mary moved fast. One moment she was distant, the next her hands smacked against the mirror. Her fingers flexed, and then the clawing began, a shrieking squeal of razors cutting across glass. I jerked back, forcing myself to maintain the handhold. There'd been no noise during the last summoning. Now, the sound was undeniable.

"Why? Why can we hear her?" I asked, my voice warbling.

"I changed a few things around. Watch," Jess replied, her voice barely above a whisper as Mary's hands slid down the mirror. The fog thinned, and for the first time, I saw her. All of her.

She was dead. That wasn't a surprise, but I hadn't expected her to be *so* dead. Her mouth gaped open in a rictus grin, revealing a row of jagged, broken teeth that grayed along the gum line. Her face was gaunt, like her skin had been pulled taut somewhere behind her head. It reminded me of papier-mâché, when the first layers of tissue are on top of the balloon and the colors of the latex underneath are still visible. Except in this case, the balloon was her skull, and the tissue paper was her too-thin flesh. A spidery network of veins pulsed along her temples and upper cheeks.

There was a hiss as her tongue lolled out. It was pasty and white, covered in film and wiggling around like a worm. She raked it over the glass with an awful groan. Her lips were so receded that her teeth clicked against the mirror, the pointy stubs black and yellow with decay.

I tore my gaze away from her mouth and up to her eyes, fathomless black orbs sunk deep into her skull with no lashes, no brows. Patches of skin had peeled away along her forehead and chin. Her nose was nonexistent; the cartilage had rotted, leaving her with two socket holes that oozed a tarlike guck. Her hair was stringy tufts of black on a bumpy, pointed skull. Her cheeks were hollow with sharp, boney edges.

Beside me, Kitty squeezed my fingers for reassurance, and I did the same back, both of us transfixed by the jerky, erratic movements of the ghost behind the mirror. We could still hear the screech of her fingernails, along with something else—a raspy, rattling breathing.

"I . . . I can hear her. God." Kitty groaned.

"I know, isn't it awesome?" Jess asked.

Jess used "awesome" way too loosely.

We kept our eyes fixed on the mirror. Mary jerked her head to the side to eye Jess. Kitty and I were closer to her, but Mary wasn't interested in us. Jess had said that she controlled the ritual, that Mary only answered to the summoning voice. Maybe that meant Mary only wanted to see the person who called her, too.

I could see the excitement on Jess's face. Kitty, Anna, and I wanted to puke, but not Jess. She was happier than I'd seen her in ages. I watched her lean toward the mirror to get a closer look. I wanted to be that cool, that collected.

"Mary, can you hear us? We can hear you," Jess said.

Mary snapped her jaws and lunged at the glass. The mirror bowed out with her. Jess reared back with a yelp, the first sign of true terror I'd seen from her. Kitty and Anna screamed. I began to hyperventilate. I had no idea what just happened. A mirror was cold glass. It was solid. It shouldn't move. But this mirror had stretched like a liquid membrane, like Mary was pushing against a sheet of plastic wrap.

"Why? *Why?* Send it back. *Send it back,*" Anna wailed, tears streaming down her cheeks now. "Enough. I BELIEVE IN YOU, MARY WORTH."

"It won't work from you, it has to be me who dismisses her. Hold on a second," Jess hissed, licking her lips and squirming. I felt Kitty jerk around and I moved my hand up from her fingers to grip her wrist. If the mirror was moving, we were already in over our heads. Kitty breaking the bond would make the situation worse.

"Mary, if you can hear us, talk to us," Jess said, her cheeks flushed red, her eyes enormous in her face.

Mary edged forward, pushing herself against the mirror. She tested the gooey mass with awkward hesitance. Her fingertips pressed on the surface, a jagged fingernail poking through, ripples flowing outward from where it emerged.

Part of Mary was no longer in her world, but in ours.

"Oh, my God," Jess gasped, then barked with laughter. *How could she laugh?* I'd gone so rigid, you could have replaced my spine with a yardstick. Anna silently wept on one side of me, and Kitty had her eyes snapped shut, murmuring "no, no" and shaking her head.

"Talk to us, Mary. Tell us your story," Jess continued.

"What are you doing?" I asked as Jess leaned forward to talk to the ghost. Jess was so bold, so sure of herself. It was like she'd known what to expect from Mary, and if she had . . .

No. She wouldn't do that. She'd never set us up like that.

"I just want to talk to you. Can you speak, Mary?" Jess prodded.

Mary ignored her, popping another finger through the mirror and cooing as she sent a third, a fourth, and finally a thumb. My throat constricted as Mary's second hand quickly joined the first. They were now free of her glass prison and waving about, her fingers curling over like talons. Mary rasped and rattled, and when I saw the unnerving look on her face, I realized she was laughing.

What would a ghost have to laugh at? I had no answers. Well, no *good* answers, anyway.

"Mary, I . . . We want to know about you," Jess continued. "About your life. We read your letter to your sister, Constance."

The moment Jess said Constance's name, Mary froze. Pain seemed to cross her face, one gruesome expression followed by another. I heard a faint trill from her side of the mirror, like the high-pitched squeal of a mewling kitten. Jess took it to mean she could continue the questioning.

"Yes. We read about Constance!" Jess paused to collect herself. It was clear by her tone that the ghost's response thrilled her. I jerked my face Jess's way. She was shaking—almost vibrating. It wasn't fear pulsing through Jess's body, it was excitement.

"Jess, stop," I pleaded, but she ignored me.

"We read about Constance's marriage and her move to Boston. And how you thought you'd marry a sheep farmer. And we read about Pastor Starkcrowe and Elizabeth."

"NGGGGAH!" Bloody Mary dove at us, her chittering replaced by furious, punishing bellows. It was hard to tell whether the mention of the pastor, of Elizabeth Hawthorne, or of both had enraged her.

Mary's face tore through the mirror, twisting and writhing feet away from me. Her jaw snapped like a rabid dog's, a string of green saliva hanging from her maw like she hungered for flesh. The candlelight was dim, but I could see every fine line on her face. I could see the dead leaves strewn through her dripping wet hair and the pounding black vein in her temple.

And the smell. When Mary crossed into our world, she polluted the air with a scent too sour, too sweet, and too wet.

There was earthiness, too, like mud and moss. And rot. So much rot.

"Stop it! This isn't safe. Send her away," Anna pleaded. "Please, please."

"We're fine. She can't cross the salt barrier," Jess snapped. "It's moved out a little, but she still can't cross it. Look. *Look!*"

I looked. The salt line was there, but Jess hadn't put it flush to the glass like last time. The line was five or six inches away from the bottom frame of the mirror. Was Jess *trying* to coax Mary out?

If so, Jess and I were going to have some serious problems.

But first, the ghost.

Mary let out an angry shriek. We reared as far from the mirror as the tiny bathroom would allow, clinging to one another's hands in desperation. Kitty wriggled like she had during the last summoning. I slid my fingers up to her elbow, gripping hard as she gasped in surprised pain.

"J-Jess, I c-can't...make it stop," Anna stammered.

But Jess was relentless. As she watched Mary test her new freedoms, her smile was gone but her expression was no less intense.

Mary pushed her arms through the glass, her left hand reaching toward the wall, smearing her palm over the beige tiles. The sludge from her open wound drizzled down the crevices of the grout.

Mary rolled her head, shifting her gaze among the four of us, hissing and flicking her tongue. She peered down at the salt line and groaned before reaching her desiccated fingers toward it. The tip of her middle finger grazed the line. Mary screeched, snatching her hand back, like she'd been burned. She ducked behind the mirror with a growl, crouching so we could only see the top of her head and the few fingers she'd looped over the bottom of the mirror's frame. A puddle of water pooled on the counter from where she'd been leaning, tendrils of it snaking its way toward the salt line.

"Almost done, I swear," Jess said. "Mary, can you speak? Can you say something before you have to go?"

Mary's eyes darted to Jess's face. I watched her mouth open. Her lips twitched, like she was trying to make a word, and formed a cracked, misshapen little *O*.

"You can do it. Tell us," Jess said, encouraging Mary with the gentleness of her tone. Jess tried to move closer to the mirror, but Anna yanked back on her arm, keeping Jess pinned against the opposite wall. Jess snarled, but Anna kept her hold even when Jess jerked Anna forward, forcing them closer to the ghost.

Mary's mouth wavered, her lips still puckered. Despite my terror, I quieted. I wanted to hear Mary, too. Mary stood to lean from the mirror, her head popping through the liquid glass as she moaned. Her lips quivered and receded, showing her broken teeth and worm-riddled gums.

Puff.

Mary blew out the candle on the vanity with a tiny puff of fetid air, plunging us into blackness. We screamed, but it was Jess's voice that rang the loudest. "I BELIEVE IN YOU, MARY WORTH."

The bathroom went silent. My heart pounded in my ears, my temples threatening to splinter apart. I wanted to be somewhere where the light never faded. I wanted to erase the name Bloody Mary forever. I wasn't sure I'd ever forgive Jess. She'd put us up to this. She'd moved the salt line. Every awful feeling swarming inside of me was Jess's fault.

"Never. Never again. Do you hear me? Never again, Jess. You're lucky if I'll ever talk to you again." Anna sniffled and began to cry, heart-wrenching sobs.

Jess sighed into the darkness. "Come on, guys. We're fine," she said. "It was scary, but—"

"Turn on the light," I yelled. A rivulet of sweat coursed down my face and over my cheek. I was drenched in sweat. I dropped Kitty's hand to brush my forehead against the back of my arm.

I never should have let Kitty go.

A wail ripped through the room. Mary was there. Somehow, some way, Jess's dismissal didn't work. Maybe it was because the candle was snuffed out. Maybe it was because the salt line was moved, or maybe Mary's murky water had melted through the defense. Whatever the case, without the handhold in place, there were no protective wards left to contain the beast. Kitty scrambled away before I could stop her, stumbling into a wall with a pained thud. I was now closest to the mirror.

Closest to Mary.

Jess flicked on the bathroom light just as Mary's claws raked down my shoulders. It was razor blades through butter, bloody cuts splitting my flesh in crimson tracks. I tried to flinch away, but Bloody Mary reached around my front and jerked me off my feet, dragging me toward the glass, toward the world we had woken behind Anna Sasaki's mirror.

I was going in.

I tried to struggle, to wriggle and fight and slap at Mary's hands, but she'd hooked me too tight. There was no way out. The glass surface rippled and bowed as Mary pulled me in, headfirst, my face pointed at the ceiling. My back struck the sink. I screamed as Mary scraped me across the ledge beneath the mirror, fire shooting along my spine.

Behind me, there was only the ghost and the fog. Mary hoisted me again, and the top of my head crested the surface of the mirror. It slurped on me like a frigid, toothless mouth. Over my forehead, over my brows—the mirror swallowed me into its gullet. Gel flooded my eyes, plunging me into darkness. My friends' panicked screams cut off as my ears were drawn through the quivering glass.

From chaos to empty silence.

I cried out for help as the undulating liquid spilled into my mouth. Farther in, to my shoulders, my chest. The mirror gel had slipped to my waist and was spilling toward my hips. I held my breath as long as I could, until the desperation for air overwhelmed me. Instinct forced my mouth open again and that sour, brackish water rushed into my throat. I gasped, but only to choke. I was going to drown halfway between Mary's world and my own.

Until hands grabbed my feet and pulled. As I slipped back out of the mirror, Mary dug her fingers into my flesh, her nails shredding at my chest. I screamed, gagging as my lungs filled with fluid. A twisted game of tug-of-war pulled me back and forth between my friends and Bloody Mary. My world was shrinking by the moment. It wasn't until my friends gave another mighty haul that the stalemate ended. The ghost lost her grip, her claws torn from my flesh. I spewed onto the floor of Anna's bathroom like the mirror had birthed me from its foul womb.

Anna screamed then, the kind of terrified shrieks reserved for horror movies and personal tragedies. I forced myself up onto my knees, expecting my back to spasm with the movement, but shock had settled in. Though my vision was blurry, I could still see Bloody Mary heaving her way out of the mirror, her blood-smeared fingers clutching onto the frame. She lifted her leg over the bottom, her foot sloshing down onto Anna's floor like she'd emerged from a swamp.

Mary was out.

She chuckled as she forced her way into our world, her movements slow and lumbering one moment and fast and jerky the next. Stringy black hair hung to her elbows, the strands caked to her neck and shoulders. Pale, gray skin hugged her knobby bones, the flesh at her joints worn through. A tattered white dress covered her, splotches of my blood staining the fabric along the ragged sleeves and bust.

"I BELIEVE IN YOU, MARY WORTH! I BELIEVE IN YOU!" Jess screamed from her position near the linen closet, but the words did nothing. Our defenses were obliterated.

Mary's head tilted back as her nostril holes flared to scent the air. Anna shoved past Kitty to get to the door. The two of them fumbled with the knob, but it wouldn't turn. We hadn't locked it, but even if we had, it was to keep people out, not in. Something else was at work here.

I coughed and shook my head, wanting desperately to escape the bathroom, but I had to pause to let my body convulse, my lungs dispelling more of the rank liquid. I glanced up at Jess, hoping she'd stall Mary, but Jess was frozen, staring at the terror lurching our way. Anna was screaming and pounding on the door. Kitty was throwing her weight at the door, trying to rip it from the hinges, but not Jess.

Mary peered down at me and groaned, her hand lifting toward my head like she wanted to stroke my hair. I did the only thing I could think of to protect myself: I reached for the salt box on the floor and whipped a handful at Mary's face.

The moment the salt crystals struck her face, Bloody Mary thrashed and bumbled away, her flesh sizzling, sour-smelling smoke wafting off of her in oily clouds wherever the salt had touched. Mary clawed at her cheeks and forehead in a frantic attempt to remove the salt stuck to her wet skin. I clapped my hands over my ears to block out Mary's deafening wails.

"Go back, GO BACK!" I ordered, my voice cracking.

Mary dropped her hands and fixed her black eyes on me, her thin, leathery lips receding with a hiss. She swung her arm at my head. I took another handful of salt and flung it. She screeched and writhed, smoke fizzling off her body.

I threw more salt, trying to force a retreat. It seemed to be working. Mary turned to put her hands on the mirror frame and began climbing back inside, her foot perched on Anna's sink. Once she had good purchase, she leapt, the watery glass sucking her into its depths. Somehow, I was winning. I scrambled to my feet, my hand rapidly firing salt at the mirror. The gel thickened, the crystals suspended halfway between Mary's world and ours.

I'd hoped when the mirror swallowed Mary, she'd disappear, but she rose up to fill the glass again, the fog behind her whipped into a frenzy. Mary pushed her hands out like she'd grab for me, but there was too much salt embedded in the mirror. Her hands burned on contact. She wrenched them away and shuddered, smoke billowing from her palms, the tips of her fingers peeling like blackened onion skin.

I don't know what shook Jess from her stupor, but something penetrated the fog. She relit the candle by the sink and grabbed the salt from my hands, placing a thick line beneath the glass. Whenever she got too close to Mary, the ghost lashed out, but the mirror had solidified enough that Mary couldn't cross. The salt thickened the glass to a tar-like consistency.

"Everyone, come here. Turn off the light. I want to try to dismiss her again," Jess said.

"Oh, screw you. Like w-we're going to trust you again," Anna snapped just as Kitty gave the bathroom door another shove. It popped open like it had never been locked. Kitty and Anna thrust themselves into the hall, Kitty wheezing, Anna thanking a higher power for getting her out alive. I glanced at the mirror behind me. Mary remained, staring at me, hungry for my blood. Her lip curled and twitched, her eyes devoured my face, burning my features into her memory.

I could hear Anna sniveling as she climbed the stairs, but Jess's voice rang out, stopping her short. "If you don't help, this thing is going to live in your basement forever. Let's finish this." Anna erupted in stomps and a series of nonsensical threats—she was furious at Jess. But living in a house with an open link to Bloody Mary was sufficient motivation for Anna to return. She resumed her position, taking a moment to wipe her tear-stained face with a towel.

Kitty continued up the stairs, and Jess darted after her to drag her back down to the bathroom. They reappeared a minute later, Kitty stumbling in Jess's wake, her inhaler plugging her mouth, cheeks and eyes red. She looked puffy, too, like she had so many tears swelling inside of her, she might rupture.

Kitty pocketed the inhaler, and Jess herded her into position by the sink. Kitty stood there shaking, her tongue skimming over her lips. No one wanted to do this, but we reformed the summoning circle after Jess flicked off the light. I laced my fingers with my friends', this time leaning as far away from the mirror as I could.

I could still hear the wet rattle of Mary's breath from behind the glass.

There was little ceremony this time. "I believe in you, Mary Worth," Jess said, and we waited for the fog to usher Mary away. Except it didn't. Mary bashed her forehead against the glass, black smears of her blood streaking down in curling rivers. Her fingernails shredded at the pane, two nails snapping off, exposing raw, tender flesh—but Mary remained trapped inside.

She refused to go.

"I believe in you, Mary Worth!" Jess shouted again. Mary plastered her face to the mirror, giving us an unadulterated view of the mushy insides of her nostrils. It was Jess who had given all the summoning commands, but Mary's gaze fixed on me. I'd become the object of her fascination. I shuddered as she eyeballed me, her tongue slithering over the glass to lap at her own blood.

"Oh, my God. Gross," Kitty rasped.

"Wh-what if she never goes? N-never leaves?" Anna stammered.

Jess took a deep breath before jerking her hand away from Anna to break our bond. She braced, probably expecting the mirror to soften and unleash the monster again, but Mary stayed on the other side, her hands pressed to the glass as she stared at me. Jess relaxed, her hand smoothing over her blond head. "We'll figure it out. There's got to be a way to get rid of her. Shauna, are you okay? Does your back hurt?"

My back didn't hurt until Jess mentioned it—then it hurt *a lot*. Mary had scoured those talons over my flesh. A burning pain exploded across my shoulder blades. I swallowed a whimper, feeling faint. I wanted to sit down. I needed to sit down. I let go of Kitty and Anna and sank onto the toilet, my butt scooted forward so I didn't brush my back against the tank.

"I don't feel very good," I admitted.

"She should go to the doctor," Kitty said. Jess waved her off, crouching to peer at me. Jess's thumb and forefinger grabbed my chin, her sharp fingernails biting into my jaw.

"You're pale," she said.

"I'm always pale. Fresh off the slab," I returned, but the joke fell flat, especially when I glanced to my right and saw Mary hovering, her body half-hidden by the mirror frame. She was trying to follow me, but the glass would only let her get so far, so she wedged herself against the side.

Jess inspected my injuries. She leaned over my shoulder to tug my shirt away from my back, but the moment she pulled, I twitched. I was wet, and the fabric had adhered to my open wounds. The slight tug nauseated me enough that I placed my hand against the wall, using the cold of the tile to distract me from my queasiness. It wasn't until Jess let out a groan that I suspected the shirt wasn't stuck to me with water so much as with blood.

"She needs help," Jess said. "But a doctor is going to ask questions. Let's see if we can do anything first. Maybe, like, clean the cuts and bandage them? If it's still really bad we can make something up about an accident or . . . I don't know. Something."

I was furious with Jess but in too much pain to argue. We could fight later, when I wasn't about to bleed to death in Anna's basement.

"Let's get out of here," Kitty said as she turned on her heel and raced up the stairs.

"Good plan," Anna agreed, her eyes fixed on the mirror.

Jess wrapped her arm around my waist to help me to my feet. I sagged into her side. We shuffled from the bathroom like the slowest three-legged race ever, leaving Mary squirming and hissing in the mirror behind us. Jess managed to get me out of the doorway, but we had to stop when I got dizzy. The exertion made me want to throw up all over again.

"I'm not staying here. Not with her here," Anna proclaimed. I glanced back in time to see Anna grab a sheet from the linen closet and throw it over the mirror. It didn't hang quite right, and she darted in to adjust it so she couldn't see Bloody Mary anymore. When Anna neared the mirror, Mary growled like she knew Anna was there even though she couldn't see her. Anna looked terrified, but she persevered, tucking the sheet under the frame until Mary was fully hidden from view.

Anna closed the door and ran into the hall behind us, her face expressionless. "Let's get out of here. The house. I don't want to be here right now. Let's leave and then figure this mess out." She wriggled her way past me and Jess to go get Kitty.

I wasn't going to stop her. As much as I wanted my back tended, I wanted to get away from Bloody Mary even more.

Kitty wedged a folded towel behind my back so I wouldn't bleed on Jess's car upholstery. Another towel covered the seat so my pants didn't drip everywhere.

We drove toward my house. Every time Jess took a turn, I tensed, and tensing flexed my back, which hurt. Kitty insisted I needed a doctor, but I didn't want to end an already traumatic day in the emergency room. Getting home, and safe, was my top priority.

We said little during the ride. We were too upset, too freaked out. Jess's brow was furrowed like she was deep in thought.

Kitty had her head tilted back with her eyes closed. Anna sat wide-eyed with rage. I'd never seen her look so mad and be so silent.

I was mad, too. I'd nearly gotten killed by Jess's game. I couldn't say for sure Mary had broken free because Jess had moved the salt line. I suspected as much, but really, we hadn't fully summoned Mary on our first attempt. Maybe she would have been able to cross over our way even without those extra inches between salt and mirror. Maybe the water would have come through and eaten away at the line like it had this summoning. There was no way to know.

I wasn't ready to drop Jess as a friend. Not yet. Jess was as upset as the rest of us. Whether it was because I'd gotten hurt or because everyone was going to blame her or because the whole thing had gone so wrong, I didn't know, but it didn't matter. Jess's misery bought her a little slack. Probably not with Anna, though. Or Kitty.

"I still see her. Like, even with my eyes closed, I see her," Kitty said from the backseat.

"Now imagine her in your basement bathroom forever. I'll be able to see her whenever I want," Anna returned.

Jess stayed quiet as she took the last turn to my street. She pulled into the building parking lot and eased into the guest spot. I went to put my hand on the door to let myself out, but Jess insisted on helping me. Pain cut across my shoulders, making me gasp. Jess held me still until I was steady on my feet.

"Her bag's in the trunk. Grab it. House keys are usually in the front pouch," Jess said to Kitty. Kitty ducked behind the car to rummage for my stuff. She pulled out my backpack and pawed through the front section for my keys. Anna plucked them from her hand and jogged ahead of us, first to let me into the base floor and then up into the apartment. Jess and I hobbled after her, Kitty behind us with her hands up to catch me if I fell.

Inside, the apartment wasn't much to look at—boring beige walls, matted beige carpet. The entrance opened into a living room with floor-to-ceiling windows and a small kitchen with a round table and four chairs. Past the living room was a hallway with a bathroom on the right and at the end, a split into two bedrooms. Mine was on the left, Mom's was on the right.

Anna headed down the hall to open my bedroom door, and Jess eased me inside toward the bed. She tried to get me to lie down, but I stopped to drop Anna's towel and peel off my shirt. Putting my arms over my head hurt too much, though, and Jess had to strip me down to my bra and underwear. I felt weird standing around almost naked, but the girls didn't care. Anna tossed my wet pants into the hamper and my shirt into the trash.

Jess helped me onto my bed. I sprawled facedown, and she lifted my hair to get it off my neck. From the doorway, Kitty gasped. At first I thought she was reacting to the cuts in my back, but instead she pointed to my mirrored vanity, her cheeks ballooning out.

"Something flickered. Her. I think I saw her," Kitty said.

My head swiveled and I braced to see Mary's face in the

glass, but there was only the reflection of Anna's head, Jess's back, and my pale pink drapes.

"We didn't summon her here. I don't think that's possible," Jess said.

Anna snorted. "Yeah, she's hanging out in my downstairs forever, remember? Thanks for that, by the way, Jess. Thanks. Not only did you nearly kill Shauna, you've made my house uninhabitable."

Jess whipped her head around to glower at Anna. She'd been quiet to this point, but by the look on her face, that was about to change. "Stop," Jess snapped. "We both know being angry won't fix anything. It's not going to make Shauna's back better. And it's not going to get rid of the thing in your basement. We can fight later, after this is over, but for now, cut the crap, Anna."

"Oh, so *I'm* the one who needs to cut the crap," Anna said. "Me, not you."

"Yeah, you. You're being a bitch. Shauna needs help."

Anna seethed. She stalked a few steps forward, her finger pointing at Jess's face, but Kitty reached out to grab her shoulders, reeling her in like a fish. Kitty turned Anna until she faced my vanity. Anna spun, but not without another shooting glare in Jess's direction. "What?" she demanded.

"J-just watch. Please?" Kitty pleaded, her voice thick with fear. "I swear she flashed by."

The two of them stayed stock-still, peering into my mirror, as Jess disappeared into the hall. I heard her in the bathroom opening cabinets and drawers. I craned my head to see what

Kitty was talking about, but there was nothing in the mirror other than their reflections. There were no shooting lights, no fog, no scary dead faces.

"I don't see anything," Anna said.

Kitty frowned and settled at the foot of my bed, the mattress shifting beneath her weight. She rubbed her palms down her cheeks and rolled her head around on her shoulders. "Maybe I'm seeing things. Sorry. I'm worked up."

"We all are," Anna said, sliding a hand to Kitty's shoulder and squeezing. "I'm going to jump at my own shadow for a long time."

Jess came back into the room with a wet facecloth, my mom's first aid kit, and some antibacterial ointment. She dropped everything on my nightstand except for the washcloth, which she pressed against one of my cuts. It burned like she filled the gash with molten lava. I gritted my teeth, willing myself not to cry out. My hands grabbed handfuls of the blankets beneath me, wadding them up into a tight ball.

"I'm covering this stupid mirror," Anna said a second later. She walked past the bed to tug my bathrobe from the peg on the wall and slung it over the vanity. It was probably for the best; when I got around to being vertical again, I'd planned to do the exact same thing.

Jess pulled away from the first cut and moved to the second in the same agonizing manner. It was an unpleasant few minutes, the room silent. I dropped my head when my eyes began to water. Jess stopped mauling me with the washcloth, but then came the ointment, and that was worse in some ways.

Her finger didn't go into the cuts, but it did press down on the tender skin around them.

"You're not bleeding anymore," Jess said quietly. "It's clotted. She got you good, but I don't think you need, like, stitches. I mean, we can go to the hospital if you want and say you got attacked by a cat, but..."

"A cat? Really? More like a freaking tiger," Anna said. I nearly laughed, but then Jess smeared my wounds with more ointment and I forgot how to be happy about anything, ever.

"She should risk the doctor. Bloody Mary's fingers were dirty and gross," Kitty said, her hand coming to rest on my calf. She gave it a squeeze before pulling up my blanket to cover my bare legs. "She could get a nasty infection. Remember that girl who got that flesh-eating disease on the news? They had to cut off her hands and feet."

"That's up to Shauna," Jess said, opening the first aid kit and pulling out a pair of the big Band-Aids. She tore the packages with her teeth and then placed them over my cuts, gently prodding them to lie flat. "But they are going to ask how she did it. We bring her in for stitches, she says a ghost attacked her, they'll think she's nuts or lying. If she's lying, then they're going to wonder why. Who's abusing her. Her mom? Her boyfriend? Us? It's just... I get why you're saying it, and if Shauna wants to go I'll drive her, but it's a big, ugly can of worms. We need to come up with something they'll believe before we go."

I glanced at my friends. For all that we didn't like admitting it, Jess was right. Bloody Mary was something the world should know about. She was something we should be able to talk about and warn people away from, but we couldn't. No one would believe us.

"I'll wait," I said, dropping my head down into one of my pillows. "If I need a doctor later, we'll go, but for now let's see how I do." Everyone nodded, all of us wearing matching frowns. Earlier, I'd feared my friends would be torn apart by what happened at Anna's house, but I realized then it wouldn't happen for one reason. We shared a ghostly burden.

8

Jess flung the red notebook onto the floor with a frustrated sigh. She'd been leafing through it in hopes of finding something that'd help with Bloody Mary, but she'd come up empty. It wasn't surprising; most of what she had in there was for making Mary appear, not disappear.

Kitty also tried to help by scouring the Web on my laptop. Searching for Bloody Mary yielded a bunch of Halloween sites, so she switched to a general ghost search. I was prone in bed with Anna wedged onto the mattress at my side while we looked for clues on her phone.

Sadly, the Internet failed us.

A lot of what we found involved sites charging exorbitant fees to purify a house against negative spiritual activity. Many claimed to be professionals, but it was hard to take them seriously when their Web sites had horror movie sound tracks and blinking cartoon ghost banners. Also, their "real ghost" photography sections were typically floating orbs or mysterious shadows. Nothing we found was Bloody Mary–caliber.

"I think I'll head home for a bit. Call Aunt Dell and maybe try to talk to Cordelia Jackson again," Jess said. "I don't have any leads, but they might."

"Why not call them from here?" Anna asked, her tone sharp. "If we're suffering, it's only fair you suffer with us."

I could tell Jess wanted to yell by the way her molars ground together, her cheek twitching like she had a nervous tic. Her eyes swept to me for a moment before she took a deep breath, her nostrils pinching together. "Because, smart-ass, I don't have Aunt Dell's number on my cell."

"Who's Cordelia Jackson?" Kitty asked, cutting Anna off before she could provoke Jess again.

Jess whipped her head around to eyeball her, her expression not altogether friendly. "She's a girl from Solomon's Folly who summoned Bloody Mary a while ago. She hung up on me last time I called, but maybe if I explained what happened to Shauna..." Jess's voice trailed as she swiped her stuff off the floor. "You cool if I go, Shauna? I'll call you tonight."

I nodded and glanced at the girls. I was afraid both of them would ask for a ride home and leave me alone to suffer horrible Mary paranoia and an aching back, but neither Kitty nor Anna looked inclined to follow. Maybe it was a safety in numbers thing. Maybe they were too mad at Jess.

"Drive safe," I said. Jess nodded, heading for my front door.

"Later," Kitty called after her.

Anna said nothing.

The front door clicked, and Anna shot up from the bed next to me with a shriek. She went to my doorway and peered down the hall, staring at the closed door like it had grown fangs and a tail. "Thank God. I want to smack her for being so stupid. I get it, we agreed to do it, but if we knew what we were in for? Yeah, no. No, never."

"I'm not sure Jess knew what we were in for, either," I said, slowly pushing myself up from the bed. "I guess we should have asked better questions." My wounds felt tight and sore, but I ignored the pain and forced myself onto my feet. Kitty reached out to steady me, and I cast her a grateful smile when her hand cupped my elbow. "Thanks."

"I have the right to be mad," Anna insisted. "You can't tell me I don't."

"You do. I'm mad, too," I said. "I will be for a while, but I'm not going to say this is all on Jess. Mostly, yeah, but not all." I felt sticky and gross from my bath in Mary's mirror, and all I wanted to do was shower in steamy hot, fresh water until I was clean again, but there was no way I was doing that in a bathroom in an empty house. "Do you guys mind sticking around while I take a shower? I'll borrow Mom's car later to drive you home. I just . . . you know. In case I need help."

Anna nodded before going into my living room and throwing herself on the couch. I heard the TV turn on a moment later. "That's fine. But I swear, Shauna, I don't know if I want to hang out with Jess again," Anna called down the hall.

I had no answer for her, so I tottered my way to the bathroom,

Kitty at my side to keep me steady. I was about to go in, but the moment my foot crossed the threshold, my body tensed. I didn't want to take another step. That stupid brass mirror over the sink. It was nearly as big as Anna's, and all I could picture was Mary lurking inside its depths, ready to pull me back into her world.

"Guys? Can you come in with me when I . . . not when I shower, but when I go into the bathroom? I'm afraid," I admitted.

They understood. Anna got up from the couch to grab the salt shaker from the kitchen. She shook the salt at me when she trotted down the hall. Kitty stayed at my back as the three of us shuffled into the bathroom as a collective, terrified unit. My heart was in my throat when I glanced at the mirror, but it quickly sank when I saw a normal reflection. Behind me, Kitty and Anna let out their own relieved sighs.

"Here, let me," Anna said as she brushed by me to place a thin salt line beneath the mirror. She was meticulous, shaking out the grains once, twice, three times.

"Thanks, Anna. I appreciate it," I said as they headed back to the living room.

Even though we'd checked the glass, even though Anna had salted, I kept my attention fixed on the tile floor as I undressed. It felt better to avoid reflective surfaces—less chance of seeing something I didn't want to see.

I stepped over a basket of Mom's bubble bath stuff to get into the tub, sliding the shower door along its golden runners. The panels had textured, wavy glass, so I could see colored shapes through them but not details. I was fine with that—the door acted as a great, blurry barrier between me and the mirror. I turned the shower on full-throttle, anxious to burn Bloody Mary's taint from my skin. As soon as the water hit my bandages, I yelped; that much heat on my cuts was more than a little unpleasant. I bore it, though, focusing on the water swirling down the drain rather than the discomfort.

The bathroom slowly filled with pale gray steam. My face tilted toward the showerhead and I sighed, relieved, but then a mystery glob hit my forehead and slithered down my face. My eyes flew open. I reached up to touch my cheek, dismayed to find mud smearing my fingertips. The showerhead sputtered and coughed, water gurgling and struggling inside the pipes. The spout twisted in its base like a furious metallic serpent.

There was another burp from the pipes. A rank, rotten odor spilled out into the bathroom. I recoiled, my hands covering my nose and mouth, the hairs on the back of my neck bristling. I recognized this stench. It was decay. It was sour and sweet and meaty and wrong.

It was *her*. I smelled *her*.

"No. No," I moaned, whipping my head back and forth. She couldn't be here. This had to be some horrible cosmic joke, a terrible coincidence that the building's pipes backed up exactly the same day we'd summoned a ghost. Another wad of sludge spewed from the shower to splash my shoulder and front. I reached for the faucet to turn the water off.

That was when I saw her.

Mary stood on the other side of the shower door. Her image was distorted—a blur of black hair, white dress, and gray and yellow skin. How? How had she come out of the mirror past Anna's salt line? Was it because we had no handhold or candle? I could reason out how she'd gotten through the mirror earlier, how we'd failed. But how was it she was here now with no summoning, no candle, no hand-holding?

She didn't move toward me. She didn't make a sound. But I screamed at the top of my lungs, backing into the corner of the tub, banging on the wall for my friends. Panic bubbled up inside of me, a geyser of confusion that left me feeling light-headed. I heard Kitty and Anna scrambling down the hall. They were coming to help, and had I not been so terrified, I'd have appreciated exactly how brave that was.

"Open the door," Anna yelled. I could hear the doorknob twisting and rattling as they fussed with it, but it wouldn't budge.

I hadn't locked it.

They hadn't locked it.

Mary had locked it.

Kitty and Anna shoved at the door with all their weight, but the hinges wouldn't give. They squealed and bent, but the screws held tight. "It won't . . . it can't," shouted Kitty. "SHAUNA! ARE YOU OKAY?"

No, I wasn't okay. The pipes of the shower groaned in agony as the showerhead vomited thick mud. I wanted to turn the faucet off, but I was too scared to move. I whimpered and huddled down in the tub, my hands covering my face, but I kept peeking over them. I was too scared of dying *not* to peek.

Crouched as I was, I caught sight of my mom's bath supplies, including a slim tube of bath salts leaning against the basket.

Scented Epsom salts. The crystals were purple, but hopefully their color and purpose didn't matter.

Kitty and Anna were still pounding on the door, and I could hear something hard slamming against the wood like they were trying to knock it down, but it wasn't going anywhere. I was alone in this, and that meant I had to stop shrinking. I let out another sob and stood, steeling myself to open the shower door with shaking fingers.

As I touched the handle, Bloody Mary let out an earsplitting cry.

I screamed and thudded down into the tub as she pressed one of her hands to the door, smearing the pads of her fingers against the panes. I got a close-up look at the black gouge across her palm. The skin near the cut bubbled with moving lumps. My stomach churned as a beetle wormed its way out of her flesh.

I had to get to the salt before things worsened. I wrenched the door aside and dove for the basket. My chin was tucked to my chest so she couldn't slash my throat if she swiped at me. I left my back exposed despite my injuries. It was better than giving her access to my front. My fingers wrapped around the lavender-colored tube of salts. I ripped off the top, frantically flinging the crystals around the bathroom.

But Mary wasn't in the bathroom. I heard a hiss. I craned my neck toward the sound. Mary was gazing at me from inside the shower door. She'd never been freely standing in the room. The hand, the beetle, all of her was trapped inside the glass.

I fumbled my way over the edge of the tub, tossing salts at the glass door so she couldn't follow. She writhed as the salts struck the textured glass, but she never tried to poke through the door. Behind me, clumps of mud continued to sputter and spew over the tub.

The moment my bare feet touched the linoleum floor, Mary moved. She left the shower door and reappeared in the mirror above the sink. Before she'd been a blur of shapes and color in the textured glass; now she was as sharply defined as my own reflection. She glared at me, the sliver of her upper lip twitching, the flesh cracked open, oozing a trail of yellow slime down the corner of her mouth.

"Go away," I shouted, tossing another handful of bath salts at the mirror. *"Go away!"*

Mary smiled, the thin skin of her cheeks stretching tight over her skull. The veins at her temples pulsed black, as if a twisted, distorted life still fueled her body. Her dry, reptilian laughter grew louder and louder. My misery amused her. I couldn't take it anymore. I couldn't stand her being there. I couldn't stand her finding my fear so very entertaining.

I whipped around to grab the freestanding toilet paper holder from the floor. The heavy iron hit the mirror like a baseball bat, and shards of glass rained down around me.

9

As soon as the glass stopped falling, the door unlocked. Mary was appearing without a summoning, manipulating objects, haunting glass, and skipping from surface to surface. None of this were we prepared to handle. I could explain none of it.

Anna and Kitty barged in but stopped short when they saw me standing muddy and naked in the middle of the floor. I yanked a towel off of the towel bar and wrapped it around myself, shivering when it brushed against my bandages.

"Is she in here?" Anna asked, waving the shaker of table salt back and forth from the doorway. I shook my head and motioned them back into the hall so I could leap over the shattered glass to join them.

Kitty stuck her head inside to peer around the bathroom before moving. She looked from the tub to the shards on the floor. I followed her gaze, frowning at the sharp, spiky pieces of glass. One mirror down, but there were so many others. Would

I have to shatter them all? My vanity? The tall, standing mirror in my mother's bedroom? What was stopping Mary from climbing out of them right this instant?

"Kitty, move," Anna said from the hall. I leapt over the remnants of the mirror and onto the hallway carpet. Anna pressed past me with her salt to stand in the doorway, like she expected something else to go wrong. I expected something to go wrong, too. My eyes drifted down the hall. She could be anywhere. Here now.

Good God.

"Why is this happening?" Kitty asked, her voice sounding strangled.

"I don't know." I sank down onto the floor, my body smeared with mud and gunk, my stomach so tense it cramped. I dropped my head into my hands and stared through my splayed fingers, my attention fixed on the broken shards of mirror. I wished Jess had known what could happen so she could have prepared us, so we would have known to run long and run far to get away from Bloody Mary.

Then it hit me. Maybe Jess *had* known. The pictures on the wall. She'd taken the pictures down. Why would she suspect Mary could be anywhere other than a proper mirror? She'd said safety, but that was a bizarre leap to make.

"Oh, no. Come on," I whispered. "No."

I propelled myself off the floor and jogged to my room, frantically searching for my phone, never once turning my back on my covered mirror. My cell was still in my backpack, and I tugged it out and dialed. Kitty and Anna ran in after me, but I ignored them, pacing until I heard Jess's voice over a loud rap sound track from her car stereo.

"She's here, Jess. Mary was in my bathroom taunting me. How'd you know to move the pictures off Anna's wall?" I demanded.

Jess turned the radio down. I could see her expression in my head—the knitted brow, the pinch at the corners of her mouth. "Oh, my God, are you okay?"

"Why did you move the pictures, Jess?" I repeated.

She sighed. "Okay, so I . . . Cordelia," she blurted.

"Cordelia what?" I eased down onto my bed. Kitty came to sit beside me. Anna hovered in the bedroom doorway, glancing over her shoulder every once in a while, convinced Mary would come lurching after us from the bathroom. She gripped the salt container in her hand, her thumb skimming back and forth over its top.

"She was haunted by Mary for a long time," Jess answered. "Like, I didn't want that to happen. That wasn't what I was trying to do."

"I thought Cordelia hung up on you when you called," I said.

"She did after I told her I wanted to summon Mary, but . . . Look, Shauna. I didn't want anyone to get hurt, I swear. It was supposed to be a cool thing, but it went weird. Cordelia said Mary was after her. That she could see Mary in glass and shiny stuff. So that's why I took the pictures down."

"Why was she haunted for a long time?"

The silence on Jess's end grew uncomfortable. "I don't know. She just said Mary never left her alone. She followed her in mirrors and glass. For years. Mary was still following her the last time I called."

I went silent. Mary was following me in mirrors and glass, too. If Cordelia was stuck with her for years, was I? In a terrible, selfish way I hoped Mary was stuck on Kitty or Anna. But they'd gone into the living room while I'd showered. I was the one Mary had come after.

Me.

Mary was on *me*.

"I'm sorry."

"Shut up, Jess."

I sucked in a deep breath and counted to ten. I felt tears welling; I didn't want to cry. Not anymore. I'd cried enough already. Instead I clung to my anger, feeling it swell hot and bright behind my eyes. Jess had put our lives at risk because she wanted to play a stupid game. "Here's what you're going to do, Jess. Text me Cordelia Jackson's phone number. Then find out everything you can about Bloody Mary. Origins. Everything. And Jess, if you screw me over again..."

I didn't finish the sentence. I didn't know how to finish it. I'd what? Not talk to the person with the most information about Mary? I needed all the help I could get.

"Yeah, of course. I'm going to help, Shauna. I'll figure it out. I'll help you with anything you need," Jess said.

"Right now I need to not talk to you. If you find anything out, text me," I barked before ending the call. Anna and Kitty peered at me, questions all over their faces. My phone buzzed with a text message—Cordelia's number. I glanced at the numbers. Cordelia had information that I wasn't sure I was ready to hear.

"This woman, she was haunted by Bloody Mary for a long time. That's why Jess knew to take the pictures down. Cordelia saw Mary in glass and other shiny stuff," I explained before dialing the number. Anna and Kitty shared a look, but they stayed quiet as I waited for Cordelia to pick up. I waited. And waited. It rang six or seven times, and I was about to hang up when a deep female voice rasped a hello at me.

"Cordelia? Cordelia Jackson?"

"What?" was the flat response.

She wasn't a kind-sounding woman. Her voice was gravelly, like she'd smoked for too long or talked too little.

"H-hi," I stammered. "My name is Shauna O'Brien. I'm friends with Jess McAllister, who called you about summoning Bloody Mary."

The line went dead in my hand. Kitty reached out to pat my shoulder, and while I appreciated the sentiment, I brushed her aside. I didn't want comfort right now. I wanted answers, and this woman in Solomon's Folly was the only one who could give me any. I redialed. It didn't take Cordelia long to pick up a second time.

"Go away," she snapped.

"Mary's on me. She followed me after we summoned her. Please, help me," I said, talking as fast as I could to get it all in before she hung up.

"Are you local like your friend?" she demanded.

The question took me off guard, but I nodded in response. "Yes, I'm from Bridgewater."

Cordelia went quiet. I could hear her deep, even breathing. "Forty-seven Nickel Street in the Folly, gray house. Black windows. Until then, avoid everything shiny. *Everything.*" And she was gone again.

Part of me wanted to go see her right then, but Mom had planned a night of tacos and Sandra Bullock movies. If I bailed, she'd know something was wrong. The other problem was a ride. Mom needed her car, and relinquishing the keys required an explanation.

"Hey, can either of you drive me out to Solomon's Folly tomorrow after school? I know it's far, but I want to talk to Cordelia. It sounds like she might help me." I jotted down the address on a piece of paper by my nightstand. I could have asked Jess to take me, but I wasn't ready for her company. Apologies or not, she'd screwed me over.

"Can't. Dentist appointment at two tomorrow. I'm getting dismissed from school," Anna said. She murmured an apology before disappearing into the hall. A moment later, I heard her in the kitchen shuffling around, the door to a closet opening and then closing.

"I can," Kitty said. "No problem." Kitty didn't often drive because Jess was our chauffeur, but she did have one of her dad's cars at her disposal whenever she needed it—usually the red SUV with the sunroof.

"Thanks."

I retucked the towel and went out to see what Anna was up to. I found her standing in front of the open bathroom door with a broom and dustpan in one hand, the salt shaker in the other. She scowled at the sea of glass in front of her.

"Man, your mom's going to be pissed," she said.

"Maybe." I didn't have an excuse for the mirror, though I was leaning toward telling her it happened while I was at school—like it fell off the nail because our downstairs neighbors got too rowdy again.

Anna stopped eyeing the wreckage long enough to turn around to offer us salt. "I'll get this cleaned up if you guys will watch me in case...you know."

Kitty snagged the salt from her and sat on the carpet, her gaze swinging my way. "Y-yeah. I'll watch. I'm...Shauna, are you okay? What did Cordelia say?"

"She gave me her address and said to avoid all shiny surfaces." After seeing Mary in the shower doors, the suggestion made sense. At least she hadn't passed through to grab me, so maybe regular glass restricted her more than straight mirrors? Her possession of the showerhead was more understandable, too, since that was stainless steel, which was reflective. The doorknobs were brass, so maybe that's how she locked us in and out at Anna's place and here.

I glanced down the hall. Family pictures—shiny frames. The television in the living room—shiny screen. The windows— shiny panes. The more I looked, the bigger the problem grew. Silverware, computer screens, the stove. The microwave. The car. My cell phone. My hair clips. Anna's glasses. Anything plastic, anything glass, anything metal. Which was everything. Mary could be anywhere.

What was I going to do? I couldn't escape all of that! I was exhausted, scared, and in pain. Was I supposed to pitch a tent in the middle of the woods? Even then, wouldn't the zipper be shiny? Did she really mean *everything* shiny?

"Holy crap," I whispered. All I wanted to do was lie down on my stomach and go to sleep. I hated Mary, I hated what we'd done, I even hated Jess. I was covered in mud, I couldn't shower, and . . .

"Shauna?" Kitty's voice stopped me from spiraling deeper. She smiled tightly and nodded at the bathroom. "When Anna's done sweeping, if you want I'll sit in the bathroom with some salt so you can shower. I won't look, but you're all . . . you know. I'm sorry about the shiny thing. I'm sorry about all of it."

"Yeah, it's . . . I still want to punch Jess," Anna said between sweeps.

I swallowed hard and nodded, my face turned away from them so they couldn't see that I was two seconds from losing it. "Thanks, guys. Thanks for sweeping, Anna," I said. "I'll be right back." Before either of them could follow me, I went back to my room and threw myself into my computer chair, wheeling it as far away from my vanity as possible.

I looked out my window to stare at Mom's empty parking spot. She'd be home soon, and I realized I'd never warned her that we had company. She'd be pissed if I didn't tell her and she only had tacos for two. Plus, I had to borrow the car to drive Kitty and Anna home. She deserved fair warning.

I called her at work and left her a disjointed message. "Hey, Mom. Uhh. Came home from school with the girls and the bathroom mirror was broken. I'm cleaning it up now, but we'll need to get a new one. And Jess left Anna and Kitty here with no ride, so I have to borrow the car when you get home. We can do tacos after still, if that's cool. Bye." I hung up, glad my mother didn't have to work tonight.

10

Clean and rebandaged, I sank into the couch with Anna and Kitty, exhausted. The TV droned on, filling in for our silence. Words couldn't quite capture how messed up our situation was.

Mom walked in a little while later with a family-sized box of tacos and a movie. She must have gotten my message about Kitty and Anna. I hadn't asked them to stay for dinner, but by the longing looks they gave the Taco Bell box, it was clear they planned on sticking around. I didn't mind. Two more people to fight off the pop-up ghost.

"Soup's on!" Mom said, slinging her coat over the back of the chair and leaving our dinner on the table. She ducked from the kitchen to inspect the bathroom. Anna had done a great job cleaning it, so there wasn't much for her to see. "Damn. I guess we'll get another mirror this weekend."

"The glass is in the garbage," I said, abandoning the couch to grab plates from the cabinet. The girls followed me, both of them familiar enough with my apartment that Kitty went for the silverware and Anna poured us drinks.

"Soda, Mrs. O'Brien?" Anna offered.

"No, thanks. I'll grab a water," Mom said, coming out to join us. She paused by the refrigerator to get her own drink. "How's everyone doing?" Our silence spoke for us. "That good, huh?"

"Drama. Stupid girl drama," I said, piling three tacos onto my plate and loading up on hot sauce.

Mom motioned to the three of us to eat without her; she was unpacking her bag from work. "You're short a body. I take it Jessica's the girl drama?"

"Jess is channeling her demon side again," I replied.

"It'll work out. It always does," she said, sliding into the seat across from me. Her shoes flew out from under the table to thud against the opposite wall. The sound made me, Kitty, and Anna flinch. Mom rubbed her nylon-clad toes. "Today was a real bi— bear. At least we get to watch some quality TV tonight, huh? End the day the right way."

"What movie did you get?" Kitty asked, and the conversation drifted from Mom's movie to romantic comedies to what we last saw in the theaters. I tried to concentrate on the chatter instead of my looming dread, but it was hard. Especially when I picked up my chicken taco and saw Mary's face on my white dinner plate.

It was fleeting—a glimpse of black eyes and stringy hair— but it was enough to make me choke. Chicken taco flew down the wrong pipe, and I coughed and wheezed for air. Mom jumped up from her seat to whack me on the back, her hand striking my new cuts. It hurt so much, I spit guacamole at Kitty, accidentally blasting her cheek with green goop.

"Shauna, are you okay? Honey?"

I pointed at my throat and gurgled, though it wasn't a breathing problem so much as I couldn't believe what I'd just seen. In my plate. All that panic and worry about Mary being everywhere returned twofold. I dropped the remains of my taco and reached for my soda to swallow past the choking sensation.

I stopped. The glass. If Mary was in my plate, what would stop her from being in my glass?

Desperate and miserable, I went to the sink and turned on the water. I could feel my mom watching me as I splashed my face, cupping water in my palms to drink. Yes, the sink was chrome, but there was distance between the faucet and the base. I could keep my hands midway without touching anything.

Was this how it had to be from now on?

"Are you okay?" my mom repeated.

Another splash of water and I nodded. "Be fine. Just a long day. Sorry about the guac, Kitty."

"It's okay," Kitty said in a slightly disgusted tone.

"It's been a crappy day. Seems appropriate," Anna said.

Face soaked, cheeks so warm they felt like they were on fire, I retook my seat. I nudged my plate away and grabbed another taco, holding it over a napkin. In a way, I hoped Mary would pop up somewhere my mom could see. The group had agreed to keep it quiet, but if Mom had a good, hard look at Mary by no fault of mine, it'd be hard to refute my rampaging ghost claims.

It was like Kitty psychically caught my vibe, because I felt her hand brush my leg under the table. It was a small pat, but I knew what it meant, and my eyes flicked her way. We shared a look before going back to our food, much quieter now, my mom's gaze ping-ponging around the table.

"I'm not getting something," she said.

"Jess is a jerk," I said, though my voice was ragged from choking. It reminded me a little of Cordelia's voice, all grizzled and hoarse. If Cordelia looked anything like she sounded, she was one terrifying woman.

"She's always been a little difficult, but you've smoothed it out before. I'm sure this will be fine," Mom said.

I had to wonder if Mom would say that if she knew what Kitty, Anna, and I knew.

"You okay over there? You're off tonight," Mom asked after we drove Kitty and Anna home.

"Yeah. Just stressed," I said.

Mom pulled the car into our parking lot right as the peepers started screaming, a telltale sign summer was around the corner. She stifled a yawn behind her hand before rooting through her purse for the house key. I saved her by producing mine from my pocket, and she took it with a grateful smile. "Movie time! Hope I don't pass out on you. Your old lady is feeling pretty old right now."

"It's okay if you do. Just don't snore."

We walked into the house side by side, Mom looping an arm through mine. We walked up the stairs like that, and strangely, it was the only time I'd felt even slightly relaxed since Mary came into my life. Mom made me feel safe despite the things I'd seen and done, and I desperately hoped whatever Mary wanted from me, she kept my mom out of it. She shouldn't be my collateral damage.

Mom opened the front door and stepped aside to let me in. Every light was off in the apartment. I expected a corpse to lunge at me from the darkness, but it was still. Then I felt a soft brush of lips across my temple. My hand swung up on instinct to knock away whatever it was. Except it was Mom. I'd just thwacked her upside the head.

"Oh. Oh, crap. Mom, I'm so sorry. I—"

"Shauna! I was just going to kiss you! What in God's name is *wrong* with you?"

She flicked on a light so I could see her death glare, and I melted into the floor. "I'm s-sorry. You startled me."

"Apparently. You're awfully jumpy tonight. Is something going on? Between this and doing the tango in your seat at dinner, you're worrying me."

"No, I'm fine. I'm sorry I hit you."

"Spill it," she demanded, arms folding over her chest.

The way she looked at me, I knew I wasn't wriggling out of it. I was so tired from the day and so annoyed with Jess and scared of Mary that I shrugged and walked toward my room. When Mom protested my leaving midconversation, I lifted my hand for her to follow. Fine. She wanted to know? I'd show her. Jess had told me we couldn't tell our parents because no one would believe us. Well, if Mom saw it, how was she going to dispute it?

I went straight for the vanity and tugged off the robe. There was no hesitation because I had a point to prove. My reflection looked back at me. Mom stood at my side, looking between me and the mirror like one of us would sprout wings. I backed onto my bed and sat, waiting for the horrible face to appear.

"Yes?" Mom pressed.

"Just give me a minute," I said.

And she did, but nothing happened. Either Mary was off mauling other unsuspecting girls or she was toying with me. *Of course* the one time I wanted her here, she played coy. I raked my fingers over my scalp.

"Jess walked away from us today. Not, like, permanently, but it's hard. She's still hanging out with Bronx because of Marc and there's drama. Kitty's upset and blah, blah. It's all super dumb. I'm not sure she's going to be our friend for much longer," I said. It was all true so I didn't feel totally awful saying it, but it didn't come close to the snarling, hissing, blood-hungry bulk of my problem.

Mom peered at me. She knew it wasn't that simple. I must have looked suitably forlorn, though, because she came to sit beside me, her hand rubbing over my thigh. "You guys have been friends for a long time. I bet she'll think about it and come crawling back."

"Sure," I said, but really, I didn't care if Jess fell off the face of the planet. Thinking her name was enough to make my jaw clench.

Mom gave me a couple minutes to brood before she stood up and offered me her hand. "Let's go. That movie was burning a hole in my bag earlier. There's nothing you can do about Jess now, so let's hang out. Maybe you'll feel better by bedtime, okay?"

I laced my fingers with hers and followed her into the living room. I didn't care about the movie, but I wasn't going to pass up an opportunity to cuddle with my mom, especially knowing what could be waiting for me on the other side of the glass.

Mom passed out halfway through the movie. I watched the rest of it with her head propped against my arm, my eyes pointed at the TV but not really seeing it. When the credits rolled, I gently shoved her shoulder to wake her and glanced at the clock. It was almost eleven, and I hadn't touched my homework.

Mom yawned and shuffled her way to her bedroom with a muffled, "G'night. Love you." I told her I loved her and ducked into my room. Normally, I'd close the door and kill the lights and sprawl into my pillows like an overtired toddler, but as I started to follow the routine, I thought better of it. I left it open. If something else happened, I wanted to be able to call for her. I was afraid of the monster in my closet for the first time since I was nine years old.

I tossed the bathrobe over the mirror again. For good measure, I grabbed the salt from the kitchen and lined the bottom of the mirror. My hand shook as I poured. I tried not to notice.

Behind me, my cell phone vibrated. There were two messages. The first one was from Bronx, saying I should call him. It had come in two hours ago. I didn't respond for two reasons, the first being the hour, the second being that Kitty and Bronx's dating drama was pretty much the last thing on my mind with my big fat Mary problem. I'd handle their boyfriend-girlfriend situation another day.

The other text message was from Jess. *So sorry. Go to this site.* The link was to the Solomon's Folly Historical Society. Despite my fatigue and the glare on my computer, I was curious. I swallowed past my trepidation and typed in the address. An old photograph loaded on the screen. A dozen people stood in front of a stone church. I could tell by the dress of the parishioners that this was taken a long time ago. It reminded me of the Civil War portraits I'd seen in my American history textbook.

It was an imperfect photo; the background, the church, and the left half of the group were clear. The people on the right side, though, had small water spots on them that distorted their images. It reminded me of Mary Worth's letter. Why did everything to do with her have to be so very *wet*?

I studied the picture. On the far left was a handsome man with a tall hat, a hand clasped on a walking stick, a long black jacket hanging to his knees. The way he'd tucked his other hand beneath his coat lapel suggested pride, like these were his people. I glanced down at the picture description. *From left to right, Pastor Edmond Renault, Mrs. Hannah Worth, Miss Mary Worth, Miss Constance Worth (Simpson), Mr. Thomas Adderly, Miss Elizabeth Hawthorne (Jenson), Rest Unknown.* My gaze skipped from the names to the faces. Hannah Worth was as Mary described her mother in her letter—blond and perfect in a fairy-tale princess way. Her hair was wrapped around her head in a fat golden braid, her nose was long and thin over wide lips. Her arm extended to her side to loop around the shoulders of a girl.

Mary Worth. She was holding on to Mary Worth.

I stared. The girl in the picture looked nothing like my nightmare-come-to-life. She was pretty like her mother, but darker all around, with hair that looked black or chestnut. Her eyes were big and dark against her pale skin. She was not overly thin, but not big, either. She was healthy, robust, so at odds with the skeletal ghost from the mirror. The most startling thing about her, though, was how young she looked. She was my age in this picture. How could a girl like Mary end up so monstrous?

One by one, I studied the rest of the faces. Constance resembled her mother with her flaxen hair, though she had a rounder face like her sister. She clasped Mary's hand, the gesture telegraphing their affection. Thomas Adderly was somewhat goofy-looking, with a too-serious face and slumping shoulders on a wide, heavy frame. The picture was enough to make me believe he had warts and onion breath as Mary described. As for Elizabeth, she was plain, with dark hair and dark eyes. Her cheekbones were a little too high, her face a little too angular to be traditionally pretty. Her expression was flinty, too, and cold.

I e-mailed the link to myself so I could print a copy at the school library tomorrow. A squealing noise from under my feet seized my muscles. It took a moment to recognize the sound of the toilet flushing in the downstairs apartment, the pipes shuddering in the walls.

It was going to be a long night.

I climbed into bed, my hand reaching for the lamp beside my bed table, but I couldn't bring myself to turn it off. Complete darkness scared me, so I dug my head in between my pillows and turned my back to the mirror. The thick comforter went around my shoulders, and for a moment, I imagined that blankets covering my body and my mom sleeping down the hall were enough to keep me safe.

I almost had myself convinced until I heard the scratching. It was faint and slow at first, but as the seconds ticked by, it grew more intense.

Scree.

Screeeeee.

Screeeeeeeeeee.

It sounded like the fingers of a tree branch squealing over a window pane. I tried blocking it out by huddling deeper into my mattress, the pillow bunched up around my ears to stifle the noise, but it was too shrill, too high-pitched to ignore.

Scree. Scree scree screeee. SCREEEE.

She was back. A terrible part of me had hoped she'd gone after Jess or Kitty or Anna tonight, but no, it was me again. Mary was in my room, and the only thing that separated me from her was a bathrobe and a line of Morton salt.

Scree. Scree.

THUD!

I shot up in bed, the cuts on my back screaming. My vanity trembled. My plastic bucket of makeup tumbled over, tubes of lipstick, gloss, eyeliner, foundation, and perfume scattering across the tabletop and rolling to the floor.

I picked up the salt from my bedside table and swung my legs over the bed. My eyes darted to the hall, half expecting my mother to run in and yell at me for making too much noise, but she was fast asleep, the lull of her radio drowning out Mary's return.

My fingers itched to fling salt at the vanity, but I couldn't waste such a precious resource. I slid out of bed and edged toward the mirror, but the moment I neared it, the vanity stopped rattling. I waited, expecting Mary to shriek or shake the mirror or do something else to screw with me, but she'd gone still.

I brushed the tears off my cheeks and lifted my hand toward the robe. There was no way I could sleep in this house if she was in the mirror. I counted down from three and jerked the robe aside. There was no face there, but written backward in sludgy black tar was a single word that sent me falling to the floor and sobbing.

MINE.

It was not a restful night. Three hours of sleep on my couch, and every thump, thud, scratch, and creak in the building sent me scrambling for the salt container. If I wasn't quick on my toes, Bloody Mary would scoop me up in her claws, the field mouse to her big, dead hawk. When Mom saw me on the couch at six the next morning, she gave me a nudge. I jumped up like she'd electrocuted me.

"You're being weird again. I don't like it. What the hell are you doing on the couch?"

"Had a nightmare," I said, knowing it was a weak answer and not caring. I shuffled to the kitchen, pretending I couldn't see her concerned scowls.

"I'm off," Mom said. "If you need me, call me. I'll leave my phone on. I'm worried about you, kiddo."

I was on my way to my third class when a hand clapped on my shoulder from behind. I yelped so loudly, a hallway of heads turned my way. Bronx muttered an apology as he fell into step beside me, a stack of books tucked under his arm. "Hey, sorry to scare you. Needed to ask you something."

"Hey," I said. I didn't want to talk to Bronx, but there was no way to say that without sounding like a bridge troll, so I stepped out of the way of the crisscrossing traffic, angling my back against the wall. Bronx followed, and for a moment, I looked up and down the hall, paranoid that Kitty would see us together.

People cleared out as the bell rang again. Apparently, I was going to be late to my third class. I dropped my bag to the floor as Bronx moved to stand opposite me in the now-empty hallway, his back pressed to the windows.

The main body of our school was two floors of classrooms, the gym, the auditorium, and the cafeteria. Between the main building and the recent addition, there was a long, curving hallway, where we currently stood. One side was all windows, overlooking the football and soccer fields. The other side had two bathrooms and a computer lab.

Bronx leaned against the glass like it wasn't a big deal. I envied his calm, but then, he hadn't just spent the last day warding off ghost chicks. "I got a weird-ass message from Kitty last night. Haven't heard from her since our split, but that doesn't mean . . . you know." He stopped talking to rub the back of his neck, his eyes drifting to the floor.

"Why'd you break up with her?" I blurted. "You clearly care. So why?"

"My family's moving back to New York in June," he said. He frowned and shook his head. "My mom misses it too much. I didn't know how to tell Kitty. Long distance never works, and Kitty . . . I dunno. She'd want to try but how would we work it? We're seventeen. College is coming. I thought it was better to cut ties."

That explained it. It wasn't a particularly satisfying answer, but at least it was something. "Don't you think you should let her know your reasons? She's killing herself thinking she did something wrong," I said.

He frowned and nodded, running his hand over his hair. "Maybe you're right. Last night, she left me a message and said something about ghosts. I swear she never mentioned anything like that before. That's why I stopped you. I wanted to know if . . . you know. I wanted to know if she's okay, I guess."

I had to think about what to say. We'd made the agreement not to tell our parents, but nothing about peers. Bronx reacted exactly how Jess said he would—disbelief that we'd be so dumb as to believe in ghosts—which was understandable, but disheartening. I opened my mouth to defend Kitty, but I paused. The windows were reflecting Bronx's back. I could see his big body, the white of his T-shirt, and the black of his hair. But there was something else there, too. Black eyes staring out. Stringy hair, a crooked smile on a gaunt, graying face.

"Come here," I whispered at Bronx, waving him toward the safety of the solid wall at my back. But he didn't move when I stretched out my hand to him. Fear left me cold. I shivered from head to toe. "*Now*, Bronx!" I snapped, watching Mary tip her head up to peer at him, one of her hands lifting to paw the back of his skull.

Bronx reached for me and I tried yanking him my way, but he's a huge guy, and huge guys don't move easily. Instead, he took a few steps and then turned around to glance at what had me so transfixed. Mary lingered. She'd shifted positions so she was clear now, her palms against the glass, the pads of her fingers smushed like she'd pressed too hard. She watched us with her sunken eyes, a small stream of yellow pus oozing from her tear ducts.

"Holy shit," Bronx squealed, his voice cracking. "What the hell is that?"

"*That* is the ghost Kitty called you about, Bronx!"

Mary's staccato laughter echoed from the window. No, the

windows—it wasn't just the one pane, but all the panes in the hall. We were assailed by a chorus of cackling Mary voices. There was no one around to hear her but us. I tugged on Bronx's sleeve before sprinting toward the main building. The halls there had no windows—they were lined with lockers, and if we could just get away from the glass, we'd be safe.

I couldn't see Bronx, but I could hear his sneakers stomping and squeaking across the floor behind me. Mary's dark shadow careered through the windows to keep pace with us. She skipped from pane to pane, never losing ground no matter how hard we pumped our legs.

I sprinted around a corner, ignoring the pain in my back, my breath coming in short pants. Bronx skidded up beside me, actually running into me and nearly knocking me over. We had made it to the main stretch between the cafeteria and the front entrance to the school. It was a long, windowless corridor, lockers and closed classroom doors lining either side. My feet planted on the black-and-white-checkered tiles. I was ready to keep running if need be, but maybe we were safe here. I looked around. No mirrors, no glass, just the dull gray surface of the lockers stretching the length of the hallway. Even the paint on the walls was a drab, institutional green.

BANG! BANG! BANG! BANG!

It sounded like rapid firing, like someone had shot an Uzi in the middle of the hall. I crouched low to the ground out of instinct, my hands going over my ears as a loud, angry clanging exploded from every direction. I didn't understand what was happening. Then I saw the locks on the lockers. The shiny locks. They lifted and slammed against the metal, up and down, over and over, as if invisible hands smashed them.

Over the clamor, I heard her gravelly, dry voice.

"Mine. Mine. Mine. Mine."

12

I thought the racket would draw every human being in a mile radius of the school to gawk at the phenomenon playing out around me. The problem was the nature of the noise. It *had* sounded like gunshots. There was protocol to follow. We'd all been put through drills: lock the door, shut off the lights, hide against the wall not facing the door, keep completely silent. Mary kept clanging and banging because every teacher and every student in that high school believed someone was there with a gun.

It wasn't until Mrs. Reyes, one of the Spanish teachers, turned the corner to the hall with a cell phone to her ear that Mary's tantrum stopped. Every lock stilled, plunging the hall into uncomfortable quiet. Mrs. Reyes clearly didn't think the danger had passed, though, as she ran our way to usher us toward the nearest available door, which just so happened to be a janitor's closet. She was stone-silent as she shooed us inside, the phone stuck to her ear.

"Yes, yes, the high school," she whispered. Beside me, Bronx let out a strangled noise, and Mrs. Reyes shushed him.

I didn't know what to say. Neither did Bronx. We couldn't tell the truth, so we were stuck going along with an enormous misunderstanding. Mrs. Reyes finished her call, presumably to 911, and closed her phone. After that, we waited. And waited. And waited. We were in that closet for what felt like ages waiting for someone on the PA system to tell us we were all clear. It gave me a long time to think about what had just happened. About what Mary had just done to the school because of me.

At what point was it unsafe for me to be around people?

The answer was clear when the three of us were still in the closet an hour later, cramped, sweaty, and miserable. There was a light with a string above us, but we weren't allowed to pull it, so we were stuck in the dark. Mrs. Reyes's perfume was cloying. The sirens screamed outside while instructions were yelled out over megaphones. Sometimes I heard the grinding whir of an overhead helicopter.

This was my fault. I was the liability. I wanted to melt into a puddle of shame. I sank down onto the cold floor, my arms wrapped around my knees as I stared straight ahead. I could hear Bronx shuffling around behind me. Mrs. Reyes was coughing and sneezing, assailed by the dust in the closet.

Finally, the principal's voice piped through the overhead

speakers. "We have an all clear. I repeat, all clear. In the wake of today's event, the school will be closing early. Buses are running, parents have been informed via community outreach phone calls."

Mrs. Reyes opened the closet door. The other classrooms opened one by one. You'd think a bunch of students who'd been forced to sit silently for an hour would have a lot to say, but no one said a word. They were all too freaked out. I pulled myself to my feet and wandered back toward the hall where we'd seen Mary. I didn't want to go there, but I had to; I'd abandoned my bag there with my cell phone.

Bronx stayed with me. In fact, even when I ducked into the hall, my eyes scouring the windows for a sign of Mary, he stayed with me, his elbow touching mine. I wasn't sure if the contact was for my benefit or his. People were making their way to the parking lot, and we fell into step beside them. Outside, the school was still surrounded by police cruisers, most of them positioned so concerned bystanders couldn't block roads. There was a cluster of parents outside, too, all of them watching the doors.

I reached into my bag for my phone to call my mom, ducking away from the doors so the clamor of concerned parents reuniting with their kids wouldn't overwhelm my conversation.

"Hey, kiddo," Mom said in greeting.

"So you didn't hear?" I said back.

"Hear what?"

I explained what had happened as best I could. At least, I

explained the story of the school in lockdown after suspicious noises. She'd missed the emergency phone call because the school had our house number, not her cell number, for contact.

"I . . . wow. You must have been terrified," Mom said. "That's awful. Are you okay? You've been so stressed."

"I'm fine," I said, though my response sounded hollow even to my ears. "Freaked out, but I'm okay."

"You're sure? I have a late night, but I can leave early if you need me. Luanne owes me a shift."

"I'm okay. I'm going out with Kitty for a while, but I've got my phone. I'll call if I need anything," I said.

She grumbled under her breath and sighed. "All right. I left twenty bucks on the counter if you want a pizza. Love you. Glad you're safe."

"Love you, too, Mom." Bronx was still nearby, on the phone with his parents, too. At one point I spied Jess in the parking lot, though she hadn't seen me. Mrs. McAllister was one of the parents who'd come, and mother and daughter were standing next to Jess's car. Mrs. McAllister was fretting and stroking Jess's hair, and Jess was shooing her away like a fly. Typical Jess stuff, and for a second, I forgot I was mad at her and found a small smile.

"Shauna! What the heck?" I heard from the steps. I craned my neck and saw Kitty stumbling outside, a fistful of papers in hand, like she'd spilled her backpack and hadn't taken the time to reorganize yet. She pointed the papers at the parking lot, toward the little red SUV I liked so much. Well, normally liked—right now it looked like a shiny death machine, but so did most things.

Bronx closed his phone and looked at Kitty, frowning. "Hey."

Kitty handed me her backpack, and I held it open for her as she crammed her papers inside of it. Her eyes skipped to Bronx. She licked her lips before reaching up to pat her hair into place. It was up in a bun today, and she looked pretty enough, but being around Bronx made her self-conscious.

"He saw Mary," I said.

"Wait, he did?" She stopped primping and glanced between us. Bronx nodded as I offered an abbreviated account of what happened with the lockers.

"So the lockdown was *her*?"

"Yeah."

"I didn't believe it until I saw it, and man, that's freaky shit," Bronx said, running his hand down his face. "Got your call last night and thought you were nuts, but now...man."

Kitty scowled at him and jerked her bag out of my hands, hard enough that I stumbled a half step toward her. "Right, because our breakup is going to ruin me." It kind of *had* ruined her, but friendship solidarity said I couldn't point that out now or later or ever. At least she was sticking up for herself. She'd never do that with Jess. I supposed there wasn't much left for her to lose with Bronx, though.

"That's not what I meant. Who believes in ghosts? Really?" Bronx frowned and looked over at his car. I followed his gaze and saw Marc waiting for him. Bronx nodded at him, Marc nodded back, and Bronx shuffled a few feet forward. "I should go. But if you need help with anything, let me know. That's . . . Be careful, I guess," he said. He cast Kitty another glance, frowned, and then headed off.

"Later," I said to his back. Kitty shook her head as she turned toward her dad's car.

"I hope Mary eats him," she said.

"Kitty!"

She sighed. "Sorry. I'm just mad. Mad's better than depressed, I guess. Maybe. I don't know."

I debated telling her about his moving back to New York then, but I decided to hold off. If Kitty got hung up thinking about Bronx, we'd never get to Solomon's Folly, and I really needed to talk to Cordelia Jackson.

We climbed into the SUV and I immediately put the window down. One less shiny surface to worry about. Kitty did the same on her side, and then peeled back the sunroof. "Did you see Anna today?" she asked.

"First period," I said. "She didn't sleep well, but I guess Mary left her alone last night. She wasn't in the downstairs bathroom anymore. I just wish she'd left me alone, too, but not so much." I took out my cell phone to show Kitty the picture of the writing in the mirror. I'd snapped it before heading to the couch. I was glad I did, too, because in the morning, there was no sign of it. Mary had either wiped it off or let it disappear or . . . whatever it was ghosts did with their unsettling mirror writing.

"Holy crap. Man, I hope Cordelia has some answers for you,"

Kitty said, easing the car out of the parking lot to avoid the milling parents, students, and police.

I glanced at my phone. Half past eleven. "I really hope so, too."

Cordelia's house was easy to spot. Where other houses in her neighborhood were painted light colors with perfectly mani-cured lawns and attractive landscaping, Cordelia's house was a forbidding charcoal gray. The lawn was of hip-height grass, and her purple Volkswagen, rusted and with two flat tires, was parked on a moss-covered driveway. The shades were drawn and there were black squares of paper taped to the insides of the glass. The steps leading up to the screened-in porch had a sizable hole in them, like someone had fallen straight through, and there were empty wooden buckets everywhere, their insides stained maroon.

Kitty and I stared at the wreck, the sun beating down on our heads through the SUV's sunroof.

"Do you want me to go in with you?" Kitty asked.

I did, but Cordelia hadn't struck me as overly friendly. I doubted she'd take kindly to my dragging an additional stranger into her house. "Better not. She barely wanted to talk to me on the phone. I don't want to give her a reason to kick me out."

"Okay." Kitty rooted around in her backpack, looking for her phone to entertain herself while I climbed from the car. The front stairs were perilous-looking, and I leapt my way to the top step, neatly avoiding the broken boards. My fist pounded on the dilapidated screen door. There was shuffling from inside the house. A chain lock slid open. A single green eye in a sliver of pale face peeked out through the crack. I couldn't see anything beyond the hint of a woman, although I could hear the loud, static humming of a television.

"You're the haunted girl?" she asked, her voice just as crusty and grizzled as yesterday's phone call.

"Yes. I'm Shauna O'Brien."

She slammed the door shut. Confused, I knocked again, but there was no response save for a soft thudding and a muffled curse. I waited a minute, two minutes, three minutes, but nothing. Another knock and still she ignored me.

"Cordelia? Hello?" I called. Angry and scared, I headed back down the stairs, avoiding the rusted nails and deceptive bows in the wood. Halfway down the steps, the front door swung open behind me. I turned back to look. Standing in an ankle-length skirt covered in hand-sewn patches and a threadbare Gatorade T-shirt, her hair cut ragged around her ears, was Cordelia Jackson.

She was older than I expected, maybe midthirties, although her brown hair was shot through with steely gray. Her skin was pale. Pink, slicked-over scars slashed almost every piece of visible flesh. Her arms looked like they'd been forced through a paper shredder. Her face looked like she'd been mauled by a raccoon, and worst of all, she had a patch over her left eye. Three of the fingers on her left hand were missing, and two of her toes were gone, too. Either she'd fought in a war . . . or Mary happened. I didn't want to believe it was the latter; I didn't want this to be me.

"I had to go check, to see." Cordelia's voice cracked, her eye dewing and her lips trembling. She looked away from me for a moment before a small, tight smile played around her mouth. "I checked the glass and she wasn't there. For the first time in seventeen years, she's not staring back at me. My God. I'm free. I'm finally free."

I sat on a spindly wooden chair in the corner of Cordelia's living room. The chair legs were off-balance and wobbled whenever I shifted my weight. Fifteen feet. That was the distance Cordelia insisted be between us at all times. It was the only way she'd allow me inside her home.

"I'm sorry," she said, "but I'm not going to lose her only to get her back because I let you in."

I didn't take it personally. I was too busy taking in the condition of the house. Three steps past the door and I was besieged by a rank, coppery odor. I gagged. With the windows and doors closed, it was stuffy inside, and that made the aroma meaty and thick, like breathing slaughterhouse air. The humming I'd mistaken for a TV was actually the buzzing of flies. Everywhere. Clouds of them crawled over the black paper covering the windowpanes as if they were trying to escape. A dozen swarmed up when I sat down, and I had to keep swatting them away as they darted in front of my face. There were flypapers strung like streamers from the ceiling—curled, yellowing strips covered in shriveled black dots.

"It's the blood," Cordelia said, seeing me watch the flies. "I paint the windows with pigs' blood. No matter how many fly strips go up, they keep coming back. You'll get used to the smell."

"What? Why would you . . . Why pigs' blood?" I asked, my stomach churning, threatening to revolt on me.

Cordelia sank into an ancient upholstered chair across the room, next to an industrial-size sack of salt. Her fingers toyed with the burlap's fringe. She twitched then, a nervous tic in her cheek that she tried to hide behind her maimed hand. "Because it's effective." Cordelia leaned forward, staring at me intently with her one eye, her mouth pursed into a grimace. It put one of her worst scars into clear focus. The laceration bisected her thin top lip and traveled up along her cheek to curve into her nostril. "She gets better the longer she hunts you. Every scratch is a way to familiarize herself with your scent. The only thing that throws her off is to inundate her with another kind of blood. Pigs' blood is pungent. Works for inside the house. It's not like you can smear yourself in animal blood and go walking down the street, if you know what I mean. Bad enough the local butcher thinks I live off of blood sausage with all I have delivered." She cackled, a dry, reedy sound that reminded me of Mary's laugh.

"So, wait, I'm stuck with her?" I asked.

"That depends. What happened?"

I told her everything. Cordelia listened with her head tilted to the side, her eye at half-mast. Her fingers twisted in her hair before she grabbed single strands and plucked them out only to drop them on the floor beside her chair. "That's how it starts," she said. "A scratch. And losing her grip on you is why she's following you now. If you'd gone into the mirror as she intended, I'd still be haunted, but because you didn't she wants you. It's an obsession." She lifted the stub of a finger to point at her eye patch. "She took that as a trophy years ago and has been with me ever since. She hunted me and now you because we lived. The scent of your blood is the way she finds you—through any glass, any mirror, any reflective anything."

There was a groan that sounded like a dying animal. It took me a second to realize the sound came from my own mouth. My shoulders slumped and my head fell forward, my hands sliding up to cover my eyes. Bloody Mary was truly haunting me. I was her meal of choice. Not Jess or Kitty or Anna, but me.

Cordelia stood from her chair, walking through the living room to one of the tall bookcases she had lining the walls. Hardcovers and paperbacks stuffed on every shelf, additional books lying horizontally wherever there was space. "I'm not wrong, am I? She tried to pull you through a mirror and you got away," she said.

"Yes, ma'am. I mean, Cordelia," I managed, though I sounded broken. I felt broken.

"Cody. No one calls me Cordelia. Well, Becky did, but Becky's dead now." She paused, then shook her head, banishing a memory. "Something you need to understand, Shauna. Mary won't be content taking just you. She wants you alone and vulnerable. She wants to punish you for escaping her." I watched Cody pull a photo album from the shelf, her thumb skimming over the faded binding. "People like us have to make sacrifices to protect the people we care about. If you love them, leave them. Now. It's a lesson I learned too late." Her face softened, the strain of her admission making her mouth flatten into a grimace. She bent down and pushed the album across the carpet toward me. It came to a stop by my feet.

I scooped it up, my hands shaking. The idea of losing my friends because they'd suffer for the crime of knowing me scared me. I was a leper. A dirty little secret they should thrust away before they got my disease all over them. I wanted to shriek and wail and throw things at the unfairness of it all. But I needed to stay calm. I needed Cody, the only person who could help me.

I concentrated on the photo album. It was full of pictures of Cody when she was a teenager, most of them with friends or people I assumed were family members. The first few pages were normal enough; Cody's happy, smiling, unblemished face appeared in stark contrast to how she looked now.

I turned the page. There was a picture of a different girl with dark hair and a date written on the edge. Beside the date was the word *Love*.

"Her name was Jamie. She was my best friend and one of the girls who summoned Bloody Mary with me. A few weeks after Mary marked me, she took Jamie through the mirror in my parents' living room. I watched it happen. I watched her pull Jamie through. I begged, I pleaded, I even offered to go in Jamie's place, but Mary wanted my suffering. Struggling was useless— Mary is too strong. She thrust me away and took Jamie."

Trembling, Cody paused to run her hand across her brow. Even after all these years, the loss still weighed on her. "I reported it to the police, but no one believed me. I was a goth girl, and Jamie was the only openly gay kid in the school. People thought I was making it up because of how I dressed, how I acted. Jamie and I were oddballs. They tried to blame me for her disappearance, but when they ran the DNA from the scratches on my face, they realized they had no case."

"I'm sorry," I said.

Cody let out a harsh bark of laughter. "For that? Oh, please. There's a lot more to be sorry for. Becky was taken a few months after Jamie. Moira lasted the longest, but it was still less than a year after our summoning. Mary took my cousin John for the sin of coming to visit me a couple years after that. It's not just the summoning people who are in danger here. It's everyone around you."

If I had known Cody better, I would have told her how sorry I was for what she'd been through. Pity is a funny thing, though; some people want it, others don't, and Cody had proven prickly enough that I didn't risk insulting her. I delved deeper into the photo album, spotting more dates along the edges of pictures. I peered at the faces of people I didn't know, feeling despondent.

"Damn it," Cody muttered. I peeked at her over the top of the photo album. She twitched and her hand snaked out to snatch at the air. Her fingers curled over as she brought her fist close to her chest. She whispered under her breath, dark hair sliding down to cover her face.

"Pardon?" I asked.

"Fly," she said. She grinned at me. Her hand lifted and she stretched out her fingers. A smear of dead fly decorated her scarred palm. Cody pointed at the remains like this was some great feat. I didn't know what to say as she flicked the bug bits away with a raspy giggle.

She'd seemed so normal for a few minutes. Now I wasn't so convinced. Mary had done a number on this poor woman.

"I miss them, you know." She lifted her skirt to wipe away the last of the bug goo, acting for all intents and purposes like the fly incident had never happened. "Every day I wish I'd gone into exile sooner. But I thought if I could hold on, eventually someone would summon her and get hooked liked I'd been. I knew I'd be free one day. I just didn't know it would take so many years and cost my friends' lives. For what it's worth, I'm sorry it happened to you. I don't wish Mary on anyone. I warned your friend away, but she didn't want to listen."

Jess never listened, and because of it, I'd gotten haunted. The desire to curse was so overwhelming, my teeth clenched on the sides of my tongue. I wouldn't lose it here in front of Cody. She had enough to worry about without my throwing a tantrum over my best friend.

"Sounds like Jess," I spat. "That's how she is." I glanced back down at the album. When the pictures finally stopped, I let out a long sigh. I hadn't known any of the people shown, but I felt sad for them all the same. Cody, too. She'd had a life, and Mary had put that life on hold. She'd robbed Cody of what should have been her best years. At least it was over for her now.

For me, it was just beginning.

"Is there . . ." I stopped talking to take a deep breath, hearing the warbling in my voice. "Is there a way to put her away for good? A way to beat her? There has to be something I can do."

"Probably, but I'm not sure what it is. I'd guess it stems from her background." Cody pulled one of those manila envelopes with a string tie at the flap from between two thick books. She removed a piece of paper and flung it my way. I immediately recognized it as the picture on the Solomon's Folly site.

"I've seen this. It's online. That's Mary Worth."

She nodded. "Moira hit the Solomon's Folly library right after I got haunted. The original picture has water damage. If you haven't figured it out yet, Mary's tied to water. I think it has to do with the flood. That picture was recovered after the Southbridge River flooded back in 1962. The flood destroyed the Southbridge Parish—the church you see there. The town did what it could to salvage the church's older artifacts, but most of the collection was moved to storage for protection. Moira conned the librarian into letting her take a look. She was always good on her feet like that. Much better than me, anyway."

Cody settled into her seat with a notepad she'd pulled from the bookshelf. She opened it, flipped to a page, and then left it on her lap, like she'd long ago memorized what she was about to say. "Moira also uncovered a few local articles. They explained a lot—about why Mary chooses young girls to haunt, anyway."

"She'll only haunt girls? I thought she pulled your cousin John through the mirror," I said.

"She did, but she'll only haunt girls like you or me because she'll only answer a summons with four girls. Mary's father died of fever when she was a child. And Hannah Worth drowned in the Southbridge River when Mary was seventeen. Mary insisted it was murder, but she refused to name a suspect."

It looked like Cody was going to keep talking, but she jolted out of her seat and spun around, head whipping from side to side. Her hands flew down for the burlap sack of salt. She shook it around her, salt flying all willy-nilly. She mumbled and groaned. "Mary, Mary, Mary," she said over and over, the salt crystals spraying, some careening across the room to strike my legs.

I stood from my chair and braced for the ghost. My eyes scoured the room, looking for Mary's ugly face, but there was nothing shiny nearby. There was nowhere for her to hide. Cody had covered everything with masking tape or black paper.

"Where is she?" I yelled.

Cody ignored me, scurrying through the room with her salt pointed at the floor, a thick line trailing behind her.

"Mary, Mary," she said again.

"Where, Cody?!" I barked.

Cody stopped in her tracks, one foot in the living room, the other now in the kitchen. Her head swiveled toward me. She looked so empty for a moment, so fragile, but then she snorted and glanced away. Color blossomed in her cheeks like she was ashamed of her outburst.

"I thought I heard—no. No, I didn't." She lifted her salt sack to her chest, cradling it like a baby. Her cheek rubbed against the coarse burlap. "Sorry, so sorry. This happens sometimes, after so many years. You hear something or see something and you react, because if you don't react, you die. It's that simple."

I sank down into my chair, my eyes never leaving her as she returned to her seat. She fell back into the old upholstery, the salt bag pressed to her heart. She never relinquished it, not even when she leaned forward to retrieve the notepad and envelope she'd dropped in her panic.

She still looked embarrassed. I tried to smile, but it fell flat, and my attention drifted back to the picture in my hand. Hannah Worth. I traced my fingertip over her pale, plaited hair. "She was beautiful," I said.

"Yes. Yes, she was. Unfortunately it cost her, and in the long run, Mary, too." Cody let out a sigh. By the stretching silence, I knew that our meeting was over. I wasn't going to wait around for her to kick me out, and I didn't want to give her a reason to hang up on me if I had to call her back.

"Thanks for everything," I said, standing and dropping the picture of the Worths onto my seat. "I should go, though. I need to get back for dinner, but you were really helpful." Cody looked like she'd get up to show me out, but I lifted a hand and shook my head. "No, you stay over there where it's safe. You've had enough of Mary. It's cool."

I started for the door, but then she called my name again. I looked back at her. Clutched in her maimed fingers was a white envelope.

"Mary dislikes big groups of people," Cody said. "At first, anyway. The longer she hunts you, the less of a deterrent groups become. She also tends to avoid adults—especially women, especially moms. She was attached to her own mother. You might catch a glimpse of her here and there, but she won't stay. Never underestimate her. Never."

She said nothing else as she tossed the envelope at me. It struck me on the side of my knee. I bent to retrieve it, pulling out a stack of photocopied pages.

April 9, 1864

Beloved Constance,

I am so glad to hear that Boston is treating you well. I wish circumstances would have allowed for a visit before now, but Mother counsels patience. I think she tires of my exuberance. I've mentioned the possibility of leaving this horrid little village for good and moving closer to the city, but Mother insists that she prefers the quiet of the country. I think her resolve is faltering, though, especially lately. We tire of the nonsense.

The town's histrionics continue. It's gotten awful enough that Mother begged the pastor to intervene on my behalf, though his cure is possibly worse than the illness with which he afflicted me. After my morning lessons, I report to church and he has me sit in his private quarters copying scripture. I write until my hand aches. When I ask for reprieve, he strikes my knuckles with a switch.

At first, it was only an hour or two of daily tedium, but now it is four, and I can feel his eyes boring into my back all the while. He never leaves or moves. He simply stares. His attention is disconcerting. I am simply thankful that he looks upon me with loathing and not lust, as he looks upon our dear mother. I've deduced he keeps me near as a way of keeping her near. It is unnatural.

You know my disposition, Constance, and I am not one to silence my tongue under the best of circumstances, but this man's influence over the town is such that I fear I must abide his ridiculous rules or suffer dire consequence. When I refused to attend his lessons a few weeks ago—if such mindless labors can even be called lessons—Mother had difficulty selling her poultices. Mrs. Grant said "the store didn't need them." She's been buying them every week for ten years! I cannot prove that Pastor Starkcrowe swayed her, but you know how devout Mrs. Grant is. You'd think that store of hers was built by the Lord Himself.

If my suspicions are correct, the pastor punished Mother for my rebellion, which is a wicked, evil thing to do, especially with how little we claim. Halving our income is devastating. It's the sole reason I returned to him; we simply could not afford the alternative. Mother says I shouldn't assume the worst of Pastor Starkcrowe, that I have no proof of his interference, but I do find it strange that the very day I returned to his instruction, Mrs. Grant sent her son to buy Mother's goods again. It was a Wednesday, which is definitely not their usual Monday delivery. Does that not cross you as odd?

If it does not, perhaps I am the lunatic Elizabeth Hawthorne claims. I am convinced she is the force behind the wagging rumors of my mental instability. The pastor has done me few favors since his arrival, the wretch. He's slurred my character and, most recently, given me a terrible fear of the dark, something that has not plagued me since I was a child.

The first day of my return to the church, the pastor berated me for abandoning my lessons. He yelled so much that spittle struck my face, and he does not have the most pleasant breath, I assure you. The spring church festival was upon us, and Elizabeth and her awful coven were decorating the pews with flowers when I arrived. I was able to ignore their unkind whispering, but when the pastor shouted at me, they had the audacity to snicker. I glanced at them, but instead of punishing them for their rudeness, the pastor grew more incensed with me because, as he put it, I "lacked the necessary discipline to listen to holy instruction."

There was no instruction, Constance; he only shouted at me for avoiding his company a week, but before I could say as much he dragged me through the church and to the basement door.

I will not tell you that I didn't struggle, for that would be a lie, but the basement is foreboding, more a dungeon than not. It frightens me. It smells like Mother's herbs when they go to rot, and the stone walls are covered in mold. He thrust me down the stairs, and I stumbled into all sorts of strange miscellanea: a mirror, an old pew, an old bookshelf, a box of idols. I'm surprised I didn't break my neck upon the refuse. The floor had puddles of water, and there were awful beetles everywhere. Some of them even crawled on me. I doubt I'll forget the feeling of them scuttling over my skin.

"You'll be lucky to see the light of day again," he told me as he closed the door. I begged for release, thinking perhaps he lingered on the other side, but he was gone. There was laughter instead. It was Elizabeth and her odious friends. She called to me through the door, mocking me as I sat in the cold wet. It injured my pride, but I pleaded with her to let me out. She insisted she couldn't do that else she make the pastor cross. Her assurances that I would be released sooner or later were hollow and cruel.

I spent hours in the dark, my eyes fixed upon the empty mirror. Do you remember Mother's insistence that we cover the mirrors when Father took ill? Her superstitions about his dying before the glass? I thought it ridiculous at the time, but during those bleak hours, I came to understand her fears. A lightless mirror is a terrifying thing. There is no reflection, only black glass. Like an abyss. It's endless and consuming.

I haven't told Mother about what happened with the pastor. If she confronts him for his cruelty, he could contact Mrs. Grant again and we will be destitute. If she confronts the Hawthornes about Elizabeth's behavior, they bring their own complications. Mayor Hawthorne is not a nice man, and I doubt he'd believe ill of his Elizabeth.

I am sorry that my letters are so glum lately. The prospect of visiting you brightens every one of my dark days. I sometimes dream of staying in the city with you, but I am not sure I could leave Mother alone, especially with Pastor Starkcrowe's lascivious gaze upon her. Perhaps your letters will convince her that the air in Solomon's Folly grows toxic. You always were more influential than I.

Write soon, and give Edward my love. I adore you, Sister Mine.

Mary

Cody watched me leave from the porch, her hand lifted in a half wave of stubbed fingers and scarred palm. Her eye flitted over her yard, like she couldn't believe she was actually outside of her door without having to worry about Mary's assailing her from every angle. I couldn't tell if it was relief or fear on her face.

"Thank you," I called to her. Reading Mary's letter, hearing Cody's story, I felt worse than I had before I'd come. Everything looked so bleak. Seeing Cody holed up in that run-down house with those flies, that smell, the blackened windows...It was a sobering peek into my future.

"Don't forget the pigs' blood. And the salt," she called out.

"I won't," I said, approaching Kitty's car. Kitty had fallen asleep in her seat, her phone propped on her chest, face pointed at the sunroof. It wasn't until I knocked on the door that she darted up, her sunglasses flying off her nose to strike the window. Seeing that it was me and not a killer ghost come to maim her, she relaxed and unlocked the door before fumbling for her sunglasses. I started to climb in, but Cody called to me again. I paused, glancing back at the woman standing on the porch.

"One thing: tell your friend to stop calling me. I warned her."

Cody ducked back into her house. A moment later, I saw her tear a sheet of black paper off of the front window.

"So how did it go?" Kitty asked, easing the SUV out of the driveway and onto the empty street. I didn't answer her. Cody's gray house slipped out of view. Leaving felt wrong. Cody knew more about my situation than I did, and there was an illusion of safety being near her. I couldn't stay with her, of course, but a part of me desperately wished I could.

"Not good. I'm haunted, which I sort of knew, but I need to talk to Jess and Anna, tonight maybe, though I have to . . . ugh. Jess." It was more a ramble than a sentence, but Kitty nodded all the same, her hands tightening on the steering wheel.

"Did she say what we could do about Mary?"

"No, just how I got haunted. She only got rid of Mary when I got marked, which I guess is how the haunting is passed. It's messed up. She also gave me another letter from Mary to her sister. It's dark. You can read it tonight with Jess and Anna," I explained. Kitty was fine with waiting, which made me grateful I'd gone with Kitty instead of Anna or Jess. They were far less patient.

The only information I didn't share was that Cody told me

to leave my friends. I didn't want to freak Kitty out or make her think she was going to die being in the car with me. It wasn't like Kitty would leave me on the side of the road, but like the letter, it was another conversation to have with the group. It'd hurt enough to say it one time, never mind multiple times.

I hesitated before texting Jess. I knew I shouldn't talk to her. She'd endangered me. She'd heard the warnings from Cody and ignored them. The thing was, I knew Jess. She was my oldest friend and she hadn't meant to get anyone hurt—especially not me. She was reckless, but Jess had always been reckless. She screwed up a lot, but she always made good on it later. Maybe she could make good on this, too. Maybe she could help me survive the ghost.

Need to talk. Your place tonight? I typed.

Seconds later, my phone buzzed.

Bring overnight bag. Call for ride. TTYL.

I was willing to give Jess a chance, but I didn't want to be alone with her right now, either. I wanted normal people around me to buffer whatever crap she threw my way, and there'd be crap. Excuses, apologies, lies.

Kitty and Anna? I sent.

Sure.

I tossed my phone into my bag and leaned the car seat back so I was as far away from the windows as I could be. "I'm going to Jess's tonight to talk about Mary. She wants to help. You want to come?"

"Okay," Kitty said, easing the car onto the highway.

"Cool. I'll let you talk Anna into it."

Kitty groaned. "I'll talk to her. We don't need to be fighting with one another right now."

"No, we really don't."

There were no Mary sightings in the car or in my apartment. I wasn't naive enough to believe she wasn't nearby, watching and waiting. I grabbed an overnight bag, keeping my eyes away from my vanity. It was still covered, but I knew what could be under there. Some people might be tempted to lift the robe to check, but I wasn't. I never wanted to lift the robe again.

Before I left, I snagged my salt shaker from the nightstand. Cody said to keep salt on hand at all times, and unlike Jess, I tended to listen to the people who were trying to keep me alive.

Kitty had to swing to her house for clothes, too. I waited for her in the middle of her long driveway, the salt in the cradle of my folded legs. The pavement was warm on my butt, and I tilted my head to the sun, keeping my back to the wall of shrubs. Kitty took her sweet time in the house, but I was all right with that. Outside felt safe, free from shiny surfaces.

I messaged my mom while I waited so she'd know where I was going tonight.

<3 u, staying w/Jess 2nite, I said.

Call if going out. Have fun. Love you, was her reply.

Kitty stormed outside with a duffel bag on her shoulder and a cell phone pressed to her ear. "Yes, I know Jess is a jerk, but . . . Okay. So don't come. We'll go." Kitty frowned at me and sighed, shaking her head, obviously listening to a tirade. "So come then. You're invited. Anna. Anna! Am I picking you up or not?" The closer Kitty got, the more I could hear the shouting. To her credit, she didn't look too browbeaten. Just like I was used to Jess's particular quirks, Kitty was used to Anna's. Being Anna's best friend meant stomaching a lot of vitriol.

"Okay, fine. I'll see you in twenty." Kitty hung up and motioned me to the car. I slid in beside her and resumed my laid-back position to keep my upper body away from the window glass. I wedged the salt shaker in one of the cup holders just in case. "Anna's a little mad," Kitty said.

"Oh, good. Ought to make tonight more interesting," I said.

Anna was waiting for us on her front step, her clothes wedged into a tote bag that rested between her sneakers. She slid in behind Kitty without a word. Kitty eased the car onto the road, and I kept quiet. We knew this drill. Anna burned hot when she was mad, but if you gave her a little space, she'd simmer down. Jess didn't abide that much because she was either brave, stupid, or insensitive, but Kitty and I knew to respect Anna's boundaries.

That didn't mean I couldn't be friendly, though, so I craned my neck to smile at her. Anna turned her head, nodded, and the sun flashed across her glasses. That's when I saw the two black eyes peering out at me. There were no whites, only almond shapes of emptiness. I squealed and reached for Anna's glasses. Anna saw me sailing at her face and flinched, but my hand was faster than her recoil. I grabbed the glasses and flung them onto the seat beside her, my free hand fumbling for the shaker of salt.

"In the glasses. *In* the glasses!" I shrieked. Kitty jerked on the wheel to pull the car over onto the side of the road, nearly running into a mailbox. I flew forward and bit my tongue hard enough that I tasted coppery blood. I still managed to fling a handful of salt at the glasses in hopes of exorcising the ghost.

"Miiiiiiine."

The word warbled from the rear window and over to Anna's car door. The car windows started to rise despite no one touching the control buttons. I tried to push mine back down, but had to jerk my hands away at the last moment, afraid that Mary would pin me between the glass and the roof. There was a click as the locks snapped into place around us, ghostly hands forcing the mechanisms.

Mary's voice traveled from window to window as if she danced her way around the vehicle. There was an empty, hollow quality to the sound, too, like it came not from the depths of the car, but from a much larger, more cavernous chamber.

"What the hell is that?" Anna demanded, but both she and Kitty knew. They had never heard Mary's voice, but they knew. They screamed and reached for their car doors. I did the same, my hand sliding down to grip the plastic. For all that I'd had the pleasure of Mary's voice, it didn't prepare me for this. Familiarity didn't make it easier. I wanted to get out. I *needed* to get out. I gripped the handle and pulled, but nothing happened. I did it again, and again the door wouldn't unlock.

"No, NO!" Kitty shrieked as the three of us pushed on the doors like we could brute-force our way out to safety. The voice amplified before fracturing—instead of one Mary voice, there were six voices whirling around us, all staking their claim at once. I watched the glass of the car fog over, small rivulets of water coursing over the panes.

"Mine. Mine, mine, mine, mine..."

"Make it stop," Anna squealed, the words jumbling together as she threw herself flat onto the backseat, her face hidden against the upholstery, her hands clasped over her ears. I wanted to join her, but I froze when I saw Mary's gray fingertip press against the windshield like she was perched on the hood of Kitty's SUV.

"Wh-what... Is she coming? Is she..." Kitty's voice broke off in a whimper as Mary started writing in the condensation, the letters dribbling water. I expected to see the *M* of *Mine* again, but this time it was an *S*. Followed by an *H*. My hand flew to my mouth as Mary wrote out my name, the letters crooked and ungainly, the *N* backward.

The voices around us died at once, cut short as if someone pressed stop on a stereo. A moment later an ear-shredding scream pulsed from the glass, high-pitched and shrill. The car began to shake. We huddled down into the seats, screeching and pleading for Mary to stop. I wanted it to be over, for Mary to go back to wherever she came from, but she wasn't finished yet.

Her ragged, ruined hand flattened on the windshield in front of my face. I could see the skin moving, the gash in her palm burping out a pair of tiny black beetles that scurried down the car. She swept her hand to the side. The flourish erased my name, the phantom letters now replaced by a smear of black tar raining inky tears down the glass.

It was the school bus that did it. We were locked in a shaking car, drowning in terror, when the yellow bus pulled up to the street corner. The doors opened, unleashing a small herd of elementary school kids on the neighborhood. Mary fled as soon as they appeared.

Kitty threw open her door the moment it unlocked and bumbled into the street. I saw her whacking at her pocket. There was a wheeze just before she yanked out her inhaler, stealing a drag and falling onto her butt on the pavement. Anna crawled from the backseat, her whole body flat on the road. I dove for the sidewalk, finding a safe spot next to the trunk of an oak tree. I stared at the car unblinking, afraid that in the millisecond it took to close my eyes, the nightmare would come back.

I felt sick. I think we all did. One of the little kids stopped to peer at us, looking from Kitty to Anna to me. She was petite and blond, with big green eyes and a pink unicorn backpack that matched her jacket.

"Are you guys dying?" she asked. "If you're dying, I'll get my mom."

She couldn't have been more than nine or ten, and for her sake I forced an unconvincing smile. "No. Not dying. Just had a...an accident," I said, pointing at the car. "Just scared."

"Oh. Okay. I'm glad you're okay."

I wasn't sure how okay I was, but I wasn't going to say as much. The girl ran off to join her friends while the three of us got our collective nerve back. Anna was the first to recover. She stood from the road and wiped her pants off before turning to eye me, her cheeks flushed and stained with tears.

"Where's the salt?" she demanded.

I still had it in my hand, and I tossed it to her. Anna stepped over Kitty to fling salt over the inside of the car—in the back of the SUV, on the dashboard. She put it in the little grooves between the window glass and the rubber guard things. She put it on the seats. She rubbed it into the vents. She used every last granule on that car before stepping back and whacking her hands clean, the empty cardboard shaker abandoned on the passenger's side floor.

"W-we can't avoid driving, but we can avoid dying," she said.

Anna was right. I didn't want to get back into the car, but when I saw Anna help Kitty to her feet, I knew we had to keep going. We clustered together, Kitty's hands reaching out to either side of her so she could give me and Anna half hugs at the same time. We moved toward the car like we were walking to the gallows. When Kitty turned the engine over, we held our breaths and waited for Mary to return with her whisper games.

Nothing.

Kitty wasn't a speeder, but she got from Anna's street to Jess's house burning smears of rubber on the pavement. I held my breath for long sections of the drive, only noticing I was doing it when I'd start to feel faint. I'd breathe, then something would flash across the glass of the windows and the cycle would perpetuate. Anna refused to wear her glasses. They stayed abandoned on the seat beside her, granules of salt pooling in the curve of the lenses. She didn't touch them, not even when we got to Jess's house and she threw herself from the car.

We collected our bags and hurried up Jess's front steps, not bothering to knock. Jess's house had a kitchen, a bathroom, a big living room, and an office downstairs. All the bedrooms were upstairs. I walked through the foyer and past the stairs to look into the kitchen. Mrs. McAllister was there with Todd, handing him a paper towel full of a snack.

Seeing me, she grinned and motioned me close. "I made brownies. You should have one," she said. "Especially after that crazy day at school. I got the call and my mind jumped to the worst-case scenario. I hope they find the little bastards with the fireworks and expel them, pardon my French."

Fireworks. Right.

Mrs. McAllister cut a slab of brownie and lifted it at me as an invitation. I didn't have an appetite after the car ride, but

I liked the idea of being near Jess's mom. It felt safe. I went so far as to plunk myself down at the kitchen table beside Todd. Mrs. McAllister slid me a tall glass of milk. I murmured my thanks as I nibbled, my fingers brushing the crumbs away from my lips. Todd blabbed at me, and I nodded like I understood, but I didn't hear a single word he said. I was too busy watching Mrs. McAllister sweep back and forth across the kitchen. At that point, had she tried to go to the bathroom, I probably would have followed her.

I could hear Jess pounding down the steps. She didn't come to the kitchen right away, probably pausing to talk with Kitty and Anna, who were still in the other room. A minute later, she shuffled into the kitchen. She looked as tired as I did, and I wondered if it was fear of Bloody Mary or guilt that had kept her awake.

"Hey, how you holding up?" she asked.

Mrs. McAllister turned to look at me, her face falling into a frown. "Is everything all right, Shauna?"

"Yeah! Yeah. I'm just having a rough patch," I said, understating it by a million. "I'll be okay."

Mrs. McAllister gave me one of those tight mom smiles that said she understood even though I hadn't said a word about the problem. Our problem. *My* problem. She cut another half brownie from the pan and brought it my way, dropping it onto my paper towel. "That's when you spoil yourself with a little extra chocolate, honey. Trust me. It works." She gave my cheek a pat and then stroked my hair, reminding me of my own mom. I felt my eyes water. I was getting awfully weepy these days.

Seeing my extra brownie, Todd scowled and sat up in his chair. I watched him wipe his mouth on his arm, leaving a long chocolate smear between his wrist and elbow. "Mama, can I have more brownie?"

"No. You'll spoil your dinner."

"Won't Shauna spoil *her* dinner?" he returned.

Jess reached out to flick his ear. He batted her away like he was shooing a fly, but she ignored him and flicked his other ear, making him erupt into a series of whines.

"Come on, Shauna. I think that's our sign to retreat."

Jess led us to Todd's toy room. There wasn't much in the way of real furniture, but at least there was carpet and a couple of beanbag chairs. I walked past the G.I. Joes and coloring books to get to the windows. A big bowl of salt was already on the floor, and Anna placed a salt line on the left window while I did the same to the right one. Someone had already pulled down the shades. It made me think of Cody with her black construction paper windowpanes.

"Is your brother going to barge in here?" Kitty asked Jess. Anna hadn't quite graduated to making polite conversation yet, but Kitty made the effort.

"He'd better not, if he knows what's good for him," Jess replied.

I sighed. "You realize if he goes and tells your mom we're in here, she's going to kick us out. You need to make sure he's okay with it or we'll have to move. Why not your room?"

"My closet doors are mirrors. I was being careful." Jess *fwump*ed down into the red beanbag chair before kicking off her flip-flops. "I can handle Toad if it comes to it."

Jess had zero intention of talking to her brother about using his room. How couldn't she foresee the looming disaster? No kid wanted anything until someone else had it, and that was especially going to be true when it was his older sister. This wasn't much of a Mary sanctuary if Mrs. McAllister was going to boot us out when Todd whined.

"No, Jess. We need Todd's approval. I'll be right back," I announced. I walked to the door. The doorknob's gleaming glass surface should have caught my eye, but it didn't.

I reached for the doorknob.

It reached back.

Two slimy, cold-fish fingers stabbed out from the rounded center, scraping my fingers and ripping into the skin. The jagged edges of Mary's nails jerked down, lashing at me so hard, they sliced the webbing between my thumb and forefinger.

My hand felt like I'd plunged it into a nest of fire ants. I stumbled back, blood running down my arm and onto my jeans, dripping onto the white canvas tops of my sneakers. I dug my teeth into my lip to stop myself from screaming.

Anna rushed over with the salt and flung it at the blood-smeared fingers wriggling from the knob. The moment the crystals struck dead skin, a sizzle sparked, and Mary retreated into the glass. Blood splashes ran over the curve of the doorknob and down onto the carpet. Jess found one of Todd's SpongeBob T-shirts on the floor and threw it at me. I was in too much pain to catch it, but Kitty snagged it and wrapped it around my hand, putting pressure on the wounds to stop the bleeding.

"Clean it, we've got to clean it and bandage it," Kitty said. She grabbed the doorknob without a thought for her own safety, but the salt kept Mary behind the glass. Kitty steered me out of the playroom and across the hall to the bathroom.

"Kitty, n-no, the bathroom," I said, but she ushered me to the door anyway. Anna trailed along behind while Jess ran off toward the kitchen, presumably to get more salt. Mrs. McAllister called upstairs to see if we were okay. Jess yelled something back. All I could think about was the pain.

When we got to Jess's bathroom, Anna darted in to salt the mirror. It was flush against the sink, like it was in Anna's basement, so she was able to leave a thick line along the edge. Jess ran in with a second box, and the two of them worked together to finish it.

"Okay, it's clear. Come in," whispered Anna.

Kitty started to put my hand under the faucet, but it was chrome silver. I jerked back, afraid to get too close. Kitty understood, filling the sink with hot water for me. The faucet was still right there, but at least there was enough distance between it and the bottom of the basin that I could avoid any more finger jabs. I dipped my hand into the warm, steamy water, gasping and slumping at the fire racing up my arms. I watched through tear-swollen eyes as the water turned a red-swirled pink.

"God, we need to...do something. This, the car. I don't know. Do the 'I believe in you' thing again or something," Anna said. "We need to brainstorm."

SLAM.

One moment the mirror had our reflections, the next Bloody Mary was there, her face smashing against her side of the glass. Bones crunched, like she'd broken something in her own face, but that didn't stop her from bashing her head against the glass again and soiling it with her thick, crusting fluids.

I yanked my hand from the sink and the four of us huddled against the bathroom wall.

"G-get your mom," I rasped at Jess. "GET YOUR MOM!"

Jess looked confused, but she didn't ask for an explanation. She darted from the room to shout for her mother, asking her to come upstairs. Kitty and Anna and I remained, staring at Bloody Mary, who grinned and licked at the smears she'd left on the glass. She stopped and looked straight at me, her head tilting to the side. It forced the muscles in her neck to go taut, the stretch of skin bursting a small gray pustule along her collarbone. A flurry of black beetles poured down her dress. I could almost hear the click-clicking of their jaws.

Kitty gagged and Anna whimpered, but I was frozen, pinned by Mary's black-as-midnight eyes.

Mary stretched up and down as if her body were elastic. One minute she was tall and impossibly thin, the next low and squat. Repeatedly she pushed her palm to the glass to see if it'd give, but the salt kept her contained.

Then she lifted her hand and splayed her fingers. The tips were covered in my blood. Mary raised them to her nostril holes. I realized with sickening dread that she was *smelling* me. She was sniffing my blood.

"Oh, God," I murmured. Mary smiled, showing us a row of yellow-gray stump teeth. Slowly and deliberately, she popped a finger into her mouth, sucking it clean. Her tongue ran along her knuckle and underneath her nail to capture every last drop of my blood. She lapped at her palm and then slurped the tip of her finger before moving on to the next finger, her eyes fluttering in perverse rapture.

"Why? Why is she doing that?" Anna asked.

Mrs. McAllister rushed into the bathroom and came straight for me. She reached for my hand and hissed when she saw the blood swirls curling over my wrist and forearm. I glanced past her leaning blond head at the mirror; it was empty. The moment Jess's mother arrived, Mary fled. I wanted to cling to Mrs. McAllister and never let go, like a little kid on the first day of school.

"Oh, hon. How did you manage this one?" she asked, pulling me toward the sink. She put my hand back under the faucet, turning the water on cold as she rummaged through the drawers of the vanity for bandages and Neosporin. I wasn't thrilled to be so close to the chrome, but having Jess's mom there was as close to safe as I was going to get.

"I broke a glass," Jess said from the hall. "It's my fault."

Mrs. McAllister cast a sharp look at Jess before dabbing ointment on the shredded flesh between my thumb and pointer finger. It hurt enough that I cringed. "Easy, girlie. If this doesn't stop bleeding, you might need the hospital for a stitch or two. Keep an eye on it. Do you want me to call your mom?"

"No. It's okay. If it doesn't stop bleeding, I'll call her myself."

She nodded and layered some gauze on the injury before wrapping me in medical tape.

"Did you clean up the glass?" Mrs. McAllister asked.

"Yeah. It's fine. Sorry, Shauna," Jess said, stepping aside as her mother ducked back into the hall.

"Good. I'll come see you in an hourish, Shauna. We'll check how you're doing, okay?"

I followed her into the hall, eager to put the mirror behind me. "Sure, thanks. Oh, hey, Mrs. M? We're working on a project tonight and need extra room. Is it okay if we use Todd's playroom? If he needs stuff, it's cool. We can go somewhere else," I said.

She nodded. "Sure. I'll tell him to grab a couple toys for the night and scram."

Jess opened the door wide so I could sidestep the knob and settle back down on the floor. I felt stiff and old; my throbbing hand made my back spasm, too, like my body decided my hand needed sympathy pain.

"What the hell is going on?" Anna demanded, following me inside. She still had the salt with her, clutched to her chest as she peered from me to Jess and back again. "This is crazy. What is going *on*?"

I looked between my friends. Seeing their weary, terrified expressions, I knew it was time to talk.

16

The car haunting had Jess on edge. I watched her drift to the window to peel back the shade, looking out at the cars in the driveway like they were monsters lying in wait.

With all of us together, I detailed what I knew about Cody's haunting, how Mary was passed to me from a blood tag, and how Cody's friends and cousin died. I warned them that they were in danger, but none of them made any motion to leave. I should have told them this was it, that I had to go away after tonight, but I wasn't ready yet. It was selfish, but I was too scared to go it alone. Maybe one day soon I'd have the will to insist they go, but today wasn't that day.

Finally, I described Cody's fly-ridden house and the pigs' blood. Jess snatched the second letter from my hands, insisting on reading it aloud and refusing to relinquish it when she was done, her fingers smoothing over the paper and flattening the curled edges.

"Everything okay?" I asked.

She laid the letter flat on the carpet. "Don't you think this is sad? Like, what's said here? He abused her. No wonder she ended up becoming a crazy bitch." I could see the inherent tragedy developing in Mary's letter, but I had a hard time assigning pity to her. She was trying to kill me. One day, she'd try to kill every person in this room. Feeling sorry for a would-be murderer was stretching it.

"I'm not sure," I admitted.

Anna wasn't so diplomatic. "I don't. Bad stuff happens to everyone in life. That doesn't mean you have to turn into a jerk. Not to the people who don't deserve it. Those guys?" Anna pointed at the letter with a snort. "The pastor, that Elizabeth girl? Fine, haunt them. But what did we do to her?"

Jess was about to reply, but Kitty cut her off. "I don't think that's how ghosts work. Not in the movies, anyway. Think about it. They die and then something disturbs their resting place or someone breaks their stuff and they come back. I just don't think they can see right or wrong anymore."

Kitty made me think about Mary's rising. The mirror. The darkness. The bugs. Mary must have died somewhere around the church, I thought. Maybe she died *in* the church. Pastor Starkcrowe had threatened to lock her downstairs indefinitely.

"Hey, anyone got a laptop?" I asked.

"Yeah, give me a second." Jess got up to head to her room. Before she touched the doorknob, she bunched her shirt into a wad to form a makeshift glove. It sucked that we'd been reduced to such maneuvers, but there was nothing to do about it. Adapt or die.

Jess reemerged with her computer. I eyed it, checking for shine, but it was constructed of brushed silver and matte plastic. I felt relatively safe having it in the room. I motioned for Jess to fire it up. The screen had a reflection, so I kept my distance by pressing my back to the wall on the opposite side of the room.

"What are we looking for?" Kitty asked.

"You said that thing about the ghost being disturbed, and you're right. That's how it works in books and movies. Maybe something happened to her body. Cody mentioned that there was a flood in the sixties. If Mary's remains were in the church and something disturbed them, maybe that caused her to start haunting people."

"The legend did start in the sixties," Jess said. I remembered her texting that to me the other day. Anna must not have gotten the same information. She looked surprised Jess would know that fact off the top of her head, but before she could ask about it, Jess offered an explanation. "I did some research. Mary Worth died in 1864, but the legend of Bloody Mary didn't start until the sixties. There was a hundred-year gap."

Anna scowled. "Seriously? You knew all these things about Mary Worth and you still thought summoning her was a good idea? Wow. Great plan, Jess. Well done. Ten out of ten." The sarcasm was palpable. I glanced at Anna, then over to Jess, hoping for a peaceful resolution, but neither of them noticed me.

They were fixed on each other. Anna was squinting, a combination of no-glasses and annoyance. Jess looked furious. Her eye twitched and her ears were the color of a cherry tomato.

Finally, Jess broke the silence. "I said it before, I'll say it again: I screwed up. I know it. We all know it. But being sorry doesn't fix this. So here's how it is, Anna. We play nice until Shauna's Mary-free, and then you get the hell away from me. Or if that doesn't work, leave now. I'm here to help. If you're not going to help, go home." Jess never raised her voice, but she didn't have to. There was enough fire in her tone that I cringed. I understood what she was saying in spite of it, though. The Mary problem was bigger than our personal gripes. If we wanted to solve this mystery, we needed to work together.

I was about to ease the tension, but Jess cut me off with a muttered, "Of course, then you'd have to get back into a car to go home, and we know how that goes right now, don't we?"

It was mean; Anna hadn't been the only one in that car. It'd certainly scared me to death, and thinking about it again was enough to make my heart skip a beat. Kitty shrunk down into her beanbag chair, drawing her knees to her chest and hugging them. The lower part of her face was hidden behind her crossed arms, and her eyes jumped from shadow to shadow.

Anna started throwing her stuff back into her tote bag with a dry, humorless laugh. "You're *such* a bitch sometimes. If that's your attitude, fine. I'll call my mom and go home. I can help Shauna from there."

"Whatever," Jess said, thrusting the computer aside.

"Wait," I said to Anna. "Wait. You know what, Jess? I get what you're saying about putting Mary first, and I appreciate that. I really do. But you keep saying you're sorry, but you've never actually apologized to us. And that matters. This is scary stuff. And while it'd be more convenient if Anna stopped copping attitude"—I braced, expecting Anna to snarl at me for that, but she remained quiet, her hands wedging her clothes back into her overstuffed bag—"it's her right to be mad. We were all scared out of our minds in the car—she looked like she was on the hood. She shook it and...whatever. Either apologize *to* us instead of *at* us or I'll figure out this stuff at my place."

Jess looked like I'd struck her. Her eyes bored through my skull. Anna's lips were pinched in a flat line; she expected Jess to start screaming. Kitty snagged the computer, avoiding the fight. I had no idea what she was doing hunkered down behind the screen, but her fingers were loud on the keyboard.

Jess let out a shrill whistle like a teakettle boiling over. I stiffened, ready for a tantrum, but something dissuaded her. There was a soft sigh followed by a groan. She dropped to the floor beside me with a hard thud. "Fine. Fine, I get it. Yeah. I guess I...I am sorry. I'm sorry you're all scared. I'm scared, too. I'm scared for Shauna and myself and you guys, so for what it's worth, I'm sorry. I do really want to help Shauna now."

Anna rolled her head back to peer at the ceiling. She took a few long breaths to clear her head and nodded. "Fine. Let's just figure out what Shauna needs. She's the priority." She shoved her tote bag aside and slid down next to Kitty, leaning into her side.

"Thanks, guys," I murmured.

"Hey, come here," Kitty said. "I found Mary's church on the historical society site."

It was a black-and-white picture of an old church with a tall steeple. A brunette woman stood before its double doors smiling, holding a rake and wearing overalls. The caption read, *Adeline Dietrich, Southbridge Parish, 1961, two months before the flood.*

We'd seen a snippet of the church in the Mary Worth picture, but not the whole deal. It was a beast of a building, with large cathedral windows and two side chambers that sprouted off the main body like arms. The stone looked dark, almost black, but it was hard to tell the true color by the picture alone.

Jess reached out to tap the screen. "Oh, holy crap. I know where that is," she said. "It's right next to my grandparents' place near the river. It might have flooded, but most of the structure is still standing. Maybe we should check it out?"

The idea was interesting, though I did remember what Cody had said about Moira's library research. "We could. I'm not sure what we'd find. Isn't most of the stuff in storage?"

"Yes, but if the pastor locked Mary in the basement like he threatened . . . I doubt they'd move a body. There would be some reference if they found the bones, right?" Anna asked.

I nodded. "That'd be noteworthy, yes, but there's no information beyond the caption."

"Or maybe the body's still there," Kitty whispered. I looked at her. We all looked at her, and then we all looked back at the picture. If that was the case, we had some hunting to do.

Jess wanted to spend Friday night climbing around the church. She had the patience of a toddler. Anna was the one who told her we needed a Mary break, that I'd just been stabbed by dead-girl fingernails. I wasn't convinced it'd get better than this—I'd seen how Cody looked. But a night's reprieve sounded nice.

Instead of racing to the church, we researched over pizza. There wasn't a lot of progress, though. Anything we found about Bloody Mary related to variations on the summoning—how people claimed to summon her, the different names associated with her legend. By the time midnight came, we were tired and frustrated and too cheese-inflated to move.

Jess sighed and flopped back to stare at the ceiling. "We should have gone to the church. We need a better lead."

"Maybe tomorrow?" I asked.

Kitty frowned. "I can't. My dad's dragging me to visit my grandparents during the day, and I have plans tomorrow night. You guys can go without me if you want."

"I've got a family cookout tomorrow during the day," Anna said.

"So let's go at night," Jess said.

I didn't love that idea. If Mary was there in some guise, did we really want to face her in the dark? We were at enough of a disadvantage in the daylight. "Are we sure that's a good idea? What if she lives there?" I asked.

Jess shook her head. "She'd be cutting up everyone in Solomon's Folly if she lived there. Why would she bother with the mirrors if she didn't have to? Besides, we're better off going at night. Less reflection if there's less light. The car's less of an issue that way, too. Plus I doubt the locals want people climbing all over their historical buildings. This gives us a little cover."

"I hate to admit it, but she's got a point," Anna said. "And I can go tomorrow night, but I don't think we should leave Shauna alone between now and then. We've gotten lucky so far—the kids showing up with the car, Mrs. McAllister with the bathroom. But if we leave her on her own, it could get ugly. We should take shifts this weekend."

"I can help on Sunday during the day," Kitty offered.

Jess nodded. "Cool. I can take tomorrow day, so Anna's off the hook with the cookout. But tomorrow night when she gets home, let's hit the church and see if we can find anything. Sound good, Shauna?"

None of it sounded good. I was happy for the company, of course, but the idea of crawling through a deserted church at night with a monster haunting me wasn't high on my list of Awesome Things to Do. I was running out of options, though. We'd already tapped the Internet and Cody. We needed more.

"Sure," I said hesitantly. By Anna's less-than-enthusiastic expression, she was in accord. Jess was the only one energized by the possibility, but then, she'd been Mary-obsessed since we started.

Which reminded me.

"Hey, I meant to ask you earlier. Why do you keep calling Cody?"

Jess dropped her head, blinked, then shrugged. Her fingers returned to the second Mary letter. She reached behind her back to retrieve her red notebook and jammed the pages inside the top cover.

"Trying to find out if we can put her away for good," she said. "I have questions. I want to help you."

"Well, stop. I don't want to alienate the only other person in the world who survived Mary Worth." Jess started to say something, but stopped herself, her brow crinkling and her teeth digging into her lower lip. I knew that look. Jess had a secret. We were too far into this Mary thing for her to pull punches now. "What?" I pressed, and she squirmed beside me like a worm on a bait hook.

"There's one other girl who survived Mary. Well, not a girl anymore, but, like, you know," she said. "Elsa Samburg. She was haunted in the seventies. She's still around, but Cody's more accessible."

"How do you know that?" Anna demanded.

Jess ran her hand over her mouth nervously. "Aunt Dell mentioned her in passing. It's not like Elsa would be much help. I don't know how we could talk to her."

"Why not?" I asked.

Jess looked away from me, her eyes fixing on the blood-stained SpongeBob T-shirt on the floor. "She's in a mental hospital. She lost her mind."

17

The Elsa Samburg news surprised me, but it shouldn't have.
I'd seen Cody. And I'd had Mary on me for only a few days and
I was already questioning my sanity. Mary was perfect paranoia fodder. What I found more alarming was Jess dropping
another "Oh, by the way" on us. There were too many of them.
If she'd had all this information, why had she ever suggested
we summon Mary?

Recklessness, yes. Selfishness, yes. Her worst traits all tied
up into one huge, horrible idea that was going to get me killed.

Jess's motives were on my mind as we huddled into a pile
to sleep. We were like puppies—no one was comfortable being
alone, so we curled together around our pillows. I could feel
Anna's leg against mine and Kitty's elbow grazing my arm.
Jess stayed out of her room and slept with us on the floor, too.
She was so close, I could hear the soft cadence of her breaths.

Sleep eluded me. Part of it was the footsteps in the hall as Jess's family shuffled around the house before settling down for the night. Part of it was the wind through the trees. Part of it was the howling of a neighborhood cat and the barking of a dog. All of it conspired to keep me awake as long as possible. My last conscious moment was the thought that, yes, Mary could send anyone over the edge.

Mrs. McAllister woke us at nine the next morning with a dozen doughnuts and orange juice. It was way early to be up on a Saturday, but she stepped over our prone bodies to set the food in the middle of the room, like we were a pack of wolves. I pushed myself up to snag breakfast. Anna and Kitty joined me while Jess snored. After we ate, Kitty poked Jess's shoulder, narrowly avoiding Jess's morning flails.

"Hey, I'm taking Anna home," Kitty said. "I'll talk to you guys later. Good luck at the church."

Jess grumbled and nodded, her hands sliding down her face to rub the sleep away.

We needed to move out of Todd's space for the day. Jess came out to the hall with the salt clutched in her hands. "Sit here," she said. I slumped down onto the floor while she went to anti-ghost her room. She crossed from her bedroom to the linen closet a few times, using sheets to cover the closet's sliding glass doors. I could hear her moving furniture around before she poked her head out and motioned me in.

The room looked safe enough. The windows were salted. The

mirrors were covered or turned toward the walls. She'd even taken her pictures down so there wouldn't be anything staring at us from the frames. I stepped over a heap of dirty clothes on the floor and flung myself onto the bed. The carnival pony was there and I hugged it to my chest, my chin resting on its fuzzy pink mane. Jess eyed me and smirked, sinking down into her computer chair, the monitor on her desktop covered by a sweatshirt so there was no reflection.

"I'm glad I've got you to myself. I had an idea I wanted to run by you without the extra ears." She paused to think, tilting her head to the side. "It's not a nice idea, but I have to throw it out there. I don't want you stuck. I won't lose you. I refuse."

She sounded so fierce, I found myself smiling. Jess was an idiot, but there was something to be said for unrelenting loyalty. "Okay?"

She pulled her feet up onto the seat of her chair, her toes sticking out over the edge. She'd painted her nails a bright, cheery teal. "I was thinking we could get someone to take the tag from you. Someone who deserves it, though, so we don't feel bad."

"WHAT?!" I hadn't meant to yell, but I was too shocked *not* to yell. "No!" I shouted. "No! I'd never . . . not to anyone else. How would I live with myself? Jesus, Jess. Use your brain."

Jess reached out to pinch me, hard, on the bicep. I smacked at her and rubbed the sore spot with my bandaged hand. "I *am* using my brain. If the choice is living with yourself or too dead to live with anything, I'm picking living with yourself every time. Guilt goes away. Being dead doesn't," she said.

I shook my head. It wasn't an option. I'd rather chisel away at Mary Worth's legacy to uncover her secrets than pass the problem to someone else. There had to be a reason for all of this, and when we found that reason, we'd have a solution. I had to believe something from Mary's past was the linchpin to this whole terrifying mess. We just hadn't found it yet.

"Well," I croaked, my voice cracking from strain, "I didn't think there was anything in the world that'd make me want to go to this church tonight. But congratulations, you've managed it."

Jess sighed, resting her chin on her knee. Her eyes skimmed to her sheet-covered window. "Don't be stupid, Shauna. You want to live. I want you to live. I'm not going to let you die."

Anna returned after dinner, when the sun was past the horizon and the skies were more gray than gold. Her glasses were off, so either she'd put in contacts or preferred temporary blindness to having her eyes poked out by ghost fingers. I talked to my mother briefly, assuring her I'd be home later tonight. She said be in by midnight, but she wouldn't walk in until after two— she tended bar at McReady's until closing, so I wasn't worried about missing curfew.

I texted Kitty to be sure she didn't want to be in on this madness. She sent me a message back, saying *Out with Bronx,* followed by a smiley emoticon.

"Kitty's talking to Bronx," I said as we waited for the last light to disappear. I wanted to avoid the deathmobile as long as possible. "I'm wondering if he texted her after the Mary thing at school yesterday. Either way, I'm hoping good things come of it."

"Same," Anna said. "Except I'm mad she didn't tell me about it herself. I wonder if she thought I'd try to talk her out of going out with him again?"

I shrugged. "Who knows? But if she thought you'd fight her on it, probably. You know she doesn't do confrontation."

"I, for one, thank God they're talking," Jess said. "Maybe if he sticks it in her she'll stop being such a huge drain. One more guilt trip and I was going to feed her to a crocodile."

Anna reached out to whack Jess's forearm, her face scrunched up like she smelled something foul. "That's so crude. Did you have to put it that way?"

Jess's smile was unrepentant.

We piled into the car at nine, this time with Anna in the front passenger seat and me sitting center in the back, my legs straddling the bump between the two foot wells. I slouched down, a box of salt in my lap. Anna had devised an ingenious method to prevent us from being Mary mauled: clear packaging tape. She drizzled salt crystals over the sticky part before laying strips across the glass on a diagonal. It wasn't a solid line, but at least we knew the granules were enough to keep Mary from pushing through.

Jess got us to Solomon's Folly before ten. There was something different about the town after dark. During the day, the Folly was any other small New England town with its picket fences and quaint storefronts, but at night, it took a turn. The narrow streets had no lights. The drive was one tiny, dark, curving road into the next. Fog spread over the land in a thick paste, casting a dank pallor over the sprawling fields and farmland. The trees were clawed behemoths looming over the roads, a canopy of foliage blocking the moon and any vestiges of its light.

"Good God, this place is creepy," Anna said. We passed a gas station on the main stretch, a neon OPEN sign blinking in the window. The lights above the gas pumps were lightbulbs on strings, each swinging with the breeze.

Jess said nothing as we turned onto a stretch of dirt road that made the car shimmy. She guided us away from civilization and toward . . . I didn't know what. Nothingness. We were in the middle of nowhere, our car bouncing over the divots in the gravel beneath us.

The road narrowed until it was only suitable for a single car. It sloped downward, too, though it was too dark to see what it sloped toward. Jess killed the engine and plunged us into perfect darkness. She fumbled around in the front seat until a circle of light blasted her in the eyes. A Maglite. She handed me and Anna flashlights as well, each a fraction of the size of her own. Jess threw open her door, and Anna followed suit. I climbed out next with a flashlight in one hand, a salt box in the other. Neither gave me any comfort.

Jess aimed her flashlight down on the ground. I heard rushing water and the call of a night bird. Anna paused to swing her flashlight toward the river. The water was black and angry, the banks steep. The trees nearby were all dead, their branches dry and emaciated—like Mary's spindly, bony arms. I shuddered and stepped to Anna's side. She trembled beside me.

We stood that way awhile, peering at the river, until a light turned on across the water. I jumped in surprise. There was so much darkness here that a flash of light was startling; it was a sun against a blackened canvas. It took me a second to realize it was a porch light. There was a house on the opposite bank, and though I didn't like the idea of being seen tromping around the old church, it was good to know we weren't far from the outside world.

"We should go," I said. Anna nodded and turned her flashlight away so we wouldn't be spotted. A screen door slammed across the way. It may have been too late for secrecy.

Jess's footsteps were fading in the distance. We scrambled to catch up, Anna stumbling in a hole hidden in the knee-high grass. I looped my arm around her waist to hold her upright. Once she was steady, she continued to cling to me, the salt box wedged in between our bodies. Jess walked deeper into the night, her path keeping us parallel to the river. The walk went on and on, taking us uncomfortably far from the car. Finally, Jess stopped. My eyes adjusted to the light as I took in the enormous black lump of a building twenty feet in front of us.

Churches are supposed to be pointy things that stretch to the sky, but this church had long ago lost its steeple and portions of its roof. It looked like a dome now or, with the rooms extending from the sides and the shadowy trees surrounding them, a hulking wood tick feeding from the ground. Jess swung the Maglite up to the entrance where double doors once stood. There was an open archway inviting the unsuspecting into its maw. That's how I saw the church—a monstrous, living creature that wanted to swallow us alive.

"Oh, this can't be a good idea," Anna said.

Jess walked on. "It's necessary."

Jess approached the front of the church and pressed her hand flat against the stones. She pulled back and rubbed her fingers together as she craned her head back. "It feels wet. Like, slimy-wet. Be careful. Don't fall."

"Be care..." Anna's voice died as Jess ducked inside the passageway, taking the light of her big flashlight with her. Anna and I shared a moment of solidarity standing there together— until we heard the rustling overhead. The trees lacked the foliage to make any sound. I swung my flashlight up just in time to catch them. Bats.

"Oh, holy crap. Let's get the hell out of here," I said.

Catching a glimpse of flying furballs, Anna grabbed my hand and dragged me toward the church. For better or worse, we were going in.

18

"How did you ever find this place?" I asked into the dark. I could barely see, but I could hear Jess fumbling around nearby. She cursed as something skittered across the stone floor. It struck the wall next to me with a loud clack.

Anna swung her flashlight in a wide circle. The main room of the church was smaller than I'd expected. The congregation must have only had about a dozen pews for worshippers. At the altar, there were two arching holes where windows used to be, but the panes were devoid of glass. A tree branch had grown in through one of the gaps, its ends spearing through the roof. Slivers of moonlight cast silver shadows across the black walls.

"We're near my grandparents' house. It's a ways up the river. I'd come out here as a kid with my cousin to play," Jess said.

I eased farther inside, following the sound of Jess's voice past piles of rubble. There was a smell I couldn't identify—almost like cleaning solution. My sneakers crunched through leaves and debris. I slipped. It wasn't just the moisture that sent me colliding into the walls. There was a layer of muck smeared across the floor stones, too. Bracing, I swung my flashlight down to examine the murky, lumpy texture on the floor. I wasn't sure I wanted to know what it was.

Anna reached out to steady me, her hand gripping my elbow. I saw Jess duck through an open doorway to our right.

"What are you looking for?" I called out.

"Mary talked about a basement doorway. I'm trying to find it. There's nothing in here but grit and broken ceiling, though. A few bookcases."

"Didn't she say Elizabeth watched her get locked inside? She was decorating the pews when he dragged Mary off. This main room is where the pews would be. The door's got to be somewhere in here," Anna replied.

Anna was right. I turned my flashlight to sweep the area. The back wall beneath the windows was solid—there was no door to be found. I edged farther to the left inside the main room. There was a door opposite the one Jess had crept through that I guessed to be the entryway to the second side room. An old bureau was pushed flush to the wall. The bureau was wide enough and tall enough that something could be hidden behind it. I eased my way across the cold, slimy stones, taking Anna with me.

"Hey, Jess. Come here!" I called out. Anna and I shuffled together, our feet moving like we were skating. As we neared the corner, the smell intensified. Now I recognized it as ammonia. Why ammonia here? Was it from the dresser? The dark wood *was* covered in a pale green mold, and there were distortions and lumps riddling the surface.

"Now what?" Anna asked.

"We move the dresser, I guess," I said.

I held the flashlight in my mouth and put the salt on top of the bureau so I could get a grip. The bureau was layered in decay. I tried to push it away from the wall. It wouldn't budge. Anna went to the opposite side to help, and the two of us managed to wriggle it a half a foot forward. Once Jess joined us, we maneuvered the bureau far enough out to see behind it. A narrow door was wedged in the corner.

"It's real," Jess whispered. She reached out to touch the planks of the door, reverent when she slid her fingers over the rough wooden surface. There was an old-fashioned iron latch in place of a proper doorknob. Jess reached for it. A faint grinding noise rattled the air as she pressed the button tab at the top. The door wouldn't open. The latch was rusted shut or the lock had been jammed.

"Here, hold this," I said to Anna, handing her my flashlight. She angled both beams at the door as I reached for the lock. My feet slid across the floor, but I found some purchase by wedging my leg against the wall. Jess and I fussed with the latch. The tab finally gave, a mechanism inside squealing in protest as we bullied its gears after so many years of disuse.

"On three," Jess said. She counted and the two of us pressed and pulled, forcing the latch to open. The good news was, it worked. The door swung toward us, sending us skidding. Jess stumbled back and landed on the floor.

The bad news was more bats. *So* many bats that hadn't left for their evening feeding. A chorus of high-pitched squeals rang out, and then the flutter of a thousand wings beat the air as the bats blasted up from the dark. I dove for the floor and Anna huddled on her haunches, the flashlights dropping and skittering away. My hands sailed up to protect my head as bats skimmed across my hair with their wings and feet. I cowered lower, my only defense against the aerial assault.

The explosion of bats was over as fast as it had begun, the last of them squeaking off into the night. Anna fumbled around to collect the flashlights. Jess, however, whimpered behind me.

"Oh, *God*, nasty. Nasty," she groaned. I glanced over at her to see what was wrong. Jess still had her Maglite and was pointing it at the sludge on her fingers. The sludge we'd been sliding in all this time. The sludge I now realized was bat guano. Not only was the basement full of the creatures, but they must have been living in the remaining eaves of the church as well, which explained the ammonia smell.

Disgusting.

"Don't think about it," I said. I reached out to help her to her feet. She clasped my sleeve and smeared me in some of the muck. I struggled to take my own advice. She skidded into my side and we stepped toward the top of the steps to peer through the door, our free hands clasped together, fingers laced in apprehension and fear.

Stairs leading down into an unfathomable dark—stairs with no railing and no walls to support a would-be visitor. This had to be the place. My pulse pounded. Jess edged forward but stopped herself at the threshold. The stairs were steep and narrow, and there was a glistening sheen on the stone that indicated a long, slippery trip if she misstepped. She swung the Maglite around the room to get a better look. It was maybe fifteen feet long by twenty feet wide. Water covered most of the floor, though I could see dry spots at the corners of the room. Directly across from the stairs, there were crates stacked against the far wall, most of them covered by drop cloths in various states of decay.

The ammonia smell was thick and concentrated in the basement. Jess pointed to a crumbling break in the wall along the ceiling, a gap no bigger than a bowling ball, with a tiny bit of moonlight shining through. The bat entrance.

"I'm going down," I said. I knew I had to do it. Jess was right; this was necessary. Daylight and shovels would suit me better, but I was willing to risk the darkness to search for answers.

Jess swung the flashlight my way, blasting me in the eyes. I lifted my hand to block the light, and she jerked it away with a deep breath.

"You sure? It's . . . Not sure how safe it is," Jess said.

"Are *you* actually asking about safety? Who are you and what have you done with Jess?" Anna asked from behind us. Jess grunted; I tittered a little.

I was careful where I put my sneaker. Jess held out her hand to steady me. For a moment, I thought she'd descend into the basement too, but she stayed at the top to anchor me as long as she could. Four steps. Five steps. The stone was slick, but my going slowly and Jess's hold kept me upright with minimal slippage.

When I was halfway to the bottom, Jess followed, easing her way down while Anna took position in the doorway, her dual flashlights illuminating the path into the recesses. We were like a chain gang, with one of us near the bottom, one hovering midstairs, and one at the top. I extended my toe to check the water's depth. The floor beneath felt solid, though I felt a tire-size dip caved into the middle, like the stones were sinking into the ground. If I avoided that portion, I thought I could stand without too much problem.

I tugged away from Jess and took the last step. The slope was harder to avoid than I'd presumed. I was standing in cold, black water up to my ankles. I forced myself to concentrate on the crates ahead of me.

"You okay?" Jess asked as I sloshed toward the crates. If Mary's body was down here, it wasn't in the crates, but I was curious what *was* inside them. The first drop cloth disintegrated upon touch, some of the fibers sticking to my fingers. A chunk of cloth fell into the water by my feet. I shivered and brushed off my hands before rooting through a crate.

"A little light over here?" I called to Jess. She lifted the Maglite enough that I could see a stack of books inside the crate, though the covers were too decayed to touch. I eased my way over to another crate and peeked over the edge. This one was half-collapsed, its contents oozing onto the floor. What

remained inside was rotten, but among all that moldy, uniden-
tifiable sludge, I spotted something shiny.

I remembered the mirror from Mary's letter and wondered
if this might be it—if that tiny glint from within the crate was
a missing piece to the puzzle that was Mary Worth. I carefully
slid it out and lifted it up. A part of me wanted it to be a clue,
but another part wondered what I'd do with it if it were. But
looking at it in the dim light, disappointment quieted my fears.
It wasn't a mirror, just glass.

Something scurried across my hand. I glanced down and
saw a black beetle—the same beetle I'd seen worming its way
out of Mary's skin. Black, shiny carapace, too many legs. I felt
it skitter over my arm and I flicked it away, shuddering. Didn't
bats eat bugs? Yet this one somehow flourished down here in the
dark. It was another thing to add to my Do Not Think About list.

I returned to the crate of books. I picked it up and moved
it aside to look at one of the middle crates. The topmost layer
would likely be damaged from the bats above, and the bottom
layer would likely be drenched by water. The best place to find
something useful was somewhere in the middle.

This crate was not as wet as the others, though the stack
of papers inside was still impossible to read. Next to the stack
was a small metal box. I pulled it out, taking a moment to brush
the slushy remnants of old papers away from its top. The front
had a loop for a miniature padlock, but there was no lock there
anymore. Maybe there never was one.

"Point the light right on me?" I called up the steps.

Anna aimed both flashlights in my direction as I tugged

open the lid of the metal box. It squealed, its hinges hungry for oil. Inside was a stack of black-and-white photographs that were surprisingly undamaged. For a moment I tensed, thinking I'd discovered more pictures of Mary, but the images were too modern. I did, though, recognize the person in most of them. It was the Dietrich woman from the church picture. She was smiling and posing for shots, sometimes in groups, sometimes on her own. She was no more than twenty or thirty in most of the pictures. For a moment, I stared at her. There was something oddly familiar about her smile.

Before I could place the smile, something quick and small scuttled across my arm. I dropped the pictures back into the crate just as I felt another beetle crawling up my calf. More crept on me, tickling me with their thread-thin legs. I returned the crate and reached into my sleeve, grabbing on to a hard shell attached to a set of violent, hairy legs. I flung it across the basement.

"Uuuuugh. Bugs," I cried, hiking my pants up and itching where I'd felt one scour my ankle. The beetle had climbed up to my knee. I reached for it, right as I felt another one wiggle its way across the back of my neck. And another one graze my cheek to run down my front, into my shirt and under my bra. "Jesus!"

"Are you okay?" Anna asked.

"Yeah. No. Maybe—I . . . Beetles. Like, the black ones that come with Mary. I bet she's here. Maybe under my feet. There's a dip in the stone, so maybe she's buried—" My voice cut off on a squeal as another bug crawled down my back and another across my hip. I wanted to get out of here. I turned back for the stairs, but I couldn't move because of the *hands* that tore from the water, anchoring my legs in place.

The jagged edges of Mary's fingernails punctured through my thin socks, jabbing at my skin. I tried to kick her away—to walk toward Jess who was reaching for me, screaming instructions I couldn't understand in my panic—but those hands jerked on me and I fell forward. My arms stretched out, stopping me from smashing my face against the cold steps. I landed hard and wailed, my forearms and knees throbbing in pain from the impact. My legs were in the puddle from the knees down, and her iron grip moved from my ankles to my calves.

"Take my hand. TAKE MY HAND," Jess shouted.

"The salt. Anna, get the salt!" I yelled, my fingers clenching on Jess's forearm. Jess locked her grip on me and pulled up while Mary pulled back. I swiveled my head around, scanning the water's surface from the light of Jess's Maglite. Mary exploded up in a spray of rancid black rain. She was covered in wet leaves and strings of dead vines, her torso above the water while the rest of her remained hidden below. Strands of hair were plastered to her lumpy scalp, her dress glued to a skeletal frame.

Mary let out a wheezy chitter of laughter as her hands locked around my knees. She jerked me back and away from Jess. I sailed through the air and landed in the water, splashing the walls as my body made contact with the floor. The air was forced from my lungs, another stab of pain shredding its way through my already-bruised arms.

We were stupid. Stupid to be there. Stupid to be unprepared for the worst. Mary snarled and I felt her fingernails raking over my legs. She was trying to cut me through my jeans. She let out a furious squeal as I felt her fingernails rip into my sides. Instant anguish, those little razors digging into my stomach and twisting. I squirmed and tried to crawl away, but Mary clutched a hand into my hair. I felt cold, wormlike fingers slithering along the back of my scalp before she took a fistful of my curls and pressed my face into the water.

My nose hit the floor stones. White fireworks burst behind my eyes. I heard Jess screaming my name, I heard Anna shouting. I held my breath. I held it so long, my lungs ached. Just as I was about to open my mouth and let the flood in, Mary screeched behind me, her hands falling away. I tore my face up with a bellow, furiously gasping for air, as Mary snarled and thrashed behind me.

"Shauna! Come to me. Come on," Jess hollered. I opened my eyes, squinting against the water drops running down my face. I crawled toward Jess's voice. My vision swam, but I was able to make out two sets of shoes on the steps—Anna had come down too, and when I lifted my gaze, I saw she was rapidly firing salt at Mary.

Jess tugged me to the stairs. I cleared the first two steps without slipping, but Mary lunged at me again, her fingers tangling in the hem of my T-shirt. I kicked out at her, my heel striking her arm with a loud snap. She let go with a rattling snarl. The three of us made the perilous climb upstairs, Anna tossing salt the entire way. It was enough to keep Mary away, though each time I looked back at her, a little more of Mary had spilled out of that black puddle on the floor.

"I'm almost out of salt. It's almost empty. We have to go," Anna croaked. Jess reached for my wrist, grabbing it and dragging me through the church and toward the front doors. I looked back to make sure we weren't abandoning Anna. She stayed a few steps behind to rifle the rest of the salt, but when Mary crawled out of the basement, dragging herself up by her hands, Anna tore past us to get to the car. I couldn't blame her—Mary erect was fearsome. She was more spider than ghoul right now, one of her elbows bent in instead of out, her feet flat to the ground so she scurried instead of walked. Her back was arched too low. Her head dangled at an unnatural angle while her white serpent tongue thrust out from between her lips, licking our scent in the air.

Jess and I ran, the Maglite swinging back and forth with Jess's frenzied gait. I hurt all over. My chest ached from gasping. I was dizzy with fear, but I kept pace with Jess even as Mary snorted and groaned at us from behind. We crested the front steps of the church and stumbled into the grass, Anna only a few feet ahead of us.

Four steps out of the doorway, two enormous lights blasted us in the face. We stopped short, stuck between the apparition and the disorienting lights ahead of us. Then it registered— those were headlights. It was a car. A car with flashing blue lights on the roof.

19

"All right, kids. Rein it in. You're not supposed to be out here," a disembodied female voice said from behind the car. "This is Ms. Dietrich's private property."

I put my hands up and walked toward the car, trying to look inconspicuous. I wanted to get away from the church and be near the person with the gun as quickly as possible. I couldn't hear snarling behind me anymore, but I didn't trust the dark. The dark had too many secrets.

"Hi! Hi, we saw . . . something, but it was . . ." Before Anna got too far into an explanation, she noticed me edging away from her and followed. I saw the policewoman's outline and then I saw the policewoman herself. Tall, thick through the shoulders, a little heavy; she was older than my mom, with short black hair peppered with gray and a pair of glasses on her face. She had her hand on her hip, but not near her weapon. I let my hands drop to my sides.

"Ms. Dietrich called me out when she saw you drive up. What are you girls doing out here?" she demanded.

Jess trotted up next to us. She was pale, her eyes a little bigger than they ought to be, but she faked being okay better than me and Anna. Anna looked green, her arms wrapped around her middle as if to hold her insides inside. The wind had picked up, whipping the grass around our feet into a frenzy. My wet clothes clung to my skin. I shivered, my teeth loudly chattering. "We were playing Truth or Dare," Jess explained. "Go into the church at night."

"Got ya. Well, how about you show me a license and registration so you can Truth or Dare your way back home?" the cop said.

The officer drove us back to the car, remarking not once, not twice, but three times about how bad we smelled. Anna had shared our bat encounter. The cop grunted, regretting inviting us into her cruiser. This was the type of stench that lingered.

At the car, Jess handed her paperwork to the officer. My eyes swung back in the direction of the church. Mary was there somewhere. Or maybe she wasn't. It was hard to tell which thought was more terrifying. She'd either slithered back through the water and into her glass world or she was here, in this world. Maybe she was hunting me. Maybe she was tearing up Ms. Dietrich. I felt sick from the smell and the fresh gouges in my sides. My arms ached. My legs itched from the memory of beetles dancing over my skin.

The cop tapped Jess's license. "Are you related to—"

"Gus McAllister. He's my grandfather," Jess interrupted.

The officer nodded and handed the ID back. "All right, here's the deal. You're going to get in that car with your friends and you're going to drive straight home. Massachusetts law still has a curfew for teenagers, and if you want the privilege of driving, you honor it." The officer turned to point at me and Anna like we were Jess's shameful secrets. "And no more trespassing, girls. That church isn't a playground. Someone could have gotten hurt."

She didn't know the half of it. "Thank you, officer," I said.

The silence was oppressive during the ride home. When Jess got us back to the section of the highway that had things like streetlights and modern buildings, she turned on the radio. Anna reached out and snapped it off. Jess glared at Anna. I caught a glimpse of Anna's furious expression through the passing lights.

"Just take me home. I'll get my stuff from you tomorrow," I said, my voice ragged from screaming. My throat felt like I'd gargled with dust.

"Are you staying with her tonight, then?" Jess asked Anna. Anna hissed a confirmation back. Jess shrugged off Anna's anger, but I knew Jess was bothered—her shoulders were tense and her jaw clenched.

I was wet and scared. The salted tape was securely on the

windows, but I wanted more. I wanted every ward we could muster to keep Mary away, and right then, we had nothing else.

"Do you think she's . . . Is she free? Did we free her?" I asked, my voice warbling.

Anna groaned, a feral whine that sounded more animal than human. Jess shook her head.

"No. I've never heard of that happening," Jess said.

"But you don't know for sure," I added.

"Well, I'm taking an educated guess. Mary went away the moment the policewoman showed up. So she probably disappeared or—"

"But if she disappeared, does that mean she blinks out like you flipped a switch? Or does she physically have to go back to the place she passed through?" I asked.

Jess hesitated and then sighed, defeated. "I don't know. Maybe Cordelia would, but I don't know."

Silence filled the car as Jess pulled into my driveway to drop off me and Anna. Jess lifted her hand in a half wave; I returned the gesture. Anna ignored it. I put my key into my house lock, doing my best to overlook the flickering lightbulb in the building's hallway. I'd never noticed the light or heard its low-grade hum before, but I noticed a lot of things lately that I hadn't a week ago. Perpetually searching for a ghost had heightened my senses, like a rabbit living among wolves.

"Can I borrow some clean clothes? After a bath? It seems safer," Anna said. "You first, of course, but . . . please?"

"Yeah. Absolutely."

We took turns bathing. I stayed alert, waiting for Mary to stare back at me through the water, but we were alone. Had we unleashed the devil upon Solomon's Folly?

"I have to call Cody," I said. "I know it's late, but in case Mary's out. She should know."

"Yeah, you do. I was just thinking the same thing," Anna replied.

I finished my bath. The warm water on my battered body felt wonderful. Well, it felt wonderful everywhere that wasn't my arms, my hand, my shoulders, or my sides. Mary hadn't gotten my gut too badly, but there were scrapes and scratches there. Less than a week in and I looked like I'd been maimed by a blender. I was the scraggly neighborhood cat that got into too many fights.

"Hey, so, I don't know how to bring this up, so I'm just going to come out with it," Anna said, peering at the wall, her eyebrows low over her eyes, her mouth tight. "I'm not sure I can make the Jess friendship work. I know she apologized, but each time she reveals something she knew, each time something bad happens with Mary, I can't deal with it. She threw us into a *seriously* dangerous situation. I'm terrified all the time—for me, for you. If we're doing stuff to help you, I'll be there. I don't want to lose you as a friend, but I need to stay away from Jess awhile."

Anna had the right to feel angry and scared. I wasn't going to try to talk her out of it. Not again, anyway. Just like Kitty's situation with Bronx—the stuff I'd found important a week ago no longer seemed like such a big deal. Right then, getting out of the bathtub without another wound took most of my concentration.

I wrapped a towel around my sore body and drained the tub so Anna could take her turn. While the water ran, I called Cody, but she didn't pick up the phone. I left a voice mail and warned her about the church and Mary. For Cody's sake, for the sake of my conscience, I had to hope Bloody Mary was back behind the glass.

20

Anna slept in my bed with me. Or, well, she *stayed* in my bed with me. Sleep didn't come easily for either of us. I looked at the clock at least once every hour. I felt Anna moving next to me, sometimes hugging one of my pillows to her chest, sometimes rolling close to me. Human contact was one of the few things that gave us comfort. I had to adjust her arm once or twice because it grazed the gashes in my side.

Mom's Sunday schedule was kinder than the rest of the week—she only had the day shift at McReady's, so she'd be gone from eleven until six. Mom chattered through our pancake breakfast, only commenting three or four times on how tired and unresponsive Anna and I were. Perkiness was impossible.

"All right, well, I'm off. Don't do anything too crazy without me. And Shauna, make sure you take out the trash today. There's something really stinky in it," she said, brushing her lips across my temple before heading for the door. "I'll see you soon, Anna. Have a good day!"

"Bye, Mrs. O'Brien," Anna called after her. My mother's footsteps pounded down the building stairs.

It was a quiet few hours. I checked the news to see if there'd been a murder spree in Solomon's Folly. Nothing. Jess texted to check on me, and I sent her a small, inconsequential update. I didn't mention what Anna had said; I figured I'd let the two of them sort out their friendship. I also didn't bother changing out of my pajamas. For that matter, Anna didn't bother changing out of my pajamas, either.

Anna's parents collected her a little earlier than Kitty's scheduled arrival. I was alone, hugging my supply of salt. I'd covered most of the shiny surfaces in my room, including socks on the doorknobs and paper bags over the windows. Glass bottles were bagged, pictures were all removed and tucked into the closet.

Kitty arrived just after twelve. I came out of my room in the same checkered pj pants and tank top from last night to discover Kitty wielding a large pizza in one hand and holding Bronx's hand with the other.

Bronx waved at me, looking around the apartment. He'd never been here before, and I always got a little self-conscious when people visited for the first time. It wasn't really a showcase, but he smiled and motioned at the floor-to-ceiling windows. "Those are cool. They remind me of church windows."

"That's because it used to be a church way back when," I said.

"Ah, cool," he said.

"Sorry we're late. Figured we'd pick up some stuff on the way," Kitty said. She put the pizza down on the coffee table and then dropped her pocketbook on the armchair. It was a huge leather bag—the type that weird girls carry small dogs in. Kitty didn't have anything living inside her bag. Just salt. Lots and lots of salt. She brought out three canisters and lined them up on top of the entertainment unit.

"How are you holding up? How was last night?" Kitty asked. I waited for both of them to sit before picking my spot on the floor next to the table, purposefully keeping my back to the television. Kitty and Bronx claimed the couch, Bronx eagerly diving into the pizza. "Bronx and I were talking. This Bloody Mary thing is so unreal. We've got to figure out a solution soon. I've covered all *my* mirrors and I'm not the one haunted. I can't get her out of my head."

Bronx nodded. "Yeah, I think I'm a tough dude, but after that insanity Friday in school, I just...yeah. This is messed up."

"Thanks, guys. Last night was...I don't know if it's the worst that it's been, but it was right up there." I proceeded to explain all the details, from the drive to the abandoned church, the haunted basement, and the cop who kicked us off of Ms. Dietrich's property. Kitty forgot to chew through the telling, the slice of pizza suspended halfway to her mouth. Bronx managed to continue eating despite his stunned expression.

"Holy crap," Kitty said, putting the slice down to wipe her face with her shirtsleeve. Realizing Bronx was there, she cast him a quasi-guilty look before picking up a napkin and repeating the gesture.

"The worst part is we learned nothing," I continued. "Zero. We could go back today, but it wasn't safe the first time; it won't be safe the second time even with daylight. I wish Cody would call me back. I'm worried about her."

"I'm sure Cody's fine," Kitty said. Her hollow reassurance did little to boost my confidence.

"You did learn something, you know," Bronx said a moment later. "If that church is on private property, maybe you can trace who owned it—you've got the current owner's name. My dad's big into tracking family ancestry. He's up to three hundred years ago in Greece now with our family history. There's a lot of information on the Web. The town hall would also help. They track everything, man—births, deaths, land purchases. You could maybe tie something back to Mary that way."

I nodded along as Bronx spoke. It was worth a try. I wasn't sure what I'd find, but compared to the big pile of zero viable solutions I had, it was another lead. A better idea than Jess's solution to find a new victim.

It was also a better idea than going back to the church.

"Why not?" I said. "Mary might be buried in the church. Or might have been. If so, maybe the person who owned the church knew something about her death. Or maybe Ms. Dietrich owned the church when it flooded and could tell us if any remains were disturbed. I'm grasping at straws here."

"Ugh. Yeah, but good luck talking to her if she's the one who called the cops on you," Kitty said.

I shrugged. "It was dark, and we were far enough across the river that it would have been hard to see us. I don't have to tell her I was the one trespassing. Either way. Thanks, you two. I might try to research more before I go back to the basement. Although I'm not sure I've got the guts to go back now. There's more to see in the daylight, I know, but it was so..." I couldn't finish the sentence. Thinking about Mary tearing up out of the water, the bugs, the bats. I shuddered.

Bronx forced a smile for my sake and slid the pizza box my way. I took a slice, hoping it was enough to distract me from the memory of last night. And the night before that. And the day before that. Kitty reached out to thread her fingers through his black hair. He batted her away, but she kept going at his bangs and giggling. He smirked at her, and when she wouldn't stop fussing, he put his pizza back into the box to tug her into his lap. She squealed as he half turned her so her legs were dangling over the side of the couch, her sandals falling to the floor with thuds. I watched her offer him a bite from her own slice. He unhinged his jaw to devour half of it in one go.

"Wow. Hungry much, you hog?" Kitty asked. Bronx tossed his head back to laugh.

"I'm an athlete. We have big appetites," he said. Apparently she bought into it because she fed him the rest of her slice before grabbing herself another. When he lunged forward to try to steal that, too, she bopped him on the nose with one of her acrylic nails.

This was more like the Kitty I knew. The morose girl we'd been shouldering for the last month lacked this sunshine. Maybe it was kind of dumb that it took a boy to get her back on track, but I wasn't going to complain. She was happy. I needed a little happy around me.

"Glad you two are better," I said. Both of them turned to smile at me, then at each other, and I suddenly felt like an outsider in my own house. They were doing that mind-meld couple thing people who'd been dating awhile did, and it gave me a third-wheel complex. I got up to get myself a drink, but paused to grab one of Kitty's canisters of salt before heading into the kitchen. The moment my back was turned, I heard what sounded like a lip-smacking kiss. I smirked as I approached the fridge. Brushed steel surface or not, I had to drink. Fortunately, Mary wasn't inside the shine.

I grumbled, unsure of how to express dread and relief at the same time.

I tugged open the door and grabbed an iced tea. Right as I latched on to the can, a loud bellowing rang out from the parking lot. It took me a second to identify the siren sound as an obnoxious, whirring car alarm. Bronx gently shoved Kitty aside before heading for the windows. He rummaged through his pocket to pull out his car keys, his thumb hitting a button on the plastic alarm thing.

"If someone bumped my dad's car, he'll kill me. I'm going to go check it out," he announced, turning around to head to the front door. Except Bronx never got the chance.

Spindly arms of yellow bone and gray flesh burst out from the windowpanes and wrapped around his torso. Bronx's eyes bulged, a high-pitched squeal ripping from his throat. The biggest, strongest guy I knew was yanked off his feet like he weighed nothing. He hovered there a second, thrashing and kicking against the windows. The arms jerked him back. Hard. The windows exploded as Bronx was thrust outside, hurtling through the air, body spiraling to the ground amid a rain of sparkling glass.

I had no idea how she'd done it. So far, Mary had struck out through the glass or pulled things into the glass when the surface had softened. This time, Bronx hit something solid. The only explanation I could come up with was maybe it'd been jelly until he collided and she chose to let the surface harden. By then, the force of her pull was enough to send him sailing. Which meant she'd done it this way on purpose. Mary wanted Bronx to fall.

I stared at the empty space Bronx had just occupied. Kitty's screams echoed around the room, heart-wrenching and shrill. I never made a sound, not even when I raced to the window to see what I could do to help. Yes, Mary could still be near, but I had my salt. I hadn't dropped it, and I opened the top and sprayed it around as I neared the man-size gap, waving it back and forth like a fire extinguisher.

My imagination had already painted the world red, Bronx landing on his head and smashing his brains across the pavement. I forced myself to look. Bronx was sprawled on the ground below, but there was very little blood. He'd landed in such a way that his upper half was cushioned by shrubs. The problem was his legs. They were bent at odd angles, and one of his feet pointed in the opposite direction it was supposed to go.

She'd crippled him. Bloody Mary had crippled Bronx simply because he was near me, in my house. I pressed the back of my hand to my mouth so I wouldn't cry out, hot tears streaming down my cheeks. I felt horrible. I barely knew Bronx, but my ghost had managed to hurt him all the same. I wanted to throw up, to scream and tear down the walls around me, but Bronx needed me calm, not bugging out and shrieking in panic like Kitty. It was my fault he was down there. It was my fault that I hadn't insisted my friends leave when Cody told me to let them go.

This was *my fault.*

It was then that I heard him. It was faint, but I could hear him calling for us. He needed my help, not my self-recriminations. I made for the door, grabbing Kitty's arm and dragging her behind me as I ran for the steps. "Call 911," I said, but she was too busy screaming to hear me. I stopped on the second flight to shake her hard enough to rattle her teeth, my tear-stained eyes boring into hers. *"Kitty, he's alive.* Call 911 now!" I yelled at her.

She whimpered and fumbled in her pocket for her phone, following me as I raced for the building's foyer. I heard her talking a second later, her voice cracking when she had to tell the operator the nature of her emergency. I nearly ripped the front door off its hinges as I ran outside, vaulting over trash barrels and thrusting bags of recycling aside to get to Bronx.

He turned his head to look at me, face pale, eyes glassy.

"What was that? The arms. Was that her? Was it *her*?"

"Yes," I said, crouching beside him. Bronx grabbed for my hand, squeezing my fingers so hard, I was afraid he'd shatter them. "Kitty called the ambulance. They're on their way."

"My legs hurt. Real bad. They hurt, Shauna."

"I know. I'm so, so sorry." I considered telling him it was good he felt pain, that we were lucky he wasn't numb from the waist down or dead, but I was pretty sure he didn't want to hear that. Bronx gave my hand another squeeze and I winced. Kitty caught up with us, tears streaming down her cheeks and dribbling off her chin.

"Oh, Bronx. Baby," she said, collapsing onto her knees beside him. She reached for his other hand and slid her fingers over his. He turned his face to stare at her. She managed a watery smile, but then his body convulsed, his spine arching up off the pavement as he let out a wet gurgle and a roar. Kitty climbed on top of him then, sprawling her body over his as she wept hysterically.

"Kitty, be careful. He's fragile. Just be careful, okay?" I whispered. Anything else I could have said was cut off by the siren of an approaching ambulance.

21

Kitty hugged me and climbed into the ambulance with Bronx. I watched the lights disappear around the street bend before going upstairs. I hadn't noticed the glass on the pavement before, but now, when I wasn't hyped up on terror and adrenaline, I saw how lucky I was that I hadn't ripped my heels to shreds running outside to get to Bronx. I glanced up at my apartment and peered at the shattered opening in the wall. From here, it looked like a jagged wound in the building's side.

I called my mother to tell her what happened, repeating myself several times through tears and hysterics. She told me she was leaving work now and to stay put. I hurried inside to wait for her. She was going to kill me. It was an accident, yes, but one I couldn't explain. She'd asked me how it happened on the phone, and I just kept saying I didn't know over and over again. But I did know. I just didn't know how to make her believe me.

Mom flew into the apartment twenty minutes later. I was curled on the couch around a box of salt, sobbing. I heard the door slam. I lifted my face to her, my eyes so bleary with tears I could barely see. I was able to catch Mom's expression, though. Fury. But seeing me crumpled and limp and weepy, she softened and rushed to my side. She sank into the cushion next to me, stroking my hair. I hadn't cried like this since I was a little kid, but I didn't care. There was no shame. I cried for Bronx. I cried because of what happened last night. I cried because I was afraid I was going to get everyone killed. I cried because I was going to die.

It took a while for me to regain control. My mother crooned to me all the while and, when she was convinced I didn't have a tear left to shed, repeated her questions from earlier. I went with the simplest explanation I could conjure: he was leaning against the windows and they broke. It was an old building, it was plausible, which was probably why she didn't drill me too much. "No, Mom, no one was horsing around. And no, Mom, no one pushed him." It was good enough for her.

"Why don't you go lie down?" she said, her lips skimming across my forehead. "I have to make some calls, clean up around here. We'll check on your friend later, okay?"

"Yeah. Okay. Thanks." If she thought it was weird that I was hugging a box of salt like a teddy bear, she was good enough not to say so. My thoughts were on fire, hopping from one terrible Mary thing to the next. Lying on my bed, I replayed the events of the last week over and over and reduced myself to a quivering, sniffly mess. My temples pounded from all the crying, but I reached for my cell to call Cody again anyway. This time she answered. It wasn't the relief it would have been an hour ago; I knew Mary was on me now, back in the glass where she belonged. I knew because I'd watched her fling a kid out a window.

"Hi, Cody," I said, hiccupping at the end and gritting my teeth. "Hi. Sorry to bother you again."

"No, no. Hi, Shauna. I called you back a little while ago and you didn't answer. Is everything okay?"

"No. No, everything isn't okay." I told her all the same things I'd told Kitty and Bronx earlier about the church, but now there was an epilogue to the story, and I told her that, too. I heard her suck in air on the other end of the line before she groaned, like I'd gut-punched her.

"You need to get away. I told you this, and I don't say things because I like to hear myself talk. For their sake as much as yours, get rid of your friends. I lived with that guilt, that survivor's guilt, and it's awful. You need to split off now before it gets worse."

"I know, I know," I said. I'd known it before, too, but now that someone had really, truly gotten hurt, I couldn't procrastinate any longer. As much as this Mary thing was going to suck solo, it'd suck much, much worse if I dragged my friends down with me.

I took a deep breath and nodded like Cody could see me. "I'll do it. Today, after I hang up with you. But even without them, I just want . . . I need to figure this out. To beat Mary. I want to beat her so badly. And if she's in that basement, if her body's there, maybe there's a way. I can't lose that hope."

There was a long pause on Cody's end of the line before she said, "I understand that. I never lost hope, either. It was harder at the end, but it was still there. If you want, I'll go with you when you go back to the church. I know the situation you're in, and I'll help. The floor wasn't like that when we went years ago, but if it is now, maybe there really is something under there." She paused to take a deep breath before adding, "And when we go, we go during the day, we go with salt. But after you get situated, after you get a plan in action, we'll go together."

To volunteer to help me was brave after so many years of being haunted. But it made sense, too. Mary had tortured Cody for almost twenty years. Anyone would want the opportunity for closure, to even that score. "Thanks, Cody. Thanks a lot."

"You're welcome. If you need anything else in between, let me know. And thank you for warning me about last night. As far as I know, Mary always goes back to the mirror. It calls to her. I've never heard of her staying on this side, but I'm not sure if that's good or bad."

To be honest, neither did I.

I promised I'd cut ties with everyone right after the call, but that was a lie. I did craft an e-mail I could send to all three of them, but then I spent a few hours rereading it while I mustered the will to send it. It wasn't poetic or drawn out. It was the bare essentials:

Hey. I'm sorry everything is so messed up. Mary
threw Bronx out a window. Between last night and
today, it's clear it's no longer safe to hang out. I
love you, I appreciate your help, but you have to
stay away.—S

So simple and yet so final. The draft blinked at me, taunting
me to send it, but I couldn't push the button yet. When Mom
came in to get me for dinner, I told myself I'd send it after I'd
eaten. Mom had been busy while I'd been sequestered in my
room. She'd boarded over the hole in the wall with flattened
moving boxes and thick tape to keep out drafts and bugs.

After a salad, I went back to my room and drifted between
half sleep and staring at the ceiling. What I didn't do was press
Send on the message. Not until right before midnight—Kitty
had just sent me a text that said Bronx was going in for emergency surgery on his spine.

She said he might not walk again. Bronx's bright promise of
a football career was gone because Mary wanted to punish *me*.
I couldn't do that to other people. I had to protect my friends.
I sent it. Jess would try to call to yell at me for being so dumb,
so I shut off the phone. I kept the light on when I climbed under
the blankets. Mom visited one last time, spending a lot more
time fussing over me than usual. I liked the attention, the feel
of her hands toying with my hair. It made me feel loved, which
was something I needed right then. Being haunted by Bloody
Mary was proving to be pretty isolating.

"I love you, Mom," I said.

"I love you, too, Shauna," she returned before leaning down to give me a good-night kiss. I hugged her tight, then she wandered off back to her room, closing my door in her wake.

I stayed home from school the next day, telling my mom I was sick. I should have informed Jess, too. Her car horn blasted at quarter of seven. I hadn't answered my phone, so she came for me in person. When I didn't emerge from the building, Jess blasted the horn again, and then a third time, probably pissing off all my neighbors. There was no way I was going to venture downstairs to tell her that I was staying in, so I turned on my phone to text her. There were many messages from Jess and Anna, and a couple from Kitty. I ignored them all to tell Jess to go to school without me. Her response was, *no fuk u.*

"Oh, come on, Jess. Don't fight me on this," I said, about to send another response, but I heard the slam of the downstairs door followed by feet on the steps. A minute later, she pounded on my front door, laying siege, her fist a battering ram behind every knock.

"Cut the crap, Shauna. Open up." When I ignored her, she did it again. And again. And again. "Shauna, open the goddamned door!"

Realizing she wasn't going to leave until someone called the cops on her, I got out of bed and stormed down the hall, my salt tucked under my arm like a security blanket. I yanked open the door and glared at her. She gave me a critical once-over and frowned. Admittedly, I looked terrible: my teeth weren't brushed, and neither was my hair. I wouldn't normally let anyone see me like this, but my care factor about my appearance was nonexistent.

"Get dressed," she said. "You're not doing this."

"Doing what?"

Jess was not amused by the question. She shouldered past me into the apartment, sending me staggering back in the process. She gave me her best death glare before tromping to my room and waving her hand around. "Let's go. Dressed. Now. I'm not letting you ditch me. Us. We got into this together, we're getting out of it together."

I closed the door and glowered at her back as she disappeared around the corner to rifle through my bureau. "I'm doing this for your safety. Look at what happened to Bronx," I protested.

"It sucks, but we're in this together until the end. Here." She came out of my room to throw jeans and a T-shirt at me. When I let them fall straight to the floor, she pushed them toward me with her sandal. "Come on, Shauna. You can't hide. Our odds of figuring this out are way better as a team. You've got to keep your shit together. Now *get dressed*."

I stooped for the clothes and eyeballed her. "Why are you doing this? I'm trying to protect you."

"Let me worry about myself. I know the risks; so do Kitty and Anna. If they bail, they bail, but I'm not going anywhere. You need a bra and panties. Go." She circled around to herd me into my bedroom. I tried to push back, my feet skidding over the carpet, but Jess was strong thanks to years of playing sports. I wasn't going to win this fight.

"I'm doing this for you!" I finally snapped, but Jess gave me a sharp look before her arms folded over her chest. Her legs braced like she was settling in for a long, nasty battle.

"No, *I'm* doing this for *you*. Go. Now."

I stopped fighting. Deep down, I didn't want to. Yes, I had heard Cody, but what I wanted most in the world was a friend, and I had one standing in the hallway threatening to kick my ass if I tried to ditch her. It was bossy and ballsy and stupid, but that was Jess's way. And right then? I was glad for it.

22

I stared at the windows of my classroom, expecting to see something wicked inside the panes. I was sorting life into two categories now: time between Mary attacks and actual Mary attacks. My teacher was reduced to background noise as I counted the number of glass beakers lining the corner storage station.

Kitty texted mid-class to say Bronx got through surgery, but they wouldn't know his prognosis for a while. I took that to mean she wasn't in school today, and that made sense. You didn't recover from watching your boyfriend take a three-story nosedive overnight.

I was shuffling my way to my second class when Anna caught up to me in the hall. I didn't see her coming, and she greeted me by resting her hand against the flat of my back. I let out a screech and dropped my books. Other students in the hall turned to stare at me. Anna apologized for startling me as she stooped to help me pick up my stuff.

"You ignored my texts last night," she said, stacking my papers into a neat pile.

"I turned my phone off. I meant it, though. You really should stay away. She's always around now."

Anna stuffed my homework at me before gathering my books. I watched her do it, not helping in the slightest, though I wasn't sure why. I think my brain was just that gone. "Yeah, well, deal with it. I'm sticking around. It's not your fault you're haunted."

"You sound like Jess. I tried to stay home this morning, but she dragged me here by my hair." I winced. Comparing Anna to the person she'd sworn to avoid forever was probably a bad plan.

Surprisingly, she smiled a little and nodded, like somehow, this had bettered her opinion of Jess. "Well, that's the first smart thing she's done in a week. What kind of friends would we be if we ditched you?"

"Smart ones?" I returned.

She fell into step beside me as I meandered toward my next class. Other kids were running to make the bell, but I couldn't be bothered. Anna seemed content to keep pace with me.

"Maybe, but either way I . . . Look." She stopped talking and walking at the same time, her brows pinching together with strain. There was gravity to whatever it was she wanted to say to me. She shuffled her feet, looked down, and then back up. It was still weird to see her without her glasses on, but I'd get used to it sooner or later. "After you messaged me last night, I got really worried, especially when you didn't text me back. Jess was in the same boat, and she called me. We talked. Forget everything I said yesterday. *You're* more important. I was listening to Jess talk last night, bugging out about what's happening to you and insisting we have to help you, and I realized I need to be more like that, you know? More focused on what's going to get us through this. So that's what I'm going to do. With Jess, because she really does care." She smiled a little ruefully, lifting her narrow shoulders in a shrug before adding, "I get mad too easily. But I'm going to try to chill."

"You do. But we like you anyway," I said.

She snickered and turned back toward the hall. Her hand came out to graze my arm, fingertips tracing over the black bruise near my wrist from when Mary tripped me into the church's stone steps. It was a gentle touch, not hurtful in the least, but it set her to scowling. "We'll figure it out, Shauna. Just don't leave us. And I promise, we won't leave you. At least, I won't. I'll always have your back."

Jess didn't sit with me at lunch. I saw her in the cafeteria; she saw me, too, then put her tray at another table anyway. Anna slid in opposite me and we both watched as a few of Jess's softball friends sat with her: Laurie Carmichael with her spiky black hair and high-pitched shrieker voice, Becca Miller with the biggest attitude problem this side of the Mississippi, and Tonya Washington, who was actually funny.

"They have a softball game later. Jess mentioned it last night," Anna offered. I nodded, but the timing struck me as odd. Just this morning, Jess had insisted we stick together, but by lunch she'd already screwed off? When she glanced my way, almost like she felt the weight of my stare, she frowned and looked away.

Was Jess mad at me? Maybe. Maybe she was pissed I'd tried to ditch her. She wasn't normally sensitive, but this whole experience had certainly changed me for the worse. It wasn't so hard to believe it'd changed her, too.

Anna and I ate in silence. Halfway through lunch I realized that I had to go to the restroom. Every bathroom in the school had mirrors and steel doors and steel everything. I wanted to hold out until the end of the day, but after five minutes of squirming, I let out an exasperated sigh. Anna lifted her head to blink at me.

"I have to pee. And I'm afraid it'll . . . you know. With Mary."

Anna put up a finger to indicate I should sit tight before she headed over to Jess's table. She bent down, whispering something into Jess's ear. Jess nodded, excused herself from her friends, and jogged out of the cafeteria. Anna came back to collect me, offering me her hand like she was the mom and I was the kid and this was totally normal. I grabbed my book bag and took her hand without a second's hesitation.

"I left some packing tape in Jess's car Saturday," Anna said. "She's going to get it and meet us in the locker room. It's the closest bathroom to the parking lot."

We sped along, still holding hands. When we got to the gym, Anna let go of me to scout out the locker room. She emerged a minute later and we waited for Jess, who showed up with the roll of tape in one hand and a fresh box of salt in the other.

"Hey," Jess said in greeting. "We good to go?"

"Yeah," Anna said. "The locker room is empty."

They ushered me inside and told me to sit on a bench next to the lockers while they prepped the other side of the room. I tried to wait patiently, but the combination of a full bladder and nerves meant I fidgeted and scooted across the wood.

The high school locker room is shaped like a *T*. On the left-hand side of the long portion, the top of the *T*, are about a dozen shower stalls with skimpy white shower curtains strung up for privacy. The right side holds all the lockers and the door that leads into the main school building. Between the showers and the lockers is a floor-to-ceiling mirror almost eight feet wide. Next to it is the door that opens out to the soccer field. The bottom part of the *T* connects to the gym at the end, with a supply closet on the left side and three bathroom stalls on the right.

Anna worked on the big mirror near the showers using the box of salt I had in my bag. Jess took the bathroom mirrors and used her own stuff. I watched Anna cut off strips of tape and make a big *X* across the glass before laying a line of salt on the floor. I could hear Jess working in the other room, and when she finished, she came out to claim the tape from Anna, probably to treat the smaller mirrors over the sinks in the same fashion.

I waited as patiently as I could for them to finish. Every few seconds I'd eyeball the padlocks on the lockers around me, expecting them to explode in a creepy ruckus, but they stayed dormant. After what seemed like days, Jess came and directed me toward the toilets.

"That's as good as it's going to get," she said. It wasn't much consolation, but there wasn't much else we could do to make it safe. I scurried away from the lockers, my hands already fiddling with my pants as I took the corner. Jess had salted pretty much everything in the bathroom, including taping the chrome stall door for me, and I mumbled my thanks as I closed the door. I could see Anna's and Jess's sneakers outside, both of them waiting around to protect me in case things got weird.

I finished as quickly as possible, managing a grateful smile for them as I approached the sink. My hand darted out to turn on the water, but then reared back like something inside it might bite. Nothing happened. It was just a boring old sink with boring old water. I washed my hands and grabbed a paper towel, feeling a little better that we'd made it unscathed through something so simple and yet so complicated as taking me to the bathroom.

"So much work for such a stupid thing," I said to them, and they both laughed, though it wasn't so much a humor thing as it was exhausted resignation.

"Should we clear the tape?" Anna asked Jess.

"I guess. Let's get Shauna out of here first and then we'll strip it down."

Anna nodded and led me out like she'd become my personal Seeing Eye dog. I gave the lockers a furtive glance as we passed them on the way to the exit. I placed my hand on the long silver bar to the door and pushed. There was no click to indicate that it released. I pressed the bar again and again. Nothing happened.

I looked at Anna. She blanched and reached out to shove the door with me. It was useless.

My eyes pounded in their sockets like they might propel out of my skull. Not now. Not again. "Jess! Check the door to the gym!" I called. Anna slammed her body against the door as I darted through the locker room to get to the door leading to the soccer field. A chorus of groans from the shower section stopped me short. I knew that sound. I'd heard it in my own bathroom right before the mud and gunk. This time, though, instead of one shower under duress, it was twelve. The pipes shrieked in strained agony as the showerheads quaked and rumbled inside the fiberglass shower walls.

"She's coming," I whispered, my voice drowned out by a series of earsplitting whines. "She's here."

Clang. Clang. Clang. Clang.

The pipes screeched with a rhythmic banging, like some-one was pounding on them from the inside with a hammer. Yellow clouds rose from the metal shower drains, the ghostly fog pouring over the tiles and wafting across the floor. The showerheads gave a collective squeal as hot, black water blasted into the stalls.

"Let's go!" Anna said, rushing past me to throw herself against the soccer field door. The padlocks on the lockers behind us sparked to life, rattling and slamming like they had in the hall last week. Jess was making a thudding noise around the corner. Anna started kicking the door.

"Shit. Shit. What did she do?" Anna shoved at the door one last time as if this time it would magically open. But I knew it wouldn't. She knew it wouldn't, too. The bar wouldn't work because it was aluminum covered in chrome. Shiny things were Mary's domain.

"What's . . . Why . . ." Anna brushed past me, inching toward the showers. I followed her gaze, watching the geysers of black sludge shooting up from the drains. Water flowed from above and below now, creating an unnatural, fetid bog that oozed its way across the floor. The first tendrils of encroaching water curled around Anna's tennis shoe before splintering off into the checkerboard grooves of grout in the floor. It wasn't until the runoff was a few feet away from me that I recognized the danger: the salt line underneath the big mirror. The water was only a few feet away from the salt line.

"The line. She's going for the line. She's going to dissolve it," I said. There was a crisscross of salt across the glass's surface, yes, but without the salt line on the ground, was it enough? I glanced at the taped mirror. At first, I couldn't tell if the condensation on the glass was on our side or Mary's. Then Mary appeared through the moist gray haze to slam against the mirror. She hissed at the salted tape upon contact before neatly sidestepping to one of the wedges of open glass where the tape didn't reach.

Mary's eyes fixed on me, her fingertips dragging down the flat surface. She was so close, I could hear her rasping and rattling, like she was trying to breathe through phlegm. Anna dashed for the gym door, shoving the box of salt at me as she passed. I heard her talking to Jess, but I couldn't make out what they were saying. The sound of bodies banging against metal resumed. They were trying to force the door open. I stared at the mirror with my heart lodged in my throat, my feet itching to *run, run, run*. But to where? Bloody Mary was still trapped in the mirror behind the salt line, but soon, much too soon, the water would wash it away.

I stood there, frozen, as the water slithered across the floor. In the past, when I'd watched horror movies because I thought being scared was fun, I always got angry at the characters whose hands shook so badly they dropped the car keys when the monster was chasing them. It felt unbelievable. If someone wanted to survive, she would keep it together long enough to get away. Now, standing in the locker room like a frightened lamb, I understood. Fear shut my body down, like it had done to Jess the first time Mary came through Anna's mirror.

Jess and Anna ran up from behind me, Jess straddling the bench next to the bathroom so she could salt a fresh section of tape. I watched her work, wanting to tell her it was too late, but the words got stuck in my throat. I was too scared to talk. My mouth opened and closed, but no sound came. It wasn't until Anna clapped a hand on my shoulder that I found my voice again.

"There's no time, Jess. Look," I said.

"Bullshit. No ti—" Jess wanted to argue, but then she saw the water creeping steadily along. Her eyes flicked to the mirror. Mary bobbed her head and smeared her face against the surface, her nostril slits flaring.

"No, no, no, no. NO." Jess grabbed her salty tape and scrambled back.

"We're stuck," Anna announced, her voice dripping misery.

"No shit, we're stuck." Jess barreled her way toward the gym supply closet and rifled through it. Kickballs, softball gloves, and safety equipment flew out the door. A moment later, she made an *aha* noise followed by a loud metallic clang. She came out with an umpire mask covering her face and an arm of baseball bats. "Come here. Take one. If she gets near..."

I didn't know what effect swinging a bat at a ghost would have, but Anna and I took our bats anyway. The extra bats dropped to the floor, the water now deep enough that they splashed when they hit. Jess wrapped her bat with her tape strip, the salt facing out. Clever. I wish we'd thought of it sooner.

As we armed ourselves, the water crested the salt line and dissolved our defense. Mary's hands poked through the glass where Anna's tape didn't touch. It was that easy for her. The mistake we'd made was leaving a section of glass big enough for her to pass through. Circles rippled across the mirror's surface, the quadrant of glass quivering as it turned to gel. Her wrists came next, then elbows and arms, followed by her head. When her foot crossed from her world into ours, splashing down in the black drain water, she let out a gurgling chuckle.

I'd seen Mary in Anna's bathroom when she tried to climb from the mirror. I'd seen her scuttling up the steps of the Southbridge Parish. But I'd never been close enough to get an unadulterated look at her. Her upper body was how she appeared in the mirror: her head was balding, her black eyes never blinked. Her rubbery half lips sported tiny pus blisters. Her neck was too thin over her clavicles, skin graying with patches of green and purple. Her arms were winter branches, bare and knobby and too pointy.

What I'd never properly seen was her lower half. Her once-white dress was brown from too much time crawling through muck, the hem of the skirt tattered and torn and ankle-length. It was hiked up to her knee on the left side, exposing the bones of her leg. The skin had worn so thin, her tibia and fibula were visible, the nerves and muscle long since rotted away. Her left foot was swollen and blue-tinged, like a moldy sponge that had absorbed too much water. Her right leg was whole, but a gash along her calf released a steady stream of onyx beetles into the water on the floor, like her fleshy bits only served as a festering ground for insects.

There was no hint left of the girl from the photograph. Instead, there was five feet of ghoul. If Mary and Jess stood side by side, Mary would barely crest Jess's chin. She was so tiny, and yet I knew what she was capable of doing with that body. Death had given her a strength that her frail frame had not. I took a step back from her, my breath coming in short, panicked pants as Mary stretched her arms to her sides, testing her freedom.

"Stay together. Try to stay together," Jess said, snagging her box of salt from the bench and backing toward the showers. I followed because I didn't have any better ideas. Part of me wanted to hide. It was a childish instinct to assume the monster couldn't see you because you couldn't see it. But that wasn't how this worked. Mary would find us anywhere.

"Matter of time," I murmured, my hand squeezing around

my pitiful arsenal of salt and a softball bat. Jess glared at me from behind her umpire mask. I turned my head around to see what Anna was doing, but she wasn't there. She'd ignored Jess and gone her own way, toward the bathroom. It was just Jess and me in the shower section, the showerheads above blasting scalding water, the drains below spewing frigid black sludge. Half of my body sweated, the other half was riddled with goose pimples.

I heard Mary's labored breathing around the corner. Her feet shuffled along as she cooed and trilled, sounding far too pleasant. *Splash, splash, splash.* Her footsteps neared, then the sounds stopped. Jess and I looked at each other, wondering what could possibly interest Mary enough that she'd pause her hunt.

"Are you two all right?" Anna asked from the toilet stalls. Her voice drew Mary like a siren's song. The ghost let out a hiss and barreled away from us to find Anna. All I could picture was Mary shredding Anna apart.

She wasn't going to hurt my friend.

I ran out of the shower room, screeching at the top of my lungs. Mary trundled toward the bathroom, her arms swinging wildly to either side. Her fist tangled in a shower curtain, and she yanked it down before kicking the plastic away with a snarl.

"MARY! COME ON. IT'S ME. COME ON!" My voice cracked halfway through, but I continued to shout, waiting for the dripping dead thing to turn around and look at me.

She spun, her eyes wide. Her head tilted back as she sniffed the air, the growl that escaped her throat pregnant with menace. A beetle climbed from her right nostril to scurry across her cheek before disappearing into the neckline of her dress.

"That's it. Come get me. You want me, not her. Come on." I readied the salt and bat. I expected her to dive at me, but she moved forward slowly, like she wanted to savor the moment.

"Mine," she rasped. I shook the salt box at her, trying to keep a distance between us, but she lurched my way with grim determination. I'd had every intention of facing my fate when I'd come around this corner, but as she closed in, my feet moved back. My survival instinct had kicked in, telling me to run.

Mary was a few feet away now. I had to choose: bat or salt? I picked the bat, the salt splashing down to the floor by my feet when I dropped it. I swung the bat, hoping to maintain a gap between me and Mary, but she grabbed the end and jerked. The bat flew from my hand. Mary peered at it for a second, like she didn't know what it did, before tossing it behind her.

I picked up the box of salt. The bottom had gotten wet, but I ripped off the top and grabbed some of the dry salt. I was about to fling my first handful when a blur of motion drew my attention. Running at us with her bat raised above her head was Anna. When Mary stopped at the cross section of the locker room *T*, Anna had a straight shot at her and she took full advantage, her weapon poised and ready.

Before Mary could react, Anna slammed the aluminum bat down in an arc. It crashed into Mary's shoulder with a sickening crack. Mary wailed and staggered, almost dropping to a knee. I took my opportunity to throw the salt. It struck her on the left side of her face. Mary slapped and clawed in agony. One of her fingers squished into her eye, and a stream of viscous black goo oozed down her cheek and over her chin. She thrashed like she was on fire, her feet sliding across the wet floor as she retreated. We had a small advantage, and we had to take it if we wanted to live.

More salt. I threw as much as I could as fast as I could, some of it damp and clumpy from the box's dip in the water. Mary blindly lashed out with her claws, but Anna brought the bat around again. There was a snap as Mary's wrist took the brunt, her hand crunching and skewing off at an odd angle. By then, the locker room was almost completely full of steam. I could barely see Anna wielding the bat next to me, but every one of her swings gave me a brief glimpse of her face. Her lips were pursed in concentration, her face splattered with a spray of Mary's tar-blood. Around us, the padlocks rattled and the shower pipes groaned.

"Jess, come on. She's moving back. We need you!" I called, but Jess never came. I didn't know where she was or what she was doing. I was too busy trying to shove Mary back to check on Jess. I advanced on the ghost. She retreated toward the mirror, unable to go left for fear of getting hit with the baseball bat, unable to go right for fear of another fistful of my salt. For a moment, I thought we had beaten her, that we'd all live through this fight. I thought Bloody Mary would be forced into the mirror and we'd lock her away with the salt from my stash.

The next time that Anna swung the bat, Mary charged. Anna gasped. The steam swirled up, blocking my sight. Anna's bat rattled to the floor. Anna cried out in a muffled scream. I didn't think, I reacted. I ran at Mary and Anna with my salt, hoping to save my friend, but Mary reached out for me and . . .

thrust me away. She sent me sprawling onto my butt in the water with a single push to my chest, the salt box splashing away to my side.

The motion of my body sailing back dispersed the haze for a second. I glimpsed Mary dragging Anna toward the mirror. Mary had Anna by the hair, her moldering hand wrapped tight in Anna's long tresses. Anna thrashed and screamed, but it was no use. She was hooked tight. Anna was pulled to Mary's body—as close as I'd been when Mary had captured me with her nails during the second summoning.

"SHE'S GOT ANNA. HURRY. SHE'S GOT ANNA!" I screamed to Jess. I crawled across the ground and managed to grip Anna's ankles with my hands. I pulled on her, trying to stop Mary's progress, but the ghost was so unnaturally strong that I was pulled through the water as though I were weightless.

"No!" I howled, my voice breaking when Mary stepped over the bottom ledge of the mirror. She was going back to her world and taking Anna with her. I tightened my grasp, but it made no difference. Mary gave another hard tug, and I watched through a wall of tears as Anna was pulled over the ledge and into the mirror's surface. Anna's screams cut short as liquid glass rushed into her mouth.

"JESS, HELP!" I shouted, still pulling on Anna's feet.

Jess was suddenly there. Her bat dropped by her feet before she opened her box of salt and began tossing handfuls at the mirror. I thought it was a good idea at first, that she was forcing the ghost into retreat and we'd pull Anna to safety, but the moment the crystals touched the glass, the surface began to harden. If she continued, it'd get too thick for us to pull Anna out.

"No. *No!* Stop! It's going solid! You're using too much! Help me pull!" But Jess ignored me, firing the salt instead. As the last of Anna passed through the undulating glass, my hands went with her. I remembered the cold jellylike feel of the water from when Mary had dragged me through. This was thicker, more rigid. Salt clusters were drying on the surface. The glass was crystallizing. If I didn't pull my hands back soon, the surface would go hard and I'd either be stuck between the worlds forever or lose my hands.

"No. Please, no..." I wept, but there was nothing I could do. The pressure around my forearms became unbearable. I was forced to let Anna go. I wrenched my hands from the glass seconds before it hardened. Fog rose up inside the mirror far thicker than the steam in the bathroom. A second later, a long arc of crimson splashed across the glass followed by another. And another. Rivers of blood rained down on the wrong side.

Anna's blood.

24

It didn't seem real. When the showers stopped spewing, when the black water sank back into the drains, when the fog cleared from the room, I kept thinking that Anna would come back. Except that wasn't the reality. The reality was that Anna was gone. Forever.

I sat a few feet from the mirror without flinching, catatonic. My guts ached, my eyes burned. Mary could have hauled me inside the glass right then and I would have been too stupefied to do anything about it. But she didn't come. She left me there to snivel, my pants wet, my knees hugged to my chest.

Jess stood beside me crying softly. She put her hand on my shoulder, but I pushed her away. If she'd listened to me, if she'd pulled Anna instead of salting the mirror, Anna might have had a chance. But Jess never listened to anyone. She did what she thought was best—her ideas trumped all ideas—and now Anna Sasaki was dead.

In the end, I ran. It wasn't brave or noble. It probably wasn't the right thing to do, but after what felt like hours of sitting on that wet locker room floor, I climbed to my feet, grabbed my bag, and ran. Jess called my name, but I kept moving. I ran from the locker room. I ran from the school. I ran until my legs ached. I ran until they stopped aching and I felt like I could run forever. My apartment was miles from the school, but I ran all the way there without pause.

By the time I hit my parking lot an hour later, I was covered in sweat. My clothes and body had fused together; my hair was matted to my skull. My lungs hurt. I didn't care. Stopping was the worst thing I could have done. While I'd been punishing my body, I wasn't thinking about Anna, but the moment I climbed the stairs, the moment my key slipped into the lock of my door, I started bawling.

I dove into my bed. I buried my face in my pillow and screamed myself raw. When my throat felt like I'd swallowed a porcupine, I stopped to tear off my damp, sweaty clothes. I rolled into a ball beneath the covers. I stayed that way until the calls started. It was Jess, furiously blowing up my phone before resorting to sending texts that I refused to read. I shut it off. I didn't want to hear from her. If I had my way, I'd never look at her again. All the sorrow and rage I felt at losing Anna was directed at Jess. She'd put Bloody Mary before common sense—before our safety. Anna had been right to be mad at her. In the end, Anna was the only one of us who had had any sense.

It took them a day and a half to realize Anna was gone. Her parents called the night of her disappearance to ask if I knew where she was, but I told them I hadn't seen Anna since school lunch. I went to bed after that, sleep my only reprieve. Even then, I was plagued by dreams of Anna, of Mary. It wasn't much of an escape. I woke to tears running down my cheeks.

Tuesday morning, I told Mom I still didn't feel well. She took my temperature and despite the lack of fever, she let me stay home again. I rarely asked. I left my room only to use the bathroom, the box of salt never leaving my side. Mary never showed. I immediately went back to bed—not hungry, not thirsty, not feeling alive at all.

Mom was supposed to work a double, but at suppertime, there were feet pounding up the apartment steps and then the slamming of the front door.

"Shauna? Are you here?" I heard from the other room.

"In bed," I said. "Headache."

Her purse hit the floor. She ran to my room, her keys jingling inside her pocket. She thrust the door open to peer at me, her eyes huge. I sat up a little to look at her, the blanket tucked to my chest, and she crossed the room in three strides to hug me. It was sweet at first, affectionate, but then it grew stronger, more a clutch than an embrace.

"Why didn't you pick up your phone?" she barked at me.

I blinked, cringing as she gave me another hard squeeze. "My phone was off. Sorry."

"Oh. Oh, honey." She sank down on the mattress beside me and put her palms on my cheeks, her thumbs stroking my cheekbones. Her eyes narrowed. I probably looked awful. I'd been crying so much, my face felt hot and there were splotchy hives all over my upper chest. "So you heard, then. All right, at least you know. Luanne at work pointed out the AMBER Alert, and when you didn't pick up the phone, I just . . . I came straight home. I'm so glad to see you, but don't shut your phone off again. Don't, please," she said, and she pulled me back into her arms, forcing my face into the crook of her neck.

There was an alert on Anna. For a moment, I worried that the police would come pounding on my door, demanding answers, but that would mean they'd have to know Jess and I were the last people with her. And how would they find that out? Someone may have seen us leaving the cafeteria, but we were always together. That wouldn't raise any suspicions. No one had been around the locker room when it went down, either. The halls were empty because of lunch.

I couldn't worry about it. Even if the police came sniffing around, they wouldn't find anything except salty water. Jess had torn the tape from the mirrors before she bailed. There was nothing incriminating to find. Anna wasn't just dead, she was gone. Permanently. I clung to Mom and burst into more sobs. She stroked my hair, her lips grazing my temple.

"It'll be okay. Anna is fine," she crooned. I wanted to scream at her that, no, Anna wasn't fine, that she'd been killed in front of me.

Mom made me tea and brought me toast that I wouldn't eat. Her phone rang in the other room and she left to answer it. She returned a minute later, her fingers toying with the buttons on her coat. "That was Luanne. Some local folks are going looking for Anna—clues or . . . well. You get it. Did you want to go?"

"No, thanks," I said. I didn't want to see all those people. I didn't want to answer the questions I knew were coming. I had the answers, but no one would believe me. I didn't trust myself not to scream them in someone's face. It was much safer to stay at home and grieve, and if not grieve, then to sleep forever so I didn't have to feel anything.

Mom looked surprised. "Really? I thought . . . She's your friend. Why not?" It should have occurred to me she'd ask that, and I should have had an answer prepared, but I didn't. I glanced at the wall and shrugged. She reached out to lift my chin with her finger so I was forced to look at her. "Shauna?"

"I'm afraid of what we might find," I blurted. "If she's dead and mangled and . . . you know." It was weak, I knew it was weak, but it was the best I could come up with on the spot.

I was afraid she'd see right through it. She frowned, but after a moment, she pulled away from me and sighed. "Okay. I suppose I can understand that. That'd be hard. Well, harder. It's just . . . I don't know if I should go. One of us should, I think, but I don't want to leave you alone."

"No, it's okay. I'm okay, and if you do find something, you should call me. I just can't, not right now. I want to sleep."

She watched me for a long while before shaking her head. "No, I don't think I will. Go to sleep. I'll be right outside if you need me."

I was just about to drift off when a knock struck our front door. I rolled out of bed to poke my head into the hall. Standing

in the apartment doorway in his service blues was a police officer. My pulse pounded in my ears. I forced myself to approach,
my arms wrapping around my chest so he couldn't see that I
wasn't wearing a bra.

He was nice, all things considered. He asked me when I'd
seen Anna last, and I told him in the bathroom after lunch. Had
I heard from her on the phone after that? No. Did I have any
reasons to suspect she'd run away? No. Had she been spending
time with anyone unusual? No. It took five minutes for him to
question me. He left me a name and a contact number before
wishing Mom and me a good night.

When the door closed behind him, Mom peered at me from
her seat on the couch.

"Are you okay?" she asked.

"No."

Mom woke me Wednesday with news that school had been can-
celed while the investigation continued. I rolled over and went
back to sleep. When I came out of my bedroom at nine, Mom
was on the phone, standing next to the refrigerator. She had
called in to work. Her too-loud phone conversation also informed
me that search parties had scoured for Anna throughout the
night, and scent dogs had been brought in to find her, but so
far there'd been no trace.

Nor would there be, but I was one of only two people who
knew that. Maybe three, if Jess had told Kitty. Who I hadn't
even called yet. I ran my fingers over my face and groaned.

"Are you okay?" Mom asked, her hand moving to cover the receiver on the phone.

I shrugged. She offered me a box of cereal for breakfast, but I waved her off. I wasn't hungry. I wasn't anything except numb.

"Right. I'll call you back in a bit, Luanne," she said, flipping her phone closed and sliding it into her pocket. She motioned me to a chair, and I sat in it because I had no idea what to do with myself. I drifted through the apartment like a ghost. "She asked if we wanted to join this morning's search. They're moving out from the school to the Hockomock Swamp."

"You go. I'll be fine," I said.

"You don't look fine, but I guess that's to be expected." She shook her head. "But I'd like to help with the search. All I can think is what if it had been you? The Sasakis must be beside themselves. But I don't want to leave you alone if you're not all right."

"I can handle being alone."

"If you're sure." She sounded hesitant, like she needed my reassurance that I wasn't going to disappear on her if she left for a few hours.

"I'm sure," I said. Logically, I knew I should want her to stay. I should want hugs and love and every ounce of maternal care that I could get. But I was too emotionally stunted to give a damn what she did. I was a hollow robot going through the motions of being human.

Mom got back on the phone, and I craned my head to eyeball the bathroom, weighing the risks of a quick shower. I really couldn't put it off much longer. I retrieved the box of salt from my bureau and prepped the bathroom as efficiently as possible, even shaking a few granules on top of the shower lever and showerhead to keep the water from turning muddy. I used face-cloths as anchors, too, so the crystals couldn't slide off.

I'd adjusted the shower temperature when I spotted Mary watching me from the frosted panels. It was that same hazy, mirage-like image it'd been the first time, like she was on the other side waiting for me. Instead of freaking out, I skipped the conditioner and got my ass out of there as quickly as possible. I didn't care that she watched me. There was no fear.

This should have been victory. For the first time, I'd mastered my terror over the ghost on my tail, but there was no joy there, only resignation. Mary watched me because she'd always watch me. It was what my life had become.

As I left the bathroom, a towel on my head and one around my body, Mom was heading for the door dressed in jeans, a long-sleeved T-shirt, and work boots. She looked like she was going to a construction site. I understood why—the Hockomock Swamp was overgrown and dense. I'd been in there for a biology field trip once, and it'd been a punishing, wet experience.

"Hey, Luanne's waiting for me downstairs. The car's in the driveway if you need it, but if you go out, text me? I don't want to come home to an empty house. I think I'd have a meltdown." I nodded. She blew me a kiss and turned to leave, but stopped before stepping over the threshold. She looked at me over her shoulder, her fingers drumming on the back of the couch. "You're sure about my going? If you want me to stay—"

"Go, Mom. I'm fine. I'm here."

She cast me another long look before rushing over to hug

me, her lips grazing the towel on top of my head. "All right, all right. Humor your old lady. She's worried about you." I hugged her back, and she took that to mean she really could go, that I wasn't going to erupt or die because she abandoned me for a few hours. She stroked a hand over my bare shoulder and ran for the door to meet her friend.

With Mom gone, I knew I had to call Kitty. I didn't want to, but I had to. I grabbed my phone from the nightstand. Waiting for me were a dozen missed calls and a series of texts from Jess, each one angrier and angrier. I scrolled through, deleting most of them until I got to the second-to-last one. It leant me pause, and I found my upper lip curling like a rabid dog about to bite.

Working to get u unhaunted and ur ignoring me. Don't b a bitch.

The insinuation that I didn't care about my well-being was a nasty grenade for her to lob. I texted her back with a simple, *Go away.* Before she could blitz me with more messages, I dialed Kitty's number. A half a ring in, Kitty picked up with a pathetic whimper.

"Sh-Shauna, I ca— I can't. I can't. Bronx and n-n-now Anna." Before she could complete the thought, she was crying, and I was close to joining her. I breathed hard, full draws in through the nose and out through the mouth to keep my calm. It helped a little; only a few tears leaked from the corners of my eyes to dribble down my cheeks.

"I know. I'm sorry I didn't call. I was so messed up. My mom just left to join a search party, and I want to say something to her but I can't," I said.

"What can you say? No one would believe....God. I can't believe she's gone. She's been my b-best friend since we were six. Six!"

The next half hour was spent doing what I could to comfort her, but words weren't sufficient. Nothing I could say would help. Kitty was entitled to her grief. So was I, for that matter. I wrapped up the call when my voice started cracking every other word.

"I love you, Kitty. I'm so sorry. I tried to save her. I did everything I could. I'm sorry," I said.

"I know. I know you did. Th-thank you. I love you, too." She sniffled and croaked out a good-bye before hanging up. I cradled my cell to my chest, feeling worse than I had when I'd called, but that was no surprise—Kitty sounded awful. We both carried the burden of Anna's death, but hers was heavier. Anna and Kitty were more sisters than not. Now one sister was gone.

I rolled onto my hip to face the wall. It took a few minutes of slow, deep breathing to get my wits about me. I'd cry again today, it was inevitable, but I had one more thing I needed to do before I let myself wallow. I had to talk to Cody.

She barked a hello a moment later.

"Hi. It's me," I said.

"I'm sorry," she said. "I saw the news."

I whimpered and dug my teeth into the sides of my tongue. That simple statement rocked me to the core. She could have chided me because I hadn't forced Anna out of my life like she'd told me to do twice already, but she didn't. There was nothing except sympathy in her tone. In a weird, twisted way, I almost wished she'd yelled at me instead. The anger would have given me something to cleave to.

"Thank you. I just wanted to let you know, and I told Jess off and I...Maybe next week we'll hit the church? I need a few days," I said.

Cody sucked in a deep breath. "Yes. We'll go when you're ready. In the meanwhile, I think that's for the best. To keep Jess away. She called me this morning and I...There's something not right there. Take care of yourself and keep her at arm's length."

"What'd she do now?" I asked. I could hear the hesitation in Cody's voice, debating whether or not she should tell me. It was strange; she was such a straight shooter that I never figured she'd hedge on anything, but something Jess had said bothered her. Jess had somehow managed to flap the unflappable. "Cody?"

"Right, I'm sorry." Cody grumbled beneath her breath. "She was asking about the tag—how I got haunted, the circumstances of it. But it wasn't so much what she was asking as how she was asking it that bothered me. Which is why I didn't want to say anything because it's hard to convey appropriately.... You know what it was? Your friend sounded excited and intense, and for a minute, just a minute..." Cody paused to suck in a deep breath before blowing it out into the receiver. It nearly deafened me, but not so much that I couldn't hear her when she said, "...for a minute I really didn't know whose side she was on. Ours or Mary's."

25

I was done crying. I was still miserable, but thinking about Jess, I was also *angry*. And anger was fuel. I could channel it and concentrate on the matter at hand—getting unhaunted. What did I know? Jess had been too invested in Mary since the beginning. I'd chalked it up to enthusiasm for something new and cool, and though it seemed like forever ago now, I felt excited about Mary in the beginning, too.

The problem was that Jess knew things we didn't and had all along. She dropped information when we absolutely needed it, but she had never been forthright with it. I sensed she had a piece of the Mary puzzle that I was missing, but how was I supposed to get it from her? Even if we were talking, I couldn't assume she'd be straight with me. She'd been lying by omission all along. It was frustrating, doubly so because I had so very little to go on. There was the church, yes, and I would revisit that hellhole soon enough, but what else could I do from home?

I abandoned my bed and turned on my laptop, keeping the
salt on hand in case Mary tried anything cute with the screen.
The search engine popped up and I stared at it awhile, wondering where I should begin. The only new development was the
Dietrich lady who'd been in all those pictures at the church. I
followed Bronx's advice and signed up for an ancestry Web site.

At first, it didn't look like much. Adeline Dietrich was born
in Solomon's Folly in 1940. Her mother's maiden name was
Abigail Brown, and she had married Richard Dietrich. Adeline
had one sister named Ruth. Following the Brown line, Abigail
was the child of Michael Brown, who was the only child of Mary
Simpson Brown, who was the child of . . .

I stopped reading and stared. Mary Simpson Brown was
the child of Constance and Edward Simpson, and Constance's
maiden name was Worth. I clicked on Constance's sister, and
there it was, Mary's name, with the dates of 1847–1864. Adeline
Dietrich was related to Mary Worth. Frantically, I jotted it
all down on a piece of paper so I could show it to Cody when I
saw her. I wasn't sure how Mary's family tree would help us,
but maybe the clue to putting the ghost away for good existed
somewhere in the names on this page.

I pored over the tree once more to ensure I hadn't misread
anything. This time, instead of only paying attention to the
mothers and fathers, I branched off to look at siblings, too.
There were a few who had died young in the late 1800s and
early 1900s, and a few others who'd died childless. The tree
didn't extend all that far, most of it contained to Massachusetts
and Solomon's Folly in particular. By the time I got back to

Ruth Dietrich, Adeline's sister, I was ready to be finished, but I clicked on Ruth's name all the same. When the screen popped up, I had to rub my eyes once, twice, three times, because I couldn't believe what was in front of me.

Ruth Dietrich maintained her maiden name as her legal name, but she had married in 1962. Why she'd kept her name wasn't interesting to me. What was interesting was who she'd married. Augustus McAllister. He and Ruth had one child together. Stuart McAllister. Jess's *dad*.

"Holy shit," I whispered. I clicked on Stuart, and sure enough, listed beneath him and his wife, Allison Jamison McAllister, were their two children—Jessica and Todd. Augustus McAllister was the colander-wearing Grandpa Gus, and Jess's Aunt Dell must have been a nickname for Aunt Adeline. In the church, I'd said there was something familiar about those pictures of Adeline. What was familiar was that she *looked like Jess*.

I didn't have the complete puzzle, but I did have one more answer. This wasn't about some stupid ghost hunt for Jess. This wasn't a game. This was about her legacy, and her legacy was that she, Jess McAllister, was a blood relative of Mary Worth.

I didn't know what to do with the information. On one hand, I wanted to confront Jess. On the other, that'd require talking to her. I tried calling Kitty back, but she wasn't picking up her phone. She'd mentioned going to the hospital to see Bronx when we'd talked earlier, and they didn't allow her to have her phone on in there. I left her a text to call me later.

After Kitty, my thumb went to Anna's speed dial digit. She was always the next one on the rotation, the third in the series of friends, but now she was gone. She'd never be here again. I climbed back into bed and hugged my pillow, squeezed my eyes closed, and huddled underneath my blankets. The vague excitement I'd felt over the Jess discovery was swallowed by helplessness and despair.

I'd said I wouldn't wallow all day, but that's exactly what I did, right up until my mother came home two hours later. I drifted in and out of sleep, my waking minutes plagued by thoughts of Jess, Mary, and Anna. I didn't wake up when Mom walked into my room at suppertime, but I almost hit the roof when she leaned over my bed to run her fingers across my forehead. She startled me so much, I almost jumped out of my skin.

"What?" I shouted, shooting up in bed so fast, I smashed my skull against the wall behind me. It hurt, and I wrapped my arms around my head. Mom reached out to pull me to her, forcing my face into her midsection. She smelled like sweat and outdoors stuff—pine needles and sap and mud. She smelled like the Hockomock Swamp.

"They called off the search for now," she said quietly. "Are you okay? Your head?"

"Yeah. Yeah, I'm okay," I lied for what felt like the millionth time. Mom's fingers stroked the back of my neck before traveling up to my newest wound. She probed it a little, and I shrank away from the touch, but the pain was already abating.

"Good. It sounds like they're going out looking again

tomorrow. I have to go back to work, but if you want to stay home from school, you can."

I shook my head. "No, I don't want to be here alone." And I didn't. For all that I'd fallen into a casual ambivalence about Mary during my shower, I wasn't stupid enough to court an early demise by staying in a house full of shiny stuff alone any longer than necessary. I'd been lucky so far, but luck wouldn't last. I was overdue for another ghostly visit.

I was silent all the way to Mom's work the next morning. Before relinquishing the car to me for the day, she made me restate my promise to call her the moment I walked into the apartment. I swore I would, and she held both of my cheeks while she kissed me, telling me twice how much she loved me.

I pulled the car out of her work parking lot and drove exactly one street down before pulling over. Packing tape and a lot of salt later, I had the car warded enough that I didn't have to fear for my life.

I didn't expect school to be so full. I figured more parents would keep their kids at home considering the potential kidnapper in our midst. Police were stationed outside of the main entrances, and there was a news van parked along the street. I walked in through the parking lot doors and made a beeline for my locker, but before I could reach it, there was a hard tug on my wrist from behind.

"I have to talk to you," Jess said.

I yanked my hand away and kept walking.

"Stop. Seriously, we need to talk. I've got something going on af—"

"Shut up. SHUT UP!" I hollered, whipping my head around to glare at her. People stopped to stare at us, some whispering behind their hands. I leaned toward Jess, my lips inches away from her ear. "I know, Jess. I know why you dragged us into this. I know why you're so hung up on Mary. I hope it was worth Bronx's legs. I hope seeing your great-aunt was worth Anna, you bitch."

She looked like I'd struck her. There should have been some satisfaction in her stunned silence, but there was only hurt and anger. Everyone had lost so much while Jess stood there without a single blond hair out of place.

I jogged away from her to get to my locker, slamming my books inside and grabbing the ones I'd need for the day. She didn't follow me, but halfway down the hall I heard her voice rising above the morning din.

"I'm going to help you, Shauna! You're my best friend."

She probably meant that as a promise, but under the current circumstances, it sounded a lot like a threat. I headed for my first class, my eyes averted so I didn't have to look at anyone, so I didn't have to see any dead-girl faces staring at me from glass windows, doorknobs, or anywhere else. They'd waxed the tile floor last night, too, so I couldn't look down. I had to stare at the books clutched in my arms and hope I'd find my way.

Shiny above, shiny below, Mary was everywhere and nowhere all at once.

I threw myself into my desk right as my phone vibrated inside my bag. It was probably Jess, but on the off chance it was my mom, I stole a peek. It was neither. Kitty texted me to tell me to call her after school, that her parents had let her stay home an extra day. I wanted to send her a message explaining Jess's tie to Mary, but it was too complicated, too messy for a text. I sent her an abbreviated *Kay* with an emoticon heart.

The school day didn't have much to do with school. The teachers didn't bother teaching so much as letting my classmates talk among themselves. At one point, our guidance counselor came in to discuss resources available to anxious students. It was a pretty glum affair, and I trudged to lunch feeling like I should have stayed home after all. But anything was better than the depression jockey on my back.

It was strange to sit in the cafeteria alone. With few exceptions, my quartet of friends had been together for years, and yet there I was in the corner by myself. Kitty was home, Anna was dead, and Jess...well, Jess was across the room sitting with her softball cronies. I didn't want to look at her, mostly because I didn't want to give her any indication that there was a way to fix us, but toward the end of lunch, I glanced her way anyway. I couldn't help it; I wanted to see if she was as sad as I was. That's when I saw the red notebook. Red notebooks weren't a noteworthy thing in general, but Jess hadn't owned one before the Mary stuff. Either this was coincidence, or she had her summoning notes on the table in front of her.

Jess nodded at Becca, Laurie, and Tonya. She opened up the cover and her hands danced all over the place, her expression animated. This was her "I have a really good idea" sales pitch. I knew it because I'd fallen prey to that very same charisma when I'd agreed to summon a ghost in Anna's basement. If that's what she was doing now, if she was getting herself a fresh batch of idiots . . .

"You wouldn't," I whispered. Except she would. I knew she would. While Becca and Laurie dipped their heads forward to take a better look, Tonya stood up and waved Jess off, shaking her head. Jess called her back, but Tonya kept on walking, taking her lunch tray to another table to sit with other friends. Jess scowled after her for a moment, then turned back to the remaining two. I had a sinking feeling watching the three of them huddled together, a smile spreading across Jess's face.

I had to warn the girls. I was obligated. But by the time I abandoned my seat and gave chase down the hall, they were gone. I saw Becca after the next class, but before I could grab her attention, she headed inside the science lab and her teacher shut the door. After school, I stood by the buses—Laurie bused in and out every day—but she never showed up. When the bulk of the students were loaded and the doors closed, I ran toward the parking lot.

My sneakers skidded through the grit just as Jess drove away with one body in her passenger seat, another in the back.

26

I called Jess, feeling obligated to warn her off of any terrible ideas before they became terrible actualities. She didn't answer because she was a horrible bitch. A *driven* horrible bitch, which was even worse.

Mom said go straight home, but Mom didn't know what I knew. I drove to Jess's house, willing Jess's car to be in the driveway when I got there, but it wasn't. I ran to her front door and knocked. Mrs. McAllister answered with a dishrag in her hands. By the lift of her brows, it was clear she was surprised to see me. It made me sad to see her face; I probably wouldn't see much of it in the future. Ditching Jess meant ditching her awesome family. Related to Bloody Mary or not, the McAllisters had been kind to me.

"Hey, kiddo. Good to see you. I'm so sorry about Anna." Before I could do anything about it, I was pulled into another mommy hug. I indulged for a moment, my jaw clenching so I wouldn't cry on Mrs. McAllister's shirt. Sympathy was nice, but it tended to leave me a soggy mess, and I didn't need that right now. I gently disengaged, my eyes glassy and swollen with unshed tears.

"Thanks. Is Jess on her way here? I need to talk to her," I said.

She reached out to stroke my forehead much like my own mom had done just this morning. And last night. And the afternoon before that. It seemed to be a go-to mom comfort gesture. "She's on her way to Kitty's. Maybe you can catch her there."

My blood ran cold. Jess had two people in her car when she left school. She'd tried for another with Tonya, but Tonya had walked away. If Jess was on her way to Kitty's, that would make four girls, and with four girls...

"Thanks, Mrs. M!" I said, sprinting for the car. I heard her call my name, but I threw myself in and peeled out of the driveway, one hand on the steering wheel and the other on my phone. I dialed Kitty, waiting for her to pick up, but I got dumped into her voice mail. I kept dialing and she kept not answering. I sent a text; there was no answer. I didn't know for sure if Jess was summoning Mary again, but between the notebook, the girls, and her earlier promise to help me, the pieces fit together.

I whipped around a corner hard enough that two tires lifted off the road. Kitty was a pushover. She would agree to anything Jess wanted. Well, maybe not a pushover—Jess was just good at getting her way. She'd bully and bully until people relented, myself included. If Jess threw Kitty a line about saving me, Kitty would want to help. I wished she'd tell Jess NO for once, but that was impossible. Kitty was too nice for her own good.

I tore up Kitty's super-long driveway, nearly hitting her shrub wall at least four times before parking. My eyes strayed to the rearview mirror. I half expected it to have a tongue or fingers or some other dead body part lolling out of it, but Mary was nowhere to be found. I almost wished she were, because then I'd know she wasn't inside Kitty's house.

I rushed inside, not bothering to knock. Kitty did all of her hosting downstairs in the media room, so I beelined for the basement door. I reached for the knob just as screams blasted up from the other side of the door. There was the thud of feet on stairs before the door swung open and whacked me in the face. I doubled over as it struck my nose, my hands covering the stabbing ache. Becca and Laurie burst from the dense blackness of the basement, both of them panicked and terrified and frantic to escape. They shoved past me and scrambled for the front door, screaming at the top of their lungs the entire way.

Rot smell wafted up from the darkness, the unmistakable tang of too sweet, too sour, and too wet. *Bloody Mary was here.*

"God. GOD!" I lunged for the light switch and ran down the stairs.

The back wall of the media room had a big decorative mirror hanging over the leather couch, which was probably why Jess chose it to summon Mary. It was plenty big enough for Mary to pass through. The couch was pulled away from the wall, and there was a salt box on the floor beneath the mirror. The lines were fully formed; there were no breaks that I could see.

Somehow, though, Mary had found a way through the wards. Maybe they'd dropped the handhold. Maybe they'd forgotten the candle.

Half the bottles from the bar were smashed, and the stools were thrown askew. A few of them were broken into pieces, long shards of wood littering the booze-drenched ground. The pool table was tipped on its side in the corner of the room, its felt top shredded by Mary's claws. The couch was gutted, the springs from the cushions exposed and menacingly sharp.

There was no one in the room. I couldn't see Jess or Kitty, and although I had heard Mary's laugh and smelled her distinctive stink, I couldn't see her, either. I panicked that I was too late. Maybe Mary had dragged them both into the mirror. My stomach knotted at the thought, but then with crunching, squelching steps, Mary trundled out of the adjacent laundry room. I actually felt a little relieved to see her. She wouldn't be here if Jess and Kitty were on the other side of the glass. She'd be too busy bleeding them like she'd bled Anna.

"Kitty! What happened? Where are you?" I called out, praying she was somewhere safe. My voice caught Mary's attention and she craned her head my way, casting me a jack-o'-lantern grin with her crooked, broken teeth. There was a crack at the corner of her lip where the pustules had been the last time I saw her. They'd erupted, and now her smile extended up too far, into her cheek like someone had taken a razor to the edge of her mouth. The flaps of skin hung too loose, explaining the wet, wheezing sound Mary made every few seconds.

"Run! You need to run! The salt's not working!" It was Kitty, her voice squeaking out from behind the upended pool table. It was smart to use it as a barrier against Mary, but it wouldn't last. Mary was far too strong for a little thing like a pool table to stop her.

"Get out of here, Shauna!" Jess commanded from the same position. "Just go. I've got this under control."

"No, you don't," I said. I made my way to the closest broken stool, my fingers wrapping around a snapped leg. The end was jagged and sharp. Under normal circumstances it would make a fine weapon, except Mary was anything but normal. I watched her walk over a sea of broken glass to get to me, some of the pointy bits wedging into the soles of her feet. It didn't slow her down, not even when each foot left a perfect footprint of sludge-blood in the carpet.

I wasn't going to lose Kitty to Mary, too. I circled the ghost and moved toward the pool table, keeping Mary in my sights at all times. I walked backward, navigating the floor debris as best I could, only stumbling once or twice in my circuit.

"*Leave*, Shauna," Jess repeated.

"You're not getting Kitty killed, too. What'd she tell you to get you to summon her again, Kitty? That you could help me? Well, you can by taking the ghost. It's a shitty deal," I said, my eyes pinned on Mary, the stool leg raised in case she grabbed for me. She was only about six feet away now. I continued to retreat, past the pool table and toward the carcass of the sofa. Mary was content to follow, as if she knew that there was nowhere I could go.

I heard Kitty whimper my name right before the pool table

flew away from the wall. It could have been Kitty trying to escape; it could have been Jess flinging Kitty in Bloody Mary's direction. Either way, Mary's attention snapped away from me. She charged the pool table, her skeletal hands gripping the side and heaving it over her head as she screeched. Jess and Kitty dove away from her, Jess going left toward me while Kitty rolled right, crunching over broken glass, as the table crashed into the wall.

I slid behind the couch. Mary sniffed the air, her eyes flitting from Kitty to Jess to me, as if she didn't know which target would prove the most succulent. When she turned toward Kitty, I let out a shrill whistle and slammed the stool leg against the couch.

"Over here, you dead bitch! Come on, it's me you want!" I tried to taunt her into coming for me by making a clamor, but Mary cast a grin over her shoulder and spun back to Kitty, her hands swiping. Kitty made a break for the bar, pieces of bottle glass breaking beneath her shoes. Mary liked the chase; she followed Kitty, shriek-laughing and lunging in a twisted game.

I moved out from behind the couch, starting toward Mary with the stool leg at the ready, when I felt an arm wrap around my waist from behind. I was wrenched back and slammed into a tall, warm form. Jess. Her free hand grabbed for the stool leg in an attempt to wrestle it away from me. I gripped it tighter, but Jess grunted and kicked her knee into the back of mine. We tumbled forward as one unit, narrowly missing the exposed springs of the couch, my elbows slamming down into the glass and splintered wood.

"No. Leave it alone," Jess growled, giving the stool leg another jerk. "Just let Mary grab her and we'll see if—*oomph.*" She snarled as I elbowed her in the gut, shifting her position so she could better sprawl on top of me to pin me. Her left hand buried itself in my hair, her right sliding under my chin and gripping hard. *"Knock it off.* If Mary cuts her, she gets her scent. It'll buy you time. We can save Kitty later."

"ARE YOU INSANE?" I screamed. *"You can't trade one friend to Mary for another."* I bucked like a bronco, but Jess had me secure. She flexed the hand in my hair and pulled my head back before tearing the stool leg from my grasp. It landed a few feet away. I heard crashes from the bar and glanced up in time to see Kitty hurling the remaining liquor bottles at Mary's head. Mary just laughed and leapt toward her, nearly catching her by the sleeve.

"I'm doing this to save you! Stop being such a pain in the ass!" Jess shouted, loud enough that my ears rang. She yanked on my hair, making my scalp tingle with the force. No matter how much I writhed and kicked, I couldn't shake her, she wouldn't let go, and I grunted my frustration, the heel of my sneaker smacking her in the shin.

"Come on, Jess! I don't want this. Let me go. Let Kitty go, for God's sake. *Let me go!*"

"Shut up, Shauna. This is temporary. Just so she doesn't kill you before we can solve it. Kitty will be fine. I promise. I promise she'll be fine. We'll figure it out!"

"No, Jess! No. GET OFF OF ME! GET OFF!"

I screamed myself raw, twisting and turning. Mary got

closer and closer to catching Kitty with every swipe. She edged
her way around the bar with a series of rasps and chitters, her
lips twisting up to reveal mold-riddled gums and yellow fangs.
Another dry rustle of laughter and she tottered toward Kitty, her
talons extended to rend flesh from bone. Kitty whimpered and
dove across the bar, trying to vault to the other side, but Mary
grabbed for her leg, her hand twisting in the hem of Kitty's jeans.
Mary jerked back, and Kitty sailed down the polished wood.

Kitty gave a plaintive wail, and I knew this was it. If I
didn't do something, Kitty would either be cursed, maimed like
Bronx, or killed. I couldn't let any of those things happen. I
had to lure Mary our way, but how? Without the bar stool, the
only things I had within arm's reach were glass shards from a
broken champagne bottle, but they weren't big enough to inflict
much damage.

But then, maybe I didn't need to do a lot of damage.

Blood. Bloody Mary loved *blood*. After the doorknob
exchange, she'd slurped it off of her fingers like it was her favorite candy. If I wanted to make Mary give up Kitty, I had to give
her an incentive. I reached for the nearest shard of glass and
slammed it into the back of Jess's hand.

"You bitch. YOU BITCH!" Jess howled, rolling off me to
cradle her injured hand to her chest. Blood welled up thick and
fast, ribbons of it running down her wrist, dripping over her lap.
It was possible it wouldn't be enough, that Mary only wanted
my blood, but if that was the case, I'd jab myself in the palm to
make her come this way. I had no qualms about offering Jess
in my stead first, though. She deserved a little pain.

The effect was immediate. Mary swiveled toward us, catching the scent. She tossed Kitty aside like an abandoned toy to charge me and Jess, a rattling wheeze erupting from her lips with every step. She stopped just in front of me, so close I could see glass poking out of the meaty parts of her feet and through her rotting toenails. A rain of swamp water droplets splashed down over my head as she leaned over me to grab Jess. I dove for the bar stool leg, Jess screaming in terror behind me. Glass tangled in my shirt, tearing the fabric and scratching my skin, but I didn't stop crawling until I had the weapon in my hand.

Mary pulled Jess close. Jess shrieked and flailed, but Mary's grip was ironclad. I pushed myself to my feet and edged away, watching them. For all that I hated Jess, I couldn't watch her get maimed or dragged into the mirror. I stumbled toward the back of the couch and spotted a Tupperware container full of salt on the floor. I picked it up and got a handful, throwing it at Mary. I waited for her flesh to burn, but the granules just hit her and fell to the floor. She lifted Jess's hand to slurp the open wound, swallowing every drop of blood with a delighted groan.

"Oh, God. Oh, God. Get it off. *Get her off of me.* SHAUNA, HELP!" Jess looked at me, her eyes wide and pleading. I tried another handful of salt from the container, and again it did nothing. I began to tremble, my teeth chattering like I'd been dunked in ice water. We had so few advantages against Mary, and now one of the staples was failing us.

"It's sugar," Jess said. "Get Kitty's stash. Hurry. She... Hurry!" Mary was rubbing her face against Jess's injury now, like a cat marking its territory. It took my brain a moment to absorb what Jess had done. Sugar instead of salt. She'd laid false lines in front of the mirror so Mary could come out and grab one of the girls. It wasn't that Mary had grown immune to the stuff, it was that *I didn't have the right stuff to hurt her.*

For a second, I almost let Bloody Mary have Jess for all the pain and hurt Jess had caused, but I couldn't be that person. *I couldn't be Jess.* I looked over at Kitty, who had retrieved the box of salt from the floor. She tossed it to me, and I tore off the top to get a good handful before flinging it Mary's way.

The salt struck Mary in the side of her neck, oily smoke wafting from her skin. She let out a furious howl and jerked away. I'd thought the pain would send her scampering back toward the mirror, but as Jess shimmied away from her, trying to escape, Mary snatched at her blond hair, wadding it in her fist. Mary's other hand pulled back before she swiped it down, her claws raking Jess's shoulder blades. Jess screamed. She was marked as I'd been marked. Those razor nails had claimed her with five bloody tracks.

Jess wept for pity, but the ghost paid no mind. Mary snickered as she leaned in to drag her white, blood-smeared tongue up over Jess's cheek, leaving a glistening snail trail of spittle across Jess's face. Jess looked like she wanted to shrivel up and die, but she couldn't—Mary held her too tightly. She'd become Mary's prize of the day.

"Help me. Help me," Jess rasped as Mary started walking her toward the mirror.

I tossed the salt to Kitty so I could better grip my stool leg. "Don't use it until I tell you to," I ordered. I circled Mary. She tittered at me, her eye narrowing as she dragged the struggling Jess across the room. I thought about hitting her with it like a baseball bat, but it wasn't thick enough to do any real damage. It was pointy, though. I eyed Mary's body to pick my spot. She must have read my thoughts, as she swung Jess around in front of her, using Jess's body as a shield.

"Don't move, Jess," I whispered. Jess stopped struggling and went deadweight, causing Mary to stumble forward. I lifted the spike over my head and ran at her, aiming for her eye. There was a wet sucking noise, a squish, and Mary's scream echoed through the basement, loud enough to shake the foundations of the house. She relinquished her hold on Jess to grab her own face, groping at the wood impaled in her eye socket.

"NOW, KITTY, NOW!" I screeched, grabbing a stunned Jess and pulling her out of harm's way. Kitty swept in with her salt, throwing handful after handful to force Mary to retreat. There was a last, ear-blasting bellow before Mary turned for the mirror and dove into its quivering depths.

27

Kitty flung salt at the mirror until it turned solid. Mary was back where she belonged, on the right side of the glass. We fell silent; the only sound filling the room was Jess's weeping. I looked over at where she lay in a crumpled heap. Her hand was still bleeding, and there were claw marks in her back, just as there had been in mine. If what Cody said was true, my tag had been replaced by the promise of a better, fresher victim.

I grabbed the salt from Kitty and walked into the adjacent bathroom. I didn't lay a line. Instead I approached the mirror over the sink and waited. I was nervous—Mary was surely pissed at me after what I'd done to her face—but she didn't come at me, not even when I put my hand against the glass in invitation. It was a normal, boring reflection staring back at me now.

"Hey, Shauna, she's out here still. She's trying to get out and she looks really mad. I think she's coming back for you!" Kitty yelled.

"No," I said, reemerging from the bathroom and glaring at Jess's huddled form. Pitiful as she was, I felt only anger. Cold, hard anger that she could be so selfish and stupid. "She's here for Jess."

While I'd been in the bathroom, Mary had pulled the spike from her face. There was a huge hole where her eye used to be. My stomach lurched when beetles crawled from the orifice to fly off into the smoky haze surrounding her.

Jess looked at the mirror and then at me. Her hand reached for me, fingers wrapping around my ankle to give it a squeeze. Her blue eyes were rimmed red, her skin paler than usual. Tears and snot covered her face. "Help me. Please. I was only doing it for you. I wouldn't lose you to her. You're like my sister."

"Shut up," I said. "Just shut up and go home, Jess."

"But—"

"Shut up and go home," I repeated, my look hard.

Jess got to her feet, her fingers skimming over the cut in the back of her hand. Two bright spots of color flamed on her cheeks as she turned to address Kitty. "I'm sorry. I wanted her to go for Becca or Laurie, but they . . . I'm sorry. I wouldn't have let Mary have you, either. It just . . . I'm sorry. Please. I can't lose everything. Not now. Not if she's . . ." Jess craned her neck back at the mirror, shuddering when she saw Mary's face pressed to the solid glass, her hands clawing at the surface like she could dig her way through. "Not if she's going to hurt me. I was trying to help. I swear."

I braced for Kitty to do the nice-girl thing and forgive her. I figured she'd take one look at Jess and then try to talk me into relenting. Kitty shook her head and pointed at the stairs. "Go," she said quietly. "Go home, Jess."

"But, Kitty—"

"Leave. Please."

Kitty's rejection sent Jess into a rage. Her face went so red it was almost purple, the veins in her temples and neck cording. Her hands balled into fists, the tension making the cut on the back of her hand ooze fresh blood onto the carpet. "Fine. FINE! I don't need you. I'll figure it out. On my own, if I have to. I'll do it on my own."

She stomped toward the steps, climbing them two at a time to get away from us. The moment she was out of sight, Mary disappeared from the mirror at our side, intent on following her newest victim. Jess's sobbing drifted down the stairs right before the house door slammed. A car engine revved a moment later, tires squealing across pavement as Jess pulled out of Kitty's driveway.

"This is weird to say," Kitty said, squatting so she wouldn't shred her pants with the glass. "But I feel like we're not done. Like we need to figure out how to get rid of Mary forever. If not for Jess, then for the people around her."

"Or the next group of girls who don't know what they're getting into," I agreed. It wasn't a happy thought, but a necessary one, and I sighed. I sank down next to Kitty to lean into her side. She slung an arm over my shoulders and we hugged. And then we cried. It wasn't just for Anna and Bronx and all the fear and misery of the past week; it was relief, too, that the nightmare was over for now. At least for tonight, I could sleep in my bed and not wonder what was on the other side of the mirror looking out at me.

I lifted my head to glance around the room, looking for a paper towel or a napkin somewhere among the debris. The room was a wreck. I climbed to my feet and started picking through the carnage, doing my best to avoid glass and wood and everything else that wanted to impale me. "Your dad is going to kill you," I said. "I'm sorry."

"Yeah, he is. I don't even know what to say to him, but... ugh. It's the least of my problems, I suppose." Kitty went upstairs to grab some trash bags, the broom, and a vacuum. We went to work cleaning after that, removing as much of the debris as we could. The couch and bar stools were ruined as well as all the alcohol. The pool table was shredded, and the carpet next to it sported Mary's tarry-blood footprints.

It wasn't until I pushed the couch back into place beneath the mirror that I found the red notebook. Jess must have brought it in with her when the girls were summoning Mary. I sat on the single remaining cushion and tossed the cover open. Kitty came to stand beside me, her hand on my shoulder as I leafed through. All of Jess's notes were there about the summoning rules, and the two letters we'd already seen, but there was an addition since the last time I'd peeked at the pages.

A picture. This wasn't a photocopy, but a real picture from a long time ago. It was Mary Worth standing alone in front of the Southbridge Parish. It was hard to believe this was the same girl from the group shot we'd seen. Her eyes were large and intense beneath her dark brows. She'd lost too much weight, the round fullness of her cheeks replaced by harsh angles. Her dark hair was tangled and unkempt, and there was a smear of dirt along her chin. She wore a white dress, but it was in poor condition, the bust covered in a series of splotchy stains.

"She looks so mad," Kitty whispered. I agreed. Mary did look furious. Her head was tilted down so she could look at the cameraman from beneath her eyebrows. Her hands were balled into fists by her sides. She was full of a fury she could barely contain.

"Jess is related to her, you know," I said. "Mary's her great-aunt times five or something."

Kitty's mouth dropped open. "She...Wait, what?"

"Yeah. That's why she's been so crazy about this. That's why she probably has this picture in the first place. Mary's her relative." I flipped the picture over. *Mary Augustine Worth, February 16, 1847–October 28, 1864* was written on the back.

"That's unreal. It explains so much, though."

"Explains, yes, but doesn't excuse," I said.

Kitty took the picture from me to get a better look, then shuddered and handed it back, her finger tapping against Mary's glowering face. "I can see the start of the ghost there," she said. "I can see the resemblance. Not in the last picture, but this one, yes."

So could I. I stuffed the photo back into the notebook and closed it. An envelope tumbled out of the back, landing at my feet. It was thick, like it'd been overstuffed. I picked it up and lifted the flap. Inside was a stack of coarse yellow papers time had worn thin at the edges. It was written in Mary's hand, but unlike the other letters, this was an original.

I glanced at the date on the first page, the ink faded but still legible. *October 27, 1864,* it said. The day before her death. Which meant clutched between my fingers, in sweeping, formal script, were Bloody Mary Worth's last written words.

October 27, 1864

Constance,

I understand why you cannot come, and while it is difficult for me to be joyful about anything these days, this baby is a blessing. Your offer to send Edward in your stead is sweet, but you are too close to delivery, dear sister, and I would not risk you or that precious child for anything in the world. Once I have a fine niece or nephew, you can sweep me away from this slice of Hell. Until then, take care of yourself and your baby.

The pastor would not relent on Mother's funeral, but he is ever incapable of decency. The stain upon her character persists despite my protests, and as such, she was not allowed to be buried with "decent Christians." I advised the constable that Pastor Starkcrowe was seen walking with Mother before her disappearance, but the constable is assured of the pastor's innocence. He, too, believes Mother cast herself into the river. You can guess my opinions on the matter. Pastor Starkcrowe is a lecher of a man far too comfortable with his cruelties. I only wish others would see him for who he is.

I mourn our mother every minute of every hour. She was far too good for this world—too kind to live amongst such injustice. She deserved better than an unmarked grave outside of town. I visit her remains daily to ensure no animals desecrate her. The rocks are piled high. I will care for her to the best of my ability while I toil in Solomon's Folly.

To answer your question, yes, there have been more incidents.

I grow accustomed to the dark, though with winter coming, it will be colder and more unkind. I plan to tuck blankets in the cellar in preparation. Boots, too, for when the water rises, and perhaps a candle and flint. It is strange the things you can tolerate given enough exposure. The basement with its beetles and bats does not terrify me as it once did.

No, what plagues me most lately is my capacity for anger. Before I was sent to "repent" yesterday, the pastor struck me across the mouth with the back of his hand. He flayed me from cheek to lip. It did not move him to pity. He dragged me to the basement despite my bloodstained dress.

Elizabeth bore witness to our exchange. She had the audacity to taunt me through the door again. I didn't answer her provocations, but I cannot claim this as an attestation to character. I was simply too enraged to speak. My hatred for the pastor, for Elizabeth Hawthorne, and for every girl like her has grown bone-deep and all-consuming. I despise that our mother was so wronged and suffered the final indignity of a non-Christian burial. I despise that God is an absentee shepherd who has forsaken me and those I love.

I am a creature born of injustice and fury.

I must finish my writing now, as the pastor has rationed my lantern oil. He was assigned my guardianship in the wake of Mother's death. Every night he locks me in my room so I cannot escape, but I do not mind. The door between us grants the illusion of separation. It keeps him out as effectively as it keeps me in.

Perhaps tonight I will sleep. Last night, my cheek ached and Elizabeth's taunts were too fresh in my mind. They still echo through my head, that singsong lilt of hers making it all the more obscene. I would scratch my ears from my skull if it would make

the memory of it go away, but I think it would stay with me
regardless.

Some things are simply too cruel to abide.

Bloody Mary.

Bloody Mary.

BLOODY MARY.

MARY

UNLEASHED

June 24, 1864

Sister Mine,
 Below, I have listed my dastardly deeds since you abandoned me for Boston. "But Mary," you say. "I did not abandon you so much as find a handsome gentleman to kiss me breathless for eternity." The result is the same, Constance. I have brought a reign of terror to Solomon's Folly. I will not be sated until I have tainted everything you love with my terribleness.

1. *I have claimed your room as my own. The pink sashes are gone because pink is an affront to all that is good in the world. I have replaced it with a shade of green you would abhor. I do this as both a declaration of war and because green is a far superior color.*
2. *I have taken over your gardening duties. This is not to help Mother but to destroy your handiwork. Plants wither in fear at the sight of my boots. I am not blessed with your green thumb but, as Mother says, a black thumb, and I shall use it to wreak havoc upon your peonies.*
3. *I have taken your place on the church choir. The psalms you hold so dear are now sung so off pitch, dogs bay thinking me their pack mistress. Our sweet mother has asked if perhaps I would like to do a Sunday reading in lieu of the hymnals, but I remain stalwart.*

(To her chagrin, I might add. When I expressed that I preferred the music, she looked much like your peonies—wilted and sad.)

4. *Despite your instruction that the shawl you knitted me last winter should not be worn with my shapeless blue frock, I have done just that. I disavow fashion! I want those who look upon me to know repulsion and fear. Your innocent lace is a weapon in my hands.*

5. *I have taken over your duties with the Spencer girls, and I believe they find me the superior nanny. What better way to vex you than to fatten up the children you love with so much shortbread, they explode. Whilst Mrs. Spencer will undoubtedly take offense to my practices, the children will love me best, and that is all that matters.*

    (I caught Agatha with two meaty fists in the shortbread pan. The child had eaten half the contents in the three minutes I took to attend her sister's nappies. I would have been impressed if I was not so horribly afraid she'd get sick.)

6. *Mr. Biscuits is a traitor. Your poorly named dog has all but forgotten you. He sleeps at the foot of my bed every night making terrible sounds and equally as terrible smells. Every morning he looks upon me like I am the sun in his furry little world. This is likely because I am the one to feed him the scraps, but let's pretend he is drawn to my shining disposition.*

7. *Not only did I not go to the summer dance, I told Thomas Adderly that I would rather wash my hair than attend. I did not do this simply because Thomas is overly ardent and annoying. No, it was to defy your terrible sisterly advice! For shame, Constance! For shame!*

(Honestly, the boy is dull, and I've seen better teeth in horse mouths. There's also the Elizabeth Hawthorne problem. Her preference for dull, horse-teethed gentlemen causes me far too much grief. While attending a dance may have been nice, the company was lacking and the repercussions weren't worthwhile.)

8. Last, but by no means least, I cancel my trek to Boston. Fie upon you and your fancy home! I shall remain in Solomon's Folly until my skin is withered and my teeth fall out!

   (I am suffering a summer cold that has wetted my lungs, and Mother says I must wait to travel. While I do not like postponing, my sickness has kept me abed the last few days. I will write you when I am less apt to play the part of Pestilence. I hope to reschedule soon.)

I hope this letter finds you miserable (blissfully happy) and that Joseph snores in his sleep. (That would be awful. Mr. Biscuits is bad enough. A full-grown man must be thrice as disruptive.)

Write soon, my beloved harpy.

Your sister,

Mary

1

The darkness has a face.

Gray skin stretched over a craggy skull, black veins pulsing at the temples and cheeks. It has no nose, no lips—only voids crusted with liquid decay. Broken teeth jut up from the gums like yellow stalagmites. A white, wormlike tongue wags to taste the air. Tufts of hair top half-rotted ears, leaves and debris tangled in the elbow-length strands.

The darkness has a voice. Sometimes it's wet, like pipes choking through a clog. Other times it's dry and slithery, like snake scales gliding over rock. It depends on whether she's laughing. Mary likes to laugh, but only if she's bled someone. That's when the raspiest rattles echo from her throat.

Nothing is normal after a haunting. School, friends, boys . . . who cares? How can you worry about the mundane when you've seen the extraordinary? When one of your best friends was killed by a ghost before your eyes?

I still can't look in a mirror, because I see her. Mary. She's tattooed on my brain. Vines swathing her thin frame, clinging to a ragged dress with a copper-splattered bodice. Talons tipping the spindly fingers, the edges as sharp as razors. One leg swollen with water and ready to burst, the other nothing but bone. Beetles everywhere, living inside a walking corpse, scurrying beneath the skin until they gnaw their way out.

The thought of her is enough to send me fleeing to my mother's side. Last week, I caught a glimpse of my reflection in a picture frame and hit the floor as if I were in an air raid. Mom doesn't understand my twitchiness. Worse, I can't explain it. She would never believe me. I hadn't believed Jess when she'd first told me about it, either.

Jess. She got us into this mess. Bloody Mary Worth was her obsession and we were stupid enough to follow. When Jess positioned us in that bathroom, when she checked her compass points and placed the candle and salt line, we didn't think anything would happen. It was just a game. Then a ghostly hand pressed against the glass. We should have ended it there, but one more summon, Jess said. Just one. I relented. No, I encouraged my friends to go along with it because I was curious.

Now I'm scarred, Jess is haunted, and Anna's dead. Regret weighs on me from the moment I wake in the morning until I drift into my dreams. I want to walk away, to let Mary be Jess's problem, but I have a debt to repay. To Anna. To other girls who'd play the game. Jess will pawn the ghost onto someone sooner or later. Mary will continue torturing girls from the mirror.

I have to do something about it.
The question is . . . what?

The letter from Mary to Constance Worth Simpson should have made me laugh. It should have warmed me to the authoress from a century and a half ago. I'd have thought her clever and charming. I'd have said something like, "I'd be her friend."

But this letter had been stuffed inside of Jess McAllister's notebook, wedged between two pages of handwritten notes about Bloody Mary. Despite the tone, it was no joke, as proven by the three other letters present. They cataloged Mary's plight from start to end—a smart, funny teenager deteriorating along with her circumstances. A cruel pastor robbing her of her mother, and in turn her humor. Anger filled the gaps, but eventually that was taken, too, when she was murdered at seventeen years old.

The ghost of the legend wasn't born evil. She was made that way. Two cups tragedy, one tablespoon cruelty, a splash of neglect. It was a recipe for pain.

We tried to stop Mary. Jess even staged another summoning with Kitty, Laurie Carmichael, and Becca Miller, "To save you, Shauna," she said to me. "To get you unhaunted." She succeeded, albeit not how she anticipated. Jess planned for Kitty to take on the curse during that last summoning, but I intervened and Jess was grabbed in Kitty's stead.

We sent Mary back into the mirror, but not before Mary spilled Jess's blood. We all knew what that meant; Mary wouldn't let Jess go until Jess died or another girl took the mark from her. It was how it had always been with Bloody Mary. It was how it would be until someone put the ghost to rest. More girls would die.

Like Anna Sasaki died.

It was hard to believe she was gone. Some days, the pain of her loss was raw, like someone branding me with a hot poker. Other days, it was a dull throb, like a bone-deep bruise. I missed Anna's intelligence. I missed her snark. I missed scribbling notes to her during math class to pass the time.

I missed *her*.

School resumed a few days after her disappearance. AMBER Alert: Anna Sasaki. The police hadn't a trace, nor would they find one: Mary dragged Anna through the mirror and into her swampy, black world.

The fog rising on the other side of the mirror. Crimson blood spraying across the glass. Too much to be nonfatal. Too much to grant any hope that Anna survived. Terror and loss and futility dropping on my head like an anvil. Grief crushing me beneath its weight.

The Sasakis would never get the closure they so deserved.

The days after the murder were a fixed reel in a movie, the same twelve-hour clip playing, rewinding, and repeating the next morning. I got up, ate breakfast with my mother, and went to school early. I didn't like being alone in the house. Every sound in the building sent me scurrying for the only weapon I knew that worked against Mary—salt. It burned her. I had boxes of it squirreled away in my closet in case she returned.

There was no reason to expect her, but Jess's tie to Mary made me uneasy. Would Jess's haunting be different because she and Mary were related? What would happen if Jess somehow allied with Mary? I put nothing past Jess. She'd sacrificed one friend to the mirror and nearly succeeded in sacrificing a second.

Jess could justify anything when she put her mind to it. Even murder.

At the end of the school day, I would go to Kitty's house until Mom got out of work. After Anna died, Mom cut her hours at her second job. It was the only good thing to come from the haunting. I loved my mom. I also loved knowing that Mary left me alone whenever Mom was near. We never quite figured out why that was, but I had my suspicions. Mary Worth loved her mother. Other mothers were safe by association.

I spent the last hour of every day alone in my room, lying in bed and gazing at the wall. My thoughts drifted to Anna, to Kitty's boyfriend, Bronx. He was a star football player before Mary pulled him through a glass window and dropped him three stories. His legs had snapped like twigs. Double casts, metal bolts, surgeries—he was lucky he'd ever walk again, never mind play sports.

Mary took so much from both of them. Thinking about my part in bringing her into this world almost always made me weep into my pillow. It would have been easy to lay it all on Jess, but I wouldn't fool myself. I'd made bad decisions, too.

Jess liked to remind me of that sometimes. She refused to fade into obscurity. Rapid-fire texts—sometimes apologies, sometimes accusations. I ignored every message. The assault died down after the first few weeks, but I'd still get the occasional plea for help. When she saw me in the halls at school—her eyes sunken in like she hadn't slept in forever, a fresh cut or scratch marring her skin—I looked away. Sometimes she followed me, calling my name. I ducked into classrooms to avoid her. I left the cafeteria if she tried to eat near me.

It wasn't just because of what she did. The cuts and bruises told me she hadn't lost Mary yet. No one near Jess McAllister was safe.

"Shauna, wait up!"

Kitty's voice sliced through the hall din. The last bell had rung, and kids were eager to exit the school. We were only a week away from summer vacation, and you could feel the anticipation in the air. The chatter was louder and more animated. The attitudes in class were more laissez-faire. I resented it. Anna's death plagued me every day, while my classmates talked about beach parties. It was too soon. I wasn't ready for life to go on.

Kitty trotted up to my locker, her book bag slung over her shoulder. Her face was flushed from gym, her heavyset body hugged by a tank top and shorts. She hadn't changed clothes from class, but then, neither of us could go into the girls' locker room. That's where Anna went missing. Kitty usually opted to change in her car. I snuck off to change in the bathrooms near the science labs, my trusty box of salt perched on the toilet tank.

Kitty swept a lock of caramel-brown hair away from her ear.

"Let's get out of here. Tennis in ninety-degree heat is not fun. I'll roll the windows down in case I stink. Sorry."

"No problem." We shouldered our way through the hallway and out the back doors. My backpack weighed fifteen thousand pounds. Finals were upon us, and though I tried to study for the tests, I couldn't focus. It was like all my textbooks had spontaneously rewritten themselves in a language I didn't understand.

"I'm avoiding the principal's office now," Kitty said as we approached her red SUV. "There's a memorial for Anna in one of the display cases. Every time I see it, I cry."

Saying Anna's name was enough to make Kitty's voice hitch. I squeezed her shoulder, doing my best to ignore the sweat slicking her skin. Kitty and Anna had been best friends since grade school. Losing Anna on top of Bronx's accident—if you can call it an accident when a ghost flings your boyfriend out a window—had ruined her. Looking at Anna's picture every day would be a special kind of torture.

"I'm sorry. At least we're almost done with school. You'll get a few months off to recoup."

Kitty tossed her stuff into the back of the car before climbing into the driver's side. "Not exactly. We're still doing that thing with Cody in Solomon's Folly."

I wasn't the only one feeling obligated to end Mary Worth. I told Kitty time and time again that I could handle it without her, that Cody Jackson had volunteered to help so Kitty could stay safe, but Kitty always threw my own words back at me: we'd walked away with our lives, but others might not be so lucky.

We had to do something.

"We started it together, we'll finish it together. For Anna," she'd say.

It was always we. It was always for Anna.

I couldn't quite look at Kitty's profile. If I'd told Jess no all those weeks ago, if I'd been less of a pushover ...

"It's okay, Shauna."

She brushed the back of my hand, her fingers tan next to my pasty, befreckled skin. It wasn't absolution, but it was enough. Kitty put the key in the ignition, opening the windows and sunroof of the truck. A breeze swept in, pushing the oppressive heat away.

As soon as Kitty inched from the parking spot, a green Ford Focus sailed around the line of cars and stopped in front of us. Kitty slammed on the brakes. My hand gripped the dash as I peered down the expanse of the SUV's hood only to find myself staring at Jess McAllister. So blond. So perfect with that narrow nose and big blue eyes. So *injured.* A ragged cut bisected her right cheek and top lip. I'd passed her in the hall just yesterday and the cut hadn't been there.

How'd she explain that to her family? A fight? A bear encounter? She tripped and fell on a shovel?

My pulse pounded in my ears.

She shouted something that the end-of-school-day chaos drowned. I shook my head and looked away, but she shouted again. And again. It wasn't until Kitty threw the truck into reverse that Jess's voice finally penetrated.

Read it, Shauna.

Read what? My phone had no messages. She hadn't given me anything in school. But Jess did know my locker combination. She used to help herself to my stuff all the time. As Kitty peeled from the parking lot to get away from our once-upon-a-time friend, I started digging through my bag. Jess was bad at things like *boundaries* and *personal space*. Why would that change now that we weren't friends?

It only took a minute for me to find the photocopied pages held together by a red paper clip. They were wedged into my English textbook between the cover and the first page. She'd written a note across the back in her familiar hen scratch:

Her last letter was dated the day before her death certificate. This was written the next day. How did Mary die?

October 30, 1864

Mrs. Simpson,

It is with sincere regret that I write you bearing more bad news. I returned from my evening walk to find your sister missing from the church. She must have snuck off before dinnertime. The constable has been informed, but thus far there is no trace of her. It is as if Mary were plucked from us by the hand of God.

I am sorry. I know how upsetting this must be to read.

I bear no ill will toward your sister, so please understand that the things I put to page are for the purposes of enlightenment, not slander. Your sister was rather angry that she could not join you in Boston after your mother's passing. However, the constable and I agreed that she was better served taking refuge in the church until your husband could collect her. She is a virtuous girl, and comely, too. Allowing her to travel unchaperoned would have left her vulnerable to the world's atrocities. My conscience would not abide such endangerment.

I explained this to Mary, assuring her that Mr. Simpson would arrive upon the birth of your baby, but she struggled against reason. She has been increasingly agitated since your mother's death. Doctor Whitten concluded her uncharacteristic aggression was a manifestation of grief. He suggested hospitalization and a steady dose of laudanum, but I respectfully declined. This is a spiritual malady, not a physical one. There is nothing wrong with her that cannot be cured by the firm yet loving hand of our Lord.

We had begun to traverse the path of holy rehabilitation before she disappeared. She continued to fight my influence, questioning my motives and accusing me of unnecessary cruelty. I do not know how your mother raised her, but I modeled my guardianship after Proverbs 13:24:

> Whoever spares the rod hates their children,
> But the one who loves their children
> is careful to discipline them.

I would not brook her caustic demeanor, nor would I "leave her alone" as she so vehemently demanded. Her insistence only steeled my resolve to see her righted. Given time and a modicum of agreeability on your sister's part, I believe we could have eradicated her discord. She could have lived the life of peace and goodness that God intended.

It is my earnest hope that we find her soon so this can still come to pass.

I met with the constable before writing you, and we are in accord that Mary has fled Solomon's Folly. This alarms me for many reasons, not the least of which is her decline. No matter what she may believe, I wish for nothing to befall the girl. Perhaps Mary will find her way to your doorstep before this letter does. Should that occur, please write to me at once. I am sick with concern.

I pray for you and yours, Mrs. Simpson.

Your humble servant,

Philip Starkcrowe

Pastor, Southbridge Parish

2

I read the letter aloud during the drive to Kitty's house. Her color rose the more I talked, pink tinging her cheeks and the tips of her ears. Her hands throttled the steering wheel.

"He beat her," Kitty said. "That's what I'm hearing."

"It sounds like it." I reread the scripture passage, my jaw clenching. "The more I learn about Philip Starkcrowe, the more I think he killed her. I guess she could have run away, but it seems too convenient after everything he put her through."

Kitty nodded. "Exactly. And when would she have had the chance? He locked her in the basement, for crying out loud."

After what Mary did to me, Anna, and Bronx, I swore I'd never feel sorry for her, but the more story we uncovered, the more my stance softened. If anyone had the right to rise as an angry ghost, it was Mary Worth.

Silence filled the car. I wrestled with my conflicting emotions while Kitty drove. She looked angry. The letter was upsetting, but it shouldn't have been enough to get her red-faced and stiff.

"You okay?" I reached out to tap her leg. "You look ready to explode."

"It feels like Jess is trying to lure us into working with her. Like, was this bait? Where the hell is she getting all this stuff?"

"Probably the same place she got the first four letters." I stuffed the newest letter into the notebook. "Jess never said specifically, but with her relation to Mary, I wouldn't doubt if there are family archives. A relative or something."

Kitty's fingers relaxed on the wheel. "As long as we're on the same page. I'm not helping her, Shauna. I won't be bribed with information."

"That's fine. Did you see that cut on her face? Mary got her good."

Kitty shrugged, but I could tell by the faint lines at the sides of her eyes that she wasn't as aloof as she wanted to appear. "If you don't want to get attacked by a ghost, don't summon one."

That was the gist of it, wasn't it?

I thought about the question Jess wrote on the back of the letter. Mary Worth's death certificate listed a date of death but no cause. If Mary ran away from home, it was possible she wasn't interred in the Southbridge Parish as we initially suspected. We knew about the church from Mary's letters, which is how we ended up on a Saturday night descending into a dark, cold basement better suited for the bats than teenaged girls. We had just found a dip in the floor when Mary appeared, cutting the investigation short.

We said we'd go back, but we hadn't. Not yet, anyway. Our research was limited to books and movies. Unfortunately, everything we read about "real hauntings" talked about the history of famous hauntings, not what to do when a murderous ghost tailed you. We were left with theatrics for inspiration, where the haunted heroes always did one of three things: solved the mystery of the ghost's death, found the body and lit it on fire, or rediscovered a prized possession tying the ghost to the mortal plane.

"Hopefully finding her tomb will help us figure out what to do next," I said, my fingers worrying the corners of the letter poking up from the notebook top.

"Then what?"

"Destroy the body, I guess."

Kitty winced. "Gross. I guess it's fine as long as we don't have to deal with Jess or actually touch dead people."

Kitty seemed different since Mary. She'd always been the soft one in our quartet—too pliant when Jess made demands, unwilling to stand up for herself when it mattered most. The haunting changed her. Or maybe it only seemed that way because she used to be with Anna all the time and I was with Jess. Now that we hung out constantly, Kitty's quiet steel was more evident. Her determination to see Mary stopped. The way she picked herself up off the floor after a particularly sad day. I couldn't help but think I'd underestimated her all along. Kitty had known the risks of summoning Mary that last time, but she'd done it anyway to save me.

That was brave. Stupid, but brave.

"We'll stay away from Jess," I promised. "And I'll text Cody later about the letter. She'll have some input."

Cody Jackson was a thirty-something-year-old woman who lived in Mary Worth's hometown of Solomon's Folly. She was also the victim before me. For seventeen years, Mary tormented Cody. Mary took Cody's eye and several fingers and toes. She scratched Cody so badly, Cody looked like she'd wrestled an alligator.

Yet Cody survived, living in squalor to keep the ghost at bay. There was no glass in her house. No shiny plastic or metal. She never went outside. She'd painted her walls and window-panes with pig's blood to stop Mary from tracking her scent. The experience had left her an anxious, surly mess. But I liked her quirks. We talked at least three times a week. She'd invited us to stay with her during the summer break so we could inves-tigate Mary.

Mom had approved the trip, though she thought I was visit-ing Jess's grandparents. I'd vacationed with Jess's family since my Girl Scout days—canoeing, bonfires, horseshoes, and bar-becues by the lake. I didn't like lying to my mother, but she'd never allow me to stay with Cody, a woman she'd never met. It didn't help that Cody was twitchier than a hair dryer in the bathtub, so introductions were off the table. Mom would have steered me clear of someone so strange.

Cody's house stinking of pig's blood. Clouds of flies covering the ceiling. Black paper on the windows. No mirrors, no glass, no reflections. Scars on the skin. Scars on the soul. Fear the only constant companion.

Mom had no idea how close to that I'd come.

We pulled into Kitty's driveway, me clutching my book bag to my chest, Kitty quiet and broody. I cleared my throat. "I'm wondering if we should bother visiting the church again. A hole in the basement floor isn't a lot to go on," I said. "The pastor could be lying in the letter, but remember what Mary wrote about Elizabeth Hawthorne taunting her through the door? People would have heard shouting." I climbed from the car and followed Kitty to the side door. Her father's wealth meant they could afford things like a Jacuzzi near the in-ground pool and summer-only cars. The first floor of their house could fit my rinky-dink apartment four times over.

Kitty unlocked the door and dropped her purse in the foyer. "Yeah, but the pastor could have gagged her and tied her up so no one could hear her cry out. I think it's worth a visit."

I shuddered. Kitty hadn't been at the church with us. I'd given her all the gritty details, but she hadn't experienced Mary lunging up from that dark water. She hadn't seen Mary reaching for me.

Cold, dead hands, her skin rubbery and slick. Fingers curling around my ankles, nails puncturing my skin. Mary jerking me into the water, my head nearly crashing against the steps on the way down. Mary's fist in my hair, shoving me down, down, down, until I saw black.

"Shauna? Are you okay?"

Kitty's voice tore me from the memory. I blinked, as if I could force the image away. As if it wasn't eternally burned into my mind.

"Sorry. I just...yeah. I hate the church."

"I know. Maybe Cody and I can go for you. You can stay at the house."

Kitty and I exchanged glances. I didn't say anything because I didn't have to. We were in it together, for better or worse.

"Dinner, kiddo!"

Mom picked me up from Kitty's at half past five. We were home by quarter of six, me disappearing into my room, Mom foraging in the kitchen for food. It was almost seven when she called out for dinner, interrupting my studying. I'd been attempting—and failing—to concentrate on my history final. Starkcrowe's letter chewed on my brain. I'd left a message for Cody, but she hadn't called me back yet. Cody liked to do things on her own timetable.

I put aside the book and rolled off my bed. My room was different post-Mary; I'd packed the vanity mirror in the closet and faced it toward the wall. Jess had told me that people once covered their mirrors in the presence of the dying so their souls wouldn't get trapped. With all I'd seen with Bloody Mary, a vanity was nightmare fodder I didn't need.

I trudged down the hall in my pajamas, keeping to the middle to avoid the bathroom on the left and the picture frames on the right. Mom stood by the kitchen table, doling out canned beef stew. She smiled as I sat. She looked better these days— less tired now that she worked sixty hours instead of eighty.

Perfect skin, rich auburn hair. Her eyes were too big, her nose too narrow, her mouth too wide, but together, the parts worked. She was beautiful. I had enough of my dad in me that I didn't come together so well, with pointier features and a wider jaw. Plus, I had the redhead's plague. Freckles.

"How's studying going?" she asked, sliding into the chair across from me. She stretched her napkin over her lap.

"Okay." I paused to think of something normal to say. "I think I bombed the calculus final."

Mom frowned for a moment, then forced a shrug. "You had a good-enough quarter otherwise. One test shouldn't matter too much."

Mom was usually all over me for grades. I was an honor roll kid, Ivy League material without Ivy League money. I needed a scholarship if I wanted to go somewhere great. But after Anna died, Mom eased up on expectations. I was sure she thought I was crazy, the way my eyes swept through every room looking for spooks and shadows. The way I pressed into her side whenever the lights were dim.

"Yeah, thanks." My spoon dipped into the gray, murky stew with bits of carrot floating in it.

We fell into awkward silence. Our post-Anna lives had taken on an awful routine. Extended quiet followed by Mom asking, "Are you okay?" "How can I help?" and "Do you want to talk to a professional?"

"I have a date on Friday," she announced instead.

My spoon clattered against the edge of the bowl.

"Seriously?"

"Yes, *seriously*. It's not that strange, is it? I'm not a hundred, you know."

Not strange, but unexpected. It'd always been just me and Mom—my dad walked out on us when I was four. He could be dead, for all I know. The notion of her playing the field again was . . . well, it wasn't bad, but it wasn't familiar.

"It's fine. I'm fine," I lied.

Splotchy hives dotted her pale neck, telegraphing her embarrassment. "His name is Scott. He's an electrician. He came into McReady's a few months ago. I've been turning him down ever since, but I think I might like him. He's funny."

"I hope you have an awesome time," I said after a minute.

She nodded.

Back to the silence.

Every few bites she glanced at me, hopeful I'd have something to say about *anything*. Her date. My day. My finals. I used to chitchat, but I'd become so consumed with Mary that I had nothing to contribute to the conversations anymore.

For the first time in a long time, I asked myself why I continued to keep Mary quiet. Fear, yes, but fear of what? Being doubted? Jess had convinced us that no one would believe it. That we'd be called liars. She used Elsa Samburg's institutionalization as the worst-case scenario. Elsa was another Mary victim, older than Cody, who'd been hospitalized after her haunting.

But my mom knew I wasn't prone to hysteria. I didn't watch

horror movies or believe in UFOs or yetis. I didn't read horoscopes or tarot cards. And I definitely didn't make up stories for attention.

"Do you believe in ghosts?" I asked.

Mom's spoon paused midway between her mouth and the bowl. She blinked at me, surprise evident in the lift of her brows. "I don't know, really. Your grandmother does. She thinks her room at the rest home is haunted."

"I was haunted. I know how stupid it sounds, but it's true. For real." I had to get it all out before I lost my courage. "That's why I've been so twitchy. I swear I'm not crazy. This isn't because of Anna. It happened before Anna and it's over now, but that week was awful."

She put down her spoon and stared at me. She didn't look afraid, just incredulous that her reasonable daughter said such an unreasonable thing.

"I didn't tell you because I was afraid you'd look exactly how you look right now," I said. "I was scared. And please don't give me the stuff about logical explanations. It was a ghost of a girl named Mary Worth, who died a hundred and fifty years ago."

Mom's mouth opened as if she was about to say something. She bit her bottom lip instead, leaving a wet smear. "I see. Well, no, I don't, but...you're not haunted anymore?"

"No. It's over. I know how insane this is, but I would really like for you to give me the benefit of the doubt. I swear it happened. Please."

I didn't realize how desperate I was for her not to turn her back on me until I heard the plaintive *please*. She heard it, too; she nodded and retrieved her spoon, turning it over in her hand. "You're safe?" she asked.

"I am now."

Mom took a bite of stew and glanced from me to the table-cloth, her brow covered in worry lines. The silence chiseled away at my confidence. I'd overestimated. Jess knew what she was talking about. Confessing to something a month old was needless and stupid and...

Mom's gaze locked with mine. "I believe you."

3

Those three words were magical. I'd shaken off a shackle that had weighed me down more than I'd realized. I looked away, my fingers curling along the edge of the table, my eyes teary with relief.

"Thanks." The lump in my throat felt like a softball. "I was afraid you'd laugh at me."

Mom reached across the table to take my hand, her fingers warm around my wrist. "I've never done that in seventeen years, Shauna. I'm not going to start now."

The questions started, though Mom was gentle. She knew how fragile the trust I'd laid upon her doorstep was. "Who was Mary Worth?" "How'd you find out about her?" "What happened when you were haunted?" I never mentioned Bloody Mary by name, mirrors, Anna's fate, or Solomon's Folly, but I did talk about what Mary looked like. I talked about how I suspected she died. I shared a version of the truth that was palatable for both of us, and more important, allowed me to go to Solomon's Folly. If Mom suspected I'd be ghost hunting, the trip would be off the table.

We sat together in the living room, staring at the TV with pillows hugged to our chests. The floor above us creaked, a rusty squeal. I tensed, but then water rushed and pipes shivered. The toilet. It wasn't phantoms or ghouls, just regular people doing regular things. I let out my breath.

"Are you still scared of the ghost?" Mom must have been watching me from the corner of her eye. I shifted my weight, trying not to squirm too much.

"Sometimes," I admitted. "But it's getting easier as time goes on."

There was another pause. "I hate to ask this, but you're not doing anything weird? No séances or witchcraft?"

I flinched. That question was one of the reasons I didn't want to say anything to begin with. "God, Mom. No." I stood up to go back to my room, but she snatched my wrist and squeezed.

"Sorry. I believe you. It's the worry talking."

I wrenched my hand away and retraced my steps to my bedroom, the door slamming behind me.

She doesn't believe me.

My fingers went to my temples, attempting to massage away the brewing headache. Mary, Mom's date, Solomon's Folly, Jess. I was supposed to study, but how could I focus with so much noise in my head?

A nap. I needed a nap. I threw myself into bed, pinching

my eyes closed. Except there were footsteps approaching and a swift knock on my door and *why couldn't she just leave me alone?*

"Shauna? Hey." Mom poked her head in, her hands clutching the door. "I'm sorry. Oh, hon. I didn't mean to upset you."

But you did. Now go away.

I rolled away from her. "Thanks, Mom. Love you."

Her breath hitched. "I love you, too. I'm heading in to read before bed. If you need anything, let me know. I don't know much about ghosts, but if you say you're safe now, I'm ... I have to believe you. You know I'm here."

I stumbled through school the next morning, my head low. There was only English left to survive before I could eat lunch with Kitty. Some of my classmates said hello as I passed, but I wouldn't look up at them. A wall of windows lined my left side. So shiny and tall. So menacing.

Running down the hall, Mary keeping pace no matter how hard I pumped my legs. That awful grin. That obscene laughter. Six Marys in the panes, all mocking me, the cackles ringing out like a chorus from Hell. Reflection upon reflection delighting in my fear. Skidding around the corner to find a hallway of locks clanging against metal lockers. BANG, BANG, BANG!

Mary had become part of the school. Every mirror, every chrome knob, every darkened corner. She was my ever-present shadow. I rushed to my locker to get my books for the next class, dancing with nervous energy. A hand clapped my shoulder from behind. I shrieked, instinctively reaching for the box of salt hidden beneath my gym clothes. My elbow jerked back, colliding with a warm, hard body.

The hand plunging through the glass. Nails rending flesh, blood rising hot and thick and smelling like copper. Mud and the stench of decay as she heaves herself across the glass barrier. Snarling, her upper lip curved, a tendril of yellow spittle dribbling down her chin. The slits of nostrils flaring as she catches her prey's scent.

"Holy crap! Shauna, sorry, you okay? Ow. Damn."

I whipped my head around. Standing there, her hand hovering midair, was Laurie Carmichael. Spiky black hair, brown eyes, a pink-glossed smile. Laurie was one of those girls that everyone liked—she played a lot of sports, was involved in a lot of clubs. She could be fake at times, and she had a tendency to gossip, but she'd never aimed any of it my way, so I didn't have too much of a problem with her.

Especially since she'd been one of the girls to help Jess in that last summoning. She and I shared a secret—something we'd probably never bring up to one another, but we both knew it was there. That meant something.

I eased away from the salt.

"I'm so sorry. You scared me. Are you okay?"

Laurie rubbed at her shoulder. "Yeah, I'll be fine. But take it easy, girl. Damn. Anyway, I wanted to let you know I'm having an end-of-the-year party Friday. You're invited. I already mentioned it to Kitty."

I said nothing at first, fumbling for a response that didn't sound dismissive or bitchy. "I'm not all that social with the Anna thing going on. Is Jess going?"

"No. I haven't seen her much since her breakup with Marc. How about you?"

I didn't know Jess and Marc had split. I had to wonder if she'd ditched him to protect him from Mary.

Maybe if I'd dumped my friends like Cody told me to do, Anna would still be here. How can Jess be a better person than me?

"No. We're not talking," I said tightly.

Laurie looked like she wanted to hear more. I turned back to my locker, not ignoring her but not inviting a second degree either. She stepped away with a sigh. "Yeah, okay, that's fair. Eight o'clock if you change your mind. Invitation's open to the whole class."

"Thanks." My voice was hollow, even to my ears.

"Maybe it'll be fun," Kitty said.

I picked at my food, my eyes scanning the cafeteria. I was looking for Jess. After the car incident the day before, I expected to find her staring at me, but no—when I spotted her, she was concentrating on a notebook. She had a bandage on her face and her hair was chopped short above her ears. Even from that distance, I could see bruises around her throat. I wondered if the teachers suspected Jess's parents of abuse.

"She looks like shit," I said, motioning with my fork. Kitty looked to see where I was pointing and grunted.

"She does. Shauna, you're not thinking of..."

"What? No."

"Good."

I glanced over at Jess to see her gathering her notebook to her chest and racing out of the cafeteria. A month ago, she was surrounded by people, the popular girl. The shining star and homecoming queen and everything high-school dreams were made of. Now, she was a shadow. No people, no prospects, no *hope*.

I'm not that girl anymore. I'm alive. I'm unhaunted.

Some things remained untainted by Mary. Parties at the end of junior year were one of those things.

"Okay," I said, looking back to Kitty. "We'll go."

4

"It's Cody. What do you need?"

Cody never opened her calls with a "Hi" or "Hello." She just announced herself with that deep, raspy voice that sometimes fell to a whisper midsentence. She sounded like she'd gargled with lit charcoals, but that was bound to happen when you didn't talk for almost a decade. Even after a month of regular conversation, her voice hadn't recovered.

I had to strain to hear her, but it was a small price to pay. Cody could be tough to handle with the paranoia and mood swings, but she was also my friend. She'd risked her neck to talk to me during my haunting. Her tips kept me alive.

If I'd listened more, they would have kept Anna alive, too.

I read her the letter from Starkcrowe to Constance after Mary's disappearance, pausing to repeat certain sentences when she asked me to.

"Starkcrowe doesn't deny manhandling Mary." Cody's voice

rose and fell on a wave. "It's not hard to imagine the abuse getting out of control. I can't...I don't—" She grumbled beneath her breath, something I couldn't quite make out over the phone line. "We need to find out what he did to her."

"That's been the goal all along." I threw myself into the chair in my room and smoothed the letter out over the armrest. "But we don't have much to go on."

"We have the letters. And the church is significant. What about that dip in the floor you told me about?"

"What about it?"

"It's possible there's something under there. Or maybe there's a grave marker somewhere on the property. If she's buried with Hannah, that would complicate things, but it can't hurt to look."

Hannah's suicide meant she would have been denied a Christian burial. Mary didn't believe Hannah had leapt to her death in the river, but that didn't stop the pastor from having Hannah interred somewhere other than the parish.

"Okay. If there's anything I can do before the weekend, let me know. We're going to a party Friday night but should be coming out on Saturday," I said.

"You're useless to me. Not your fault, but that's the trouble with being seventeen. You're limited. I'll buy the supplies." Cody sucked in a deep breath before blowing it right onto the receiver and nearly blasting out my eardrum. "I'm assuming Jess is not invited? I don't want her around. She's a risk, and she pisses me off."

I eyed Kitty, who lay on her bed texting Bronx. "No, we're

not bringing Jess. We've seen her at school, but we haven't talked to her. It doesn't look like she's escaped Mary."

Kitty wouldn't look at me, shaking her head in disgust and continuing her text.

Cody snorted. "Not surprising. She probably won't be able to pass her off on her own. It's easier to choreograph a haunting when you're not the focus. Mary's chaotic. Too many things can go wrong."

I sat up straighter in my chair, moving the phone over to my other ear. "What do you mean? She tried to tag Kitty for me. It's feasible."

"Feasible, yes. Smart, no. Not when you're the prey. With a fresh summon, any of the four girls are potential victims. Jess had a clear advantage over the rest of you. She knew how to avoid Mary. I bet she kept herself farthest away from the mirror when you summoned, right?"

"Right."

Cody continued, talking so fast it was hard to understand her. "But now, if she summons Mary, Mary is gunning for her. She wants Jess's blood. Jess knows that. It's too risky. Being the farthest from the mirror isn't enough anymore."

"But Mary *has* hurt other people when she already has a target."

"Of course she has, but think of it this way—of all the times Mary showed up in your reflection, how many times was she interested in other people? Sometimes, but not always, right? How willing were you to summon Mary when you were haunted?"

"I didn't want to. It terrified me," I said.

"Exactly."

Kitty sat up on the bed behind me. She reached out to touch my hair, her fingers twining in the strands and braiding. The gentle tug on my scalp felt nice.

I slumped into my seat, eyes going half-mast like a cat in sunlight. "I'm so sick of Mary. Hopefully we can finish this soon."

"Agreed. Stay safe." The line went dead against my ear. No *good-bye* or *talk to you soon*—Cody was just gone.

The days blurred one into the next: school, Kitty's house, home, Mom, studying, bed. I managed to stay on the honor roll for the last term, but barely. I cleaned out my locker the last day of classes, flinching every time metal clashed with metal or the door to the bathroom across the hall opened and closed. I couldn't wait to escape that building. Every turn was a bad memory.

Steam from the showers. Swampy water rising from the drains, putrid and nestling in the grout between the floor tiles. The showerheads burping filthy water into the fiberglass stalls. The three of us sloshing in it, sliding in it. Feet burning. Sweat rising. Mary laughing from the fog before the strike. Tearing Anna from my grasp. Drag, drag, dragging. The mirror closing behind her. Blood splashing across the glass.

"Get me out, get me out, get me out," I whispered.

I threw the remaining papers into the trash bin, grabbed

my book bag, and slammed the locker closed, my jaw clenching at the rattle. I passed the janitor's closet where Bronx, Mrs. Reyes, and I hid when Mary put the school in lockdown. All those chrome locks slamming against the lockers had sounded like gunshots.

Helicopters, emergency protocol, a media storm. It was a disaster.

I spotted Kitty outside the principal's office, gazing at the student-made memorial for Anna. After the disappearance, people left wreaths, flowers, and teddy bears along the football field fence—so many they'd wrapped around both sides and wound down to the soccer field. Someone had preserved some of the smaller mementos, along with Anna's school picture, yearbook photos, and some sympathy cards.

Kitty's hand touched the display case, tears streaming down her cheeks.

"I feel like I'm abandoning her. I don't know why I assume she's here, but I do. So leaving for the summer . . ." She couldn't finish the thought. I slung an arm around her shoulders and pulled her close. She dropped her head onto my shoulder and cried. Heartrending sobs that devolved into wheezy, asthmatic coughs.

My eyes skimmed the pictures on the board. Some were from class trips, others from the candid section in the yearbook. The one at the center was Anna on the tennis team, wearing her short shorts and holding a racket. Anna played only freshman year and she hated it, but it was a good solo shot, her head turned to the side, her lips tipped up into a smile. Her black hair was back in a ponytail, the glasses on her nose glinting in the sun.

Emptiness crept into my gut. Not the kind that suggested emotional numbness, but the kind that said I desperately needed something to fill the space her loss left inside of me.

I miss my friend.

We lingered awhile, my eyes stinging with unshed tears, Kitty taking hits off her inhaler. She was purple in the face and shaking. Eventually, I guided her away from the display and toward the parking lot.

"Do you want me to drive?" I offered.

She shook her head and climbed into the driver's side of her car, flinging her book bag behind her. It exploded in a flurry of paper and clutter.

Kitty checked her reflection in the rearview mirror, dashing at the mascara tracks raining down her cheeks. I tensed beside her. One of us had reconciled her relationship with mirrors. It wasn't me.

Mary in Jess's car windows, surrounding us, her fingers curled over into meat hooks as she lashed from the depths of the glass. Her visage shifting to the windshield, the ghost looking like a big, dead hood ornament. Raising that finger to write a single word across the condensation on the window. SHAUNA. My name. Staking her claim with a hissed litany of "Mine, mine, mine . . ."

"Glad we've got a few hours before the party," Kitty said.

"Yeah. Yes," I stammered.

The high school shrunk as Kitty drove away from the parking lot. I didn't share Kitty's fear that we were leaving Anna behind—not when I knew that Mary's world could be reached through any mirror anywhere. Anna wasn't in the locker room. Anna was in that swamp with the rest of Mary's victims. Sometimes I tried reasoning out where that was exactly—Ghost World, Purgatory, Hell. Wherever it was, I never wanted to see it.

The drive was silent, Kitty and I lost to our private burdens. I remembered to text Mom to let her know I'd be staying at Kitty's overnight. Her *have fun* reply popped up right as Kitty pulled into her driveway. Instead of climbing out, she tilted her head back so she could look out the skylight, her eyes still swollen from crying at the school.

"Do you still want to go?" she asked.

"I thought you wanted to."

There was a long pause before she nodded and climbed out of her car. "I think *something* needs to make my bad feelings go away."

Seeing the strain around her eyes and the slight jut of her chin, I was pretty sure she needed it, too.

5

Laurie's house was off of a side street, making it the perfect location for a party—no streetlights, long distances between houses. It was one story, baby blue, with a deck, a porch swing, and potted plants dangling from the roof overhang. The windows were open, the screen door propped with a garden gnome to let air in and music out. I could hear the dance track the moment I stepped out of the SUV.

People talked in clusters around the front and side lawns. "Bronx said to take pictures," Kitty said. Before I could escape, she kissed my cheek and snapped a selfie. The flash blinded me—white lightning burned into my eyeballs.

The world shifted into focus once we entered the house. We were in a kitchen with half a dozen kids talking in front of the sink. Within ten seconds, I knew every reflective surface within arm's reach: the dishwasher, the refrigerator, the faucets, the window facing the backyard. I stiffened seeing my reflection staring back at me from the glass sliding doors. My hands reached into my pocket for my Tic Tac container of salt.

Just in case.

Laurie Carmichael separated herself from the kitchen pack. She'd dressed up for the party, all cute blouse and skirt, her makeup perfect, her shoes too shiny to be anything but new. I'd barely taken the time to brush my hair and put on ChapStick before coming out. Kitty cared more about her look, but not by much. Our standards were a lot lower than they used to be.

Laurie motioned us farther into the house, through a living room with a flat-screen TV and past five kids piled on the couch. Down the hall, a bathroom to my left, a closed door to my right, until we entered a study with dark paint and darker wooden floors. Bookshelves lined an entire wall. A desk with a computer was nestled into the corner. A black leather couch with a glass coffee table occupied the bulk of the room. I eyed the table suspiciously, briefly glancing at the squat stone fertility statue at the center.

"Bags on the couch if you want. Glad you could make it," Laurie said. "I know it's been hard for you guys."

"Thanks, Laurie." Kitty smiled at her. Laurie patted her on the shoulder and ducked back into the hall to welcome more guests.

Kitty put her coat, purse, and sweatshirt on the pile. She checked her reflection in the glass of the coffee table, patting her hair into place. I flinched for her. She caught it, and her eyes drifted from me to the table before she backed into the hall.

"I forget sometimes," she said.

How?

We rejoined the party. Waves, hugs. Nathan O'Donnell nodded at me. Nathan and I went out last year, after Jess convinced me he was cool. He spent the whole date talking about sports and video games. I rebuffed his late-date groping attempts. Jess had given me grief for it, saying I didn't give him a fair chance, that I'd put her "in an awkward position" because he was friends with her boyfriend.

So many things I should have seen about Jess early on—so many symptoms that she was too selfish to be a good friend.

Kitty floated through the room, telling everyone to smile for Bronx before subjecting them to her camera. I watched her, jealous that she could go so quickly from sadness to functional and pleasant. And happy. I hadn't experienced happy in what felt like forever.

Every time someone wandered to the bathroom, they nodded at me like it was their solemn duty to acknowledge the grieving girl in the corner. I followed Kitty wherever she drifted, but I wasn't being part of the event. I watched the people around me as if they were specimens in a laboratory.

I was, for a time, the ghost in the room.

A keg rolled in at half past eight courtesy of the football team. There was dancing, spin the bottle, drinking games played at the picnic table out back. I volunteered to be the designated driver, so I kept to soda, but Kitty started drinking almost right away. I figured she deserved to forget. If I thought it'd help me put Mary behind me, I would have been right there with her, but what if it made everything worse? I couldn't allow myself to lose control. I kept to myself, my thumb rubbing circles across the lid of the Tic Tac box.

An hour passed and then two, everything growing louder. More kids dancing. Kids yelling. Kids making out in dimly lit corners. I stayed on the fringes, Kitty always close.

Then Jess arrived.

I was near the porch, one eye on the windows, the other on Kitty as she played another round of quarters. Jess's green car pulled up onto the edge of the lawn and she launched herself from the driver's seat. She spun around, throwing something at the car before sprinting toward the house.

Get out. Get out. Get out. Get Kitty and get out.

I ducked around the corner of the house, hoping Jess wouldn't see me, but it was too late. As I reached Kitty to pull her away from the table games, Jess called my name. My hand clapped on Kitty's shoulder. She lifted her head and smiled until she saw my expression.

"What's wrong?"

"Jess." Even drunk, Kitty knew what that meant. She followed my lead, her sandal getting caught in the grass. I reached out to steady her, letting her sag into my side as we rushed back to the house.

Jess chased us inside, winded, her cheeks apple red.

"Wait. Guys. Please," she said, her voice cracking.

"I can't, Jess. I'm sorry."

I moved quickly. Past the kids on the couch, down the hall, and into the side office with the purses and coats. Kitty broke away to paw through the pile, swaying dangerously on her feet. I heard movement in the hall and then Jess was there, her hands braced against the doorway. "Wait, both of you. Please!" Jess grabbed my shoulder, her fingers digging in and punishing.

I jerked away. "Stop, please!"

"Go home, Jess," Kitty snapped. "You'll get everyone killed."

"I needed to be around friends. It's my parents' anniversary and they left me with Todd. It was the two of us. Mary came. I can't let her take my brother. So I left him with our neighbor, Mrs. Downey. Please."

I'd known Todd since he was born eight years ago. He could be annoying, but he was a good kid. He loved Matchbox cars and SpongeBob and LEGO. He didn't deserve to be sliced up by Jess's terrible shadow.

"Let's go," Kitty barked. "I'm not staying here." I knew she was right, but I hesitated all the same, glancing between Kitty and Jess. Just weeks ago, we'd all been friends.

It's Jess's fault. You can't shoulder this. Go to Solomon's Folly tomorrow, without Jess.

"Shauna, please!" The desperation in Jess's voice was palpable, the fear impossible to fake.

"She's dangerous, Shauna," Kitty said. "Let's go!"

My best friend from my past and my best friend from the present. Both wanted opposite things of me, but the decision wasn't hard to make. Jess's betrayal forever tainted what had been a good thing for a lot of years. I offered my hand to Kitty, my jaw clenched. I couldn't shake the feeling that turning my back on Jess was her death sentence.

If Mary kills us before we solve her murder, Jess is screwed

*anyway. Save Kitty. Save yourself. Get away from the haunted
girl before something else goes horribly wrong.*

"We're leaving," I said.

Kitty staggered my way, the alcohol robbing her of her grace.
I reached out to help her, my hand cupping her elbow, when she
tumbled to the floor in front of me. I thought it was the beer,
but then I realized it was something much, much worse. The
sickening smell of overripe fruit and brine water filled the room.

Only one thing had that foul tang—that stench of rot
and death.

Mary.

My heart pounded faster than a hummingbird's wing.
I couldn't see Mary, I could only see Kitty's expression and
the purse flying from her grasp. I reached for Kitty, hugging
her chest to mine and wrapping my arms around her waist. I
wouldn't lose anyone else to the ghost. I'd anchor Kitty to the
world with my weight, and if not that, I'd go wherever Mary
dragged us.

Kitty's panicked shrieks punctured my eardrums. Her
hands balled up in my sweatshirt as she struggled to hold on.

Mary followed Jess here. Kitty got too close.

I tried to lift her, but something jerked her back and away
from me. No, not something. *Someone.* An arm stretched out
from the underside of the glass coffee table and wrapped around
Kitty's leg. Gray skin, black spidery veins pulsing beneath the
surface of the thin flesh. A clawed hand equally as dark save for
a single digit that looked cotton-candy pink next to its sisters.
A gash splayed open the arm from the inside of the elbow to

the wrist, a network of fetid tendons twining around the brittle-looking bones.

Kitty dropped in front of me, Mary wrenching her to the floor. I teetered, nearly falling forward myself, but then Jess was there. White granules flew by my face and toward the arm, but the top of the table protected the ghost below. Eventually, the salt would harden the glass so Mary couldn't pass through, but that took a lot of salt and more time than we had. Jess knew it, too. She grabbed the fertility statue and lifted it over her head. *CRUNCH.* She smashed it down on Mary's elbow. The bones snapped on impact. Mary shrieked from inside the table glass, her voice echoing as if she menaced us from the depths of a cave.

Jess beat Mary's exposed arm, one heavy strike following another. Over and over she pummeled her until Mary relinquished her hold on Kitty's leg. I pulled Kitty to safety as an arc of black blood splashed across Jess's face. Mary's blood. It dribbled down Jess's cheek and stained her blond hair, but she never stopped her onslaught. Not until the ghost pulled her wounded arm back into the rippling depths of the table.

"Get out," Jess said, her voice oddly flat.

I didn't reply. I couldn't. Fear filled my mouth and throat like liquid, drowning any words I may have wanted to say. Kitty hauled herself to her feet to stumble from the room. Finding the hallway barred by curious classmates, she screeched at them to move.

Jess reached into her coat and pulled out a box of salt,

spraying the top of the table in a thick layer so it'd solidify. "I'm sorry. Tell her I'm sorry. It's my fault. Again," she said.

"Go home," I rasped. "There's too much glass here. You're going to get someone else killed."

I snagged Kitty's purse and ran. Tried to run. Kids lined the hall, their eyes huge. I didn't know if any of them had seen Mary. Right then, I didn't care. I had to get away. I'd made a lot of promises about saving innocents from the ghost, but faced with Mary again, all I could do was flee.

6

"Did she cut you?" I asked over Kitty's hysterical sobbing. She didn't answer. I gripped the steering wheel harder. "*KITTY*. Did Mary cut you? Did she break the skin?"

"I don't think so!" she wailed, sucking in a breath and diving for the inhaler in her purse. She fumbled, and it fell into the well between the seats. I rummaged for it, only one eye on the road, and managed to retrieve it without driving us into a tree.

Kitty breathed in from the inhaler as if it was her lifeline, but the moment it was out of her mouth, she slapped at the car's window.

"Pull over," she croaked. I eased the SUV onto the curb. Kitty threw open the door and staggered into the tall grass, doubling over at the waist before collapsing to the ground.

I unbuckled my seat belt and let myself out of the car to help her.

"Why'd Jess come?" Kitty asked. She lifted swollen eyes to me, her face pale, burst blood vessels riddling her cheeks. I looped my arm around her waist and guided her back into the car, careful where I put my feet.

"She was scared for Todd," I said. "Mary showed up, and she had to bring him to the neighbor's house."

"But why'd she come to the party?"

"She wanted her friends. Mary doesn't like crowds. I don't know, and I'm not sure it matters." The mistake *we'd* made was going into that side room. We would have been safe if we'd stayed with our classmates.

Stupid, Shauna. Stupid.

I helped buckle Kitty into her seat. Her eyes swept the windows around her, searching for Mary in the blackened shine. I reached into my hoodie and produced the Tic Tac box with the salt, cramming it into Kitty's fist. She stared at it stupidly, but then nodded, wrapping her fingers around it.

We pulled into Kitty's driveway at just after eleven, terrified her father would be waiting. Mr. Almeida wasn't the nicest guy under the best circumstances. Under the worst, he was a bully and a screamer. The darkened windows and closed front door meant we stood a chance of getting in undetected.

I helped Kitty inside, trying to make as little noise as possible on the way up the stairs. Kitty sniffled and whimpered, but I didn't begrudge her the fear. I suffered, too. I just hid it better than she did. Around the corner, down the hall, and into her room. I eased her onto her bed before dropping to my knees and rolling up her pant legs.

"What are you doing?"

"Looking for lacerations." I was pretty sure Mary hadn't caught Kitty's blood scent, or we would have seen her already, but I needed to check. I pulled off Kitty's socks and shoes and rolled her feet around.

No claw marks. My shoulders sagged with relief.

"You're okay," I said.

"No marks?"

"None." I crawled to Kitty's bureau, rifling through the bottom drawer for pajamas. As I pulled out a tank top and a pair of pants, my cell phone beeped in my pocket. I tossed the clothes onto Kitty's bed. "Do you need help getting dressed? If not I'll go see who this is. It might be Mom. Or Cody."

Or Jess.

Kitty nodded and reached for the tank top. I ducked from the room, the phone already in my hand as I shut the door. *Please call,* Jess wrote. I started texting back, but then dialed instead. A short conversation would take twice as long in text.

One ring in, Jess picked up.

"Thank you for calling."

"Hey, how are you?" It slipped out before I remembered I was angry at her.

Old habits.

"Okay? I guess?" Jess sucked in a deep breath. "I have another letter you should see. I'll e-mail it." Something slammed on the other side of the line, and she whined. It was a broken sound, so foreign coming from her. Jess was brazen and confident and fearless.

Or used to be, anyway. Mary stripped everyone to their last nerve.

I walked through Kitty's house and out the front door. The summer peepers were out, screeching their night songs while flutters of moths dove at the front porch light. I watched them, waiting for Jess to collect her thoughts.

"We can beat Mary, Shauna, but if I'm constantly fighting for my life, I can't make headway. I told Aunt Dell what happened. She wants to help, but she's really old and can't do much except share information. She gave me the last few letters. She's lived in Solomon's Folly all her life. With her on our side, we could make this stop for good."

Aunt Dell was Jess's great-aunt and the woman who owned the church where we suspected Mary was buried. I'd never met her in my travels to Solomon's Folly, but Jess had talked about her fondly in the past. She'd called the cops on us the last time we trespassed on her private property, not knowing it was us, but I couldn't be mad at her for it, especially considering the arrival of the police officer saved me from a Mary attack.

Jess went quiet. I could hear rustling on the other side of the line, and then a growl. There was a thud followed by a clatter. "Bitch. You think I don't see you?"

Slam.

I waited. I could hear heavy breathing on the other end of the line, followed by pounding footsteps. A rattle. A hiss. Mary was there with Jess. I would recognize those wet, gurgling groans anywhere. I tensed, clutching the phone. The adrenaline from the party surged again, the hairs on my body prickling.

"Jess?"

"I'm fine," she rasped. "She's contained. The offer stands. You help me, I help you. I'm running out of ideas, Shauna. It's only going to get worse."

I'd shut Jess out after Anna—after the revelation that she'd set us up. After what she tried to do to Kitty to save me. I still didn't want to be her friend, but no one deserved Mary. Not even Jess. She'd done a lot wrong, but she was only seventeen, and seventeen-year-olds weren't supposed to die.

And yet.

My voice wavered. "You had us summon Mary without telling us the real reason you wanted her around, Jess. You never spelled out the dangers. You didn't share half of the information we deserved to know—that people had been hurt. That people had died. Why would you risk your friends like that? Why would you risk me? I was your best friend."

Jess hesitated. I thought she was avoiding the question, but then there was more racket on her end of the line.

Slam. Crack. Squeal.

Jess panted into the receiver. "I didn't want to, Shauna. I didn't. There's so much more to it than that. You don't even know."

Before I could ask what that meant, she hung up.

The text to Jess blinked at me from my phone, my thumb hovering over the SEND button.

Are you okay?

What if Jess took it as an indication that we were fine? Or, worse, what if she didn't answer at all? Would I call her parents? Tell them to check to see if their daughter had gone missing? How would I explain if she was?

I tucked away the phone.

A coward twice in one night, but I had to think about myself. About Kitty. About my mom, and Anna, and everyone else who needed me to get through the Mary gauntlet.

I made my way back to Kitty's bedroom and found her sound asleep. I curled in beside her, watching the alarm clock tick off the hours, rolling over from PM to AM. The dread faded some, but not enough to let me sleep. Then I spied the outline of the Tic Tac box in Kitty's jeans pocket on the floor beside me. I fished it out. The salt calmed my nerves enough that I managed to drift off, but not before I thought about Jess.

Don't be dead. Please don't be dead.

I was angry with her, but I wasn't done caring about her. Kitty wouldn't like that.

A blast of sunshine woke me early—before six on a Saturday. My mother said she wanted to see me before we left for Solomon's Folly. I could have asked Kitty for a ride, but she snored at me from her cocoon of bedding. I scribbled a Post-it note to call me before she picked me up, sticking it to her cell phone so she couldn't miss it.

The walk home helped clear my head. It wasn't hot yet, the last traces of spring dewing the grass and crisping the air. I buried my hands in my hoodie pockets, winding my way around the back roads of Bridgewater. While I wasn't keen on extended exposure to Jess, I didn't want to discount her as an avenue for information. I'd talk to Kitty and Cody about it first, though. Kitty hated Jess more than anything in the world, and Cody didn't trust her. I was the weak link. I was the one who still had memories of sleepovers and Girl Scouts and going to Disney with Jess's family when we were twelve.

I picked up my pace, jogging the rest of the way to the house. I took the front stairs two at a time and unlocked the front door. Unsurprisingly, Mom was awake—she was always an early riser. What *was* surprising was that she was wearing purple lingerie and an open robe making breakfast in the kitchen.

She spun, her eyes huge, a spatula clasped in her left hand. I blinked at her. She blinked at me. She was bare down to her belly button, but she quickly rectified that, bundling up and tossing her spatula aside.

"Shit. Hi, Shauna. Let me..."

"Bonnie? Do you have a spare toothbrush? I didn't think to get—" A tall man with dark hair, a goatee, and green eyes walked from the bathroom and into the living room, his fingers fussing with the fly on his pants. My face colored, and he nearly jumped out of his skin.

"Shauna. This is Scott. I didn't realize you'd be home so soon." Mom's fingers toyed with the dangling belt of the robe. "I would have warned you, but...I'm sorry."

"Yeah, that's...It's cool," I lied. "Kitty was tired and you said you wanted to see me before I left for Solomon's Folly, so I figured I'd walk home."

Mom forced a smile, her attention swinging to Scott. He'd fixed his pants and spun around, palms turned up toward the ceiling.

"Sorry to meet you this way, Shauna. Did you want to have breakfast with us?"

"No. Not really hungry." I glanced at my mother and motioned at the skillet on the stove. "You're smoking." Mom nodded at me. Then nodded again. I gestured at the stove. "Smoking," I repeated.

She clambered for the spatula, maneuvering the bacon around the pan. "Are you sure?" she called out. "There's plenty. Eggs and toast, too."

"No, thanks. I have to pack and shower and stuff." My phone buzzed inside of my pocket. Relieved for the distraction, I pulled it out, expecting it to be Kitty. Instead I saw an e-mail notification from Jess McAllister. The letter. She was alive.

"I should take this," I said weakly.

Mom peered at me from under her brows, mortified. "Sure. We'll talk later."

"That works." I nodded at Scott and took off toward my room.

November 21, 1864

Darling Constance,

Week three in this place and all I can think of is your smiling
face. Your sweet kisses. Your laughter. How is my son? I fear he'll
be twice as grown upon my return. If only my business was not
so mired in stalemate. Solomon's Folly is not friendly to outsiders
seeking justice.

I have twice as many questions as answers.

The pastor of whom your sister wrote took a wife this last week.
Elizabeth Hawthorne. She is one of the girls who distressed Mary
if I recall my names correctly? It was not a long courtship and I have
reason to suspect—if only because of Miss Lucy Chamberlain's
rambling monologues—that Miss Hawthorne was ill-prepared for
matrimony. According to the baker's daughter, the nuptials came to
pass because Mr. Seymour Hawthorne insisted upon the match.

While Miss Chamberlain is not an intellectual, she is pleasant
and willing to speak to me. That is more than I can say for her
brethren.

(Also, she extends her congratulations on the baby and says she
grieves for our family. She has a sweet heart, I think.)

I find the pastor uncooperative. Pleasantries turned sour when
I explained why I'd come to The Folly. The constable is not much
help either, but at least my warrant got me into the church after
Starkcrowe turned me away. It was all rather suspicious; if there

was nothing to hide regarding Mary's disappearance, why would the pastor bar me from looking in her bedroom and the church basement? I asked this of the constable. He said the pastor was an old curmudgeon in a young man's clothes.

I wish I had more to report. The basement is every bit as dark as Mary described and infested with beetles. How a man of God could lock a young woman in such a cold, joyless place, I do not know. I had to bring three lanterns down with me. It was sparse: some stacked cartons and a mirror. The floor was disrupted, the bricks askew, which Starkcrowe explained was a result of water and structural damage. I searched it but found no trace of your sister. I do not know if I am relieved or disappointed.

Tomorrow I will explore the river and nearby swamp to find your mother's grave marker. The constable says she was buried inside the marshland. When I asked him why she was cast so far from her townsmen, he told me that it was Starkcrowe's will. The pastor wished to show his contempt for the spiritually weak. I feel terrible putting that to paper, but I know you appreciate honesty. Starkcrowe wanted to make an example of a suicide. Your mother is that example.

I will write again soon, hopefully with news of your sister. I still have hope that she will appear. Kiss our baby as I cannot, and think of me fondly.

Your husband,

Joseph

7

"You're sure you're ready to go?" Mom hovered as I swept through my room packing a duffel bag.

No.

"Yes," I said as brightly as I could. "It's a summer vacation! It'll be fine."

She stood in the doorway in a belted-off purple robe, her hair in a clip, her bare toes peeking out from below the hem. Every time I looked at her, she looked away. We were both embarrassed, but I had too much on my mind to sweat her personal life right now.

Like Mary coming at us from the coffee table. Like Joseph Simpson's letter to Constance. He said he had more questions than answers. I did, too, now that I knew Starkcrowe married Elizabeth Hawthorne. It was too convenient.

I wonder if they worked together to kill Mary.

"What are you planning to do while you're there?"
Mom asked.

"The usual. Bonfires, canoeing. Summer stuff."

That's how it used to be, Mom. Before I knew how scary The Folly was. How did I not notice it for all those summers?

I brushed past her to collect my toiletries from the bathroom.

She followed. "And Kitty will be with you the whole time?"

"Yes."

"Jess's parents are fine with this?" Mom stayed on my heels, closer than my shadow.

"Yes," I lied. "It's only a week, Mom. Enjoy yourself while I'm gone." Mom had her hand over her eyes, the tips of her ears blazing red. "Spend some time with your friend. He makes you happy?"

Mom peered at me through splayed fingers. "Yes, but not at your expense."

"My expense what? I made it through my junior year. I'm alive."

Barely. Barely alive. I came so close, Mom. You have no idea.

I zipped my bag closed.

"Are you and Jess still fighting?" she pressed.

"No."

Mom frowned as I hauled my stuff to the living room. I looked out the windows and down at the parking lot, waiting for Kitty. The glass was all new, the panes replaced after Mary grabbed Bronx and splattered him across the pavement.

Two surgeries to fix him so far, at least one more to go.

Mom hovered behind me. "I know I'm being clingy, but after everything that's happened..." She shuffled across the carpet and then her arms were around me, squeezing me in a fierce bear hug from behind. "I don't feel good about this. I'm not going to stop you, but I'll miss you. Text me every night?"

"I promise. Every night." I threaded my fingers with Mom's and leaned back against her, my head settling in the crook of her neck. "I will. I love you, Mom."

Kitty had on the blackest sunglasses I'd ever seen. She insisted she wasn't hungover, but by the green hue to her skin and the way her lips puckered whenever I sipped my coffee, I didn't believe her.

I rotated my phone to look at Jess's e-mail. I'd read it aloud to Kitty twice already, but she hadn't said much about it yet.

"Are you okay?" I asked.

"No. Mary grabbed me again. I have PTSD going on," she snapped.

I stopped examining the letter to blink at her profile. Crinkled brow, pinched lips, flared nostrils. She was angry. "Sorry. I didn't mean, like—I know that. Sorry."

Kitty's cheeks ballooned before she exhaled a steady stream of air. "I'm sorry. I feel like crap and I'm jumping at shadows. I can see the reflection of my eyes in my sunglasses and it's bugging me out."

"Been there, done that. It's no fun, but at least we're together," I said. "Do you want me to take the glasses?"

Kitty shook her head. "The sun is killing me. Headache."

No hangover, my ass.

The GPS beeped on Kitty's dashboard when we reached Cody's street. Kitty eased onto the curb across from a gray house with dingy white trim. Some improvements had been made since our last visit. The lawn had been mowed. The windows were clear, and all of the buckets Cody had used to transport pigs' blood were washed and stacked in a pile. Boards covered the hole in the front step, and the rusted-out Volkswagen was gone from the driveway.

The front door of the screened-in porch swung open. Cody emerged holding two Home Depot bags. She was still as pale as paper, her scars slick and pink and crisscrossing her face like a hash mark. Her dark hair had been cut short, in a boy cut, the sides and top sprinkled with gray. She wasn't old—in her thirties—but the years with Mary had aged her.

Cody stopped at the end of the driveway. "I'm ready. We should go to the church now, when the light is best," she said. Her good eye skimmed my face before jumping to Kitty. "You'll drive."

It wasn't a question.

Kitty stared. "Yeah, sure. Hi, nice to meet you."

"Hi. I'm Cody. You're Kitty." Cody opened the back of the car and threw in the bags.

"How are y—"

"Do you need directions to the church?" Cody interjected in her low, raspy voice. Kitty looked as if she didn't know if she should laugh or be offended. She had seen Cody only for a moment the last time we came out to The Folly, when Cody was a wreck. Cody was better groomed now, with new jeans, a new T-shirt, and a black patch on her face, but her demeanor was as unpolished as ever.

"Yes, please," Kitty replied. "I wasn't with everyone else the last time."

Cody climbed into the backseat and buckled up. She looked at the windows surrounding her and appeared to melt into her seat, keeping her body low and hunched like a squatting troll. "Get back on the highway, take the next exit. I have salt, lanterns, sledgehammers, shovels, and buckets for the water. Muck boots, too, so we won't have to deal with bat shit."

As Kitty guided us out of the quiet neighborhood, I handed my cell phone to Cody. She looked confused, but seeing the letter from Joseph, she started reading. Before long, she was shaking the phone. "How do I see the rest of it?"

I gawked at her for not knowing, but then I remembered she'd been inside of that house for seventeen years. Smartphones weren't a thing when she went into reclusion. She'd never e-mailed me or talked about a computer, because she'd been totally cut off from the outside world.

"Like this," I said, taking the phone and swiping my thumb across the screen. She scowled and took the phone back to read the rest of the letter.

"Interesting," she said. A passing car flashed in the window beside her and she yelped, pancaking herself to the seat. Her hands slapped at her pockets until she found a Ziploc bag full of salt. She opened it and palmed some granules, eyeballing the glass beside her and twitching.

I did a sweep of the car looking for phantom faces. "It's okay. She's not here. We're safe."

Cody hid her face into her shoulder, her eyes cast to the car floor.

Kitty got us back on the highway, or what counted as a highway in Solomon's Folly—one lane in each direction, thick trees to either side of the road, and beyond that, green stretches of undeveloped land. I could see cows in the distance, a smear of gray clouds threatening to cloak the summer sky, and a deep valley dotted with small lakes and brush.

Cody skimmed a hand down her face as if she could replace her scared face with a more assured one. "That's the swamp from the letter. The Hockomock swamp. You've heard of it?"

"I don't know much about it," I admitted. We sometimes drove past it on the way to the grocery store. At night, the fog roiled from its depths, oozing across the road and blanketing everything in eerie white. "I know it's big and wet and there was a war between the Native Americans and the settlers there a long time ago. King Philip's War."

Kitty nodded. "My dad hunts there. Or hunted, a long time ago. He says it's gross. Like, thick and hard to get around in."

Cody snorted. "He's right. It's also haunted, which should make looking for Hannah Worth's gravesite interesting. That's the plan, after the church."

The idea of a haunted swamp cramped my brain. It wasn't

that I didn't believe it so much as I didn't *want* to believe it. Ghosts drifting through the marshlands? Monsters howling at the moon? What was next—aliens and Sasquatch?

Cody caught my incredulous expression in the window and shook her head. "How is *that* ridiculous and Mary isn't?"

"It's not," I admitted. "I just don't know what to do about it."

"There's nothing you *can* do about it." Cody leaned forward to point at an approaching exit. Her nails were bitten down so far, they'd bled. Rust smeared the peachy fingertips. "We're sticking to the plan. Look for Mary's body, then find Hannah. I don't want to go into the swamp. No one wants to go into the swamp if they have half a brain, but we have to. I have to." Cody paused and looked out the window. "Moira was brave enough. My cousin. She had this idea that the swamp was why Mary rose. The curse on the land."

"What do you mean by cursed land?" Kitty asked, steering the car off the main drag.

"The swamp is bloody. Thirty-six hundred people died in or near it during King Philip's War, a lot of them Native Americans. People say the spirits of the dead linger there, which is why Solomon Hawthorne was able to settle there. No one else wanted it."

"Wait, the town's founding father was related to Elizabeth Hawthorne?"

Cody nodded. "The Hawthornes are all over The Folly, and most of them are assholes, like their ancestor. Solomon emigrated from England over three hundred years ago. First thing he did was seduce a girl already engaged to someone else. The Puritans kicked him out, so he struck out on his own. There wasn't as much unclaimed land left as he'd hoped, so he ended up building in the swamp. He's lucky he survived. The Hockomock is dangerous. Wild dogs—coyotes bred with domesticated dogs that rove in packs. Quicksand the locals call Black Betty. Undergrowth, overgrowth. Somehow, Solomon's Falls rose to prosperity anyway. The question is how?"

"You mean Solomon's Folly," I corrected.

"No, I mean Falls. It didn't become Folly until half of the town was butchered twenty years after it was founded. Hockomock means 'where spirits dwell' in Wampanoag. Considering how many people have died here over the years? Considering *Mary*? It's appropriate."

8

Daylight did little to strip the church of its ominous veneer. Gray stone blackened by time, mildew growing in the cracks and stretching toward a half-collapsed roof. The steeple was gone, but I could see the crumbling remnants of it at the back of the property. The side was collapsed as if it'd been punched in by a giant. A cracked bell lay on its side amidst the rubble, the loop at the top disintegrated to rust.

There were no front doors, so we could see directly into the church's empty belly. Broken stone littered the floor. A moldy bureau was pressed against the far wall, though how it got there I didn't know. We'd pushed it aside last visit. The door that kept Mary Worth locked in darkness was behind that bureau.

Someone's been here since our last visit.

Someone looking for Mary?

Jess?

The windows along the south side of the church had no glass.

A tree poked through the time-ravaged frames, new buds clinging to the branch tips. Twin archways opened up into side rooms that we hadn't explored.

Cody boldly entered the church. Kitty eased along behind her, her hand skimming the walls. Her head swiveled like a cat exploring a house for the first time. No matter how hard I willed myself to follow them, I couldn't make my feet go.

Mary lunging up from the cold water. My body smashing against the stone steps. Mary's fist, slimy and fishlike, clenching in my hair, pulling my head back. My screams echoing through the basement as Mary tried to drown me in a pool of water. Blackness in my vision. Water in my nose. Water in my ears, muffling my friends' terrified shrieks.

"Shauna?"

Kitty turned back and offered her hand. I stared at it, swallowing hard. Five feet felt like five hundred, but when I couldn't go to Kitty, Kitty came to me, pressing our palms together, tugging me through the doorway.

Side by side, we walked into the church. It had been wet last time, the stones slick and covered with bat refuse. Now it was drier, everything baked to caked mud from the sun.

Cody tromped from the left room to the right. She never looked at us, her Home Depot bags clunking at her sides. "Nothing except broken lumber in the last one. Stones in this one from the collapsed side wall. Let's head down."

We pushed the bureau aside until there was only the old wooden door with its rusted lock between us and the basement. Cody dropped one of the bags so she could fiddle with it. I heard the click, the grinding of the gears of the lock, and the squeal as she forced it ajar. I ducked, expecting a bat stampede. The air was still.

Cody donned our single pair of boots. She pulled out a series of lanterns and eased down the narrow stairs, placing a light every three steps. I stayed up top, my arms crossed over my chest. Kitty hesitated, but then followed Cody, handing her whatever she needed from the orange bags.

I glanced at the ceiling, expecting to see the beady, onyx eyes of a thousand mini-predators, but it was flat stone and mildew. I'd read that spirits perfumed their haunts with a certain type of energy. Happier spirits could make the air warm and smell like flowers. But we'd woken Mary down here. Her rising poisoned the atmosphere, too much for even the bats. And, it seemed, too much for the beetles; there'd been a small-scale epidemic of pincher bugs the last time, but I hadn't spotted a single one so far.

"Buckets," Cody said. "We need to drain the puddle so we can look at the floor." What followed was an assembly line, with Cody scooping buckets of water, handing them to Kitty, and Kitty handing them to me. I splashed them over the stone floor of the church, watching the water settle into the cracks between the stones.

It took a while to get anywhere. I kept thinking Cody would call up to tell us she could see stone, but then Kitty would hand me more water. After what felt like forever, Cody crouched to examine the floor.

"Gloves. I think we're finished."

I pawed through the supply bag to hand down gloves and a three-pronged hoe. Cody started to dig, shoving broken bricks, pebbles, and grit aside as she prodded the dip in the floor.

I moved farther into the basement, down three more steps so I could watch. Without the water, the divot became more defined. Seven feet long, three feet wide, and a foot deep at its lowest point. Cody squatted at the corner of it, still working on removing the topmost pieces of stone. The crusty layer slowly peeled away, revealing thick, sodden mud.

"Hand me the sifter," she said.

It was the last thing in the bag. Cody loaded it with mud and shook it out, letting big droplets of gook splash down on the stones outside the crater. She panned, like a miner looking for gold, but uncovered nothing. She took the hoe to the ground, clawing through the earth with so much ferocity, she spattered her face and Kitty's jeans.

Kitty and I couldn't do much to help, so we waited in silence.

Cody abandoned the hoe to work with her hands, her fingers raking through the muck. "I see something. Bring another lantern down."

The mud squished and burped as Cody dug through it. Brown-black smears stained her from fingertips to wrists, the sludge climbing toward the opening of the gloves near her elbows. She scooped handful after handful, throwing the mess at the stacked crates against the opposite wall from the stairs.

Cody continued working. I leaned forward to watch, but then I heard a sound from behind. My head jerked around, eyes narrowing as I peered out up the stairs.

Tap, screeeee.

Tap, screeeee.

Tap, screeeee.

It was rhythmic and getting louder.

Getting *closer.*

"Guys. Do you hear that?"

Mary heaving herself from the basement's depths, limbs bent at odd angles as she skittered onto the church floor. The strange animal chitters as she gave chase. The rat-a-tat of palms and feet striking stone as she rushed us, moving more like a spider than a human.

Kitty lifted her head. "Hear what?"

"Don't move the lantern," Cody snapped. "I see gold!"

"Sorry!" Kitty leaned forward to cast better light on Cody's dig.

Tap, screeeee.

Tap, screeeee.

I reached into my pocket for the salt, my thumb popping the top off the mint container, just as Cody let out a whoop behind me.

"Look at this!"

I wanted to, but a figure had appeared at the top of the stairs. Tall, slender. The way the sun hit, I couldn't make out features, but by its approach—her approach—I knew it wasn't Mary. Unless Mary had gotten herself a cane, a purple track suit, and a shock of short, silver hair.

"This is private property," the stranger said in greeting. "Though I'm guessing you're Jessica's friends."

The woman moved into proper light and I got my first good look at her. Deep lines around her eyes and mouth, putting her well into her seventies. Blue eyes, a narrow nose, a wide mouth, and only one ear. There was a hole on the left side of her head instead of cartilage.

"Aunt Dell?" I'd seen pictures of the woman in her younger years, but I hadn't noticed her disfigurement before.

"You must be Shauna. Yes, hello. I'm Jessica's aunt." She shuffled my way, one foot stepping like normal, the other lagging behind. The noise I'd heard was her walking stick striking rock followed by the drag of her leg.

She stopped at the top of the stairs, peering down at me and the other girls. Pinched between two of Cody's fingers, roundish and dull gold beneath smears of thick mud, was what appeared to be a locket embossed with an ornate *W*.

9

I looked from the locket to the others surrounding me. Everyone had a claim to the treasure—Cody and me because of our hauntings, Kitty because of Anna, Dell because of her blood tie to Mary—but Cody wasn't relinquishing it. I desperately wanted to snatch it from her fist to examine it, but I was pretty sure Cody would have fought me. Considering the trowel in her other hand, she would have won.

She pulled the locket to her chest to stake her claim. Kitty and I wouldn't challenge her, but Dell was another story. We were on her private property trespassing for a second time in so many months. If any of us had the right to demand Cody hand it over, it was the woman who held the deed to the land.

Instead, Dell's hands clasped the pommel of her walking stick. "If you want answers about Mary Worth, I can help," she said. "Will you join me for tea?"

Cody looked from the dip in the floor to the necklace. "We're not done here. And we were going to try to find Hannah Worth's grave today, too. We need daylight for that."

Dell nodded. "I can help with that, too. Please, come with me."

Cody twitched and muttered to herself, distressed. I understood; Jess couldn't be trusted. Why should we assume her aunt was any better?

"Fine. If it's quick," she relented.

Dell smirked and tapped her cane on the floor. "It's as quick as you choose to make it, Miss Jackson." Aunt Dell knew who we all were, it seemed.

Cody pocketed the necklace and gathered her digging tools. Kitty snuffed the lanterns. Dell hobbled outside and stood off to the side to stay out of everyone's way. I went with her, relieved to be out of that basement. Too many bad memories lived in the shadows. The trapped, musty smell turned my stomach.

Cody and Kitty followed, sludgy mud trailing behind Cody's boots. The Home Depot bags clunked at Kitty's sides.

Dell motioned at the river with her cane. "Wash the boots so they won't soil the interior of your car."

I waited for Cody to take off the boots and brought them to the riverbank, careful not to get too close to the steeper mud. Within seconds of plunging my hands into the water, my fingertips went numb, the joints in my knuckles aching. It was freezing. I sloughed off the mud as fast as I could, gritting my teeth against the stabbing cold.

Poor Hannah Worth, drowning in such a frigid place.

A hard rush of water nearly tore the boots from my grasp.

I scrambled away from the river, the boots clasped to my chest and raining cold water down the front of my T-shirt.

"I can drive you home if you'd like," I heard Kitty say to Dell. I threw the boots in the back of the SUV alongside the Home Depot bags.

"It's a short walk. Your car is safe here." Cody, Kitty, and I shared a look before falling into step behind Jess's aunt, rats to her Pied Piper.

We walked parallel to the river until we came to a small bridge. Three arced coves let water run through, the walls constructed of stone and packed cement. Posts at either end allowed people and bikes to pass over, but no cars. A faded orange sign read UNDER CONSTRUCTION, but it was evident no one had serviced the bridge in a long time.

Dell paused halfway across, pointing up the river at an exaggerated bend. "The constable's men claimed they found Hannah's body in that elbow. The report mentions the bridge being not far south from the corpse and tucked inside a bend. It's the only one on this stretch of the river."

"Did she really kill herself?" Kitty asked.

"No." Dell's curt reply didn't invite further questions.

We walked. Dell's house was an old New England farmhouse with white shingles and black shutters. The fence had seen better days; there were as many planks on the ground as there were connecting the posts. A shed that looked suspiciously like an outhouse occupied the left side of the lawn. A barn converted into a garage took up the right. The tree in the front yard was spindly and dry, its bark gone black, the branches barren.

The inside was cluttered with furniture. It was also dusty; silver picture frames were dulled to gray from a thick layer of grime. Black soot smudged the walls above where Dell burned candles, and the corners of the room dripped with lacy cobwebs. It still managed to be homey, though—overstuffed mauve couches in front of the fireplace, crocheted blankets folded in neat stacks, and shelves upon shelves of knickknacks.

Dell motioned us toward the living room, her cane waving at a fat orange cat with long hair. "Make yourselves at home while I steep the tea. Don't mind Horace. He runs the place."

Kitty ran her hand along Horace's spine while I wandered toward Dell's curio cabinet. Family photos sat propped along the back, surrounded by ceramic cats and angel statues.

"It smells like dead flowers in here," Cody griped.

"Potpourri," Kitty said. "On the coffee table."

Cody grunted and settled into the chair by the fireplace, her head tilting back to examine the portraits on the walls. The necklace chain looped around her knuckles, the links caked with dirt. Her thumb swept over the dented gold case, a ragged thumbnail prying dried mud from the creases.

Jess's smiling face loomed from the mantel. Her junior year yearbook photo. She looked fresh-faced and pretty, with her flawless complexion and long, flowing hair. Not at all like the scarred, terrified girl I'd seen at a party the night before.

"Notice there's no glass," Cody said in a low voice.

She gestured at a painting of a cottage in a field of pastel flowers. "No glass in any of the frames." My eyes jumped from picture to picture. No glass protection.

"That's because Mary appears in reflections, of course," Aunt Dell said, pushing a wheeled cart into the room. There was a china set with a steaming pot, delicate ivory teacups, and a platter of jammy cookies.

Kitty glanced up from the cat. "You worry about Mary?"

"Every Worth girl does. We'd be crazy not to. Help yourselves." Dell poured herself a cup of tea. The process of adding a sugar cube, a dash of milk, and two cookies to her saucer looked like a long-practiced routine. She settled into one of the chairs, peering at all of us over the rim of her teacup. Her eyes were cornflower blue. Jess's shade. It was disconcerting.

"But your niece was the one who summoned her. If you all know about her, why would she do that?" Cody demanded. She opened her hand and the necklace dropped, dangling from her fingertips. Dell leaned forward in her chair to take a closer look.

"Did you want to wash that? The bathroom is down the hall to the right," Dell said, pointing behind her.

Cody shook her head. "I will, but first, tell me—us—why the Worth girls fear Mary."

Dell returned her teacup to the saucer, the china clinking. She lifted a cookie and examined it, as if it had somehow become more interesting than her guests. "Let me ask you and Shauna something." Dell glanced up. The lines on her face were so deeply etched into her skin, she looked like a leather purse. "When Mary appeared, did you hurt her? Ever do her any harm?"

Cody answered before I could. "I slashed her arms with knives. I went through her hand with a butcher's knife once.

I struck her with mallets and hammers, but she always came back."

Dell nodded but continued to peer at me. I wanted to answer, but the words wouldn't come. My tongue was a slab of granite in my mouth.

Kitty's basement, Mary holding Jess hostage. Screams. So many screams—Kitty and Jess both more terrified than I had ever seen. Kitty throwing salt, the room littered with broken bottles and shattered furniture. Jamming the broken stool leg into Mary's face. Connecting with the eye socket. Mary's flesh yielding, like moldy pudding stuck to bone.

"Shauna took out her eye," Kitty said. "With a stick."

Dell nibbled the cookie, her head tilted in thought. Her hair shifted, letting me see the ear hole without the attached ear. I tried not to stare, but it looked so strange, like her head was off-balance. Was she was born that way or . . .

"She took it," Dell said.

Heat flooded my cheeks. I could hear my mother's voice in my head, chastising me for being rude. "Sorry. I—yeah. Sorry. I didn't mean to . . . you know."

"Quite fine." Dell lifted the hair and turned her head so all of us could see, though Kitty couldn't bring herself to look. "Mary took it thirty years ago." Dell let the hair drop, using the half-eaten cookie to gesture around the room. "She needs to fix herself, you see. It's not really magic. It's more"—Dell paused as she searched for the proper word—"harvesting."

"Harvesting," Cody repeated. "Like . . ."

"Oh, God." I wished I didn't understand what Dell meant,

but I did. The previous night, Mary's arm was rotten and gray except for one tiny sliver of pink. A finger. A finger that looked at odds with the rest of the steel-blue parts.

A *new* finger.

"Anna," I whispered.

Kitty's sobs filled the room. She puffed on her inhaler before collapsing into a pile of misery beside me. I stroked her hair and waited out the storm.

Cody hunched in her chair, her dirty fingertips stroking the satin of her eye patch every few minutes. She'd lost the eye to Mary some years back. She'd never mentioned Mary recycling parts because I was pretty sure it never occurred to her. To find out she'd become part of the very monster she loathed...I couldn't imagine it. Mary had cut me, but she'd never taken a part of me and made it her own.

"I saw a pink finger last night," I said quietly. "It looked out of place on her hand. Are you saying that belonged to Anna?" I reached over to squeeze Kitty's knee in reassurance.

"No. Your friend died a month ago," Dell said, "If it's pink, it's fresh. The replacement parts deteriorate like any dead flesh. Mary must have bled someone new. Not Jessica. I spoke with her this morning. But if there's a new part and Jessica's tag remains—" Dell cleared her throat. "Someone got pulled into the mirror, God help them."

I ran my hands down my face.

Another missing girl on the five o'clock news.

"So what does that mean?!" Cody rasped. Her body twitched every few seconds, the fury too much for her to contain. "You said the Worth girls fear Mary. When are you going to explain?"

Dell's look wasn't friendly. "I was getting there, Miss Jackson. Don't rush me."

Cody clutched the armrests of her chair as if they were necks she wanted to strangle. The necklace dangled from her fingers to sweep the floor. Dell's cat readied to pounce, but Cody jerked it back and pocketed it before Horace could attack.

"I've waited a long time for some answers," Cody spat.

Dell retrieved her tea, sipping daintily with her pinky raised. She took her time replacing the cup onto the saucer, her expression guarded. "Mary haunts those she bleeds but can't pull into the mirror. She obsesses, tracking them by the scent of their blood. It calls to her and sustains her. But sometimes no one summons for a long time and her body deteriorates. She's ghostly, yes, but she's something more, too. Ghoulish. She preserves her physical form by recycling parts from her victims."

Dell wasn't looking directly at any of us. "If Mary doesn't get fresh stock, she finds what she knows, and what she knows is her own blood. Worth girl blood. Jessica summoned the ghost so she didn't succumb the way my aunt did in the sixties. The way I almost did a decade later."

I stared at the old woman trying so damned hard to not look any of us in the eye.

"Your aunt died to Mary?"

For a fleeting moment, Dell looked sad. "Yes. Like so many others, which is why Jess summoned Mary. She wants to end the family curse. Our family has been dying to Mary Worth for almost as long as she's been dead."

It took a half hour, an Ativan, and a call to Bronx to relax Kitty. She sprawled across Dell's couch, body cocooned in an afghan, Horace the cat perched on her hip. Her eyes were half-mast and swollen, her nose Rudolph red. I could hear the rush of water as Cody rinsed the necklace in the bathroom. Dell swept through the house, collecting manila envelopes, photo albums, and notebooks. She dropped them on the coffee table beside the serving cart.

"Why now?" Kitty asked from the couch, sounding sleepy and content. It was a chemically induced calm, but I was envious of it all the same. "Did Jess just find out about Mary?"

Dell settled into her seat, her joints sounding like dry sticks snapping. "I'm old and tired. Without me, Mary falls to Jessica. I had to warn her. She took it better than I expected. She wanted to make Mary move on to the afterlife, so she'd stop hurting people. I believe that's her ultimate goal, but she's taken grave risks in her pursuit."

"Anna was that risk," I said quietly. "She tried to sacrifice Kitty, too."

Dell swept the back of her hand across her brow like the revelation made her faint. "She was scared and wrong. I'm sorry. I don't really know what I can say."

Silently, Kitty reached for the tea cart to fix herself a cup, but I did it for her. Kitty had been fierce since Anna's death, but there was a frailty there, too. Maybe I was like Aunt Dell— fruitlessly apologizing with tea and shoulder rubs because I hadn't had the foresight to stop Jess when I had the chance.

Dell looked at the pile of envelopes, pictures, and binders. "I don't know where to start." She bent forward, grunting as she produced a black-and-white photograph of a woman dressed in an old-fashioned nurse's uniform. By the curled style of her blond hair and the way she'd painted her lips dark, I guessed the picture was from the thirties or forties. "This is my aunt, Prudence. She was the Worth afflicted before me, and the one who accidentally unleashed Mary on the world at large in the sixties. Instead of waiting for Mary to find her in the glass, Pru gathered her friends and called for her. She was impatient, like Jessica. And me, I suppose. Impatience is a Worth woman failing. Anyway, it didn't work the first time, but the second. Well. Mary claimed her first free-world victim—Pru's friend Gerdy."

"What changed between the first and second summoning?" I asked.

"Pru figured out that imploring Mary to come didn't work, so they mocked her, like the girls had mocked her in the basement years ago. That got Mary's attention."

Dell punctuated it by producing a copy of a letter I'd already seen. It was Mary's last, the one she wrote to her sister explaining how Elizabeth Hawthorne and her friends had teased her through the basement door.

Dell's fingertip grazed the last lines.

Bloody Mary. Bloody Mary. Bloody Mary.

"We're taunting her like her bullies taunted her," I whispered. It was awful in a way, almost like we deserved—

No. No one deserved Mary. But there was an undeniable cruelty to the summons.

The water stopped running and Cody reemerged, the clean necklace lying flat across her palm. "Look what I have," she said, wagging it back and forth. The locket gleamed despite its long years buried beneath the church floor. "The picture inside is completely rotted, but the gold is intact."

Dell stirred behind me. She removed photographs from the albums, some of the pictures so old they were printed on wooden plates instead of film paper. She gestured at the curio behind her.

"Second drawer, Shauna. Get my magnifying glass? We're on a necklace hunt. I don't want to assume this is Mary's locket without some evidence."

I quickly found the magnifying glass in a nest of colored yarn and knitting needles.

"Thank you."

"You have so much stuff," Kitty said in wonderment. "Family stuff. We have some old pictures, but this is something else."

Dell squinted at her first picture, using the glass to examine the finer details. "I'm a steward of sorts, Miss Kitty. I was the one saddled with Mary, like my aunt was before me. None of my relatives have been able to put Mary to rest, so we care for these relics in hopes that the next generation will figure out what we didn't. Constance lived her whole life trying to help her sister but was never successful. The only thing she could do was preserve Mary's things in hopes that something would eventually change."

Dell tilted her picture this way and that before handing it to me. It was an image of a younger Mary, before all the tragedy, wearing a dark dress and holding the Bible to her chest. Her hair hung long and straight to her waist. Beside her was an older girl with blond hair pinned to her head. Constance.

The sisters looked so happy with their faint smiles and bright eyes.

Cody sidled up to the coffee table, sitting cross-legged on the floor as she sorted the pile, not only the photographs but notes and letters, too. Kitty scooted over on the couch to help, all of us falling into library silence, passing noteworthy discoveries back and forth.

It didn't take long to go through the photographs. I held up a picture of Mary standing with a group of girls her age, perhaps fourteen or fifteen. I recognized Elizabeth Hawthorne immediately. She brooded at the camera, whereas Mary was, once again, smiling. The girls were bundled in their winter coats; snow frosted the ground and shrubs to either side of them. The collar of Mary's dark overcoat was parted enough that I could see a hint of something at her neck. I'd seen her wear a cross before, but that necklace wasn't the right shape.

"Aunt Dell, look at this?" I offered Dell the picture so she could examine it with her magnifying glass. As I stretched across the table, Cody snatched for me, her cold fingers almost cutting off the circulation in my wrist. I yelped, more surprised than hurt, but Cody waved a photocopy of a letter under my nose.

"Read this," she demanded. "Now."

Joseph,

I'm writing to tell you my sister is dead. She did not run away as some have claimed. I know this as I know the sun will rise. There's been no news from the local authorities. No one from The Folly has contacted me. No, I've seen Mary's ghost with my own eyes. She's dead and gone and haunting me in any surface that reflects light. I implore you to read on before assuming that I'm mad.

I was rocking Edward to sleep when I first saw the face. It looked like someone standing outside of the house windows looking in. It was pale faced and small framed, and at first I thought it was a child.

I have done as you instructed—the doors are locked in your absence, and the new groundskeeper, Mr. Hallingsway, is always beside me. After seeing the stranger, I asked him to look around the property. He took the dogs on a tour but found nothing. What was curious, however, was that the dogs refused to enter the house. They stopped in the doorway, snarling. Mr. Hallingsway walked the halls to ensure no one had forced their way in, but the house was empty.

Two days passed before I saw the face again. I had just bathed. Edward was with your mother and sisters at a picnic in the park. I dressed myself in our room. As I passed the vanity mirror, I saw the face peering out at me. This time, there was a hand pressed against the glass as if pushing out from the inside. Spectral mists cloaked much of my vision. I screamed for the staff, but the figure vanished as soon as Miss Winchester dashed into the room.

This happened a half-dozen times over the next few days. Each time the stranger hid from me. The only constant was the hand upon the glass. I thought it a ghostly trick, but then I noticed that the pads of the fingers were flattened. It really did appear that someone was trapped on the other side.

Details became easier to discern thereafter. The body deteriorated between visits, going from peach and pink to shades of gray, green, and blue. The veins turned black, and the flesh cracked open. There were insects, too! Black water beetles that crawled all over. It made my skin itch to see them.

I didn't believe at first that it was my sister. Perhaps that was stupid, but hope is all I've had to cling to since your departure. Last evening I was forced to reconcile what in my heart I think I already knew. I rocked Edward in his nursery, humming a song my mother used to sing to Mary when she was a baby. Edward slept upon my breast. I stood to put him in his cradle when I spied the figure in the window, peering in. The fingers pressed to the glass, streaking down the pane as if pawing. Again there was a strange, swirling mist blocking my view.

Every previous visit, I'd run from the room, fearful of the phantom. Last night, I held Edward to my heart and waited. This must have been what the ghost wanted, as the fog cleared and I beheld my sister's face. I wept. It's bloated in some parts, saggy in others, and her eyes are sunken and black. She wears a white dress that drips with water. Her hair is tangled and matted with leaves and mud.

Part of me wanted to flee, but I forced myself to stay. Mary lingered, too, her hand stroking the windowpane. Tears streamed down my cheeks as I approached. She didn't speak. I lifted my hand to hers, expecting only cold glass between us, but I swear on our son that she reached through the window and clasped my hand, her fingers locking with mine. Dead flesh, Joseph.

She released me and faded into the glass. I have not yet seen her today.

You'll want to come home upon receiving this letter, I know, but I beg you to continue your business in Boston. The trial is so close to conclusion. Perhaps when you are done we can revisit Solomon's Folly and search for Mary and Mother's remains together? The baby is old enough to stay with your mother awhile I would think. It would soothe my soul to know I put this uneasy spirit to rest.

Thinking of you always and forever, beloved.

Constance

10

"He never found Mary that first visit," I said more to myself than anyone else. "That's so sad." Kitty took the letter, skimming the lines. She tapped the upper corner of the page, thinking. "Mary didn't appear for six months after her death? Why? And why can she see Mary if she's a mother?"

"I don't know for certain," Dell said. "And Mary is willing to make exceptions for Worth girls regarding the mothers. The blood calls to her too strongly."

She handed me the picture and the magnifying glass so I could look. Only half of the necklace was visible beneath Mary's collar, but it was the same ovular shape, the same relative size with an initial. A match. Cody quickly snatched the photo from my fingers.

Dell continued. "The necklace means one of two things. One, that it fell off while Mary was down in that basement and it somehow got covered lat—"

"No," Cody interrupted. "I had to dig. It was a foot and a half down, maybe two. If it'd been kicked under the rocks, it wouldn't have been so deep."

Dell cast me a look, an eyebrow raised as if I was supposed to explain Cody's demeanor, but I wasn't telling a woman twice my age to be polite. It wasn't my place.

Dell glanced down at the jacket of her tracksuit, plucking lint from the velvet. "Well, there you have it. There is no option two according to Miss Jackson."

"That letter is unbelievably creepy." Kitty reached out to haul Horace up onto her chest, her fingers trailing along his spine. "At least Mary didn't attack Constance."

"No. Mary still had some sense of herself then. It worsened over time." Dell's eyes strayed to the wall clock, an old-fashioned Felix the Cat affair with ticktock eyes. "It's two. If we want to look for Hannah, we should leave now. She's along the outer edges of the swamp, toward Samoset's Perch, I believe. That's not a place you go at night. I hope you all have sneakers. Shauna, Kitty—take the pictures with you if you want. You can look at them tonight as long as you promise to return them in the same condition you received them."

That seemed like a good idea. I doubted there was much we'd find that Dell hadn't already, but my experience with Jess taught me it was better to do the research myself, not count on others being forthright with information.

"Wait, you *believe*?" Cody said. "How are we going to find Hannah if you don't know for sure? We should know where we're going. The Hockomock is a hellhole." Cody licked her lips and twitched. Her hand smacked down at her arm as if she was smushing a bug no one else could see.

"I have a good idea of where we're going. I've been out looking before. Joseph left some notes that were helpful."

Cody and Dell shared a long, intense stare that made my skin itch. I organized the pictures and papers, half so Dell didn't come home to a mess, half so I didn't have to get involved in the escalating tension. Kitty joined my tidying efforts without a word.

Cody's uncomfortable. She doesn't trust Dell. She knows something I don't.

I'd just gotten the last note tucked into the accordion folder when I heard tires on gravel followed by a car door slamming. Kitty tensed beside me. Cody went to the front windows and thrust the curtain aside to get a clear look at the driveway.

"Hell," she spat.

I glanced up. "What?"

"Jess."

Feet pounding, the wail of oil-starved door hinges, and deep, heavy breaths. Kitty reached for me, digging her fingernails into my forearm. Her eyes bulged from their sockets. *We need to get out of here*, her expression said. I'd just offered my hand in a show of solidarity when Jess careened into sight.

The blood was everywhere.

It oozed from the side of her head, matting her hair to her scalp and dribbling in rivers down her cheeks and neck. The ragged tatters of her shirt hugged her body, the fabric so saturated it was stiff in parts. I could see gouges in her sides, the slashes parallel like a claw rake. Her eye was puffy and black, her nostril crusted with rust. Purple bruises covered her face, her chest, her arms. She smelled like blood—that coppery tang that reminded me of pennies or steak that had been on the counter too long.

Fear ricocheted through my body. My legs were so weak, it felt like my bones had melted. This hadn't been a minor scuffle. Mary had *pulverized* Jess.

"Oh, Jessica. Oh, no." Dell's voice was whisper soft. Her hand flew up to cover her mouth and she stared, as shaken by the sight of Jess as the rest of us.

Jess didn't answer. I wasn't sure she could. Dell maneuvered her into a chair, tutting and fussing the entire time. Her hands slid through the gore, but she didn't hesitate. She touched Jess on the head, on the neck, examining her wounds with bloody fingers. "Did you drive here from Bridgewater? How? Good God. Someone get me a towel. Talk to me, Jessica."

Kitty and I were too stunned to move. Cody shook it off first; she dashed for the bathroom to get towels and hot water. Kitty broke away from me to go to Jess's side. She used Kleenex to dash at Jess's bloody cheek. Even after everything Jess put us through, Kitty was quick to help.

"She's out," Jess mumbled. Her fingers lifted to her mouth, prodding at her fat, rubbery lips. They looked twice as big as usual. "Mary's out. She came for me and chased me and she's out now."

"Shhh. Sit still while I look at you," Dell said. Cody rushed in with the towels, and Dell began cleaning the head injury, meticulously moving Jess's hair around so she could better see the extent of the damage.

"No, you don't understand. She's not trapped in the glass anymore. She's out. I broke the mirror she passed through. When she didn't disappear, I locked her in the basement and drove here. She's out. I freed her by accident."

I didn't understand. I looked to Dell, hoping for insight, but she'd gone still, the towel poised above Jess's scalp. "What do you mean you broke the glass?" Dell asked, voice so soft I almost didn't hear it.

Jess whimpered. "She came from the sliding porch doors. I'd just gotten home . . ." Jess stammered, fumbling her words before letting loose with a sob. Jess wasn't a crier; when she broke her ankle during junior high softball sliding into home plate, she'd never shed a tear, but this was different. She slumped in her seat, blood gushing onto the mauve upholstery.

"She chased me, and I managed to get her into the basement. I locked it. I thought if I broke the doors she came from she'd go away forever. I hardened the glass with salt and then smashed it with a chair. But she was still there. She didn't find another mirror. She stayed. So I ran. She must have broken the door down. I watched her chase my car in the rearview mirror. She was so fast. I didn't lose her until the highway. She chased me down the street!"

I could picture it all too clearly. I'd seen Mary move. She'd scuttled up those church steps far too fast. She'd kept time with me in the hall of the school without difficulty. The thought of her given free rein to run—an unstoppable force—made my muscles tense, my feet itch to escape. All I wanted was to flee forever.

Cody dabbed at Jess's wounds with surprising gentleness. Dell limped toward the phone on the wall. "Did you warn your parents, Jessica?"

Jess nodded, or tried to. It was more a head jerk. "Dad knows. He's taking Mom and Todd away. He told me to come here."

"Wait, what?" Jess had been adamant that none of us tell our parents, but hers had known all along? *How was that fair?* I scowled at her.

"My dad knows but not my mom," Jess explained between snivels. "She'd never understand."

"All Worths know their monster, Shauna. Including my nephew." Dell picked up the phone, her hands trembling around the receiver. Dell had lived with the threat of Bloody Mary all her life. What about this had her so worried?

"Wait," said Kitty. "If the glass is gone, how's Mary going to climb back in? Can't she go back through another mirror?"

Dell's fingers flew over the buttons on the phone. "I don't know. The only way to know for sure is to summon her."

"No." Kitty's answer was emphatic.

Dell's call had connected, and now I could see her pacing—or limping—back and forth, her hand waving excitedly as she spoke. Every few words her volume raised enough that I caught a snippet. I heard Elsa once, which piqued my interest, but Dell immediately grew quiet again, keeping the conversation private.

"If it's the only way to see if Mary's back in the mirror, we have to," Cody said. "We'll salt the hell out of it. We know what to do."

"No, no, and no!" Kitty stomped her foot so hard, the tchotchkes in the curio clattered and Horace sprinted for the steps and disappeared upstairs. "It's bad enough we have Mary's current victim here, but Jess is also a Worth girl. It's different this time. Mary's twice as obsessed. I signed up for putting her away, not for getting killed."

"You've been through enough, Kitty," Jess said softly. "The rest of you don't have to do it, either. This is pointless."

Jess believed her death was a foregone conclusion. I'd told myself I wouldn't care if Mary ate Jess alive, piece by piece, for what she'd done to Anna. The truth was more complicated. I wanted to fight for the friend I had for all those years. Not the person she turned out to be, but the person I thought I knew.

"Jess, come on. We'll find something," I said. "Your aunt is in the kitchen right now trying to figure it out. She knows a lot about Mary."

Jess's paper-thin smile was as convincing as my tone. "Sure. Thanks."

Finished with her call, Aunt Dell hobbled back to Jess's chair, shooing Cody away so she could inspect the injuries. Her finger wove into Jess's clumpy hair, parting it so she could look at the gash below. "It's not deep. No stitches. A compress and a bandage. Do you think you're well enough to summon Mary, Jessica?"

Jess shrugged. Dell grabbed her under the arm, hauling her to her feet. "We're not giving up. I called in a favor to Jonas Hawthorne about the Samburg girl. Something like this happened when Elsa was haunted. The girls ran from Mary when she pulled herself through the glass. They managed to get outside of the house. Mary chased them for a while. Obviously she went back in later, but I don't know the circumstances behind it. I'd like to ask Elsa directly if possible."

"Like, of the Hawthorne Hawthornes?" Cody asked. "Why would he know anything about Elsa Samburg?"

"There are a lot of Hawthornes in Solomon's Folly, Miss Jackson. Solomon dealt with the devil to ensure his family line would prosper. Jonas is the sheriff. His wife shares a room with Elsa Samburg in the assisted living facility. They're friends of a fashion. Maybe he can get us in. His blood owes mine, and I'm not afraid to remind him of that."

Dell guided Jess toward the bathroom, looping her arm around Jess's waist. I wasn't ready to follow them, not when they pushed open the door, not when Dell went to retrieve the summoning supplies. I didn't want to summon Mary any more than Kitty did.

"When you say he dealt with the devil, what do you mean?" Cody called out after Dell.

Dell emerged from the kitchen with a big box of salt clutched to her chest. She glanced from Cody to me and scowled. "Some things you're better off not knowing."

11

I couldn't bring myself to follow.

I stayed with Kitty in the living room, waiting for the others to finish the preparations. They'd done everything possible to ward the space: salted the mirror, taken down all the picture frames, and covered the chrome bath fixtures with masking tape.

It didn't feel adequate, but then, what would?

"Having Jess in front of the mirror should be enough," Kitty insisted from the couch. "It's bait. Why can't we try that?"

My eyes stayed pinned on the bathroom doorway. "I tried it weeks ago when Mom was there. Mary stayed away. It's not reliable. The summoning is."

It wasn't what Kitty wanted to hear. "Can they do it with three? Why does it have to be four?"

"Mary had four tormenters. I'm guessing it has to be four

to re-create what happened in the basement." I wanted to help the women in the other room, but I wouldn't risk another Mary tag. There was shame to the admission; if Cody could do it after seventeen years of haunting, I should have had the courage to follow in her footsteps.

But I didn't.

Mary's unleashed.

She was bad enough inside the glass. But free to wreak 150 years' worth of wrathful havoc? Catastrophe. We still didn't know what fueled her—blind rage at her unjust death or something else entirely. We didn't know how to stop her. All we had were puzzle pieces that barely fit together. A necklace buried in the church. A cast of villains so long dead, information about them was scarce. A family bloodline plagued by the ghost. The mystery of Hannah Worth's grave.

"She'll butcher people," I murmured. "Mary will pull them apart like Barbie dolls." She'd have a mountain of victims. A junkyard of patch parts. The old ghost would be a new ghost—a Frankenstein-esque abomination no one knew how to kill.

The bathroom door swung open. Out walked Cody, her frustration written on her face.

"Will one of you help with this? If not, we have to find someone."

I'd said I couldn't do it, but I have to. Kitty will. She'll go. No more Kitty on the chopping block. No more sacrificial friends.

"I'll go." I blurted it out before my wavering courage escaped me. I followed Cody into the bathroom, my legs feeling leaden.

Kitty called after me, but I ignored her and closed the door, blocking her from the imminent danger.

The click of the lock sent my heart racing. I braced myself against the side of the sink, my fear so potent my head spun.

Focus. You can do this. Breathe in. Breathe out.

The bathroom wasn't much to look at. Flat aqua paint above marbled white tiles. A linoleum floor lifting at the corners. Across from the door was a footed bathtub with no shower. The right wall had an alcove for towels and a hamper. Opposite that was a tiny hand mirror over the sink, disproportionate for the space but understandable if you lived with Mary. The toilet was tucked between the sink and bathtub. A pink pillar candle flickered beside the faucet, wax dripping down the sides to pool on the countertop.

Cody shoved me into the corner, between the wall and the end of the tub. She was to my left with the door at her back. Dell was to my right next to the toilet. Jess was front and center with the mirror. She looked exhausted. Dell had bandaged her head so it would stop bleeding, but the rest of her was as battered as before, her clothes torn almost beyond recognition.

Cody flicked off the light switch, plunging us into darkness.

The mirror an endless, black abyss. The glass thick but passable, allowing Mary to slip between worlds. My body hooked like a fish on a wire, Mary's claws spearing into me. Lungs tight and starved for air. Mouth opening and taking what should have been a last breath, only to swallow an ocean of cold, brackish water. Drowning. No sound. No light. Total nothingness.

"Stay with us, Shauna," Dell said. "You'll be all right."

She and Cody clutched my hands—I wasn't sure if that was because they wanted to keep me upright or keep me trapped. I knew there was no way I was leaving until the summoning was complete.

"Get it over with," Cody snapped. She sounded mad, but her hand fluttered against mine.

She's as scared as I am, I thought. Cody's fear helped me wrestle my own panic. *I'm okay. We're all okay. We know what we're doing.*

"Let's do this," I rasped. "Before I remember how dumb this is."

Jess's voice was tight. "Will she even come? I thought it had to be teenagers."

"Childless women," Dell said. "Age is unimportant."

The candlelight flickered over Jess's swollen face. She looked like an extra in a zombie film, the bruises going from red to purple at the middle.

"Bloody Mary. Bloody Mary. Bloody Mary." Her voice rang out like a bell.

My head whipped toward the mirror. A line of salt along the bottom frame. Crisscrossing tape across the middle, more salt ensuring Mary couldn't jam anything bigger than a finger or two through the glass. It was strange the way the tape fractured our shadowy reflections. Jess was an eye, a swollen lip, a chin. Cody was a tuft of hair and a nose.

Jess repeated the summons. "Bloody Mary. Bloody Mary. Bloody Mary."

The glass stayed firm and dark. No spectral fog. No condensation. No ambling figure moving our way from a swampy distance. It should have been a relief that we'd failed, but it was another reason for worry. Four women all tied to Bloody Mary, all bled by her, some of us feeding her our body parts, and she couldn't bother to come.

Why? Because she's no longer behind the glass to hear our call.

If we can't soften the glass to send her back, how do we get rid of her?

"It changes nothing," Kitty insisted as we walked back to the car. She had a scrap of paper in hand—directions for a rendezvous point outside of the Hockomock. Cody followed us, but Dell and Jess would meet us after Jess took a shower and changed. "Okay, wait. It might change one thing. Do we really have to go find Hannah? What are we even looking for again?"

"Hannah's important," Cody insisted. "Mary won't attack a girl in front of a mother. We have to assume that's because of Mary's feeling toward her own mother. I still won't rule out the possibility that Starkcrowe, or whoever, killed Hannah and Mary both. If that's the case, why wouldn't he put their bodies together? Especially if Hannah's so out of the way. Mary wasn't in the church. She has to be somewhere. It's worth the look."

"I hate everything about this," Kitty said. "I don't want to dig for any more bodies. I don't want to work with Jess."

Cody grumbled and swatted at herself, striking the side of

her neck. She kept slapping at the spot until her peach skin turned red. More imaginary bugs. "None of us do, but we suck it up. Her aunt's the best line on information we have, and if Mary really isn't in the glass anymore, Jess poses no threat. She's on our side."

Kitty got into the car, slammed the door, and tossed the directions my way. "Jess is on no one's side but her own. We can't trust her."

I reached out to squeeze her arm. She offered me a wan smile that didn't reach her eyes. "I know how you feel, but Cody's right. We need Aunt Dell. We have to tolerate Jess if we want to pursue Mary," I said.

Kitty bit her tongue and started driving. I pulled out the Mary notebook, writing about the necklace, the Worth girl history, and what Mary did to those she'd taken. I felt like everything I needed to know to stop Mary was right there in front of me, but I was missing the thread that tied it all together.

"I'd really like to find out why the pastor married Elizabeth Hawthorne," I said. "That has to be significant. None of Mary's letters suggested they were involved, and Joseph's letter made it sound like Elizabeth didn't go into the marriage willingly. Maybe Dell can ask the sheriff for some of their family stuff."

Cody grunted. "I'd like to look at the rest of Dell's collection. We barely saw anything. My cousin's missing person's report was in there. Was she keeping track of Mary's victims? I'll be curious to hear what Elsa Samburg has to say about everything, too, though I've heard she's crazier than a bucket of drunk monkeys."

The roads worsened the farther along we went, going from paved to dirt, from straight to twisty. At first there were houses and stores around us, then only houses. Eventually, trees, shrubs, and thick undergrowth were our only companions. Kitty drove until there was no road left to drive. The way was barred by two rusted-out chains stretched between a pair of oak trees. The NO TRESPASSING sign was vandalized with so much red spray paint, it was hard to see the warning underneath.

"Charming." I climbed from the car. A mosquito buzzed at my ear. I smacked it away as Cody pulled out insect repellant. She sprayed herself and handed me the bottle. I turned to offer it to Kitty, but she was still in the car, slouched against her seat with her eyes closed.

Kitty cracked open the door as I approached.

"Do you need to go home?" I asked. "It's okay."

"I'm not going anywhere." She wouldn't look at me, instead concentrating on the felt roof of the SUV. "I know I have to deal with Jess. I don't like it. It scares me. It's like walking around with a grenade in my pocket. Cody said she isn't a threat, but why would Mary stop following Jess just because she's out of the mirror?"

Cody sensed we needed a moment alone. She wandered down the dirt road, pausing every few feet to pick up rocks and chuck them into the swamp. "Mary hunts through the mirror,"

I said. "She smells us through the glass. It's a conduit. How's she going to find us without it?"

Kitty rolled her eyes. "If Mary's going to come anywhere, where do you think it will be? Solomon's Folly is her hometown. Don't tell me we're in less danger. *We're in more*."

12

Dell showed up with a compass, a map, a fanny pack, and a pair of yellow duck boots that looked hideous with her velour tracksuit. She exited Jess's car with purpose, sweeping the sides of the narrow road. Every few feet, she reached into the brush to pull out a stick. She'd check the length against her cane before either adding it to her growing collection or tossing it away.

Jess followed behind her in clothes too big for her frame. The blood was washed away, the worst of the cuts bandaged, but her face looked pulpy, as if she'd been boxing. Her sidelong glances suggested she had things to say to me, but Kitty's words had their hooks in me.

Don't tell me we're in less danger. We're in more.

Jess was a walking, talking target.

"How are you feeling?" I asked her. Kitty cast me a sideward glance that I pretended I didn't see.

"I hurt, but it's tolerable." She tried to smile at me but ended up cringing.

Her swollen lip. It hurts.

"Take it easy out there, then."

She nodded.

"What's with the sticks?" Cody called to Dell. "Are we building a fire?"

"No. Black Betty. Quicksand. Before you step anywhere, poke the ground to see if it's soft. We should watch for traps, too. People hunt here. The last thing any of us need is a foothold trap going off."

"Foothold traps. Like bear traps? You're serious?" Kitty's face screwed up in horror, but Dell was too busy gathering to notice.

"Oh, yes. This is a hunters' road. Jessica's father used to trap muskrats here as a teenager. Watch your footing and stay together and we'll be fine. But we'll want to get out before dark. Too many unsavory things come out at night." Dell handed us our sticks as if she was distributing Halloween candy, tucking one into each of our fists with a smile.

"If Hannah was buried near the church, why did we have to get on the highway?" I asked, following Dell past the rusty chains and toward a thicket of trees and waist-tall grass. She pulled out her compass, oriented herself, and forged ahead. She didn't move fast, but nobody would in a place like this. The ferns were up to my knees. Moss covered the tree trunks around me, and four steps in, I had thorns tugging at my pant leg.

Dell snapped off a branch that barred our way. Her walking

stick poked out, nudging at the ground before she pressed deeper into the swamp. "We're coming at it from the other side of the river. Hannah wasn't allowed near the church. Suicides were considered unworthy of holy ground. Women who died in childbirth, too—they were unclean."

At first, the path wasn't clear, but the farther we explored, the more obvious it became. Our sliver of dirt had less overgrowth than our surroundings. Dell was our fearless leader, followed by me, Kitty, Cody, and finally Jess. I prodded with my stick, pausing every time the earth squished. I thought quicksand was an exotic, tropical problem—not something you'd find in New England.

The canopy above was so thick the sunlight barely pierced through. It cast everything in a dank pallor, thickening the shadows and hiding the very swamp floor we needed to fear. The air smelled like fresh-turned dirt and water, the moisture making my clothes stick to my body. Every few minutes a bullfrog croaked or birds cawed in the trees, but otherwise it was quiet.

Except for the clanging.

Clunk. Clunk. Clunk.

Whatever was inside Jess's backpack dinged with each step. Or maybe it was the shovel on her shoulder striking the side of the backpack.

"What's the shovel for?" I asked.

"Hannah," she said. "Dell told me to bring it."

Kitty groaned. "We're not digging her up. I said no grave robbing, and I meant it."

"It's not grave robbing if we take nothing. It's unearthing

the truth," Dell said. "You don't have to participate, Kitty. You can go back to the ca—"

"Don't say that!" Kitty stopped so abruptly, Cody walked into her. Jess had to take a step back so she didn't accidentally impale anyone with the shovel. I reached for Dell's sleeve, tugging it so she'd pause.

Kitty addressed all of us. "Just because I bring up a concern doesn't mean I want to go home. I'm afraid, but I'm staying. I don't want to see any more dead people, but I'll go with you because I want Mary gone. I'd really appreciate someone explaining why we're about to dig up Mary Worth's dead mother, though, because, like, this is messed up. Totally messed up."

Dell didn't answer with words, just a gesture. She unzipped the fanny pack, ignoring the cell phone, house keys, and pill bottle to produce a folded piece of paper. It was another photocopied letter, but it was incomplete, the top portion indiscernible thanks to water stains and ink blobs. I'd seen the writing on the lower half before, though—Joseph Simpson. I took it from her, skimming past the smudges to the first complete line.

—he recalls little about the location beyond the cave. His instructions were to bury her somewhere the animals wouldn't disturb the remains. We know he set out from the church and went across the river into the swamp. That took him southwest.

I've asked Mister Winters to accompany me. He makes his livelihood hunting in the swamp. He thinks the cave is near Samoset's Perch. I have no idea what that means, but I follow in hopes of finding your sister. If Mrs. Carroll's account is true, the figure she saw may have been Mary looking for your mother.

"Do you know who Mrs. Carroll is? Or where Samoset's Perch is?" I handed the letter to Cody, who read it and handed it to Kitty. Jess declined, maintaining her silence at the back of the pack. The letter passed up the line and back to Dell.

She tucked it into her fanny pack. "There's no other mention of a Mrs. Carroll in any other letters I've read. I'm assuming she's a townswoman. I mentioned before we came here when Elsa had the ghost. We had to leave early because of swamp gas, but I saw the cave entrance as we ran out. I haven't had a good enough reason to come back until now." Dell barged through a pair of overgrown shrubs, surprisingly spry considering her years and the impediment. I could picture her in a safari hat slashing at the flora with a machete.

"Swamp gas?" Kitty repeated, still incredulous. "That's a thing? I mean, I believe you, but it's so messed up."

"Phantom fog," Cody said. "It's greenish. If you see it, you run or it sweeps you away and we'll be reading your obituary in a week."

Kitty's moan sounded as if she'd stepped in one of the traps Dell had warned us about. "You want me to believe in killer fog."

Cody snorted. "No, I want you and Shauna to get your heads on straight. Mary's not the end of the weird shit around here. She's the beginning. And if we say run, you'd better run."

Dell paused to check the compass, her hand batting at a cloud of flies hovering near her face. "We go east from here. If you see a stream, let me know. Samoset's Perch will be nearby. It's tallish and hard to miss." She bullied her way through another patch of tall grass, using her walking cane to pry a thick log from our path.

"What's the significance of Samoset's Perch?" I asked, crouching to help her. The log was wet and covered in green algae and moss, with feathery layers of mushrooms along the top. The moment I touched it, ants exploded from the ends to swarm over my hands. I chucked it and slapped the insects away.

Mary's beetles on your skin. Scurry, scurry under your clothes and into your hair. All over with their threadlike legs and gnashy pinchers.

"Nasty."

Dell cast me a sympathetic look before pressing on. "Samoset's Perch is a rise in the swamp named after the Wampanoag who met the English settlers when they arrived in Plymouth. Some say it's where Solomon first declared the land his, but I'm not sure I believe that. It'd be settled otherwise. There'd be more construction."

"There's some," Cody said. "You'll find gutted houses in places. Nothing intact enough to let people live there, but the building foundations are around. We used to play in them as kids."

Dell grunted but said nothing.

A glance at my phone told me forty minutes had passed since we'd left the car. The path was barely recognizable anymore, and the swamp grew less inviting with the addition of a new, invasive plant. It covered everything—the ground, the bottoms of the trees, and the darkest, shadowy bits under the rocks.

I pointed at it. "This isn't poison oak, right?"

"Peat moss," Cody said. "We're in bog land. Your cranberries come from somewhere."

"Oh." I felt dumb, but at least I wouldn't have to stress about getting a rash all over my legs.

A few minutes later, Dell gestured to our right. The stream. It wound around a cluster of saplings before veering off. It wasn't particularly big, maybe five feet across, the water no more than two feet at its deepest point. There was a separation at the middle, a lichen-covered rock forcing a fork, where a turtle with a shell as big around as a bicycle tire sunned itself.

Dell angled toward the stream, her stick still poking at the ground to see if it would give. "Snapper. Avoid her. Those jaws can and will sever fingers."

"This place keeps getting better and better," Kitty grumbled.

We followed Dell past the hissing turtle and along the stream bank, taking side paths to avoid the nastier terrain. At one point, Dell jabbed the earth and found it squishy-soft, like gritty pudding. She threw out her arm to stop us from walking past her, carefully maneuvering us to solid ground, between the dead leaves, the moss, and the network of vines stretching between the trees.

The stream led us farther into the swamp. Not too much later, I could make out a jutting rock formation on the horizon. It wasn't as big as I expected, its peak not quite meeting the treetops.

Dell whooped.

"Jessica, up here with me. We want the flashlights."

Jess shuffled past us to join her aunt. The two of them eased their way down a steep slope and toward the perch. The cave wasn't hard to find. A pair of boulders bordered a recess in the earth, the back wall formed by Samoset's Perch itself. The entrance was round and wide, the stalactites along the top looking like fangs inside a gaping maw. Such an evil place could snap shut and swallow us down forever.

"She could be out here?" I offered weakly.

Eight eyes turned to me.

If she's anywhere she's inside, and we all know it.

13

Crossing from the outside world into the cave depths was like opening the house door after a snowstorm: warm on one side, biting on the other. Kitty huddled into my side, the two of us following Dell and Jess's lantern with chattering teeth. Our one victory was that nothing flew at our heads.

"How far down are we going?" Cody asked from behind me. When I turned to look at her, she was a silhouette in the dark, the light occasionally flashing over the whites of her eyes. It made me think of Peter Pan's shadow claiming children for Neverland.

"I don't know. I won't go too much deeper, though. It narrows ahead." I couldn't see Dell, but I trusted her because I had to. Without her, I was lost in the middle of a killer swamp.

"Look over there," Jess said, her voice raspy. Almost like Cody's. Dell swung us to the right, taking the light with her. My hand latched onto the back of her jacket. Jess stepped aside to let the rest of us see the alcove. The ceiling was about five feet high. Moss blanketed the ground and walls, long-stemmed tufts of it growing from the cracks in the stone. Across the middle of the floor stretched a flat column of small, stacked rocks. At the head of the pile was a larger rock that could have easily been a makeshift headstone.

"Do you think—"

"Yes," Dell said, cutting off Cody. "Jessica, shovel."

Jess offered it to her aunt, accepting Dell's cane in response. Dell limped over to the pile, using the pointed side of the shovel to unearth the rocks. She had to break through a crust of the moss to get to them, but soon they rolled away, exposing more rocks underneath. And more rocks under that. I didn't expect the elder among us to be the one to take on the physical labor, but something spurred her.

Kitty couldn't watch. She turned away to study the rest of the cave, not that she could see anything with the flashlights pointed in the opposite direction. She jogged in place to keep her temperature up, the legs of her jeans swishing.

My attention fixed on Dell. The uppermost rocks were easy to dislodge, but it got harder once she started going into the ground itself. She'd spear the shovel in and then have to take a breath before hoisting the dirt away.

"Can I help?" I offered.

Dell motioned me near. "There's water down there. It's making mud, and mud is heavy. I doubt there will be much left, but maybe we can find a clue or two, like the necklace. I know it's a long shot, but we came all the way here and I doubt they dug too deep. Not for a woman the pastor deemed worthless."

I dug. Moving the sodden earth strained my back, but I kept at it, grunting each time I heaved a shovel full of dirt and rocks aside. The water came faster, filling the recess as I cleared mud out. I worked from the bottom part of the rock pile up, keeping everything level. There was an odor on the air that hadn't been there before we opened up the ground. It wasn't rot like Mary, but something sour and salty. Like low tide on the ocean.

"I can't believe we're doing this," Kitty murmured. "It's sick."

"You're not doing anything. Just standing there." Cody sounded annoyed.

"Leave her alone." I turned back to the task at hand. "She's right to think this is disgusting. Because it is."

"It's necessary." Cody approached the hole, crouching to peer into the large rectangle. Her hand swiped through the water. Her head tilted. "There's something under here. Something not dirt."

I tapped her sneaker with the edge of the shovel. "Disgusting and necessary aren't mutually exclusive. Move. You're in my light."

Cody smacked the shovel away. "Did someone bring a bucket? Something we can use to get the water out."

Jess dug through the backpack. She produced a stack of plastic cups, the red kind people used for soda at parties. "We brought them for drinking water, but here." Cody snatched them from her, going back at the hole to remove two cups of muddy water at a time. Dell edged nearer with her flashlight; Jess, too. Only Kitty stood off to the side, still refusing to watch.

She was the only one who didn't see the face in the water.

Hannah Worth was supposed to be dust and bones at 150 years dead. But what we unearthed were not dry, skeletal remains. The body was wet. Flesh plumped the cheeks, a discernable curvature to the lips. Her features were as plain as they were in the photographs I'd seen just hours ago.

Hannah Worth was *juicy* inside of her watery grave.

In life, Hannah was a beautiful woman with ivory skin and golden hair. The peaty bog had left her the color of soot, but there was no denying her identity. Her eyes were closed, the corners crinkled like she'd squeezed them shut. A delicately arched nose, high cheekbones. Some kind of wrap covered her hair, made of leather or soft cloth. It fastened underneath her chin in a bow. It, too, had not gone to rot.

I stumbled away from the body, my hand held up as if I was afraid she'd rise from the dead and strike me. How was it possible? I could have understood if we'd found nothing, but to discover something so disturbingly untouched after all that time—I couldn't process it.

I stifled a shriek into the back of my arm, staring at Dell and waiting for answers, but she had none. Her fingers were pressed to her mouth, her eyes wide. Jess leaned into her aunt's side, the lift of her brows telling me she was as freaked-out as the rest of us.

Cody shook her head, still crouched next to the hole, her mouth opening and closing in astonished disbelief.

"What's going on over there?" Kitty demanded. "What's wrong?"

"She barely looks dead," I managed despite my shock.

Kitty still danced to keep warm, but that made her go stock-still. "What?"

"No other way to explain it. She looks like she just died. She's discolored—blackened, like leather—but I can see a mole on her temple. She has a mole." Cody pointed at a small growth beneath her hairline. Time had robbed her of few of the finer details.

Jess eased out from behind Dell, moving to my side in the dark. Her fingers brushed my wrist, but I was too stunned to pull away. "How? Is she a vampire or something?"

Dell let out a long breath, like she hadn't exhaled in days. "N-no. I've read of things like this. Bog men. Bog corpses. If you're buried in salt water, or near salt water, and there's peat...Jesus Christ. Pardon me. It's shock. Right. At least we know she's buried alone. Mary would have been on top of her if they were in a double grave. She died second."

"She didn't drown," Cody said. "There's no way she drowned. He did it—Starkcrowe—or if he didn't, someone else did."

"How do you know that?" I looked from Cody to the corpse, the water covering only half of Hannah's ears, her face pointed at the cave ceiling. "How can you tell?"

"Her eyes are closed, like she knew it was coming. Also, if she'd been in the river, her features wouldn't be so perfect. Rivers have tides. Tides lash at the face. Water corpses also bloat. Look at her."

"How do you know all this stuff?" I asked, incredulous. Cody looked embarrassed for a moment, but she shrugged her shoulders like she could slough it off. She then proceeded to smack at her neck, at bugs she felt but no one could see.

"There wasn't much I could do when I was in the house alone. The social worker brought me library books."

I slid down the cave wall to sit on my butt, my feet stopping short of the grave. "If what Cody's saying is true, there's no evidence of drowning in the river. The account of Hannah's death was totally made up. That's another reason Mary has to be so mean."

Dell moved away from the body, pausing by Jess and holding out her hand for her walking stick, tears running down her cheeks. "I'm going to call Jonas and see what he suggests. I dislike disturbing the dead any more than we already have, but she deserves a real burial. Mary would have thought so, I think. Cover her as gently as possible, please. Dirt only, no rocks."

Looking at Hannah, I could see the sordid beginning of Mary's hate spiral.

Kitty went with Dell outside, leaving me, Cody, and Jess to rebury Hannah. I almost asked if we should take a picture for research purposes, but that felt more irreverent than unearthing her in the first place. Covering her was far quicker than digging for her. We used our hands to push the dirt back into the hole, careful to abide by Dell's wishes. Outside, Dell and Kitty stood elbow to elbow, both peering up at Samoset's Perch.

"Jonas is sending the deputy for Hannah. They'll call the coroner to be sure she's taken care of. I have room in the family plot for her. Maybe a proper blessing will put Mary at peace." Dell looked down from the rocks to force a smile, motioning back at the stream with her cane. "He can get you girls in to see Elsa in the morning, but he'd like to meet with you tonight, at the farmhouse. I'll give you directions after dinner."

"You're not going?" Jess asked.

"No, and neither are you. The last time I saw Elsa, she had a reaction. She has a talent that I . . . It's like she senses Mary's taint, and Worth women are tainted. You're staying with me. The other three have a much better chance at communicating without you there."

Jess didn't look pleased, but she didn't argue.

We fell into line to make our way back to the car. It was quiet except for the rustling of leaves and the furious hum of mosquitoes. I didn't realize how tired I was until we had to scale the slope instead of slide down it. Kitty went up first and offered me a hand. With her help, I forced my way to the top, my thighs and back aching with every step. When I pulled away from her, dirt smeared her palm. I was slathered in mud from fingertips to elbow, the guck stiffening my jeans and browning my sneakers.

Cody and Jess had just pulled Dell up with the rest of us

when a scream blasted through the trees. It was loud and high-pitched, more a shriek than a wail. The birds exploded from their nests in fear and agitation. A flock swooped down at us, so low I could feel the air pressure of their wing beats.

"What the hell was that?" Kitty demanded.

Cody grabbed her by the elbow only to take off at a dead run. "Mary!"

14

She's coming.

Get away. Get as far away as you can.

The trees shivered, the leaves whispering with the breeze.
A snap in the brush sent me scurrying ahead, but I didn't run
off, not with Dell struggling to keep pace behind me. It would
have been easy to abandon her and Jess, but getting lost in a
place with phantoms, quicksand, and wild dogs sounded almost
as bad as facing Mary.

I looked ahead, at Kitty's disappearing pastel-colored dot.

Kitty! Wait for me, please! Don't leave me behind.

She kept running.

It was strange to be in such an open area and to feel so
trapped. The shrubs, saplings, and vines closed in. I couldn't
step too far to the left for fear of traps. Too far to the right,
Black Betty. Another ghostly cry blasted through the swamp.
I ran to the stream, my heart pounding like a timpani drum.

I spotted Cody's slate-blue sweatshirt and Kitty's pink tee at the fork. Kitty stumbled back, her stick beating the ground in front of her.

"Jump over it," Cody snapped. Except Cody didn't move ahead either, eyeing the turtle that had relocated from her rock perch to the path. The turtle's head extended from her shell, beaked mouth agape and hissing. Black mud blanketed her except for her eyes, which shone like polished beads in her leathery skin.

"This is stupid." Cody sidestepped the turtle, only to have the ground gulp down her foot as soon as she put her weight on it. Sand clutched her sneaker, slurping on the dingy white leather. Kitty's last-second grab stopped Cody from falling face-first into the hidden pit.

"Holy shit!" Cody scampered back as the turtle lunged, another sibilant hiss warning us away from the territory she'd claimed. Kitty jabbed at her with her thick stick, but the turtle's jaws clamped on the end and snapped it off.

"South!" Dell called from some yards back. "Follow the stream."

"We can't. Turtle and quicksand." Cody retreated, her stick searching the ground for patches of hungry earth but finding none.

"Then it's detour time." Dell turned and led us deeper into the Hockomock, away from the straight trajectory and into a tangle of leaves, vines, ferns, and bushes. We struggled with every step through the dense undergrowth. Kitty kept stepping on the heels of my shoes, but it wasn't her fault. There was simply no place else for her to go.

We kept going until we hit a thick wall of shrubs. A steep drop-off to the right and a patch of soggy earth to the left. It was through the shrubs or turn back. Dell shoved at the branches with her cane, but she didn't make much headway. I stepped in to take her place, using my body as a battering ram. I pierced the first layer of shrubs and pressed into the second.

"Come with me, or they'll close," I said. Kitty followed, then Cody, Jess, and Dell. Sandwiched as I was, I couldn't see the ground, but if the shrubs weren't sinking, neither were we. I pressed forward, emerging into a glen with an arranged ring of rocks at the center. The remains of a long-abandoned fire were scattered across the dirt. Rusty cages formed a lopsided pyramid off to the right, a mildewed wooden rack half-collapsed from years of disuse behind them.

Samoset's Perch, the stream, the path—everything familiar was hidden by a sentry line of oak trees tall enough to touch the sky. Their roots rose up from the ground like a nest of roiling tentacles, their trunks so thick around, they were four people wide.

"A hunter's camp?" Kitty asked.

"Looks like it," I said.

Jess helped pull Dell from the shrubs' clutching branches. A fresh cut bled along Dell's jaw, but she paid it no mind. She was too intent on pulling her compass from her fanny pack and orienting herself.

"Southeast, if any of you have compasses." I didn't, but I did have a phone. As Dell retook the lead, I checked my cell, surprised to discover four-bar reception in the middle of a swamp. Kitty guided me along at a stumble while I opened the app on my phone.

I'd pulled up the compass dial on my screen when I heard a snap followed by a howl. Kitty stopped dead. I slammed into her back, my free hand bracing against her shoulder. Three feet in front of us, Cody bent over at the waist, her arms wrapped around her middle. The color had drained from her face; her single eye drizzled tears. She teetered back and forth, rocking on her heels. I didn't understand why until I looked down.

White sneaker gone red.

Oh, no. Oh, God, no.

The trap clamped on the end of her sneaker, the metal teeth buried deep into the soft leather.

"Get it off of me," Cody rasped.

We were statues in a gallery, poised but unmoving. Cody's whistling squeal, reminding me of a kettle left to boil, ripped Dell from her stupor. She offered Cody the cane, but not before Cody collapsed to the ground, forcing the trap to tilt back with her. I saw jaws and a metal chain spiked into the ground. Unlike the rusty cages, it gleamed silver.

Dell crouched to sling an arm around Cody's shoulders. Jess knelt on the other side, reaching for the trap. She paused when Cody cried into a wad of her sweatshirt. The muffled sobs broke my heart; Cody was the strong, salty one. She was the warrior. Her tears were a foreboding omen.

So was the shrill cry of a furious Mary. Another blast of birds careened past us, their survival instincts telling them to flee, flee, flee! Every part of me wanted to run with them, but I couldn't abandon Cody.

"Sorry," Jess mumbled, grabbing the trap and prying it open, her arms quivering with the strain. The jaws parted an inch, but then Jess's fingers slid through the blood slicking the stainless steel. It slipped from her grasp. *SNAP!* A second bite into Cody's foot. Cody screamed, her temples covered in sweat, the pool of blood spreading. It stained her jeans, climbing from frayed hem to ankle and rising to her calf.

Jess set her jaw, her eyes rimmed red. She tried again. Her fingers shook as she forced open the sides, her thumb and fore- finger hooked in such a way that if Cody got bit, Jess's fingers were fodder, too. She shuddered, all her strength concentrated on freeing Cody. She peeled the mouth open another inch, far enough that Cody's foot could slip out if it wasn't impaled. I dashed in to help, lifting Cody's sneaker from the bottom teeth before maneuvering her foot down and away from the top ones. She came free with another chorus of whimpers.

Kitty figured out how the trap worked. She waited for me to move Cody aside before stepping on the springs on either side of the jaws, forcing the mechanisms to click into place. The mouth of the trap stopped biting, and Jess jerked her hands away, her arms slick with Cody's blood.

"Go," Cody growled, huddled against Dell's chest. "I'll slow you down." Blood bubbled up through the gouges in her sneaker like a crimson geyser.

"No," Dell said, speaking for all of us. "If anyone will peel off, it will be me and Jessica. I'm old and slow. Jessica is marked. You have a fair shot of getting out of here."

My eyes searched the trees. I kept expecting to see Mary's haggard, gray face peering out at us, but nothing.

Yet.

"We need to move," Jess said, wiping her bloody hands on her jeans. "It's not safe here."

"She's right. Get her up." Dell took a deep breath and pried off Cody's sneaker. Cody kept flinching, so Dell looped an arm around her lower leg to hold her still. I wanted to shout at Dell to go faster, *didn't she know what was coming for us*, but it was delicate work. Cody keened as the sneaker pulled away, her sock so saturated with blood it was black. Perspiration dripped from her temples while dark sweat rings formed under her arms.

Dell wobbled on her haunches, her hand clamping on my knee to stop herself from falling.

"How is your leg?" I asked.

"It hurts, but it's manageable. I'm lucky it hasn't given out." Dell stripped down to an old tank top, using her track jacket to fashion a tourniquet. The sleeves tied above Cody's ankle, the rest swaddling the injured foot. As soon as Dell pushed away, Kitty hooked an arm around Cody's waist, bracing to take her weight.

I took Cody's other side, squatting to help her up. Cody wasn't big, but Kitty and I strained to get her off the ground. She held her foot up as we trudged along, Dell leading the pack. We moved southeast, scaling hills that looked gentle but proved challenging with Cody's additional weight. Dell paused before we dipped into a valley between two taller inclines, the furrow in the ground watery and bristled with ferns. She tilted her head back to look at the canopy. Her eyes closed and she sucked in a breath.

"It's quiet," she said.

No wind. No frogs or crickets or birds. It was perfectly still in a place that had no business being still.

"She's here," Jess said. "Mary's here."

15

Mary blended into the trees. A decrepit dead girl ought to call more attention to herself, but the shadows were thick and the dirt smearing her clothes acted as camouflage. My manifested nightmare, five yards away. Staring. Waiting.

Her skull was more pronounced than I remembered. A pointed head covered by bulging black veins, the gray skin so thin along her cheekbones I caught glimpses of skull. A nose-less void at the center of her face, receding lips exposing moldy gums and broken yellow teeth that looked as if they'd been filed to points. Her hair had fallen out except for a few dark strands above her temples.

And her eyes...

Her *eye*.

The left one was as black and as recessed as our last encounter. But the right was different. Film covered the pupil, milky tendrils threading out toward the whites, but I could see the iris underneath. Honey golden brown with dark rings around the edges. I knew that eye. I'd seen it every day for three years *in someone else's head.*

Anna's eye.

I took a step back, but I was stuck, sagging beneath Cody's weight, far too close to Mary. "We should go," I whispered. "Now."

Mary stepped toward us. Her foot sloshed as it struck the ground, the flesh full like a balloon and bulbous at the ankle. It was engorged to the knee, where it appeared to taper, her dress hiding her thigh. Beetles darted in and out of the gashes covering her body. Lumplike shapes pressed on her skin from the inside as they wriggled to and fro.

Dell held her cane aloft like a sword. "Mary, we're here to help you. We found your moth—" Mary lunged for her, arms lashing out, fingers curled over as if she wanted to peel Dell's face from her skull. Her digits were spindly and bluish, but there were two that looked fresh—the ring finger beside the pinky was pink and plump, seamlessly blending into the rest of her parts. There'd been only one yesterday.

Dell whipped the cane around, bashing Mary upside the head. The ghost screeched, bumbling back and hissing like the turtle. "Run! Go south!" Dell shouted, whipping the cane around a second time, clobbering Mary in the knee. Mary growled, but she didn't fall, instead advancing on Dell with wet gurgles.

Kitty took off running, pulling me and Cody with her. We moved fast, but not fast enough with Cody dangling between us. Cody knew it, too.

"Leave me," Cody snarled, "I'm slowing you down."

Terror choked any reply I wanted to make.

GET OUT, GET OUT, GET OUT!

We ran blind, hoping with every step to avoid traps and quicksand. I held my phone with my free hand, the compass guiding us in the direction of the car. Behind us, Jess screamed. I whimpered, scared for her and Dell. Scared for me and Kitty and Cody, too. The fear was all-encompassing—it was the only thing that mattered anymore.

Kitty headed right to avoid passing through bramble bushes with thorns the size of my thumb. Around a pine tree, a boulder, and down a slope, toward a straightaway with knee-high plants and patchy grass. Her breath came in short pants, her face so sweaty that her hair stuck to her forehead and neck.

"I need a second," Kitty wheezed. "Asthma." We didn't have a second, but she couldn't breathe. We paused at the edge of the clearing, Cody clinging harder to me so Kitty could use her inhaler.

"This is stupid," Cody murmured. "You should leave me." Her head lolled forward as if the weight was too much for her neck to support, but then she jerked it back up again, refusing to stay down. I glanced at her wrapped foot. Cody wasn't just bleeding. She was bleeding *to death*.

Kitty crammed the inhaler into her pocket and readjusted Cody's weight across her shoulders. I readied for another sprint, but when I stepped forward, my foot wouldn't lift. I tried the other one. It was too heavy, as if drowned in cement. Black Betty. But it wasn't like Cody's earlier sinking—it was slower. More insidious.

Kitty squirmed on Cody's other side, thrashing as if she were on fire.

"Don't. You'll sink faster. Stay calm," Cody said, her voice so quiet I had to crane my neck to hear her.

I shoved the phone into my jeans pocket and went perfectly still, the sand up to my ankle. "Get Cody on the slope. We're not so far in we can't pull each other out."

Kitty bit her bottom lip, tears swelling in her eyes as we readjusted our grip on the slack woman between us. With a soft, quick countdown, we tossed Cody to safety. We tried to be gentle, but Cody hit the bank with a thud, cussing a blue streak when her foot struck the ground.

"Sorry!" Kitty reached out to grip my arm, like clinging to me would somehow stop her from being swallowed.

Cody rolled onto her hip. Pale and covered in sweat, she looked precariously close to shock. She reached out her hand for me. "It's not too deep. Grab on."

My grip locked on her forearm near her elbow, hers did the same. With Cody as an anchor, I pulled one foot from the grasping muck. There was a rude squelch as I came free. I extended my leg to the slope, and Cody heaved as best she could. I launched forward, landing on solid ground beside her.

I scrambled to my knees and offered my hands to Kitty. She leaned forward, going through the same process to free herself. On our feet, we flanked Cody's sides, lifting her from the ground with twin grunts. Cody whimpered as we moved her, her hold around our necks weaker than before.

We approached the bank, determined to scale it. Up one

step, up two. It wasn't an easy climb, but if we were slow and careful, we could get purchase to push onward. We were nearly to the top when I looked over the crest of the hillside and saw Mary sprinting our way, fresh blood splotching her dress across the bodice. She moved too fast, in a blur.

"Whose blood is that?" Kitty asked, rearing back and nearly toppling the three of us. I overcompensated by leaning forward, toward Mary despite every instinct.

"Kitty, *stop*. We'll end up in the quicksand again."

"She's coming," she warbled. "We have to run."

"Yes, but not that way. Up and around." We struggled up the incline despite the futility of the situation; we couldn't outrun Mary. We'd stabbed her and beaten her and inflicted all sorts of hurt on her, but she resurrected each time. In the past, salt sent Mary retreating into mirrors, but what mirrors did we have in a swamp?

I won't stand here and die. I won't hand over my friends.

Cody refused to be a hindrance.

As soon as we were on level ground, she fought us. I'd thought her strength diminished after the trap, but her fury was such that I had to let her go or get punched in the face. Kitty had a similar problem; Cody elbowed her in the gut over and over until she released her. As soon as she was free, she shoved my shoulders so hard, I stumbled back and into Kitty.

"Run," she growled. She reached into her jeans pocket and pulled out Mary's necklace, cramming it into my fist and curling my fingers over it. "There's a key under the mat behind the back door of my house. What's mine is yours. Finish it."

"Cody, what are you doi—"

"Run!" She screamed it in my face, spittle striking my cheeks as she pushed me a second time. I didn't argue as Kitty grabbed my hand and wrenched me back. The necklace dangled from my fingers.

"We're not leaving her," I insisted. "No!"

"We have to, Shauna!"

Cody whirled to meet Mary head-on, her weight balanced on her good foot. She lifted her chin and tore off the black patch, exposing the sewn-shut socket where her eye used to be. A mass of pink-and-white scar tissue covered her from brow to the side of her nose. She was as pale as paper and drenched with sweat. Her body trembled.

She'd never looked fiercer.

"I'M WAITING, MARY!"

Mary barreled our way, a shot fired from a gun. Kitty tried to steer me away, her fingers pinching my bicep, but my feet remained planted. *Cody*, I thought. *We have to help Cody.*

"Go," Cody implored. "I'm screwed anyway. Please." It was the *please* that did me in. I didn't want to abandon her, but we needed to persevere so Mary wouldn't haunt again. If Cody had to die to make it happen, that was her decision. I hated it, but it made sense. Cody made sense. Mary was too close for any other plan.

Twenty yards between us and Mary. Fifteen yards. Ten. I bumbled back, Kitty's grip tightening on my arm. Mary shrieked with fury before veering to the left—toward me and Kitty instead of Cody. *Two for the price of one*, I realized, delirious with terror. A bubble of crazed laughter threatened to burst from my mouth. Cody remained unfazed. She crouched low, her hand swiping out to close around a fist-sized rock.

"BLOODY MARY, BLOODY MARY, BLOODY MARY!" she mocked, her voice as strong as I'd ever heard it.

The ghoul's trajectory immediately changed, the taunt too personal to overlook. She launched herself at Cody, pouncing like a wolf on its prey. Her hands struck Cody's shoulders, her weight knocked Cody back. I screamed as they rolled down the hill, wrestling like cats the entire way. Mary thrashed and punished with those razor-tipped fingers. Cody returned the violence with the rock in her fist, hitting Mary on the back of the head over and over again. They rolled back and forth; sometimes Mary was on top. Sometimes Cody.

Screams, snarls, and sobs. The last were mine.

"Let's go," Kitty pleaded. "She's doing this for us."

Still I didn't move. Not until I saw the ground opening up, the sand rising. I understood then what Cody intended—to pull Mary under the quicksand. For a heartbeat, she looked up at the slope, her face covered with fresh cuts and blood. Somehow, despite the ghoul beneath her snarling, she found a smile for me. A big toothy one that stretched across the lower half of her face.

It was enough. I took Kitty's hand and we ran.

16

We kept going until our legs hurt and then until they didn't hurt.

Cody is dead. She saved us.

Kitty never let me go, her fingers laced with mine. I'd pocketed the necklace so I wouldn't lose it, retrieving my cell phone in its place. "Southeast" was the only direction we had to go on. We'd been cautious getting to Hannah, but the retreat was chaos with Mary in the swamp. Even if Cody dragged her down into the sand, who was to say she'd stay there? Who was to say Mary didn't finish Cody and crawl out before she drowned?

We smashed our way through another thicket and toward a flat glen peppered with spicebushes and low-growing bittersweet. I let go of Kitty to snap off a stick from one of the shrubs. One thing I'd learned in my short time inside the Hockomock: if the land didn't support something big and green, the land didn't support at all.

A yell echoed through the trees. It wasn't a scream of terror, but my name followed by Kitty's. We'd lost Cody but found Dell.

Kitty climbed a nearby rock, standing on it so she could better see the wood line behind us. She yelled out, her voice cracking halfway through. The next thing we heard was Jess's voice calling back to us. My phone buzzed a second later.

Hold still we're coming.

What if Mary's looking for us? I texted back.

Dell can get us out quick.

I joined Kitty on the rock to wait. Crunching underbrush, rustling leaves—even expecting Dell and Jess, I prepared for the worst, the stick in my hand ready for Mary. When Jess's bandaged head popped out from behind a tree, I relaxed, but I never let my eyes stop skimming the landscape. I wouldn't be surprised again.

Dell followed behind Jess, her cane replaced by a piece of wet, moldy wood that looked like a broken fence slat. Her tank top was shredded over her stomach with a nasty rake of claw marks.

"Where's Cody?" she asked. Kitty and I stayed silent, though I did point in the direction of the sandpit. Dell sucked in a breath. "She's gone? Where's Mary?"

"Cody dragged Mary into the sand," I said. "She told us to leave her. They sank."

"Oh. Oh, my." Dell's jaw quivered like she might cry, too. "I'm so sorry."

I shrugged, not sure of what to say. "Are you okay?" I gestured at her middle, hoping it wasn't another Cody-scale wound.

"I'll be fine. Surface cuts only."

"It should have been you, Jess. You did this and it should have been you." Kitty's voice started off soft but grew louder by the word. Her eyes were swollen from crying, her nose red and crusted with snot. "It's your fault. IT SHOULD HAVE BEEN YOU."

Jess dropped her gaze to the soiled tips of our shoes, her nod so slight I barely caught it. "I'm sorry."

"Sorry?" Kitty snorted like a bull before the red cape. "Sorry doesn't cover it. Two people are dead. We should throw you in the pit with Mary so she won't come after the rest of us."

Jess flinched. "I never meant for any of it to happen."

It was the wrong thing to say. Kitty screamed in Jess's face—no words, just ear-punishing bellows that blasted out one after the other.

I clapped my hands over my ears. Kitty didn't stop until Jess stepped toward her. Immediately, I put myself between them, a human shield. I didn't know what Jess intended, and I didn't trust her enough to find out. Dell grabbed Jess's shoulder and yanked her back.

"Stop, Jessica." Jess tried to shake her off, but Dell held tight. "I said stop."

Jess stopped.

"I want to leave here. I hate this. I hate everything," Kitty screamed.

"Then let's get you out. Give me a moment." Dell retrieved her phone from the fanny pack. "I'll call the sheriff to get Co—" She paused to suck in a breath. "To get the situation taken care of. We'll see how he wants to progress with you talking to Elsa."

"Fine." Kitty jerked her head away so she wouldn't have to look at any of us. I glowered at Jess, the three feet between us stretching miles.

Dell led us through the swamp, droning on as she talked to the sheriff. I shivered despite the heat and humidity. A bird flew by to perch in the closest tree. I tuned in to the rest of the birds then, the tweets boisterous and cheery from the swamp around me. They'd been so still during Mary's attack; maybe their ruckus meant she was truly gone.

"I'm glad you're okay," Jess mumbled from behind me.

I couldn't say the same to her. "How'd you get away from Mary? She followed you guys first."

Jess's bark of laughter was harsh and humorless. "We found a patch of swamp gas and ran behind it. Hard to imagine, but even Mary has her limits."

If something could be evil enough to scare Bloody Mary Worth, I never wanted to see it for myself.

When Dell gave us directions to the sheriff's house, I typed them into my phone. I didn't trust myself to remember my name after all that happened, never mind an address.

"Jessica and I are staying here to meet the deputy," Dell said. "Sheriff Hawthorne is expecting you at Hawthorne House. It's the oldest building in town. They don't offer tours anymore, not since Karen went away, but... well. He's offered a meal and hot showers."

We were supposed to stay with Cody....

I had to swallow a whimper.

"Why do we have to go see him? Can't he just take us to Elsa?" Kitty asked.

"His wife is involved. He wants to make sure you won't upset her. Karen and Elsa have been roommates since they entered the hospital. When one moved to assisted living, the other followed." Dell cleared her throat, her hand pressing over her scraped middle. I had a feeling there was information she didn't want to share. Jess and she had more things in common than their blood.

"Okay, but can we trust him? He's a Hawthorne," Kitty pressed.

Dell nodded. "Yes. I do, anyway. He understands our plight. Jonas has weights of his own that make him cooperative."

I tried not to roll my eyes. I couldn't imagine anyone having a weight like Mary.

Kitty slid from her rock to tap my elbow. "Fine. Let's go."

"Where are you girls staying again?" Dell called after us.

"Cody's," I decided on the spot without consulting Kitty. Maybe there was something in Cody's stash that would help. Dell estimated a twenty-minute walk from where we were to the road, but we halved it; as soon as we escaped the Worth women, we jogged, only pausing once for Kitty to catch her breath. We never said a word. I climbed into the SUV exhausted, miserable, and scared. And then I saw the Home Depot bags in the backseat.

Cody. I'm sorry.

Grief and self-loathing bubbled up inside of me.

I could have done more.

Kitty reached out to squeeze my knee, the first she'd acknowledged me since we left the others.

"Text your mom to tell her you're okay. It'll make you feel better." I didn't know about that, but I grabbed my phone and sent a message. It wasn't much more than telling Mom I loved her and I'd talk to her the next day, but in some small way it did make things a little bit easier. Well, that and the small hope that maybe Mary had been sunk for good.

Kitty grabbed the GPS from the glove compartment and set it up on the dashboard. I peered down the SUV's hood at the crisscrossing rusty chains and the NO TRESPASSING sign at the entrance to the swamp. Every time the wind rustled the trees, I flinched. And when Kitty drove away from the Hockomock, I prayed I'd never have to set foot in it again.

17

"Did Cody ever talk about her family?" Kitty turned the car onto a back road with faded paint lines and overgrown grass poking up through cracks in the sidewalk. Every third house was boarded up, the two intact houses between wearing their age in the peeling roofs and weatherworn shingles.

I glanced at Dell's directions. "I know she has some, but she never talked about it. She was really private. Keep going straight."

We passed a diner called Flo's Joe, an abandoned vegetable stand, and a gas station with an old rusted-out car on concrete blocks out front. The GPS beeped, and Kitty turned onto a curvy dirt road with no streetlights.

"You'll miss her," Kitty said quietly.

I looked out the window. "Yeah, I will. She helped me a lot. If I'd kept her out of this, maybe she'd—"

"Don't, Shauna." Kitty patted my arm. "Cody made that choice. It sucks and I won't ever forget that or her, but she made that choice. Don't shoulder that. It's not fair to yourself."

A lot of things aren't fair, but that doesn't make them less true.

Hawthorne House wasn't what I expected. I'd pictured an immaculate home with expensive cars parked out front. Instead, it was a sprawling, run-down manor house long past its glory days. Barren, unattended fields bordered the twisting driveway. The fences were collapsed, half of the connecting posts snapped off or rotting. It was separated from its closest neighbor by miles.

Oddly, one field on the right was in perfect condition. No weeds, no plants. The soil looked freshly tilled, and the fence was perfectly maintained. Emerald grass lined the outside perimeter, contrasting starkly with the dirt drive and the yellow crabgrass carpeting the rest of the property.

Kitty parked opposite the front door of the main house. At least I thought it was the main house—it was hard to tell. Hawthorne House was two separate houses connected by an enormous barn. The one on the left looked lived-in—the screen door was propped, the windows open to let the breeze pass through. The shingles were gray with age, but someone had taken the time to replace the ones near the eaves. A fresh coat of paint covered the black shutters. A hanging fuchsia added a splash of brilliant pink to the wraparound porch.

The house on the right was almost identical to the one on

the left, except it looked like the set of a horror movie. Boards covered the windows, slatted so efficiently from top to bottom I couldn't tell the condition of the glass underneath. The front door was equally inaccessible; iron hoops nailed to the house front allowed chains to crisscross the entryway, a padlock tethering them together near the ground.

The only thing intact was the cupola and widow's walk on the roof. It was a large square—twelve by twelve—each wall constructed of three floor-to-ceiling windows abutting one another. A black, pointed roof cast shadows on the upper panes of glass. A narrow white door the same size as one of the windows faced the chimney flute. The paint was in good shape, and the fence rail stood tall despite missing half its rungs.

I glanced back at the first house. No cupola. It was only present on this house. It looked like the two roofs should have been swapped so that the cupola could join the lived-in part of the house, it was that well preserved.

"I wish this was the worst place I'd been all day," Kitty said.

"Agreed." I climbed from the SUV, reeking like a sewer. Kitty shared my concern. She sniffed her sweatshirt before pulling it off and tossing it into the truck. Dell said the sheriff offered showers. I hoped that was still the case.

Thunderous stomps inside the house called my attention to the screen door. I half expected Godzilla to emerge, but Sheriff Hawthorne was average height and average weight with what my mother would call "ruddy skin." His dark brown hair was streaked with silver at his temples, his mustache and heavy brows sporting a similar salt-and-pepper effect. He wore fawn-colored steel-toed work boots, accounting for his heavy tread. Camouflage pants and a faded gray T-shirt with a charity picnic logo printed across the chest completed the outfit.

"Kitty and Shauna?" he asked, his voice deep.

I nodded. "She's Kitty, I'm Shauna. Thank you for seeing us."

"I do what I can. LYDIA. BRAN. COME OUT HERE." The last was aimed at the house. A childish squeal preceded a little boy shoving his way outside. He had the same green eyes and dark hair as his father, though his skin was honeyed brown. He wore a Batman T-shirt and blue jeans with dirty knees.

The teenaged girl shared the boy's skin tone, but her features were softer: almond-shaped eyes, full lips, a lovely nose sprinkled with freckles. Her sundress was yellow with two big pockets along the front, and her feet were bare. She slid in behind her father, her hand extending to rest on the little boy's back. The sheriff didn't like her shyness; he *tsk*ed and drew her forward by the elbow. She looked down at the ground in response.

"Lydia's your age. Bran's seven," the sheriff said.

I waved. Kitty managed a "Nice to meet you."

"I'm sorry about your friend," the sheriff said, his hand skimming over Bran's dark head. "Officer Stone will contact Miss Jackson's family, if she has any."

He glanced at his daughter. "Food's cooking?" Lydia nodded. Bran tried to squirm from her grasp, but she held tight, her hands clasping on his shoulders.

"Can I watch *Teen Titans*?" Bran asked.

The sheriff eyeballed him. "Be polite, Bran."

"Okay. Nice to meet you, Shaunakitty. Now can I go watch *Teen Titans?*" He said our names so fast, they were indiscernible.

The sheriff sighed and shooed him off. "My son the whirl-wind." Sheriff Hawthorne forced a smile, but it was out of place on his face—strained and unnatural, as if he wasn't sure how smiles were supposed to work. "How long on dinner, Lydia?"

"A half hour, probably," the girl said. She had one of those soft, low voices that under better circumstances I would have wanted to listen to for a while, but I was too sore and smelly and miserable to enjoy anything.

"Good. You girls are welcome to stay, but I have two rules if you do." He looked between us so we could see the serious-ness on his face. "One, no saying the word G-H-O-S-T in front of Bran. He gets nightmares. Speak in code. Second, and by far the most important." He pointed past my shoulder toward the one good field among all the decrepit ones. "You don't go there. Under any circumstance." He leveled a heavy stare on us. It was hard to tell if this was a request, a warning, or a threat.

I nodded slowly and could see Kitty doing the same from the corner of my eye. The sheriff instantly relaxed.

"We understand each other, then. Go clean up before dinner. We'll talk about Elsa once you're fed."

"What's with the field?" Kitty whispered to me as we dressed in the spare room. "Is it, like, murder field?"

I looked out the window to the front yard, gazing at the near-black dirt and tidy fence. "No idea, but something's not right."

"No, it's not." Kitty raked a comb through her hair and headed for the bedroom door. She glanced at me over her shoulder. "Maybe everyone in this stupid town has their own monster."

We went downstairs to join the Hawthornes at the dinner table. Lydia had made roasted chicken for dinner with mashed potatoes. I wondered how she knew how to cook when all I could do was microwave popcorn, but then I remembered that her mother had been in the hospital for a long time. Lydia probably had to grow up fast.

"How much do you know about Mary?" I asked the sheriff, my fork dragging tracks through my potatoes.

The sheriff eyed Bran, who was cramming broccoli into his mouth. "Enough that you don't need to go into detail, and likely shouldn't because of present company." He paused. "What were you hoping to get from Elsa? She and Karen—my wife—share a room at the facility. They've been roommates for almost seven years."

I did the math. Karen had been institutionalized near Bran's birth. A fact that seemed noteworthy.

"We want to ask what happened with Mary. We know lots of things that seem important, but we don't know how they connect. If we can piece together the whole story, maybe we can figure out how to stop her." I paused to take a bite of food. "Hannah Worth didn't drown. We know the pastor quickly married Elizabeth Hawthorne after Mary and Hannah died. Why? And what does it have to do with what is happening now?"

The sheriff and Lydia exchanged a look. The sheriff motioned at me with his fork. "After supper, Lydia can take you out to the family plot."

Kitty looked up from her dinner. "It's here?"

"This is the original Hawthorne House. Or, well..." The sheriff pulled a biscuit in half and crammed one side in his mouth. "It's the replacement building from the mid-seventeen hundreds. The original burnt down with our ancestor and his family inside. But everyone since then is buried in a private cemetery in the back, including Elizabeth and Starkcrowe. Family previous to the fire is buried at the center of town, at First Church."

"Starkcrowe's not really buried here. It's just a plot," Lydia said quietly. She looked from her father to us. "The family put up a marker, but there's no one buried below."

The sheriff grunted. "Yes. An empty plot. Starkcrowe ran off shortly after the marriage. Elizabeth's father had him proclaimed dead after six months. Judges could do that sort of thing."

I filed that away. Starkcrowe had a history of bad behavior, yes, but he was a pastor. Running off on his wife would have been scandalous. And what of Elizabeth?

"I'd like to go," Kitty answered. When I cast her a side-eyed glance, she shrugged. "I'm curious."

I wasn't interested in the graveyard, but I'd go because Kitty was going.

Dinner descended into quiet—the sheriff was not the chatty type, his daughter no more inclined to speak than he was. Occasionally, I'd catch her peering at me, and she'd smile, but then quickly turn her attention to her younger brother. Bran writhed to get out of his seat halfway through the meal, but she kept him quiet with promises of cartoons and dessert. After he finished his vegetables, she let him run off to watch TV in the other room.

The moment he was gone, the sheriff got conversational again. He lowered his voice so it wouldn't carry. "I understand what you girls are up against, and I'll do what I can to help, but my concern is Karen. If you upset Elsa, you upset my wife. They rely on one another. I understand this is a difficult situation, but if you promise to keep your questioning delicate and leave when it's time to leave, I'll make the call."

"We'll be careful," Kitty swore. The sheriff looked to me for separate confirmation.

"We're not out to upset anyone. Thank you, Sheriff."

"Let me set it up, then." He got up from the table and wandered off to use the phone. His daughter stood, headed down the hall, and disappeared from view.

"Strange," whispered Kitty. I shrugged. Not as strange as everything else we'd seen in Solomon's Folly.

I cleared the table out of habit. It was my chore at home, and I tended to jump to it at other houses, too. As I scraped plates into the garbage, I remembered Mrs. McAllister giving Jess grief because I helped out and Jess didn't. It made me sad to think about—I'd probably never be at the McAllister dinner table again.

Especially if Mary catches Jess.

But that would mean Mary crawled out of the quicksand.

That was impossible, wasn't it?

If it's so impossible, why are we still searching for answers?

I gritted my teeth and stacked the plates into a neat pile. I was about to carry them to the sink when Lydia returned from the kitchen. Seeing me, she gasped and rushed over, taking the plates away and putting them back on the table.

"No, no. Don't worry about—I have it. Thank you, though. You wanted to see the family plot, yes?" Her smile was too bright as she ushered me away. I had no idea what I'd done, but it was clear something was wrong.

"Did I offend you?" I asked, not sure if I should apologize.

"Not at all." That was all Lydia said, pausing by the screen door to slip into a pair of sandals. Kitty joined us outside, falling into step beside me past the cars, the barn, and the dilapidated half of Hawthorne House.

"Why are there two houses?" My eyes followed dried vines of dead ivy as they wound around the pillars supporting the porch overhang.

"At one time there were twins in the family and they didn't want to fight over the house, so they built an addition that mirrored the original construction. The run-down side is the original building, though my great-grandfather abandoned it in the fifties when it got too hard to repair. The part we live in was built about a hundred years later and is still serviceable."

She guided us toward the woods along the property edge, a path lined with white painted stones veering off into the unknown. Lydia headed straight for it, but I turned to get a different view of the older house. An attached room on the back looked different than the rest of the house—a pile of twisted metal that made me think of a mangled jungle gym. Most of it was rectangular, maybe fifteen feet long and ten feet wide, but the top portion was domed.

"What's that?"

"That used to be a conservatory," she said.

I edged closer to check it out. The floor of the conservatory was cracked concrete, dead stems poking up through the fissures. The broken remnants of a stone fountain aligned with the apex of the dome. Abandoned pots and planters littered the shelves and ground, dirt scattered everywhere. Ivy wound around the outside frame and climbed toward the roof, some of it brown, some of it green. I followed the green all the way to the widow's walk.

There was a stained glass window on the back of the cupola. Two regular windows flanked it, as tall as the cupola itself and rectangular, but the middle window was domed-top stained glass. The glass was dark thanks to a thick layer of dust on the inside, but the design was still visible. It was a bird in flight, its wings back, its beak pointed down. The metal shaping the picture was weather-beaten and silvery.

I pointed up at it. "What's that?"

Kitty followed my gaze and frowned. "It looks like something you'd see on a tombstone."

"Yes." Lydia motioned at the white stone path. Kitty and I followed her into the woods. Past a line of trees and down a series of wide stone steps, there was a grassy clearing with lines of tombstones arranged in neat rows. The front stones weren't arranged as evenly, but they were the oldest—the earlier Hawthornes probably had no idea that their family line would roost there for the next three centuries.

"Like I said, the oldest Hawthornes are buried outside of the First Church at the center of town." Lydia drifted through the rows, looking at the dates. It was easy-ish to find people, because they were buried in the order that they died. Rows two through four were all the eighteen hundreds.

"The bird," Kitty said. "It's on all of the markers. Look." She broke away from me to approach the nearest tombstone. It was shaped like a cross with an ornate circle at the top. Inside of that circle was the same crow we'd seen in the stained glass window.

"It's a family crest," Lydia said. "It's been our marker for as long as there's been Hawthornes in Solomon's Folly."

Kitty ran her fingers over the carving. "Usually you see doves on tombstones, not crows...."

Lydia hesitated before answering, as if she had to calculate what she said. "Crows are survivors. They always get what they think they want."

"What they think they want?" Kitty asked the question before I could. "Not what they want?"

"Yes." Lydia paused in front of a simple square stone, bleached white by time. The crow was carved at the top of this stone, too, its claws clasping a broken bud. "Here."

I looked down.

ELIZABETH JANE HAWTHORNE JENSON
AUGUST 31, 1846–MAY 16, 1869
BELOVED WIFE AND DAUGHTER

Next to it was a much smaller stone, simple by comparison and lacking the bird etching.

PHILIP ELIJAH STARKCROWE III
OCTOBER 5, 1839–APRIL 8, 1865
SERVANT OF GOD

"They both died young," I said. "Elizabeth remarried? To a Jenson?"

Lydia nodded. "He's not buried here. Their marriage didn't last long, as you can see. He must be interred at First Church. That's where most of old Folly is buried."

I tried to put the dates in order; Mary died six months before Philip disappeared. Elizabeth died four years after that. That wasn't much time, and for a moment I wondered if Mary had anything to do with it. I crouched before Elizabeth's tombstone, my legs tight and sore from running earlier. "Starkcrowe ran off, but how did Elizabeth die?"

Lydia cleared her throat like she was embarrassed. "I want to give you something." She reached into the pocket of her dress and produced a folded letter. "Don't tell my father. He's funny about family things, but I—I don't know if the letter will help, but I'd rather you see it than not. We all have our problems. Ours is . . . well, strange things happen here, too, in the field.

I don't know much about your Mary, but I can sympathize. A little."

"What *is* going on with the field?" Kitty asked.

Lydia's cheeks stained red. "Nothing you have to worry about if you don't go into it. Just be careful in The Folly. Its secrets are old and ugly and dangerous." She thrust the letter at me, desperate to change the subject. "I thought you might want to see this. It might be relevant. I don't know if anyone told you, but Elizabeth Hawthorne hanged herself."

November 23, 1864

Lizzie,

There is a marked difference between what I cannot do and what I will not do. One suggests inability. The other suggests refusal to change a prior course of action. In regards to your engagement, I am of the latter category, which is how I shall remain. This is not a negotiation. You will wed Philip Starkcrowe in two weeks' time.

It would perhaps be simpler for me to explain in person, but I cannot shirk my responsibilities to the state of Massachusetts. As you are a devoted daughter of the House of Hawthorne, you will do your duty without further complaint. Anything else would prove your mother right, and she is harpy enough without that fuel.

I know you see this as a great injustice, but from my perspective, it is an instance of cause reaping effect. While the recent unpleasantness was handled, it was not without its complications, and the expediency of certain deeds requires me to make plans I would not have made elsewhere. Your marriage is one such example. I dislike having this stain under my crest. It befouls my house. I will, in due time, see to its removal, but until then a marriage guarantees the agreeability of all involved parties.

As for the rest of your concerns, I will address them because I love you best, but I have little patience for inane female blather. The Adderly boy was never an acceptable match. Your idiot dog is smarter, and I'm fairly convinced my boots could outsmart the dog, so what does that say for the oaf? I would not pair Hawthorne blood with Adderly blood any more than I would pair a champion stallion with the lowliest swine. I told you years ago this was not a realistic expectation, and I reiterate it now. Move past these fanciful notions and understand that Adderly is barely fit to polish your shoes, never mind be on your arm.

I hope I have made myself perfectly clear.

Mr. Starkcrowe is a pastor and devoted to God. Once he is married, I have no doubt he will be committed to you if for no other reason than fear for his immortal soul. He shares ideology with Jonathan Edwards (perhaps you should reread "Sinners in the Hands of an Angry God"). Philandering defies a very basic tenet. There, too, is the matter of his flaxen fixation leaping to her death in a river. I do not know how to explain to you that being jealous of a dead woman is ridiculous.

I recognize that he has a temper, Elizabeth, but I have faith you will comport yourself with dignity and decorum as befits a pastor's wife. He will have less reason to anger if you curb your barbed tongue. Should he prove excessive with his disciplines, I will speak to him, but I will not borrow a problem that does not yet exist.

Lastly, your claims that I have forsaken you are hysterical, insulting, and patently false. You dropped inclement weather upon my doorstep, and like most inclement weather, I batten down the hatches until the storm passes. I do not "sacrifice you" to Starkcrowe as you so put it. I clean up the mess you have made with the tools at my disposal. It is my duty to see that the Hawthorne *name perseveres. Without us, Solomon's Folly falls to ruin. I will not have that on my conscience.*

Whatever is on your conscience is your own doing. Perhaps next time you will exercise more caution in your affairs.

Your Loving Father,

Seymour

18

We climbed into Kitty's car armed with the sheriff's cell phone number, a nine o'clock appointment for the next morning at the Geraldine Hawthorne Assisted Living Community, and the stashed letter.

Lydia dashed into the house after a hasty good-bye while Sheriff Hawthorne stood on the porch, his arms crossed over his chest. He glanced at his watch. "I have an appointment at quarter of eight tonight, but I'll be back at half past. Are you sure you don't want to stay here? It might be uncomfortable at the Jackson house, all things considered."

"We need to look around Cody's house to see if there's anything that will help with Mary," I said. "She told us how to get in." Any hope I had that Mary sunk into the quicksand for good was overshadowed by the fear that she was still out there.

The sheriff eyed me. "You can look and then come back here. I'll be up until midnight, but call anytime."

"He's a cop, Shauna," Kitty said. "We might be safer. Plus he's a Hawthorne, which might deter Mary, if she got out of the swamp."

Or maybe she'd come looking for revenge against the Hawthorne family.

The sheriff stepped off the porch and leaned into Kitty's open car window. "I can't do a lot to help you girls. I know..." He paused. "Being sheriff in a town like this, I know things. Things that shouldn't be possible but are. I'm limited because of my responsibilities. My wife. My kids. The town. The town needs the Hawthornes more than the Hawthornes need the town. We're tied here for better or worse."

Without us, Solomon's Folly falls to ruin. I will not have that on my conscience, Seymour Hawthorne wrote in his letter. One hundred fifty years later, his great-times-many grandson was still saying the same thing.

"The point is," the sheriff continued, "I can't help you beat this thing, but I can give you beds and food while you do. I'd be happy to have one less nightmare on my conscience."

"We'll be back," Kitty answered for both of us. She cast me a guilty look. "I know you want to stay at Cody's, but it feels wrong without her. Looking around is fine, but sleeping there—no. Please."

I sighed. Of the three options—Hawthorne House, Dell's, or Cody's—it was the best of a bad lot. "Thanks, Sheriff Hawthorne." I said. "I'll text you before we come back."

The sun was setting by the time we pulled into Cody's driveway. I expected to hear the crickets heralding the dusk, but it was silent. In summer in Bridgewater, the kids played in the streets until dark. Solomon's Folly was different. Parents tucked their kids away before suppertime.

Looking at Cody's gray house, my chest grew tight. I climbed from the SUV to walk around to the backyard. I'd never been behind the house, and seeing the overflowing trash barrels, the old furniture stacked and ready to go to the dump, I understood why. It was an obstacle course of junk.

At least there was a path to the concrete steps. I lifted the dingy mat and found a key where Cody had left it. Kitty picked her way around the mess to join me as I pushed open the back door. It led straight into the kitchen. The house was in much better shape than I remembered. Flypapers no longer covered the ceiling. The furniture wasn't new, but it was new to Cody. The fake leather couches in the living room replaced the threadbare stuff from the last visit. She'd tidied the house as well—the floors were swept, the curtains washed. A fresh coat of paint brightened the living room and hallway.

She thought she had things to live for. She thought she had more time.

Kitty closed the door behind us. I made my way to the living room. I'd been to the house only once, but I remembered the shelves stacked with books and papers. They were sorted now—another thing Cody had cleaned once she was freed from Mary's curse. I tried not to think about it too much as I grabbed the photo albums and manila envelopes from the bottom shelf.

I'd gone through the pictures before, but Cody hadn't shared the rest.

The first envelope was full of newspaper clippings about missing girls. The stories of their disappearances were similar to Anna's—teenagers gone without a trace. I wondered about the missing girls' friends: how many of them lived with this same burden? Knowing what happened and not being able to talk about it? How many were chalked up as runaways when the reality was much worse—Mary had taken them and used them to fuel her own decaying body.

That's how she got the fresh fingers.

I shuddered, handing the clippings to Kitty, but she waved me off. She sat on the couch, her cell phone in her hands, thumbs flying.

"Bronx?" I asked, sorting piles.

"Yes. He wants me to text him every night. He's worried about me." She sniffled, wiping her runny nose across the back of her arm.

Which reminded me, I needed to text Mom. In a little while.

Kitty continued. "He's mad at me."

"Why?" I pulled an envelope from inside the bigger envelope and wondered if there'd be a third envelope in the second one, like Russian nesting dolls with paper. Instead, there were six paper-clipped pages, the top one a photocopy of a photo.

"Because I told him wh-what to do with my stuff if I died."

I jabbed her in the knee with my thumb. "Hey, now. I won't let anything happen to you."

"I'm not sure that's up to you so much as Mary."

"Enough, Kitty," I snapped, rougher than I intended. Mary wouldn't take another friend from me. I wouldn't let her.

The picture on top was of Elizabeth Hawthorne standing with three girls her age, all of them wearing dark, button-up dresses with belled skirts and lace collars. Elizabeth wore a decorative shawl around her shoulders. The girls clasped hands, telegraphing affection, but their spines were stiff, their smiles lukewarm. I'd read that old cameras had slow exposure times so people had to maintain their poses for a long period. If the toothy smile faltered midtake, it'd screw up the picture.

Cody had written on the page with a red marker—arrows pointing at each of the girls. The short, slight girl with the curly dark hair on the left was Sarah Ashby. She held hands with Elizabeth, who held hands with a tall, heavyset girl named Meredith Richards. The last girl on the right was pretty and of average size, the only blonde of the group. Her name was Agnes Willowcroft. They stood in front of a fencepost, but in the far back I recognized Hawthorne House—I knew it was the older side from the widow's walk.

I flipped to the next page, a photocopy of an official death certificate from the town of Solomon's Folly. The next three pages were also death certificates. The strange thing was, they were incomplete. The names were filled in, the dates of death, but the causes were left blank except for Elizabeth's, which listed cerebral hypoxia.

Sarah Ashby was born on June 2, 1847, and died April 30, 1865.

Meredith Richards was born on November 3, 1847, and died June 19, 1865.

Agnes Willowcroft was born February 6, 1845, and died August 4, 1865.

Elizabeth died four whole years later.

"Mary did it," I said, skimming through them. "She killed them. The other girls, I bet."

Kitty put the phone aside to reach for my papers. I handed them over, pointing at the empty fields. "Why else would the doctor leave them blank? You can't put *ghost* down as a reason."

Kitty surveyed the dates. "I wonder if that's why Elizabeth killed herself. All her friends were dead."

"Or guilt, maybe. That letter from earlier." I pulled out Seymour's letter, careful with the vellum. Unlike the others we'd read, it was an original from the nineteenth century. It was in excellent shape, but with a family history as huge as the Hawthornes, I wasn't surprised they'd kept it in good condition. They had a legacy to preserve.

I folded out the letter on the end table next to the couch. "Elizabeth's father was such a jerk. But notice how he keeps talking about the bad stuff Elizabeth brought back to him to handle? This is right after Mary died. He's talking in code. Like, right here. 'While the recent unpleasantness was handled, it was not without its complications, and the expediency of certain deeds requires me to make plans I would not have made elsewise.' He's talking about Mary. He has to be."

Kitty stopped to reread the letter. Finishing, she blinked at me over the top of the yellowing page. "What if Elizabeth killed Mary? All this time, we said it was Starkcrowe because he was mean to Mary, but what if Elizabeth did it?"

19

There was weight being in a person's house hours after she died. It was life put on pause, the living intending to return to her nest but denied the chance. A loaf of bread with the bag open at one end. Unwashed dishes piled in the sink. A half-filled garbage bag by the door. Toilet cleaner left in the toilet for a later scrubbing.

Signs of Cody's reclusion remained. Torn pieces of dark paper that used to cover the windows were stacked by the front door. The pictures were stuck to the wall with gum, none of them framed. Flypaper hung in the corner of the living room, curled and peppered with bug carcasses.

My unease matched my sadness.

We sifted through Cody's collection, though most of the things we'd already seen. There were some pictures of missing girls, and a map marked where disappearances occurred, but none of it helped solve Mary's death.

I swept the other rooms, trying not to miss anything. Two bedrooms with double beds, dressers, and bookshelves. A bathroom with no vanity. A small office with stacks of unopened notebooks, a transistor radio, and piles of books. There was no computer, nor were there screens, monitors, or mirrors of any type.

"I don't want to root around in her drawers," Kitty said. "That makes me feel bad to think about."

There were merits to thoroughness, though—what if Cody forgot to share something important? She told us a lot of things over the previous months. Something could have escaped her mind.

We could be looking all night for a needle in a haystack. Cody deserves some privacy.

"Okay. I'll grab what we have and we can go."

I shut off the lights and closed the doors behind me. Kitty waited for me in the living room while I finished up packing. I decided to take the paperwork but leave Cody's personal albums in case her family wanted the photos. As I stuffed them back into the bookshelf, a shrill wail echoed outside the house. I froze. It wasn't the same pitch as Mary, but it was much too close.

It can't be. No, it's not. So what is it?

It happened again, an exaggerated groan that sounded less like fury and more like despair. It was joined by a second and third voice, like a pack of wolves, but that wasn't quite right either. They were too human sounding. Frantic whispers followed the baying, the voices talking over one another more than to each other in a tongue I didn't understand.

I glanced at Kitty. The color had drained from her face. "What?"

She said nothing, only pointed at the side window. Fog. Dense and green and swirling in a series of tiny maelstroms. It reminded me of the fog in Mary's mirror, only softer and wispier along the edges. It curled around the house, tendrils licking at the front window and creeping skyward before dissipating into the ether.

"What is that?" Kitty demanded, but she knew. We both knew.

Ghost fog. Here.

Another unholy chorus of whispers and groans echoed through the living room from the window. I stood still, my eyes wide, my pulse pounding in my ears. The fog drifted away, toward the other side of the property, the thickest parts of it rolling and roiling like a nest of ghost serpents.

"Now. Go now." Kitty took off at a hard run through the kitchen door. I followed, shoving the house key under the welcome mat. Night had fallen, the sky black and empty of stars. The slam of Cody's door seemed to beckon the fog back; I could hear the whispers swinging back around the side lawn.

We sprinted for the car. Kitty shoved the key into the ignition and tore away from the neighborhood with a squeal of tires. A haunting screech followed us, the ghost fog an amorphous blob of fury sweeping back and forth across the pavement. Unlike Mary, it moved slowly.

"WHAT IS THIS?" Kitty slapped at the dashboard and shrieked. "What's going on?"

We sped to the sheriff's house. The two traffic stops were tor-
turous thanks to the creaking woods surrounding us. I scanned
the trees expecting green fog to spill out from the brush. Nothing, though the distant groaning turned to shrill, high-pitched
wails and yips. Halfway to the Hawthorne farm, gray fog crept
in from the marshes and rose to swallow the car, just as dense
and swirling as the ghostly stuff we'd left behind. It reminded
me of cauldron smoke.

"No green," I said. "It's normal fog."

"That doesn't make it easy to drive through." Kitty's hands
gripped ten and two on the wheel. We couldn't see more than
three feet in front of us, the high beams only worsening the
conditions.

"This is insane," Kitty murmured. "I hate this town."

More baying echoed from behind. I locked the doors, my
fingers trembling as they pressed the button. We drove in
silence, one terrible, terrifying question on my mind.

What the hell is wrong with Solomon's Folly?

The rain came as we settled into our bedroom at Hawthorne
House. The room was dated, the rose wallpaper faded, the window curtains threadbare and yellow from age. The double bed
had a metal headboard that looked institutional, like something
out of an old hospital. When the rain started to pelt the windows with fierce slaps, Lydia scurried in to put a pan in the
corner. She apologized for intruding, and darted down the hall
to her own room.

I hadn't noticed the leak in the roof until the *ping ping ping* of raindrops striking the pan began. It distracted me at first, but as I jotted into my notebook all that we knew about Mary, I tuned it out.

"You texted your mom, right?" Kitty asked, the glow of the phone illuminating her face.

"Yes. She said good night."

Kitty put her phone aside to peer at me. "So if we find Mary's body, are we still going to burn it?"

I shrugged. "I guess? Fire works on everything else. I don't know why it wouldn't with this. I'm hoping that if we solve the murder, Mary will be at rest and we won't have to worry."

"Maybe we should ask Dell," Kitty said. "It'd be really stupid if we went through all of this to find the body and then didn't know what to do with it. I'm glad we're figuring out what happened with Elizabeth, but there's still a lot we don't know, like what's the connection to mirrors? I understand the thing about mirrors sucking out the souls of the dying, but that doesn't explain how Mary gets in water, chrome, plastic."

I studied my list. I had everything clustered according to topic—discoveries about the Worths in one column, the Hawthornes another, Starkcrowe a third. There was another short list for miscellaneous facts, like how Mary was summoned, where she could appear and under what conditions. "She pops up in anything reflective. It's impossible."

"What do you mean?"

I tapped the page. "When we first talked about the mirror soul thing, we thought Mary appeared only there. But she doesn't. She's in reflections." Kitty glanced at me, confused. I tried to explain. "Okay, like, where have we seen her?"

"Mirrors. Glass. Water."

"Right, so limiting our search to mirrors is ignoring the other stuff, which is silly. There are too many possibilities. Trying to find one specific mirror tied to Mary isn't feasible."

Kitty tousled her hair, leaving her bangs askew on top of her head. "I get it. All the more reason to ask Dell."

I grabbed my phone and texted Jess. I meant to earlier when we got sidetracked with the sheriff, Cody's, and the ghost fog.

Hey, you awake? I typed.

It took her a minute to respond. *Yeah.*

Now that I had her attention, I wasn't quite sure what to do with it. I glanced at Kitty. "Do you want to stop over Dell's house after we see Elsa? It's probably easier to ask Dell in person than to filter through Jess."

She frowned. "Fine. As long as it's quick. Seeing Jess turns my stomach."

"Okay. Not a problem." I got back to texting.

We're seeing Elsa at nine tomorrow. Can we stop by after? Need to talk to your aunt.

Sure was all she said.

I was about to put the phone aside when I asked one last question. *Any sign of Mary?*

No Mary or Cody. Sunk. Fishing out 2morrow cop said. Need tow truck.

I turned off the cell and slid it onto the end table. I didn't make the connection of why they'd want the tow truck immediately, but then I remembered the winch on the back. I rolled over on my side of the bed, my back facing Kitty.

"Night, Shauna." She turned off the light before rustling around beneath the blankets and going still. I wanted to fall asleep, but my emotions were too tangled. Fear of Mary. Fear of the fog. Sadness about Cody. Trepidation about meeting Elsa Samburg. I was a ball of bad feelings, and before I knew it, tears dribbled down my cheeks to soak the pillow below.

We're in over our heads, but we've come so far.

We've sacrificed so much.

Walking away was smart, but I couldn't do that to the woman who'd died today—who'd put her faith in me. Though Cody Jackson was weird and surly and occasionally crazier than a bat in a belfry, she'd been my friend, and I would miss her.

"Geraldine Hawthorne was my great-great-aunt," the sheriff explained over pancakes. The rain had stopped, though the skies were an abysmal gray. I had on my Windbreaker in case of a storm, my hair tied back because my curls frizzed in humidity. "She opened the facility to care for her elderly father. It started as a private hospital, but my father changed that in the seventies. It's been an assisted living complex ever since."

I ate my breakfast, sandwiched between Lydia and Kitty. Bran was off watching cartoons in the other room, his breakfast on a TV tray.

"I hope this isn't rude, but, like, didn't they meet at the institution?" Kitty fidgeted in her seat, clearly uncomfortable. "Sorry to be, you know. Sorry." She fumbled with it, but I wouldn't have done any better. It wasn't an easy topic.

The sheriff stabbed into his stack of pancakes a little more fiercely than necessary. "Yes. You do know that neither of them talk, yes? That's why they gravitated to one another to begin with. When I pushed to get Karen relocated, the doctors worried what the separation would do to them, so they sent Elsa with her. They live peacefully enough despite all their crazy."

Lydia flinched. "That word, Daddy. Please."

"Right. Sorry," he murmured. "I'm not as careful with my words as I should be sometimes." He concentrated on his breakfast, and again a meal with the Hawthornes turned oppressively quiet. Kitty nudged my foot with hers under the table. I returned the gesture.

I tried to help Lydia clean up breakfast, but she kept me away from the far side of the kitchen. It was a very specific area near the double windows she seemed intent to box off. Strange, because an earlier peek through the hall window revealed nothing but empty cornfields, an enormous weeping willow tree, a shed, and an overgrown apple orchard.

The sheriff wagged his fingers at Lydia, the pads blackened with what looked like mechanical grease. "I'll plan on you two for dinner. Or Lydia will. I'm working at noon and have to oversee the swamp dredge. I'll call Dell with what we find. Hopefully, there will be two bodies and you can put this thing behind you." He paused. "Not hopefully. That's the wrong—if you need something, you have my phone number."

He looked uncomfortable.

"Thanks," I said. "We're visiting Dell after Elsa, but I don't think there are any other plans. I really hope Elsa has some information she can share about Mary that we haven't found yet."

The sheriff nodded.

I stood from the table and headed outside, Kitty on my heels. As we approached the SUV, the sheriff called out, his hand holding open the screen door. His silhouette looked huge, his shoulders broad and filling the doorway. He stepped outside in his grease-smeared tank top, pressed uniform pants, and too-polished boots.

"Be careful with my wife. Elsa, too. Please. Both of them have been through too much. They don't need help being unhappy."

"I will, Sheriff. Thank you again for trusting us," I said.

20

The Geraldine Hawthorne facility was lovely in a colonial Americana way. The cadet-blue buildings had white shutters and tall white pillars supporting the roof overhangs. The pink and white gardens were meticulously pruned, the pathways to each building new red brick. The sheriff told us that Elsa and Karen were in Building Three and to ask for Nurse Lacy at the front desk.

"I wonder what happened to the sheriff's wife," Kitty mused as we walked through the guest parking lot. "I really want to know what's up in that field. Or maybe I don't. It'll make me more freaked-out about staying with him."

"I was just thinking the same thing. And I'm too chicken to outright ask him, so maybe this is one of those cases where ignorance is bliss." I glanced at my phone. Quarter to nine. We had plenty of time.

We passed a line of open windows in the first building, the music spilling out a fifties pop song. It was a seniors aerobics class, twenty or so grandmas and grandpas shuffling to the beat while a perky brunette instructor shouted instructions. One lady in the back row exercised while holding on to her walker. What she lacked in hand motions, she made up for with awkward bounces.

The next room was a seniors pottery class, the students no younger than sixty or seventy. Everywhere we looked, older people partook in group activities to start the day. Elsa and Karen weren't that old yet. To get them into a place like this, the sheriff probably had to pull some strings. The Hawthorne name probably helped.

My knees knocked as we approached Building Three. I wanted to question Elsa, but I couldn't forget that she was a trauma victim. I dreaded what would happen if I triggered her anxiety. We had too much at stake to lose the sheriff's support, and he wouldn't be pleased if I upset his wife. Kitty opened the door. A man with a long black ponytail smiled at us from behind a reception desk. He wore blue scrubs and a stethoscope that dangled from his neck like a python. "Can I help you?"

"Hi, I'm looking for Nurse Lacy?" I said.

"You're speaking to him."

I stared at him stupidly, not registering that a nurse could be a guy. He laughed, his face breaking into so many lines, it was as if he'd aged twenty years in a second.

"I get that a lot. Shauna and Kitty, right?" When I nodded,

he produced two lanyards with laminated passes and a clipboard. "Sign here and I'll take you down." Checked in, we followed Nurse Lacy from the desk and through a reception room, passing stairs, an elevator, and an empty community room with Ping-Pong tables and soda machines. "A couple of rules before you go in. No mirrors of any kind. No compacts, no nothing. Do you have any birds on you?"

"Wait, what?" Kitty asked, clearly confused.

Nurse Lacy chuckled. "I meant on your clothes. If so we'll get you a sweater. Elsa obsesses over birds, and if you want a decent interaction with her, we need to keep her restricted to the birds she already has, not ones she might want to collect."

Lacy continued. "Don't touch Karen, or Elsa will get upset. Don't be alarmed that Karen doesn't acknowledge you. That's typical behavior." He stopped outside of a closed door and smiled, his hand poised on the knob. "I doubt that you would, but please don't remove any of the contact paper on the windows. It's there for Elsa's benefit. If you have any questions, press the green button for the intercom. If there's an emergency, press the red button and I'll come."

He opened the door and motioned us in. I stopped before crossing the threshold.

"She can't speak, but can she write?" I whispered. I figured if Elsa couldn't tell us what happened with Mary, maybe she could write it down.

Nurse Lacy shook his head. "She has nerve damage from her injuries. If you absolutely need it, I can make another appointment when a doctor's in attendance, but she gets frustrated when her motor functions don't perform well."

"Oh. Okay. Thanks."

"No problem." He winked at me and poked his head inside. "Elsa, Karen. Your guests are here."

I walked in. It was an open floor plan apartment. The first room was a combination living room and kitchen, the kitchen immediately to my left, the living room extending all the way back to a wall of windows. Everything was Easter egg–colored. The wainscoting on the wall, pale yellow. The floral wallpaper above, yellow and pink flowers with mint green leaves. The couches were peach; the cabinets in the kitchen, robin's egg blue.

I understood what Nurse Lacy meant about the contact paper then. Instead of regular panes of glass, they'd taken the time to apply a clear plastic overcoat like you might see in a bathroom window for privacy. It was wavy and bubbly and allowed colors in but no definitive shapes.

Mary in the textured glass of the shower door, looking in at me, watchful but unable to pass through. This is the same. Elsa's protecting herself all these years later.

I licked my lips, looking to the doors on the right. Three in a row, the first open and revealing a mirrorless bathroom with cotton candy–pink walls and seashell decorations. The next two were closed. Bedrooms, I guessed, though one of them could be a closet.

The women we'd come to see sat in front of the windows at a chess table. I recognized the lady on the left as Karen

Hawthorne. Her daughter resembled her—beautiful features, smooth dark skin. Her hair was buzzed short to her scalp, silver at the temples but otherwise black. She didn't look at us, nor did she look at the chessboard before her.

Elsa played chess for both of them, swiping pawns from the board with glee, her face brightening with every play. She was short and round—Rubenesque, my mother would have said—with a tan that suggested she spent a lot of time outside. Her hair was auburn and cut short beneath her ears, the sides pulled up in silver barrettes. Her dress was a short-sleeved muumuu with bright purple flowers and lace at the neck.

When she turned to look at us, I was surprised by her youthfulness. Elsa had to be midforties, but the woman didn't have a wrinkle on her face.

She didn't acknowledge Kitty or me at first, instead glancing back at the board, but then she swooped up a queen, held it above her head like a prize, and stood. She walked our way, the queen outstretched before she put it in my hand, closing my fingers around it.

"She does that," Nurse Lacy whispered behind me. "Tries to give you things. There's a basket in the hall when you leave. I'll stay a few minutes to make sure things go smoothly."

I nodded and looked at the chess piece, then at Elsa. Her eyes were very blue, her nose a little too big, her mouth small. She wore stop sign–red lipstick.

Nurse Lacy hovered by the door. Elsa gestured at the couches in the living room, the two facing each other and separated by a wicker coffee table. There was no TV, though there was a stereo cabinet with the glass doors removed. On the wall, shelves upon shelves of bird figures made of clay, porcelain, and plush stared out at us. Parrots, pigeons, ducks—it seemed the type of bird mattered far less than the presence of feathers.

Elsa shooed us toward the couches and headed for the kitchen, the half wall allowing me to see her put a kettle on the stove. She lifted a tin of tea in one hand and coffee with the other.

"I'm set," Kitty said.

Elsa looked disappointed.

I didn't want to get off on the wrong foot. "I'd love tea, thank you." Elsa proceeded to assemble three cups despite Kitty declining. Elsa brought a steaming cup over to Karen, setting it on the table by her elbow. She touched Karen's hand, scowled, and retrieved a knitted blanket from one of the bedrooms, adjusting it around Karen's shoulders and kissing her cheek. Karen never stirred.

I watched Karen from the corner of my eye, curious to see if she blinked. It wasn't often, but it did happen. I wondered if she knew we were in the room.

Elsa returned to the kitchen, humming quietly as she put our cups on a tray. I'd been told Elsa was mute. It seemed she could make noise, she simply chose not to speak.

There was a soft click as Nurse Lacy let himself out of the room.

She delivered the tea to me, looming as I honeyed the brew and sipped.

"Thank you," I said. "It's great."

She grinned. I expected her to sit with us, but she whisked over to her birds, selecting four from the hundreds if not thousands of knickknacks. She presented her prizes in her right palm. Black birds, all of them. A wooden swan, a plastic crow, a windup pelican, and a stuffed vulture with a bright orange head. I smiled at her, and them, and she shoved them at me, indicating I should take them. I did, though she plucked the plushie from the pile and put it on my head, only to let it tumble down.

She pointed at herself, then at me, and did it again, the bird on my head released to fall to my lap.

"Is it a game?" Kitty asked.

Elsa sighed and shook her head, sitting with her tea. She lifted her hand and tapped above her heart. A fake hand. I hadn't noticed it when she'd bustled about, but now that she was still, I could see the metal joint at the wrist, silver against the flesh-colored prosthetic.

I wanted to ask. I needed to ask, but I was so afraid of setting her off. Mary's name was a powder keg ready to blow, so I went for a subtler approach. I pulled down the collar on my T-shirt, showing off the scars where Mary hooked me. It was weird, but Elsa understood. She reached out and brushed the air in front of my faded wounds like she wanted to touch them but didn't dare.

She nodded slowly and tapped her hand. Then she put the bird on top of my head and watched it plummet. I caught it before it struck the floor.

"We want to make her go away," I said to Elsa. "Forever."

Elsa nodded, but then she rocked on the couch, back and forth, her brows knit together. It wasn't a good sign. Kitty's breath hitched and we locked eyes. A string of songs warbled from Elsa's throat.

"I love your birds," I said. "They're really pretty." Elsa sprung up from the couch and went to her shelves, her fingertip tapping every figurine on the head in order from left to right. It would take her all morning to do all of them, and I hoped I hadn't ruined my chance for a conversation.

Then I remembered that I had Mary's necklace and the letter Lydia gave me in my Windbreaker pocket. The necklace could be a problem, if she recognized it as Mary's, but the letter never mentioned Mary by name. It seemed a safer bet.

"Elsa, I have a letter that you might want to look at? If not, that's okay."

Elsa stopped with the birds and turned to look at me. She glanced over at Karen. The blanket had fallen off of Karen's shoulders to puddle on the floor, and Elsa rushed over to fuss with it, tucking the ends under Karen's arms with no help from the woman herself.

The tea remained untouched, steaming by Karen's elbow.

I slid the letter across the wicker table. Elsa resumed her position across from us. She eyed the envelope awhile before opening the letter from Seymour Hawthorne to Elizabeth. I braced for the worst, but she calmly refolded it, reinserted it, and slid it back to me.

And put the bird on my head. It fell to the floor. She pointed at it and then me.

Kitty stooped to retrieve it, her look equal parts confusion and frustration. I felt the same, but I wasn't sure what to do. In the end, it didn't matter. Elsa let out a cry, standing from the couch so fast, I was afraid she'd hit her head on the overhead ceiling fan. She whirled in a circle, the floral muumuu billowing out around her before she sailed to the windows. She started at the left window, her hands pressed against the contact paper before she inched to the right and swept across the room, narrowly avoiding Karen.

"Elsa? Is everything okay?" I was alarmed. So was Kitty. She crept off the couch to retreat toward the intercom on the wall.

Elsa moaned, the fingers of her right hand spreading over the glass. She shoved her face against the pane, nose mashing flat. Behind me, Kitty pushed the button to call Nurse Lacy. The intercom buzzed as Elsa let out a low-pitched bellow. I eased her way, hoping to bring comfort—terrified that I'd tormented her with the letter—but before I could reach her, Elsa screeched and bashed her head against the glass.

Crunch.

She sobbed and pulled back for a second strike, the contact hard enough to shake the window without breaking it.

Crunch!

Blood splashed across the contact paper, following the bubbling pattern as it dribbled down.

Crunch, crunch, crunch.

"Elsa, no!" My arms wrapped around her from behind. I heaved her back, but she was heavier than me and so much stronger. Her head slammed off the glass again and again, her nose exploding in a burst of red. She wailed, both her natural hand and her prosthetic beating on the glass above her head. I slid my hand between her face and the window to stop her, but she crushed my fingers with her next blow.

I yelped and pulled away, my forearm covered in Elsa's blood. Behind me, Kitty pounded on the buzzer for assistance, opening the door and screaming for help. Nurse Lacy burst in a few seconds later, a young, redheaded nurse on his heels. The blood was everywhere—on Elsa, on me. It covered the pane and soiled the carpet below. Splashes of it traveled far enough that they dappled Karen's cheek.

"What happened?" Nurse Lacy demanded, he and the other nurse wrapping their arms around Elsa to peel her away from the window.

"I don't know. I'm sorry. She got up and...I don't know." Tears streamed down my cheeks. My fingers ached. Elsa thrashed to get away from them, but when Nurse Lacy whispered in her ear, she went slack and sobbed. The nurses turned her around and guided her to the couch.

"Sign out," Nurse Lacy said. "Please. At the front desk. I have to take care of her. You can leave the lanyards there."

"I...right. I swear, I didn't do anything."

He said nothing. I took two steps back before Elsa lifted her pulpy, smashed face my way, her nose crushed and pointing at an odd angle. She whimpered and then she screeched, furious, blood and spittle flying in my direction. I understood then why she could hum but not talk.

Elsa Samburg had no tongue.

21

"I don't know what happened." I dropped Elsa's trinkets into the basket outside of her room, the tears drying on my cheeks. "She seemed fine with the letter. I don't get it."

"Neither do I, but you have to call the sheriff," Kitty said. "Maybe if he hears it from you, he won't be so mad."

The idea felt as bad as when I'd had to call my mother to tell her Bronx had fallen through the windows from our apartment—or been pushed by Mary, really.

The blood drying on my arms felt itchy. I wanted to stop by a bathroom to scrub, but I was pretty sure if we didn't exit immediately, Nurse Lacy would call security. We removed our lanyards and signed out at the unattended desk, baffled by Elsa's breakdown.

The mystery was solved the moment we stepped outside.

Jess stood on the brick walkway, peering at the building front. Her head was bandaged above the ears, her lip and eye still swollen from the previous day's attack. The bruises on her face and neck had faded from plum to a sickly yellow. She wore a too-big Harvard sweatshirt and sweatpants, which had to be loaners from her aunt.

Seeing all the blood on me, her eyes went huge. "Oh, God. Did Mary attack you? I'm so sorry."

"What are you doing here?" I stalked toward her, anger surging from the pit of my stomach like lava bubbling up inside of a volcano. "You were told to stay away."

She took a step back. "I'm sorry. I just wanted to talk to her myself. Probably about the same stuff you were talking to her about, but I felt useless at home."

"You were told to stay away!" My hands made contact with her shoulders, and I shoved as hard as I could. She fell back into a pink flowering bush, flailing, her feet barely touching the ground. "Why don't you listen?"

Elsa had been fine. If she was prone to violence or self-harm they would have warned me or not let me come at all. Something outside the window had set her off. Elsa sensed the Mary taint. She knew evil was in her midst and she reacted to it.

"Shauna," Kitty said from behind me, her voice quiet. "We should go."

"I cannot believe you, Jess." I closed in on her and grabbed her shoulders, my fingers digging in so hard that she flinched. I shook her, my body convulsing with rage. "Your aunt told you why you shouldn't come. You hurt Elsa."

"I deserve to talk to her!" Jess yelled it in my face, pushing me back. "She's got answers. I'm the one dying here."

"Elsa just smashed her face to bits. The blood on me is hers. Do you know why? It's because YOU showed up after Dell told you it was a bad idea. I keep wanting to forgive you—to find something redeemable about you—and you keep acting as if your life is worth more than everyone else's!"

"I tried to save you before! From Mary. I did that for you," she protested. She reached out her hand to me, to touch my arm, but I recoiled.

"No, you did it for *you*. You didn't want to lose *your* friend. It'd inconvenience *you*. Anna and Kitty were incidental to *your* needs. I guess Cody was, too, huh?" I stepped into Jess again, seething enough my fist clenched, but Kitty grabbed the back of my shirt and yanked.

"Let's go." She walked me toward the parking lot, her hand looped around my bicep. It didn't hurt, but her grip was firm enough that I didn't dare struggle, either.

"I'm okay," I lied.

"No, you're not. People are staring. Get in the car." Kitty threw me into the passenger's side of the SUV before whirling on Jess, her finger lifting to point at her face. "We're going to see Dell to tell her what happened with Elsa, and after that you're going to stay away from us, or I swear to God I'll feed you to Mary myself."

Jess dropped her head into her hands and wept, soul-wrenching sobs that echoed across the grounds. I jerked my face away, angry and hurt and sad.

Why, Jess? I want to open up to you again, but you keep screwing it up.

Smatters of elderly people watched us, some through the windows, some on morning walks. Most of them looked concerned, but a few were clearly scared. One woman gesticulated at us with a cell phone attached to her ear.

My mouth screwed into an ugly smirk.

By all means, call the cops. I'm sure the sheriff is going to love hearing this.

She hadn't called the sheriff, or if she had, he wasn't off the phone with her by the time I called. I got his voice mail instead. I rambled through my explanation, apologizing every other sentence and laying a whole heap of blame on Jess's shoulders.

"The nerve." I slid my phone into my pocket. I'd wanted to believe Jess was getting better, but a leopard doesn't change its spots. "I wonder if she tried to talk to Elsa after we left. I hope not, for Elsa's sake." Kitty shook her head, guiding the car onto Dell's street.

We parked the car at ten o'clock sharp according to the dashboard. I pulled out Seymour Hawthorne's letter and approached the front door.

I knocked, alarmed when the door swung open with barely any pressure. I pushed it all the way, and Horace rushed past me and dove under the porch. Something wasn't right. An unpleasant coldness settled into my chest.

Mary.

Kitty took a step forward, but I held her back, a finger lifting to my lips to indicate quiet. She nodded, wide-eyed.

Snort. Snuffle. Gurgle.

Wet, animalistic sounds resonated from the back of the house, Dell's kitchen. I surveyed the living room. Everything was orderly as it should be, no pictures out of place, no tchotchkes skewed. The mess we'd made with the Mary memorabilia had been tidied, the accordion folders lined up neatly. Only a single letter remained out in the open. The box of salt and the candle from yesterday's failed summoning were perched on the end of the stairs, waiting to be put away.

Another snort from the kitchen was followed by a ragged moan. Even wordless, I recognized Dell's voice.

She's alive back there.

But she wasn't alone, and by the sounds of it, Mary had done something awful to her.

Kitty and I had a choice to make. We shared a look before she squeezed my fingers. I squeezed back. She went for the box of salt on the stairs as I tiptoed toward the fireplace, grabbing the poker from the kit by the mantel. I lifted it as carefully as I could, not wanting to rattle or clang and call attention our way. The iron weight in my hands was a small comfort as I eased toward the hallway, my feet silent on the rug. Kitty followed so close behind me, I could feel the heat of her breath on the back of my ear.

Out of the living room and past the bathroom. The mauve carpet ended at the doorway of the kitchen, becoming beige linoleum. The smears were impossible to miss. Wide, thick rust smudges streaked the floor, as if someone had taken a push broom to a puddle of blood. It traversed the kitchen from right to left and curled up and around the island toward the sliding back doors. The left door was broken, the glass shattered at the top with angry, pointed shards lining the bottom.

I eased inside and immediately wished I hadn't. Mary crouched above Dell's supine body, squatting like a troll over fleshy treasure. Her feet flanked Dell's torso, pinning her arms tight. Mary's head was tilted forward hiding her expression, the gaping hole of her ear allowing a beetle to scurry in and out with wild abandon. Her dress was no longer white, but brown from crusted sand.

She climbed out of the pit. She found a way.

I bit my tongue to keep from crying out.

There was another wet squish, and Dell screamed—a strange, muffled thing that sounded off. I couldn't see what Mary had done, but Dell's legs and hands juddered, slapping against the floor beneath her. A puddle of blood-tinged water dribbled across the floor, settling into the grooves between the tiles and slithering toward my sneaker.

I cringed and eyed Kitty. She swallowed hard and nodded, encouraging me forward. I raised the fireplace poker over my head.

Another inch to the left.

Two.

The moment I had a clear view of what Mary had done to Dell, I had to bite back my screams. One of Mary's hands pried Dell's mouth open too wide. Her thumb peeled up Dell's top lip, exposing a row of gums missing half their teeth. I was frozen in terror, unable to look away as Mary reached in to pluck another tooth free with her bare fingers.

Squish.

Dell howled, body bowing in agony. Mary ignored her pain, stuffing the tooth into her own fetid maw with a series of chuffs.

She's taking Dell's teeth.

"No," I wheezed, my brain refusing to accept the scene before me. "No!"

Mary jerked her face my way and hissed, her lower face smeared with Dell's blood, the top line of her teeth red-stained porcelain.

22

I charged Mary, the fireplace poker clenched in my fists like a baseball bat. I arced it down, swinging at her head as hard as I could, but Mary jerked out her hand to intercept the blow. She tore the iron from my grasp with ease and tossed it aside like garbage. It clanged as it hit the refrigerator, rolling under the kitchen cabinets and from my reach.

Kitty rushed in with the salt. Handful after handful, smoke billowing from Mary's head where it struck cursed flesh. Mary screeched, her claws tearing tracks in her own face. The flayed flesh gaped wide, a black, tarry blood seeping from the wounds. The kitchen reeked, a cross between spoiled milk and burnt meat.

"Get the poker!" Kitty barked, advancing. Mary stumbled when Dell reached up to grab her foot and twist. It wasn't enough to trip her, but it was enough to call her attention to the floor. She snarled and reached down, face still smoking when she bunched her hands in the front of Dell's bloodied pajama top.

I darted for the poker as Kitty ripped open the top of the salt box, shaking the contents over the top of Mary's bald, pointed head. Another barrage of smoke accompanied her scream. Dell dropped to the floor with a wet thud.

Mary retreated toward the doors. The smoke pouring off of her spread across the ceiling. I grabbed the poker, holding it like a rapier as my sneaker skidded through the growing puddle on the floor. Water was everywhere. I couldn't tell if it was from Mary's time in the swamp or part of her ghostly repertoire.

I lunged at her. She swiped at me again before grabbing a kitchen chair, hoisting it like it weighed nothing. The chair sailed at my head, but I ducked, feeling the brush of air as it whizzed by my ear. The chair hit the wall and splintered apart, leaving a huge dent in the plaster.

I skittered forward with the poker in one hand. Kitty flanked from the other side, now armed with the table salt. Mary swung her head between us, gurgling before her mouth curled up into her new smile. She grabbed a chair in each hand and whipped them—one at me, the other at Kitty. I heard Kitty scream as I dove for the floor, the chair striking the cabinets above me and raining down wooden pieces.

Chair legs, armrests, and the seat pelted me on the back. Mary ran at me, her engorged foot slamming down on the wrist of the hand holding the weapon. Her claws plunged into my back. She sunk them deep, through my Windbreaker, thin T-shirt, and bra, cutting through flesh and muscle.

I screamed as she tittered above me. Mary wrested one of her hands from my back to twist it around the base of my ponytail, lifting me by it, all of my weight pulling on my scalp. She hauled me close, pressing my fleshy body against her bony one. Her head dipped close to mine as she breathed in my scent.

Or, more specifically, the scent of my blood. She twitched beside me and then she lifted her head, striking down like a viper, her new teeth sinking into the meat of my shoulder.

She bit me. The bitch bit me!

I keened. I didn't know if I was marked again, if the burden had bounced back my way. Mary reared up, a splash of my blood joining the rest on her mouth. I thrashed in her arms, but Mary squeezed tighter, her hand leaving my ponytail to stroke over the top of my head. Her fingers threaded through the strands as if to comb them. She wrapped a lock around her bony, blue finger and pulled, watching it bounce up. She repeated the gesture, chortling as my hair resumed its shape upon release. The third time, she wound it tight before jerking it from my head.

The lock ripped away. Hot blood rushed down my scalp. It coiled over my forehead and dripped along my cheek. My vision swam, refocusing in time to see Mary lifting a lock of my hair to her own head, like she'd fashioned herself a new wig.

My understanding was swift and brutal.

She wants my hair.

"NO. IT'S MINE. YOU CAN'T HAVE IT!"

Mary shook me to silence me, cooing as she gazed at the red curls surrounding my face. I kicked her knee. I pinched her sides. I fought her with every bit of strength I could claim. It did nothing.

What did do something was the knife.

Neither Mary nor I saw Kitty coming. One second she wasn't there, the next she was, jamming the butcher's knife at Mary with a scream. Mary dropped me, my legs unable to right themselves in time to keep me upright. I hit the floor with a whump, sprawling beside Dell and feeling queasy.

The poker. Have to get the poker.

I gritted my teeth and crawled across the kitchen floor. Kitty pulled the knife free, only to plunge it in again—higher and farther than the first strike. Stabs like that would have killed a person, but Mary was different. Nonhuman. She flailed, her arms swinging wildly to either side of her, knocking candlesticks and a napkin holder off the kitchen table.

My hand closed around the iron.

I swung it around as hard as I could, smashing Mary in the leg. She staggered back, twisting her body to avoid another blow. Instead of facing the kitchen, she faced the shattered sliding doors. I hit her again, aiming for the second knee. She fell forward. I didn't intend for her to hit the jagged spikes of the glass door, but that's how she landed, the longest, thickest pieces impaling her chest and stomach. Her lower half kicked behind her, her upper half pounded on the planks of the deck.

"Oh, my God. Are you okay?" Kitty sailed to my side, a nasty cut bleeding on the side of her neck.

"Yes. No. I don't know. Dell." I motioned toward Dell. She'd rolled onto her hip, away from me. Her back was unmarred, but I knew the devastation of the front. I crawled over to her, putting my hand on her shoulder. "I am so sorry."

It was unclear how long Mary would be out of commission. Part of me wanted to stab her a few hundred more times, but her powers of recuperation were so ridiculous, the better plan was to run while we had the chance.

Dell shouted something back at me, but without her top teeth, I couldn't understand her. She slapped at the floor in front of her. I scrambled around to her front side, still kneeling. She gazed at me with watery eyes, her mouth closed but seeping blood from the corners. She tried to speak again, but it came out like a moan. Frustrated, she growled before forcing herself up onto an elbow.

She dipped her finger in the blood beneath her and wrote on the linoleum.

L.

E.

T.

"Letter," I said, remembering the letter on the table in the front room. Dell nodded and cringed. I shoved myself up and glanced back at Mary. She thrashed like an upended roach, occasionally pushing herself far enough up the spikes that she'd free herself from one only to slip down to the bottom of another.

"We have to go now," I said to Kitty. "Help Dell."

We maneuvered to either side of Dell, adopting the all-too-familiar position of carrying one of our wounded when she couldn't propel herself. Out of the kitchen and into the hallway, the space was too narrow for three adult bodies and so we turned to the side, sidled our way to the living room. Once there, I broke away to grab the letter, stuffing it into the pocket with Mary's locket.

We hurried out of the house and to the SUV.

"What about the cat?" Kitty asked, helping Dell into the backseat. "Should I try to coax him out from under the porch?"

"Screw the cat. We have to go." Kitty glared at me before climbing into the driver's side, waiting for me to take my seat before locking the doors. She peeled away from Dell's house with a cloud of dust and screeching tires. "Fine. Where are we going?"

"To the hospital," I said.

Dell grunted from the backseat, slapping the headrest next to my ear. I turned to look at her. She put up two fingers, then one finger before pantomiming making a call and pointing back at her house.

"Jess," I said, my voice flat. "You want me to warn her."

Dell nodded and collapsed into the backseat. The blood at the sides of her mouth made me think of a clown with a painted frown.

I pulled out my phone, the message difficult to type because my hands shook so badly, I could barely function.

Stay away from Dell's. Mary is there. Dell w/us.

The moment I sent it, Dell tapped my headrest again. This time, she pointed at my pocket.

"Yes, the letter, but you need to get to the hosp—" She shook her head and poked my pocket, jabbing me in the hip.

January 12, 1865

Joseph,

My sweet man. Please come home. Of course I will think no worse of you for it. I know what I charged you with in my previous letters, but that was revenge speaking. If it added undue pressure, I'm sorry. I'm grateful for all you have done. Solomon's Folly is an unpleasant place in the best of circumstances. In the worst, it's nightmarish. You've spent two long months righting the wrongs done to my sister and mother. It's not your fault that you were stymied at every pass.

While I've never met the pastor myself, my sister's letters were enough to convince me that he is a demon. I'm glad you find him displeasing. It would have troubled me more, I think, if you'd disagreed with Mary's assessment. To know that he's as dogmatic and unpleasant as Mary claimed is a strange comfort. I can cast him as a villain with no weight upon my conscience.

I cannot say much about the Hawthornes other than what you've gleaned. Seymour is protective of his house and something of an ass (forgive me, I know that's awful). It's sad that a servant of justice would be so corrupt. You're likely right about the family's involvement. Elizabeth was always cruel to Mary, and her marriage to the pastor makes me believe more than ever they have something to hide. It's not so surprising, I suppose. The Hawthornes' legacy is mysterious and dismal.

The constable isn't a terrible man if you don't expect him to do his duty. Mother often had him to dinner. The best I can say about him is he's a jovial drunk and a terrible card cheat. You do know he spends his weekends at the gentlemen's club with Seymour? That would explain why your attempts to get into Hawthorne House went unsupported. He is in Seymour's pocket, as snug as a ball of lint.

I am glad you will pursue the matter beyond Seymour's authority. I don't expect the state to do much about it, but at least we tried. I don't want to give up without a fight. I already feel like we were bullied away from the truth.

Your return is joyful for you, for me, and for our son. You will be happy to know he is past his croup. He is hardy and hale and quite eager to see his father after so long. This awfulness denied you much-deserved time, and I am eager to see you reacquainted.

I will see you soon, my love.

Constance

I read the letter once, and then I read it aloud for Kitty. Seymour Hawthorne's letter came next for Dell. I reopened the letter Jess forwarded to me on the phone from Philip Starkcrowe to Constance, too. I wished I had the rest, but I wasn't sure I needed them anymore. The puzzle pieces that had been straining to fit for so long clicked together in one glorious, terrible moment of understanding.

Philip's letter to Constance after her disappearance. Joseph's letter to Constance telling her of the search. Seymour Hawthorne's letter to Elizabeth Hawthorne telling her she'd marry Starkcrowe. Constance to Joseph telling him to come home. Constance to Joseph six months later, after he'd left The Folly, telling him she'd seen Mary's ghost.

"I know where she is," I said, my voice strangled. "Oh, my God. Elsa tried to tell me, and I was too stupid to figure it out."

"What are you talking about? What does Elsa have to do with anything?" Kitty looked alarmed, as if I spoke in tongues.

"It's Hawthorne House!" I scrambled with the letters. "Okay, this last letter, Constance says Joseph was never given permission to look in Hawthorne House. One of the earlier letters—I think it's in Dell's collection—says that he got a warrant for the church. But he must have been stopped when he tried to get another one to investigate the Hawthornes. And in Seymour's letter, he talks about the House of Hawthorne all with capital *H*s. But then he says in one line, 'I dislike having this stain under my crest. It befouls my house,' with a little *h*. He means the actual house, not the family. The crest is the bird. The stain is Mary. They must have moved Mary from the church to the house."

Kitty grinned beside me, slapping the steering wheel and bouncing in her seat. "The bird in the window is the crest! Elsa kept putting you under the bird. Holy shit. Okay, okay. So now what?"

"We'll get Dell to the hospital and then I'll call—"

Another smack to my headrest. Dell shook her head at me from the backseat, stubbornly refusing to be sent away. She didn't look good; her coloring was gray, her brow sweaty. I reached out to check her for fever, and she was clammy to the touch. Every part of her drooped, as if she'd gone boneless since the attack.

"You need a doctor," Kitty said looking at Dell in the rearview. "You look awful."

Dell's hand lifted and she made her fingers walk, then mimed the phone call again. It took me a second to decipher it. "You want us to go there and then call? The sher—no, an ambulance. Right. Okay." She tapped her nose and slumped into her seat.

"Two birds, one stone," I said. "Head to Hawthorne House. Or, no. Wait. Mary. She bled me. I don't know if she's going to follow me or not, and Lydia and Bran are there. Maybe you two should go without me."

"No way." Kitty stopped driving in the vague direction of *away from Dell's* and toward the highway that'd get us to Hawthorne House. "Dell's just as apt to have Mary on her trail as you are at this point, and I don't want to go alone. Sorry, don't mean to endanger the Hawthornes, but this is not a one-man job."

That meant I needed to convince Sheriff Hawthorne to let us dig around his house *and* relocate his children.

"What if he doesn't let us in?" I squirmed in my seat, immediately regretting it when my back ached. I went stone still to lessen the pain. "He doesn't have to cooperate."

Dell slapped her palm over her chest, her brow furrowed. She looked fierce. I remembered then what she'd said when she'd first put in the call to Hawthorne.

His blood owes mine and I'm not afraid to remind him.

I called, hoping the sheriff wouldn't avoid me after the morning's episode with Elsa. He picked up after one ring.

"Hawthorne." He sounded harsh.

"Hi, Sheriff. It's Shauna. I called earlier."

"I know. The facility called, too. Karen's fine. I should have known better, but—" He cut himself off. "It's not your fault. They left you unsupervised and that wasn't—it's not your fault."

"Thanks." I sucked in a deep breath as Kitty pulled onto the highway. At most, we were ten minutes away from the manor house. I couldn't waste any time. "Look, there's no good way to tell you this, so I'm just going to get to it. I think Mary's body is in Hawthorne House. Like, buried in it somewhere."

There was a long pause on the other end of the line. "What makes you say that?"

I couldn't read his voice. He didn't sound mad, but that didn't mean he wasn't. "Letters we've read. We dug up Mary's locket in the church. We think she might have been buried there at one point. I'd love to show you everything, but there's no time now. Mary killed Anna and Cody. She beat up Dell. God, she pulled out her teeth. It's now or never, Sheriff. Please."

He said nothing for a long moment, but then I heard the whir of police car sirens. "Give me twenty minutes to collect my kids. I'll unlock the chains. If you're looking for clues, they'd be in the old house."

We waited in a convenience store parking lot off the highway. It was a run-down place with one functioning gas pump that had no credit card slider, a neon OPEN sign blinking in the window, and another sign warning shoplifters they'd be persecuted above a picture of a shotgun. A Rottweiler trotted around the back of the store on a short leash, barking at us.

The sheriff needed time to get his kids out. It occurred to me that he could be sweeping the house to try to hide evidence. Was twenty minutes long enough to move a body? What choice did I have but to believe him when he said he wanted one less monster in town? Dell shivered in the backseat. Kitty cranked the heat despite the June temperature pushing eighty. It wouldn't do a whole lot against shock.

"The minute we get there, I'm calling nine-one-one," Kitty said. A part of me could understand why Dell made a fuss. She'd been victimized by Mary off and on for fifty years—she didn't want to be sent away at the last minute.

Five more minutes. I was about to tell Kitty to head toward the house when my phone buzzed. Jess.

"Where are you?" she asked.

"On our way to Hawthorne House. We'll call an ambulance for Dell when we get there."

"Why are you waiting?" Jess sounded furious, like we were denying care to Dell just to spite her. As usual, it was all about Jess.

"I can't put her on the phone. She can't talk. Mary pulled out her teeth. She insisted she come along." I glanced at the backseat. Dell's head dipped forward, her eyes fluttering. "Or, we'll call now and the ambulance can meet us there. Either way, she'll get to the hospital."

"Fine." Jess hung up. I wondered if I should warn her away from Hawthorne House, but what good would it do? She didn't listen to anybody. My lone consolation was that she posed no greater or lesser threat than I did. Mary had bled me and I'd survived. I could be her chosen victim.

Again.

"She's going to meet us there, I take it," Kitty said, her voice flat.

"Probably."

Kitty started the car and drove us out of the parking lot. I dialed 911 on my phone, but before the call went through, Dell's hand swatted out to smack the phone away. It fell into the well beside my feet. She scowled at me and shook her head.

"You're being stubborn," I said. She shrugged. "If you die, Mary wins."

We'd just pulled onto the winding road that led to the sheriff's house when Kitty squinted at her rearview. Her eyes swept from street to mirror and back again, her spine stiffening. I looked behind me. I could see the dot on the horizon, far enough away that it was indiscernible, close enough that it lent me pause.

"Is it—?"

"I don't know," I said, cutting Kitty off. "But we'd best be prepared." I did a cursory check of the backseat for make-shift weapons. Salt. So much salt. We had the shovel and sledgehammer from the basement excavation along with the lanterns and lighters. I picked up a lantern and turned it over. Lamp oil.

I didn't know if Bloody Mary could burn, but I wasn't beyond finding out.

24

Hawthorne House vacant was dreadful.

The tall grass in the fields should have rustled. Birds should have sung from their perches in the trees. The wind should have whispered as it blew by, but everything was still. I climbed from the car, a lantern in my hand, a lighter wedged into the waistband of my jeans, my pockets bulging with salt.

I expected Dell to wait in the car, but as soon as Kitty parked, Dell started limping toward the older half of Hawthorne House. She was in better shape than I assumed, or maybe this was like her perseverance in the swamp—Aunt Dell was Herculean. There was flint under that withered exterior.

"I'm still calling an ambulance," Kitty said. "She's hurt."

"I'll go with her." I jogged across the yard. Dell was already at the house, stepping over the rusty coils of chains that had barred the way not an hour ago. She turned the knob and the door swung wide on the hinge. The interior of the house was so dark, I was sure it was where light went to die. I shouted at Dell to stop, shoving past her to take the lead.

"You're hurt and I have a light. Let me go first."

She nodded, the movement sending flakes of dried blood snowing to the ground. The crease between her lips remained a brilliant scarlet.

I searched for light switches along the wall, but flicking them did nothing. I lit the lantern, thankful for its dim incandescence. It was strange to be in a house so similar to the other while being altogether different at the same time. The layouts matched, the front room and kitchen that opened up on the right to a dining room. The stairs were on the left, a bathroom tucked in behind. The open archway in front of the staircase led into a den.

But the floorboards curled up in the corners. Dingy sheets shrouded the furniture. The chandelier above the entrance had nine broken flutes of glass surrounding nine equally-as-broken lightbulbs. I was afraid a rotten floor might send me plummeting into the basement, but a few slow, steady steps proved the construction solid. I swept the kitchen, Dell shivering all the while. Her hand balled in my shirt. She tugged too hard, forcing the fabric to brush over my new cuts.

I opened cabinets and poked my head into the bathroom. Raw pipes from where a vanity used to be. A lime-stained toilet. A moth-eaten shower curtain hid a tub with curved white feet. I whisked it aside, but the tub was empty save for disassembled plumbing guts.

Too obvious. If they hid the body, they actually hid it. Crawl spaces. Under floorboards. In closets.

I edged my way to the steps, Dell my frail shadow.

"I'm going for the basement," I said to her. "Be careful."

Dell grabbed my arm and shook her head, pointing at a broken board in the floor near the kitchen. I shone my flashlight down, only to see a dirt floor. Dell poked me again and proceeded to hold her fingers close together, pantomiming small.

"A small basement?"

She nodded. Her hands closed together one on top, one on the bottom like a sandwich.

"A crawl space?"

She nodded once.

I didn't have the resources to handle a crawl space, and our time frame wasn't exactly solid. I swept the downstairs instead. Going into the side room, I found a small door tucked in the corner that looked like it had been purposefully hidden by a chair. I moved the chair and looked inside, the dim light making it hard to see.

There was a scratching sound and I tensed, my hand poised on the short half door. A mouse scurried into my flashlight light, eyes big and whiskers twitching.

My heart is racing over a rodent. Breathe, Shauna. Get it together.

I headed back for the entryway so I could climb to the second floor. Dell had taken the other side of the house, but when I moved for the stairs, she followed.

"Nothing?" I asked.

She shook her head.

The stair rail felt solid beneath my hand. I climbed to the second story, Dell at my back. A jingle outside made me tense, but then Kitty jogged in behind us with the sledgehammer clenched in her hands. She eyeballed the stairs before whirling on the window to her left, knocking two boards away from the glassless frame. Shards of light stretched across the dark, gouged floor.

Kitty followed us up the stairs. "That's better. The operator said fifteen or twenty minutes on the ambulance. Maybe you should wait in the car, Dell?"

Dell didn't answer.

Up we went. The spiderwebs on the second story were intense, stretched from the ceiling beams to the railing on the balcony over the kitchen. I used the lantern to sweep them aside. Sticky white strands clung to my arm and tangled in my hair. A wisp flew into my mouth. "It's possible Elsa was being literal. Maybe Mary's under the stained glass window," I said. "Or maybe she's under one of the tombstones in the graveyard."

Dell tugged on my sleeve and pointed past me. At the back of the room, a slim door nestled in beside a sheet-covered bookshelf. I hefted the lantern and approached. The door opened with no trouble, though the stairs beyond were daunting. The boards were narrow and steep, twisting up into blackness.

My shoulders barely fit as I ascended. The darkness abated the higher we climbed, light peeking in through tiny cracks in the walls. Two rotations up and I had to stop. An overhead door blocked the way. I jiggled the hook latch, but it wouldn't move.

"Kitty, I need the sledgehammer." She handed it to me without complaint.

I gripped it by the handle and shoved up, once, twice. Metal moaned in protest before the door flew open with a loud rattle, kicking up a cloud of dust. I pulled my T-shirt up over my nose so I wouldn't have to breathe it in and climbed into the room.

The space was twelve feet wide but only eight deep. Windows faced the front yard and to the east. To the west, a glass door gave access to the widow's walk. The stained glass window should have been on the south side, but it was shielded by a wall. Two broken end tables, a covered couch, and a faded painting of flowers barred the way.

The stained glass wasn't dark from dust. It's dark because it's walled off from the other windows.

"Maybe she's behind it," I said. "They could have hid her there."

Outside, a screech echoed across the Hawthorne property.

Knowing who it was—how close she was—I rushed to action. When the door to the widow's walk wouldn't open, I used the sledgehammer to force it, breaking three panes of glass in the process. The sheriff's potential ire didn't matter. Nothing mattered except getting behind that wall.

"Move the furniture," I said. "We need to get at the window."

"Just toss it out on the widow's walk?" Kitty tested the couch with her foot before stepping on it and grabbing the painting from the wall.

"Yes. Hurry."

Dell stood back while Kitty and I cleared the room. The couch wouldn't fit through the doorframe, so we maneuvered it over the floor hatch as a Mary deterrent. I was afraid the wall blocking us from the window was constructed of brick, like something from "The Cask of Amontillado," but there was a fist-sized hole near the bottom. Something had scratched its way through the horsehair plaster, allowing a shred of light to pass into our side of the cupola.

I swung the sledgehammer around with all my strength. The wall gave way more easily than I'd expected, the old plaster crumbling upon impact. The second strike sent white bits flying around the room like shrapnel. Over and over I pounded, until we could see the skeletal wooden framework beneath.

Until we could see a brown leather trunk behind the wall.

It was about five feet long, two wide, two deep. Black straps at the ends held it closed, the golden buckles gleaming despite ages of disuse. In front of it was an aged, yellow envelope face-down on the floor.

"Oh, God." I cleared out enough of the bottom plaster that I could step into the hidden portion of the cupola. I tucked the envelope in my back pocket and crouched beside the trunk, the sledgehammer propped against the wall behind me. My eyes strayed to the glass window above with its black bird. The crow's beady eyes watched me.

Another bellow from outside impelled me to open the trunk. I went for the lock expecting it to give me trouble, but the moment I applied pressure, it opened. The lid parted from the base and a musty odor filled the air.

Kitty lifted the lantern, the light revealing a 150-year-old truth. Bones and cloth. Ragged yellow lace twisted around a pile of remains so long interred, there was no flesh. To the left, a skull with crooked teeth. A leg bone. A pile of dust. To the right, a rib cage, a scrap of black cloth . . .

And a second skull. There wasn't supposed to be a second skull.

My hand flew to my mouth.

"Oh, Jesus."

"Is that two skulls?" Kitty demanded. "Oh, my God. Who is it?"

My mind raced for an explanation. Names and dates streamed through my head. Constance and Joseph lived to ripe old ages. We'd found Hannah in the cave. Elizabeth was buried outside. The friends were accounted for even if we hadn't seen their grave markers in person.

Starkcrowe went missing. His tombstone said he died April 8, 1865.

Something about the date seemed significant, and I racked my brain, trying to force the connection.

"April eighth. April eighth." I murmured it to myself, my mind's eye retracing all the steps I'd made in my Mary journey.

"What?" Kitty demanded.

Constance.

"The letter!" I nearly squawked it, turning back to the remains. "From Constance to Joseph."

Mary moaned somewhere below us, the encroaching threat working her way toward the humans trapped in the small space. Kitty tossed one of the end tables onto the couch, like that'd help keep Mary out.

"Which letter? Spit it out, Shauna."

"It was dated April ninth. Constance saw Mary for the first time the day after Starkcrowe's supposed disappearance. Don't you get it?"

Frantic, I thrust my hands into the bones, searching for answers. The yellow lace was definitely from a woman's dress, but the black cloth was nondescript. I moved aside the rib cage and grabbed for what looked like a sleeve. The bones rattled as I pulled it free. The cloth was thin and yet still managed to be stiff. I oriented it as best I could, wincing when a bone dropped from inside to join the collection below.

It was a jacket adorned with brass buttons, the folded lapels reminding me of a gentleman's suit coat. Layered beneath was a clerical collar.

"It's Starkcrowe," I said. "Mary's spirit rose six months after her death. When they buried her with her murderer."

Mary chose to stay.

The Hawthornes' cruelty birthed this monster.

25

From downstairs came the crash of a marauding ghost breaking furniture. I dropped the pastor's coat and eyed the remains, my pulse pounding in my ears. There was no way out of here. The widow's walk was on the roof of the house, and while the eaves allowed us to slide down a ways, it was a long drop to the ground.

Except for the conservatory. It was tall enough. If we can get a solid grip, it'd be possible to jump.

"Take Dell to the conservatory and climb down. I'll burn the bodies. Maybe destroying the remains will send her away." I removed the cap from the bottom of the lantern, a slow trickle of lamp oil escaping the hole. I sloshed it over the bones and ancient clothes. "I really hope they send a fire truck along with the ambulance. Otherwise, the whole house will burn."

More thunderous noises from downstairs and the sound of

something heavy breaking. Mary hunted us, and the longer she went without her quarry, the angrier she grew.

"The conservatory's in ruins, Shauna. The dome's broken. The broken glass. How are we supposed to—"

"It's better to risk that than stay here," I yelled. "Just head that way, Kitty. I'll catch up to you, okay?" On the outside, I was stone. On the inside, I was mush. But we'd come too far to fail. We were closer to ending Mary's curse than anyone had ever come before.

I resigned myself to the dangers a long time ago. I can do this.

Kitty grabbed Dell by the arm and pulled, but Dell's feet remained planted to the floor. Dell pointed at me and extended her hand for the lantern.

I eyed her. "I'll do it."

She opened her mouth to speak and another torrent of blood spilled forth. A clot slithered from between her lips and spilled onto her shirt. Her jaw snapped shut. She looked pained as she pointed out at the widow's walk and then smacked her bad leg.

"She can't do the climb," Kitty said quietly. "And I can't carry her alone."

Dell tapped the side of her nose. Again, she reached for the lantern. More stomping from below, this time on the stairs. The sofa atop the hatch would keep Mary out for a minute or two, but her strength was too great for it to last.

Our only hope is the bones.

I grabbed Dell's wrist and squeezed. "I'm going to lure her out so you can escape. I promise. Hang on as long as you can." Dell nodded. Kitty offered her the sledgehammer, but she declined, snatching the lantern and lighter from me. I tried to ignore the trembling of her hands and the ashen undertone to her skin.

Kitty charged out to the widow's walk. The railing had no break in it, so she made one with the sledgehammer, the piece skittering down to crash to the ground below. We paused on the edge of the roof and eyed the conservatory. Before, I'd been afraid to touch the rusty, twisted metal, but with Mary behind us and the promise of flames, I would risk it.

I eased along the ledge and toward the dome. A *fwump* and the smell of acrid smoke pulled my attention back to the cupola. Fire and the trumpeting squawk of an enraged ghost. We'd run out of time.

I slid down the roof's edge on my butt, pain ricocheting through my injured back with every bump. Kitty followed, the two of us careening far faster than intended. I kept hoping Mary would quiet behind us, whisked away from this plane and onto the next, but she screeched while the bones burned.

Near the end of the roof slope, I put out my hands to either side to slow me down. My palms burned where they scraped over the shingles. My sneaker caught on the second-story gutter just in time to stop me from sailing over. As Kitty skidded to a halt beside me, the gutter squealed and ripped away from the side of the house, sending us both scrambling back.

"Damn it." I glanced over at the conservatory four feet away.

"I'm going to go for it," I said. "I'll find something for you to jump down onto. A table or something."

Kitty looked between me and the metal dome. "Do you want me to try first?"

"No. I'm a little smaller and you've got the sledgehammer. Just...I'll be okay." I pushed myself up into a crouch, knowing I had to jump for all our sakes, but I couldn't make myself go. A countdown from three in my head did nothing to inspire the leap.

Dell's startled shout did. I looked back. Smoke poured from the open door of the cupola. The old woman staggered outside to the widow's walk, a hand held up in front of her. Mary emerged from the gray cloud like a chittering nightmare. The fact that her last tie to this world was licked by flames didn't appear to matter.

What if we were wrong? What if burning her body doesn't stop her?

I launched myself toward the conservatory. My legs kicked in the air, gravity threatening to splatter me across the hard, concrete floor a story below. A scream burst from my lips before my hands latched onto the curved metal of the dome. Something bit into my fingertips, the underside of the frame rusty and sharp, but I managed to cling, swinging back and forth like a pendulum.

I heaved my way toward another bar, body aching. Kitty shouted above. Mary snarled. Smoke wafted from the cupola door, thick and oily and hard to see through. I worked myself toward the ground as efficiently as possible, hopping to another bar. It bent beneath my weight but didn't tear away from the foundation. I moved closer to the crumbling podium of the old statue at the center of the conservatory. I dropped onto its flat surface.

I climbed outside the conservatory through a glassless panel in the window. Kitty shouted my name. I heard a shriek followed by a growl and a thud. Mary had closed in on them. Maybe she already had Dell. I had to entice her down.

"BLOODY MARY!" I screamed at the top of my lungs, running around the side of the house in hopes of luring her out through the front door. "BLOODY MARY, BLOODY MARY."

Mary bayed, a sound of outrage and despair that shredded the stillness of the farm. There was a yelp from the rooftop—Dell, I was pretty sure—and then Kitty screamed down to me.

"Run, Shauna! She's coming. Run!"

I turned the corner of the house as Mary hurtled off the roof, crashing into the ground six feet away from me.

The pile of dead girl twitched. All her parts looked out of place and haphazard. Her leg bent at an odd angle. One shoulder was higher than the other. A thumb pointed in the wrong direction on the hand. But it didn't stop her. Her tongue flicked out, like a snake tasting the air. She hoisted herself up onto her hands, then climbed to her feet, wet gurgles rattling from her chest.

I ran away from Hawthorne House, toward the fields. Mary snarled as she gave chase, lumbering after me despite her bony foot turned backward on the ankle. It flopped with her every step, the joints destroyed in the fall.

She was crippled, yes, but a healthy Mary was twice as fast as me. A broken Mary kept time, so close I could hear her wheezing breaths. I sprinted toward the closest field. It was the sole good field with its tidy fence, freshly tilled earth, and emerald grass.

The horizontal rails were spaced out enough that I could squeeze through and into the field with no problem. Mary lunged for me but didn't give chase. She'd cleared a roof to get me, she'd walked through fire to hurt my friends, but she wouldn't cross that fence. She hissed and screeched and slapped at the fence, but she wouldn't come after me.

I stopped and gasped for breath midfield, staring at Mary as she moved around the perimeter, snarling and testing the dirt. I looked down. Rich, dark earth. Nothing unusual about it.

Until it moved.

It was a subtle rumble at first—so slight it felt like vibrations on my heels. But then something wrenched beneath me, like the field turned itself. Fields weren't supposed to ripple. They weren't supposed to quicken when someone walked upon them. I took off running again, fear scratching at my skin from the inside.

What was it Jess had said about the swamp gas? Hard to imagine, but even Mary has her limits. Whatever lives in the Hawthornes' field is one of those limits.

I found the Hawthorne monster.

26

I ran, my breath short, my body slicked with sweat. Mary curved around from my right in an effort to cut me off. She lashed at me as I vaulted the fence, the edge of her pointed fingernail skimming the underside of my forearm. I raced down the driveway and past the second field. Sooner or later, I'd run out of steam and Mary wouldn't. I reached into my pockets for the salt, grabbing two fistfuls and tossing them back over my shoulders.

Mary screamed, pausing in her chase to contend with the burning flesh. It let me put a few yards between us, but it wasn't enough. I cleared another fence, the hip-tall grass slowing my progress. Mary jimmied a slat of broken fence from the post and threw it at me like a javelin. It went wide by a few feet. The second one came much, much closer, spiking into the ground beside my sneaker.

I fumbled in my pocket for the locket. Mary's locket. I whirled around and threw it sidearm at the ghost.

"IT'S YOURS, MARY. YOUR NECKLACE."

Mary snatched the necklace from the air and stopped cold, peering at the delicate thing gleaming against her palm. Her head tilted to the side and she cooed. It was the gentlest sound I'd ever heard from her. It was also the most unsettling.

I slowed my retreat, afraid any sudden movements would draw her attention from her new prize. I watched as Mary turned the necklace over to inspect the back. The remnants of her lips receded in what looked like a grimace, but the flutter of her one eyelid suggested something else.

Mary *was smiling*. That rotten countenance with its borrowed teeth *smiled*.

I continued backing away, my movements as unprovocative as I could make them. Mary ran her thumb along the crease of the locket. One of her serrated fingernails slid inside of it, springing the ancient mechanism and forcing it open.

All good vanished the moment she saw her pictures were gone. The portraits had been destroyed by time and the water under the church's floor. Mary threw the locket aside and tore after me with a fresh scream, her pace quickened by fury.

She blames me for the pictures. She thinks it's my fault.

Again I ran, this time through hip-height grass that pushed back at me. Mary lumbered after me like a rabid beast. She'd catch me soon, and I tried to steel myself for the fight I couldn't win. I was about to dive into the grass, hoping to hide beneath the underbrush, when the green Ford Focus turned onto the driveway.

Jess pressed her foot down on the gas and sped directly at us. Grit flew and tires squealed as she surged ahead. Jess crashed into Mary, sending her flying back twenty feet. She landed facedown, legs akimbo, but Jess didn't slow. She drove at Mary's prone body and then over it, squishing Mary into the dirt.

For the first time in a long time, I was glad to see Jess.

I scampered from the field and ran for the old house, cutting a wide berth around the ghoul. She writhed on the ground but hadn't recovered enough to pick herself back up again. Jess climbed from her car, a box of salt clenched in each hand. She rushed in to wave them over Mary's head and back, the smoke from the body a shadow of what billowed from the roof.

"What the hell happened?" she demanded as I ran up beside her.

I spoke through ragged breaths. "Dell burned the bones, but something's not working. She's still here."

"Why?"

"I don't know."

Jess groaned. "So we're back to mirrors, I guess? Maybe finding the mirror that was in the room with her when she died? I feel like we've made no progress whatsoever."

"We haven't," I said flatly.

Mary wrenched her head around on her shoulders. There was an unsettling crunch, like her vertebrae had popped back into alignment. She shoved at the ground to dislodge her body from the packed dirt but couldn't quite manage it. I knew better than to hope that she was down for good.

I grabbed Jess's sleeve and ran toward the second building. "We have to get Kitty and Dell." I hesitated outside of the front door, the thick, black smoke pouring out and swallowing all the good air.

Behind me, Mary groaned.

"I'll stay down here in case she gets up again. Get Dell and Kitty." Jess whirled on the ghost, the salt boxes poised and ready to fire.

I jerked my T-shirt over my nose and barreled ahead. My eyes ached the moment I stepped into the house. The fire still burned, and it was hotter than Hell inside. I fumbled for the railing of the stairs only to find no railing. Through the smoke, I could faintly see its shape in the middle of the living room.

Mary snapped the railing off in her rage.

I hugged the wall and climbed toward the balcony. I plowed my way toward the door leading to the roof. Opening it blasted me with more smoke and I took another deep breath from under the T-shirt.

Onward I pressed, feeling faint and sick and sore. The hatch door had been splintered apart under Mary's brute force. I climbed up and into the cupola. The couch was pushed against the opposite wall. The fire licked higher, reaching toward the crow's face in the stained glass window.

I was half-blind as I bumbled my way toward the widow's walk. I could make out Dell's shape near the chimney. She'd collapsed, her mouth gaping open, a pool of blood beneath her cheek. I rushed to her, my hand sweeping over her sweaty forehead and down to her neck in search of a pulse. I didn't feel anything, but when I shifted my fingers, life thrummed against my pads.

"Kitty! Are you here?" I called out.

"Oh, my God. You're okay. I've been trying to get up the roof, but I keep sliding back. I saw her fall. Is she dead?" Kitty was still on the side of the roof I'd leapt from. I looped my arms under Dell's and pulled her toward the break in the railing, grunting with exertion.

"Mary's out front, but Jess is holding her off. Our best bet is to get Dell down from back here if we can. We have to run."

The farther away from the cupola I got, the better I could see. Kitty was halfway up the roof side, the sledgehammer abandoned behind her. Her brown hair was matted to her scalp with sweat. Her green eyes were huge. She was rosy all over, her fear flushing her from head to toe.

"I'm so glad to see you," she said, stretching up as I bent down. Between the two of us, we were able to slide Dell down the decline. Dell moaned as she hit a bump, but otherwise went unharmed.

"Hey! Is she okay?" Jess jogged around the conservatory side, her bruised face tilted up at us with concern.

"She's passed out, but she's alive!" Kitty called. "Do you think you can catch her?"

"Yes." Jess dropped the salt boxes and reached up her arms toward the roof overhang. Kitty lay flat on her stomach across the roof, using her own weight as an anchor. Getting a grip on Dell was tricky, but she figured out that she could hold on to her feet better than her hands when she lowered her down. "Where's Mary?" I shouted.

Jess jumped up to grab Dell's hands, reeling her aunt in as much as she could before Kitty dropped her. "I salted her. It's fine."

Kitty counted three, two, one and eased Dell down. I watched her body slip past the ledge and from my sight. I glanced back at the smoking cupola. I felt like a scared failure. We'd dedicated the last month to putting Bloody Mary Worth away. Some of us died for it. Solving her murder should have ended everything. Destroying her remains worked in all the movies and TV shows. But it was a lie. Nothing had changed. We were back to hunches, conjecture, and mirrors.

"Jump down. I'll catch you," I heard Jess say to Kitty. Below, Dell sprawled across the dry grass, her head tilted back, her mouth hanging open. Blood drizzled from the corners of her lips. Jess stood beside her, arms lifted up again in wait. Kitty looked back at me from the roof, her hand outstretched.

"Come on. We'll get out of here."

She probably meant Hawthorne House, but I was ready to exit the situation for good.

Enough. I'm sorry, Anna. Cody.

I was about to slide down the roof toward Kitty when the blur of motion zoomed around the corner. There was no time to react. There was no time to *run.* Jess stood on the ground, awaiting us, and then she didn't. She flew back, pinned beneath a snarling, blood-crazed Mary. She was a broken, disjointed collection of smoking parts, her body crushed and mangled, but that didn't stop her. Her gray, rotten arm lifted above her head before she thrust it down at Jess's neck. Her claws dug into the sides of Jess's throat, fingernails piercing the soft, supple skin before she wrenched her hand away.

Pink, ragged flesh sundered from its proper place.

The screams were Kitty's, not Jess's, because Jess didn't have time to scream. She gurgled wetly, red painting her chest, the ghost above her, the ground to either side of her. Her hand clutched the wound, blood surging from between her fingers with the panicked beats of her heart. Her legs and arms jolted, her body convulsed.

Seconds later, she went still.

Kitty wheezed, her asthma strangling the air from her lungs. I did nothing. I couldn't think. I couldn't act. Jess was dead. All the things I'd said to her—all the accusations. The distance between us that hadn't been there for ten years.

But I couldn't forgive. Not in time.

Jess didn't deserve the ending she got.

No one did.

"No," I whispered, shaking my head. "Jess? JESS!"

There was no answer.

Behind me, the cupola crackled. One of the regular windows had split under the pressure of the heat, fire surging up to lick at the walls. Trembling, I peered at the spiderweb crack in the glass. I looked down at Mary.

Perhaps it was the trauma of what I'd just witnessed that

made my brain twitch. Perhaps it was Mary standing over Jess and covered in her blood, her head tilting back as she watched Kitty. But as I stood there on the widow's walk, a puzzle piece rotated inside my head. I'd thought burning the bones would complete the Mary Worth picture, but it discounted something very important. Something Jess had said not two minutes ago.

So we're back to looking for mirrors.

No, we weren't. We were back to looking for *shine*—anything that shined could have trapped Mary's soul to this plane. She was in all reflective surfaces. Elsa had put the toy on my head because she was trying to tell me to look up at the bird. At the Hawthorne bird.

The Hawthorne bird made of glass.

When they'd opened up that trunk to throw Philip in with Mary, she'd cleaved to the stained glass. To the crow.

"The sledgehammer," I said to Kitty just as Mary lunged up at the roof's edge. Her fingers latched for a moment before she dropped back down again. Mary leapt a second time, getting a grip, but falling with a snarl. I could hear her harsh, dry laughter from the ground as Kitty scrambled up the slope. Mary lunged and lunged, intent on scaling the roof.

"Kitty, the sledgehammer," I repeated, my voice as calm as I could manage.

Kitty stared at me, tears running rivers over her face. I motioned at the sledgehammer. She extended it my way, yelping when Mary clung to the edge of the roof and managed to pull up her torso. She dangled from the side and growled, her mouth gaping open, her new teeth gleaming. She heaved herself up with another trill of raspy laughter. Kitty withdrew as far as she could, the angle of the roof limiting her escape path.

I ran into the cupola. It was smoky and black and awful, but I didn't hesitate. I pulled back the sledgehammer and aimed it at the stained glass bird. It cracked but didn't give. Mary screeched from outside. I did it again, bringing the hammer around with as much fury as I could muster. The metal head crashed through the Hawthorne crest, splintering the surface, shattering the crow and raining sparkling glass.

I backed from the cupola and toward the widow's walk. Mary was only feet away from Kitty, but instead of pressing her advantage, she froze, her eyes wide. She looked past us to the broken glass on the ground. There was a small whine and then she skulked away like a wounded animal.

Her foot fell off first. Then her fingers, followed by a leg. As each piece disconnected from the whole, it disintegrated to dust, floating away in the writhing smoke clouds. Mary whimpered, staring at me with her shriveled black eye and her milky stolen one before they plummeted from her skull and turned to ash.

Mary Worth crumbled to bits before us, the glass that bound her to this world shattered.

Somewhere to the south, sirens wailed. I slid down the roof to join Kitty on the eave, gathering her up and guiding her toward the conservatory. I made the first jump, no longer afraid, like all fear had been tapped from my body. I helped Kitty down, then I sat beside the still-warm body of Jess McAllister and her struggling aunt, my sneaker resting in the growing pool of blood.

Brownies and Girl Scouts and family vacations. Summers by the lake with campfires and canoes. Stories of first kisses. Secrets told. Late-night texts. Fights and make-ups and every-thing in between. We were a team, Jess and I.

Now she's Mary Worth's last victim.

The sobs took me by surprise. They made my chest and stomach ache. Kitty wrapped her arms around my shoulders, and I pulled her close, watching the smoke rising from the roof of Hawthorne House through a blur of tears.

Kitty pressed her dry lips to my cheek as the ambulance pulled up the drive.

The aftermath was a whirlwind. The EMTs tried to resuscitate Jess in the ambulance to no avail. Dell was admitted to the hospital and stabilized despite her blood loss. The sheriff was able to save most of the second house. I later learned he had it bulldozed anyway.

We had no reason to stay in Solomon's Folly after Mary's fall. The ghoul was gone, or as gone as we could make her. The only reason we lingered on Hawthorne property at all was so Kitty could ask the sheriff what we should tell our parents about Jess.

Sheriff Hawthorne eyed us from under the brim of his navy blue hat, the corners of his mouth hidden by his heavy mustache.

"There was an accident. Jessica fell from the roof."

No, she didn't. She had her throat ripped out.

It wasn't supposed to end like this.

We climbed into the car and pulled away from Hawthorne House for what I hoped would be the last time. Lydia Hawthorne stood on the front porch with her brother, Bran, watching our retreat. She lifted a hand in a wave, but I didn't reciprocate. I couldn't. I was too shaken.

So was Kitty. She didn't talk for a full half hour. The only sounds she could make were quiet snivels. They echoed my whimpers.

I want my mother. I want to go home.

I rested my head against the window and closed my eyes. Weary. Afraid. Sad.

Winning had never felt so much like losing before.

We were on the last leg of the drive when I remembered the letter in my pocket. I pulled it out, examining the thick vellum paper with age discoloration along the edges. It seemed important and yet not at all in the wake of Mary's destruction.

I opened it all the same.

My name is Elizabeth Jane Hawthorne, daughter of Seymour Hawthorne and Margaret Pepper Hawthorne. I was the wife of Philip Starkcrowe III, and then the wife of Aaron Jenson. Like all Hawthornes, I was born and shall die in Solomon's Folly.

This is my confession.

There is nothing special about me. I am not particularly pretty nor am I scholarly like my brother Matthew. I do not have Alexander's wit or sense of humor. My years walking this earth have only proved that I am a bad wife and a terrible daughter. My marriages failed with no love or children to show for my time. My father speaks of our legacy like it is a reason to rise in the morning. Solomon's Folly is our pride. It is sad then that his lone daughter is as wicked as Solomon himself. I swore four years ago that I would never again come to this box of regret, which is what these remains represent, but I feel I cannot go to the good rest without confessing my sins. No pastor wishes to listen to what would be construed as mad prattling, and when I try to speak with my father, he pretends that he cannot hear me. This secret is my burden.

My dislike of Mary Worth started through no fault of hers. I was and am foolish when it comes to my affections, and I have loved Thomas Adderly for as long as I've known the meaning of the word. He is tall and handsome and has good teeth. They are very white and straight.

As a girl, I would have done anything for him to smile upon me, and truth be told, I suspected one day he would. I am a Hawthorne, and Hawthornes always get what they think they want. I presumed Thomas's affections were a matter of time. But patience is a virtue and I am not virtuous enough. When I discovered that Thomas hung his hat upon the Worth girl, I grew incensed. The Worths were poor. Comely, yes, and the mother seemed kind, but they didn't deserve what I deserved. I was only thirteen and stupid.

Mary stood between me and the man of my heart, so I did what any petulant girl would do: I tortured Mary. For years I afflicted her with hurtful words and petty revenges that she never warranted. I should have tired of it quickly, but the cruelties entertained my friends. Their laughter made me brave.

I remember the first day Philip Starkcrowe preached at Southbridge Parish, after Pastor Renault's relocation to the Berkshires. I had no idea Philip would be my one-day husband, but then, our sin eventually brought us together in unholy matrimony. That day, I stood with my family after Sunday service watching Philip's reaction to Hannah Worth. She was the fairest of us all, too beautiful for Solomon's Folly, and despite being five years her junior, Philip could not hide his fascination. When I noticed, Mary noticed, too. She called attention to it in her own quiet way, and he instantly loathed her for throttling his ardor.

I will never say much good about Philip, but I cannot deny his craftiness. He wished to pursue the Worth matriarch, and having a bold daughter provided an opportunity to spend time with the family. He had no interest in Mary's betterment, but he claimed otherwise, and Mrs. Worth reacted as any mother scared for her child would.

She trusted that a man of God would never abuse the privileges of his station and let him tutor Mary.

Hannah was naïve.

I saw Philip's disdain as validation of my own crusade. Sarah, Meredith, Agnes, and I would go to the church after lessons under the guise of spirituality, but it was to see what awful thing befell Mary that day and delight in it. At times, Philip would tie Mary's left arm behind her back and a ruler to her spine while she copied Bible text. Other times, she would be forced to scrub the vestibule with a small brush only for Philip to stomp through with muddied boots so she'd have to begin anew. He struck her often. He threatened to have her immured with the lunatics. He locked her in the basement of the church for hours at a time.

How he thought tormenting the daughter would endear him to the mother, I do not know. Perhaps he assumed Hannah would believe his word over Mary's. In the end it did not matter. Hannah drowned. Philip never spoke of her after our marriage, and I never asked, because the truth scared me. Everyone knew that woman did not jump to her death. She went walking one night and never came home. We all had our suspicions, but the constable did not wish to call a godly man a liar. Perhaps that was fear for his soul. Perhaps it was lack of evidence beyond a body in the reeds of the river. Thus, a murderer walked free. I will not deny that I laughed at Mary's misfortune. To claim otherwise is a lie, and I refuse to perpetuate any more of those while I still have breath to breathe.

I thought Mary would relocate to Boston with her sister, but Mary was given into the care of the very man who orphaned her. It made little sense. Even my father, who rarely involved himself in lesser matters, commented that the girl belonged elsewhere, but no one made a fuss. Constance might have insisted upon her removal, but she had just welcomed a baby son.

October 28, 1864, was when my life changed for the worse. The day began like any other: breakfast with my brothers, lessons, lunch at my father's office, and gathering at the church with Sarah, Meredith, and Agnes when we grew bored with needlepoint. While Philip was horrid to Mary, he seemed to relish our company. Agnes quite fancied herself in love with him. He didn't return the affection. Agnes was given the courtesy afforded the Hawthornes and those they held dear.

Mary was locked in the basement upon our arrival. We'd seen the pastor strike her across the mouth the previous day, bloodying her before thrusting her into the dark. Sarah had come up with the moniker of Bloody Mary, and we whispered it to her through the door like idiotic children. Something was changed that day, though. Mary was formidable like never before. Philip was in a red-faced frenzy. Mary threw herself against the door hard enough that it rattled on the hinges, demanding that he release her.

"You can rot in there for all I care, you treacherous harlot," Philip snarled, not realizing that we four stood behind the pews.

Mary slammed harder upon the door.

I felt unsettled by this exchange, and Agnes fared no better. She pulled upon my sleeve, pleading for us to go. Would that I could rewind the time, but curiosity got the better of me and I thrust her away. She left with Meredith at her side. Sarah remained with me out of loyalty, clasping my hand and watching the pastor pace the church like a caged lion.

He sensed our presence then, whirling on us with a look of fury. I feared he would deliver his vengeful wrath upon us, but he exited the church instead, I assumed for a walk to placate his ire.

"You will let me out this instant. If you wish to act the lech, find yourself a doxy, Pastor!"

Mary could not have manufactured the claim for our benefit—she did not even know we were there. Philip had tried to compromise her and she rebelled against his advances. It was more proof that he was not the courtly gentleman Agnes fancied.

For the first time, I felt pity for Mary Worth. I had not quite yet come to the conclusion that I had wronged her, but I was on the path to understanding. I approached the door. Sarah tried to stop me, whispering that I could not act against the pastor, but I did not see it as defiance. I'm a Hawthorne. The only people Hawthornes must abide are the elders in their own House.

"Mary?" I called through the door.

There were more furious kicks on the other side. "Leave me, Elizabeth. I want nothing to do with you or your broody hens."

"Hush and I'll let you out." Only I had taunted her thusly not two days ago. She could not have known I had changed my song. When she pummeled the door, I hesitated, but my convictions spurred me onward and I fussed with the lock. The pastor returned at the wrong time. Seeing me at the door, he shouted for me to stop, but I did not know he approached. I did not know he was still consumed with fury. All I knew was that the door was swinging open. Mary stood in her white frock, astounded that I'd been kind. She was so very thin that the dress hung loose upon her body. It was smeared in dirt, and there were bugs on it from her tenure in the basement.

What happened next is hard for me to relay. The pastor shoved past Sarah to wrench the door from my grasp. We scrambled as he tried to close it, and I held it open with my inferior strength. Mary shouted and barged forward, surely afraid that Philip would send her back into the recesses of the church.

He pushed her.

He would call it an accident, but I saw his expression when he turned on her. None of his anger had abated when he put his hand over her face, nestled it into his palm, and shoved. The stairs were slippery. Her head struck a step and cracked open, spilling her blood across the stone. She sprawled on the floor like a broken doll.

This is not where I became an accessory to Philip's crime. That occurred when he convinced two hysterical girls that we would be punished for Mary's death if we did not follow his lead. He pulled us into the basement with him, Sarah holding the lantern as he frantically dug into the floor with a shovel. He didn't go deep; far enough that he could lay the bricks flat after Mary's burial. I watched him haul her limp body into that pit. I watched him shovel wet mud on her dress from the feet up.

I watched her eyes blink open as he covered her head.

I never told him she was alive. I don't know that it would have mattered. He likely would have finished what he started. I will not make excuses for my actions. It was an evil deed committed by a scared, stupid, selfish girl. I was so afraid my father would discover my transgression, I let Mary Worth be buried alive. With Mary interred, Philip told us we must pray for forgiveness from God, and that we must never speak of what happened. I did as instructed because I worried the pastor would put the blame on me and my friends—that my public disdain of the Worth girl would incriminate me. That a frail woman's word would never matter more than that of the man charged with our immortal souls. Philip used that fear to control us.

I barely slept at night, and Sarah was prone to fits of weeping, but we maintained our silence. Meanwhile, the pastor convinced everyone that Mary escaped his care to be with her sister in Boston. He played the bereaved guardian ever hopeful for his ward's safety.

These were the first of the lies but by no means the last. Joseph Simpson arrived in town a week later. He is Constance Worth's husband and a sophisticated lawyer from the city. His black hair and blue eyes would have set the girls to tittering had he come at any other time, but considering his business with The Folly, he was met with suspicion and disdain. It did not deter him. He had many questions, and he came armed with accusations. He knew of Mary's trials with the pastor. He also knew of my history, though he filtered his inquiries through my father.

Hours after Mr. Simpson's appearance, Philip shadowed my father's doorstep. I was at lessons at the time, but when I came home, both of them awaited me in the front study. My father reserved this room for work, but I was called before the judge's desk not as his daughter but as a potential murderess. It was the first time my father ever struck me. I had always been his sweet girl, but from that moment on he treated me as a stranger. Philip had poisoned his mind about the events in the church. It had been my hand that shoved Mary. It had been my impassioned moment that led to her demise. In his iteration, he struggled to preserve Mary's life against me. Philip painted himself my savior, the man who valiantly buried the body in the church's basement to protect my reputation and the Hawthorne name.

I don't know what my father believed, but the threat of scandal spurred him to action. Mary's body was to be moved to a less obvious location—likely the swamp, where her mother rested. Also, I would marry Philip Starkcrowe in two weeks' time. It was, as my father so coldly put it, insurance. Philip would be part of the family and thus beholden to the Hawthorne name. Our unborn children were ties that would permanently bind.

I protested, but it did no good. Asserting that Philip was responsible not for one but two Worth deaths changed little. "It's too late, Elizabeth. Had you been a victim of circumstance, you would have come to me a week ago. The innocent have nothing to hide and so they do not bother trying." At dinner that night, word reached us that Joseph Simpson had procured a proper warrant to launch an investigation. It would inevitably land him on my doorstep—my mistreatment of Mary was not unknown. Though the constable was one of my father's closest friends, there were some legalities neither of them could circumvent, which is how I ended up in the church basement after dark with my brothers digging up Mary Worth's corpse. Father insisted I go, any delicacies granted me by my womanhood no longer a consideration.

Simpson questioned Philip at the jail that night, which granted me and my brothers a slice of time to conduct our illicit deed. I remember the revolting smell and the gray tinge to Mary's skin. I remember a piece of her body breaking away and Alexander hastily shoving it into his burlap sack. Matthew replaced the stones of the floor while Alexander and I dragged Mary to the cart. No one dared to enter the swamp at night, so Mary was brought back to Hawthorne House.

I feared discovery, but Alexander assured me that Father had it well in hand. There was a trunk. They tried shoving the sack inside but Mary did not fit, and so they made her fit. I will not go into details. Into the cupola she went. I did not find it a terribly good hiding spot, but then our house man, the Greek Leopold, came into play. I was told to bathe, my clothes taken and burned along with my brothers'. By the time I dressed in my nightclothes, Leopold was at work in the attic. By morning, a pair of chairs, a bookshelf, a portrait of my grandfather, and gas lanterns affixed the wall that had not been there twelve hours before. Mary rested beneath the stained glass window, hidden from the world by a lovely retreat.

Simpson's investigations continued for some time, long past my marriage to Philip, but he returned to his wife in January of 1865 with no answers about the missing Mary. By then, I had taken up residence in the eastern half of Hawthorne House with my husband. The gossipmongers quieted for the most part.

In the earliest parts of our marriage, Philip was courteous. We acted the parts of any newly married couple, feigning a joy we did not feel. My guilt weighed heavily at first, but over time, it grew easier to live with myself. I tried to forget Mary Worth and concentrate on pleasing my new husband. While Philip was stern and demanded near constant veneration to our God, he was easily pleased with his favorite stew and ample time to himself.

Our trouble began when he grew restless. As I stated before, I am not as lovely as other girls. I am plain with milquetoast skin and drab brown hair. My nose is too long, my eyes as dark as pitch. While I cannot say for certain that Philip had walked Eden's garden enough to know the many paths, his dealings with the Worth women gave me reason to believe it so.

After two months, the violence began. It was always below the neck so my dresses would hide the bruises. My Hawthorne pride would not allow me to broach this subject with my father. He barely spoke to me anymore, our familial bond tainted beyond repair. Begging him to intervene was impossible.

It was six months into the marriage, four beneath Philip's punishing blows, when the situation became untenable. I made his stew, but he complained through every bite. When he threw the food into the fire and told me it wasn't fit for a dog, I left the table and climbed the stairs. My intent was to go to sleep. He misconstrued it as rebellion.

He chased me up the stairs and grabbed my hair, striking me across the mouth until I tasted blood. The things he screamed were hard to parse. Scripture and profanity blended seamlessly. The punch to my eye almost blinded me, but it was the shaking that scared me most. I felt my feet slipping on the landing, and instinct took over. I did not intend to shove him, but that is what happened. I must have caught him off guard as he fell backward, immediately striking his head upon one of the wooden steps.

Not unlike Mary Worth, Philip Starkcrowe died upon the stairs, his neck snapped, head lolling to the side at a wrong angle.

I did not make the same mistake twice. I informed my father immediately. While he was not pleased, he did not berate me, for which I can thank my blackened, swollen eye. The story he concocted was that Philip, dissatisfied with his plain wife, abandoned the town to seek his fortunes elsewhere. Railway tickets were purchased in his name. His bags were packed and promptly disappeared, no doubt in the swamp somewhere. I asked what we would do with Philip's body. Father cast me a withering look and again called upon Leopold.

I was not a superstitious girl. While Agnes and Meredith

conducted séances to speak with the other side, grimoires ever at the ready, I did not subscribe to such nonsense. However, even I could see the folly in putting the remains of the murderer in with the victim. It tempted fate. I protested as much, but I was promptly dismissed as the wall was taken down. Philip was dumped into the trunk atop Mary Worth. The wall closed them in together.

Opening that trunk was the worst thing they could have done. She anchored herself to this world and began her quest for vengeance.

She appeared in the glass of my mirror as I went to bed, peering out at me as if she existed on the other side of a door. I thought I would expire from fear. She was a hideous thing. The flesh on her bones sagged, a thin growth of mold covering her face and her one remaining ear. Her jaw looked loose, as if it would fall off her face if she turned her head too fast. One of her arms was cut off at the elbow. I correlated it to a cut Alexander had made to get her into the trunk all those months ago.

I ran from my room, screaming that Mary Worth had come to get me. I was alone in the eastern wing, and so I ran to the western, across the yard to my father's house. He was out, likely ensuring that the truth about Philip's death did not leak or cause trouble. My mother did what she could to calm me, eventually dosing my tea with laudanum to put me to sleep. For the first time in fifteen years, I slept upon her breast, my arms wrapped around her.

I spent all the next day convincing myself that the vision of Mary was a reaction to trauma. All of that shattered when a weepy Agnes arrived on my doorstep, claiming to have seen the ghost. My fear returned twofold. Not only had Mary appeared the very night Philip was put to rest beside her, but to one of my friends? It seemed improbable, but then both Meredith and Sarah showed up, equally frightened. They'd seen Mary, too.

This presented a set of challenges for me. Firstly, I was supposed to be grieving Philip's betrayal, not frantic about a girl who died six months previous. Secondly, my father would never listen if I told him that he had to take down the wall and separate their bodies. I did not know what to do.

The decision was made for me when the constable arrived, asking after Philip. The brevity of the questioning told me that my father had already taken care of the mess. I did not pretend to be upset. With my pulpy face, it was unnecessary. I could shed no tears for a man so wicked.

The girls stayed with me that night, all of us dreading another encounter with the phantom. Mary never came. When the next day passed and she did not come, I was relieved. Perhaps Mary had expressed her discontent with her entombment and had moved on to the better afterlife she deserved.

On April 30, 1865, Sarah Ashby went missing. Her sister reported that Sarah went into her dressing room and never came out again. I did not blame it upon the ghost, for it did not occur to me that such a thing could be possible. Oh, how I mourned my dear friend. Sarah had been as a sister to me. I felt her loss so keenly, it was as if a part of me had gone with her.

The town rallied around me, abandoned by my husband, now missing my nearest and dearest friend, but it did little for my heavy heart. No trace was ever found of Sarah, nor was any trace found of Meredith when she disappeared on June 19, 1865, or Agnes when she disappeared on August 4, 1865.

The public outcry was swift. They assumed there was a murderer in our midst. Watch groups formed, the men taking up weapons and going on patrols, but no evidence was ever found. The initiative fizzled quickly, but when the only common thread among the disappearances was that each of the girls went into a room alone and never came back, what could they expect? My father had the audacity to call me to his office and ask me bluntly if I had anything to do with their deaths. The poison dripped from my tongue when I told him that, no, my murderous ways were reserved for the abusive men he married me to.

His response to that was to tell me that I would be married again by year's end to a man by the name of Aaron Jenson, and he would appreciate it kindly if I did not strike him down, as the trunk was out of space.

I was too despondent to argue. I had, by then, lost everyone dear to me. My friends were dead. My brothers were disgusted by me, thinking me a fallen woman. My father treated me like a shadow. My mother was kind sometimes, but only when my father was elsewhere. A second husband was nothing compared with these things. I deemed Aaron an ignorable nuisance before ever meeting him.

Father informed me that I would be attending a dinner party with him and Mother to meet with Mr. Jenson. I was to act the part of the dutiful daughter, smile when I ought to smile, and not eat too much for fear of diminishing my value to a man twice my age.

As I powdered my nose, I looked in the mirror, but instead of seeing my own reflection, I saw Mary's face. It is hard to describe her as improved from the last appearance, but her skin was firmer, the missing arm replaced, and her jaw aligned. She was still quite dead and awful, but somehow more alive.

I shouted and hustled from the room to join my parents. My mother asked if I was well, but my father snapped at me to comport myself with dignity—that I would not shame the Hawthornes yet again by alienating the one man left in Solomon's Folly who would have me. I closed my eyes during the carriage ride, deep breaths helping me quell my fear.

Somehow, Aaron found me enchanting despite my plainness, my dearth of conversation skills, and my avoidance of my own reflection. I found him tedious with his grizzled whiskers, monotone prattling, and mustard-stained vest.

My father had Philip declared dead in October after his luggage was found on the edges of the swamp. Aaron and I were married in November. I saw Mary more frequently after that, sometimes in my vanity, which I had removed from my room, but most often in the panes of glass in the house windows. Aaron thought me a skittish thing, but having a dead girl gazing at you from mirrors would rob even the bravest of their resolve.

I plunged the household into dark with thick drapes and shades. My husband did not seem to mind, but he did not have a passionate disposition and was quite content to sit on the porch swing until the snows came. He was an old man with a young wife, hoping for a passel of children before death caught up to him.

Mary took to haunting other things. Plates, candlesticks, hairbrushes. I purged the household of anything that could house the ghost's visage. I was desperate to relocate Mary's remains from the attic, but I had an ignorant husband always in attendance, my *father lived on the other side of the estate and would never allow it, and I hadn't the faintest idea of how to get through the wall on my own. My one attempt with a hammer resulted in a tiny hole, through which, dear letter, you shall be thrust upon completion.*

I am quite near completion.

I cannot run from Mary much longer, nor do I believe I warrant the escape. There is little one can do without light, and I lack it so often that I have long swaths of time to ponder my life's choices. I see now that the specter is my punishment for years of unkindness. It is my comeuppance for watching Philip bury Mary beneath the mud and stone. Seeing her in the glass, I understand how my friends disappeared. She took them. Whether that was to punish them for their transgressions or to punish me for mine, I do not know. The latter hurts my heart, but it is no less than I deserve.

While I can live without windows and sterling, I cannot live without water, which is where I see Mary most lately. I drink it in the dark so there is no reflection. I bathe in the dark as well. My options run thin, and I find instead of being fearful, I am weary.

Sorry and weary. This is no way to live. All hail the great and mighty Hawthornes, a house built upon the bones of those we wronged.

E.H.

Acknowledgments

A lot of wonderful people helped get this into print.

Thank you, Christian Trimmer, for bringing me into the Hyperion fold. What a fantastic book family. Thank you, Tracey Keevan, for taking my little piece of coal and polishing it to a fine gleam. Thank you, T. S. Ferguson, who was the first editor to tell me, "Modernize this." It got me on the right path. The fact that you became my friend along the way is amazing.

Thank you, Crystal, Lauren N., Renée, Brian, Nikki, Christi, Claire, Melinda, Laurie, Lara, and Reuben, for lending me your eyes. Thank you, WFR crew, for putting up with constant cut-and-pastes. Thank you, Scott Storrier, Matthew Finn, and Marty Gleason, for always listening. Thank you, Becky Kroll, Chandra Rooney, Evie Nelson, and Sarah Johnson, for tearing me apart to make me better. I wouldn't trade your cruelties (or friendship) for anything in the world.

Thank you, Miriam Kriss, for picking up a book from the slush pile X years ago and saying, "I like them." I am forever in your debt for making this particular dream a reality.

Thank you, Greg Roy and Eric Tribou, for spending

countless hours dead-eyed while I droned on about books. You are my second family and I love you.

Thank you, Lauren Roy, my sister from another mister and best friend. I have no idea which deity I pleased to get you in my life, but I'm thankful every day that you're around. You are a spectacular person and make me better by association.

Thank you, David Finn, for tolerating me day in and day out. You've believed in me, my books, and this strange life we share. That means more than I'll ever let on. I hope you're paying attention because this line is for you: you're a superhero.

Thank you to my family, who've been so supportive. I love you all. Mike and Mike—you're two of the most wonderful dads a girl could ask for. Drew Cole, I'm so lucky you came into my life when you did and helped me grow into a quasi-normal human. And Mom—whenever someone says something good about me or my work, I want you to claim a piece for yourself. I would not be the person I am without your steel, your love, and your rapier wit.

And last but not least, thank you, Dot, for tapping away in that front room for so many years. Yours are some big shoes to fill.

Acknowledgments

I wrote this book twice.

The first time, I was in no condition to *exist*, never mind put words to paper. My mother was diagnosed with cancer in January 2014, in the early stages of this book's development. I had deadlines, and I trucked on despite the strain—despite Mom's chemo and my constant worry that I was going to lose someone so special. The end result wasn't pretty. I wrote a book that was a product of my headspace. It didn't satisfy me, nor would it have satisfied any reader who set eyes upon it. I wouldn't show it to my oh-so-patient editor, Tracey Keevan. I wouldn't even show it to my agent, Miriam Kriss, who's seen all of my word atrocities for the past five years. It was that rough.

Fast-forward eight months. Mom persevered and is, as of this writing, doing remarkably well. She's always been excellent at sassing the world at large, and thanks to an incredible team of doctors at Brigham and Women's, will continue to do so for years to come.

We were lucky. It was over for us. With that weight off my shoulders, I was able to sit down and write *Mary: Unleashed* a second time, the way it deserved to be written. I couldn't have done that without the support of my family, friends, and publishing circle. I'm so grateful to have my mother here. I'm so grateful that people helped me, so I could help her. It's funny how kindness trickles down like that, bestowed upon one person so they can share it with another—and believe me, there was an abundance of kindness. More than I can possibly call attention to in a short acknowledgments page.

So, to everyone who spared a prayer, who offered an ear, a hug, and encouragement when the fog was thickest, thank you. This book wouldn't be possible without you.